# The Iron Buddha and Other Tales

## By Rod Watson

*Complimentary copy*

This copy is a first printing and has some typos; these have been eliminated in subsequent printings.

*[signature]*

14/02/2018

Published by New Generation Publishing in 2017

First Edition

**ISBN No:** Paperback 978-1-78719-610-0
Hardback 978-1-78719-611-7
Ebook 978-1-78719-612-4

A copy is with the British Library

**www.newgeneration-publishing.com**

New Generation Publishing

# Contents

# Foreword

## Out of the Stench of Corruption Comes Forth Sweetness

Truth is stranger than fiction. All these tales are true and some of them are strange—some are very strange. Did I have a bicycle that thought it was a giant falcon? Did I come across a rat that could sing, tell jokes and had an option about the National Health Service? Yes I did. In my mind, these things really did happen. My dog also cried out for me to help her when her hour came. She did.

Originally titled, 'Tales from the Counting House', a friend asked me, "What can possibly be interesting about the dull, dry activities of the Purchase and Sales Ledger Departments?" Well, people work in these places; they may be loving gentle parents, church wardens, scout leaders and pillars of their societies, but in the fifty organisations that I have worked in, or consulted for, I have found those personae largely disappear when it comes to the workplace. In fact, there is not a single organisation that I have engaged with that I have not found some kind of fraud, malfeasance or Spanish Customs going on.

The organisation's mission statement may be full of worthy ideals, but the real drivers are *fear, anger, greed* and *self-interest;* and oh yes, *sex* and plenty of that. It was not intended to be a humorous book, but inevitably pride comes before a fall as when the pompous man in a smart suit slips on a banana skin, we all laugh. The tales are full of irony, hubris and hypocrisy and inevitably when the best laid plans of naughty mice and bad men fail, most of us smile.

*"I wish I could find a good book to live in."* I hope, at least, *this* book will *entertain* you.

Rod Watson
October 2017

*(The Bio Pic is below)*

Rod Watson was born in Hong Kong in 1948. When he was three years old his family moved to the southern tip of South Africa where he received his primary education. His secondary education took place in Edinburgh.

A Certified Accountant, he has worked in the horse racing industry, as a news agent, a cigar merchant, restaurateur and in many industries including construction, motor trade, fashion, lobbying and manufacturing.

His first book 'The Adaptive System' (How to make a thousand pounds in your lunch hour) was published in 2007 and is to be re-published in a revised edition.

Rod spends his time between Brighton (England), South East Asia and South Africa.

# Chapter One: The Rock

This is an account of the Japanese Occupation of Hong Kong. Like many others, it describes a family's descent from exotic munificence in the Far East to extremely 'reduced' and 'changed' circumstances. However, the chief characters are not the men and women but the bovine POWs, who also suffered most terribly. It also shows a side to the Japanese wartime soldiers that indicates they were not all crazed and cruel demons.

It was September 1951. Hugh Uisdean Gundle was sitting on a rock, on the edge of a field overlooking the South China Sea. The field belonged to the Hong Kong Dairy Farm, and Hugh was the Chief Veterinary Officer of the farm. This was his 'sunset hour'. The weather at this time of year was always hot and humid so, after a busy day, it was pleasant beyond words to come to the high ground and cool off slightly in the breeze. For Hugh, the sunsets over the sea were nothing less than spectacular. 'His' Rock was special to him in another way too. It was a small outcrop in what was otherwise grass, with a pond at the base of the slope to the sea. The Rock was unique in so much that it had a flat ledge backed with a vertical slab making a perfect chair. Next to this chair was a flat area that served well as a table. Within reach of these natural furnishing arrangements was a tight crevice and, within this crevice, Hugh would keep a bottle of whisky, a bottle of purified water and a crystal tumbler. It was the job of his assistant, Ah Tan, to keep the water topped up, and Hugh's responsibility to ensure the whisky level never fell below the sacred level of four fingers.

At this hour, he would pour two fingers of whisky into the glass with two fingers of the crevice-chilled water; he would smoke a cigarette (or three) and sit, reflect and think. Sometimes, he would just sit.

Two more fingers of whisky and water and then he would walk across the fields to his villa. This evening, his bottle was *Islay* malt: a peaty reek, almost tarry, with a whiff of iodine. Top notes of *Lapsang Souchong*. He was drinking Scotland. How he longed for cold Scottish rain, the clear bubbling streams bursting between granite and heather. People you could trust; simple honest folk – his 'ain folk'. If you felt unwell, it was usually the common cold, not this dreadful, energy-sapping, malignant malaria. He lit another cigarette. These were Russian cigarettes that the Russian hands on the farm had introduced him to during the Occupation: a cardboard tube with a small but extremely strong cigarette at the end. Black pungent tobacco.

Tonight, he could feel a typhoon coming – the air pressure had changed, the sky was streaked with an unusual palette of luminous colours varying from bright orange to streaks of boysenberry, violet and mauve. The usually placid ocean was now restless, choppy; angry grey waves with dirty white ruffs pounded the shore. Not a time to be at sea or anywhere else except indoors and secure. There were almost continuous flickers of forked lighting on the horizon and he heard peals of deep thunder rolling across the ocean. Sound travels far over water. Three miles off land, you could hear a dog barking on the island when the air was still. The rain would simply be thrown out of the sky in warm, heavy drops. Definitely not Scottish rain. Now, the deep thunder reminded him of the ordnance being fired on 8th December 1941. The Occupation had been over almost six years, but still the events haunted him. Most of his chums who had come out of the camps just shrugged the whole episode off, as if they had simply suffered a bad cold. They had thrived and prospered since; made fortunes in import-export and property.

Additionally, the island was being flooded daily by a tide of 'mainland' Chinese. Not only Chinese, but Russians and even Australians. It was changing, changing daily and changing fast. It was all happening too fast for him; seemed too much for him to cope with. He and his family were going to leave the Colony with its bitter-sweet memories and immigrate to South Africa.

A few days ago, this field had been a hive of activity. A piece of ordnance had been discovered by one of the farm's workers (a cowboy) in the pond at the bottom of the field. This 'ordnance' was in fact an unexploded 500lb bomb dropped by the Americans on their raid on the farm seven years ago. Hugh had been there. In 1943, an ambiguously worded notice had been brought to him by a messenger (later executed by the Japanese) of the British Army Aid Group in Free China, which indicated that all British working on the farm were *persona non-grata* with the Aid Group: "It is as well that you should be warned what is coming."

What was 'coming' was a load of fifty 500lb bombs, which the American Air Force delivered at one o'clock in the afternoon on that unforgettable day, 16th November 1943. It was said that the RAF would not bomb 'enemy' elephants in Burma, and apparently that strategy applied to the farm, but was not respected by the Americans. As the bombers came, British and Japanese jumped alongside each other into slit trenches. Tin hats were hurled into these trenches, and the Japanese offered these hats to the British, who, in turn, offered them back to the Japanese, with the result that no one donned the hats at all.

The noise of the planes was deafening. Huge bangs and thuds broke out all around. There was a strong smell of explosive and kerosene. Hugh thought wryly how it was that he was prepared to work in a dressing station for wounded soldiers, but cows? The dreadful noise faded and the anti-aircraft guns could now be heard. The last of the bombers could be seen waggling its wings in defiance. Yet, not a single animal or even chicken had been hit. One bomb had smashed through a staff house, but did not explode. The occupants were in an outhouse brewing 'hooch' at the time. Of course, the Japanese-controlled newspaper next day claimed a number of aircraft as having been shot down by the brave pilots of the Imperial Air Force.

Immediately after the discovery, the field was roped off. It was decided to detonate the bomb and a warning issued in the same local newspaper declaring the area off-limits. This announcement had completely the opposite effect. The entire colony and his wife turned up, as did numerous food and drink stalls as well as an army of photographers. Several steamers anchored off shore. The farm, never missing a trick to promote its products, had several ice cream carts doing a roaring trade. At midday, the bomb was exploded. A huge bang, the firmament shook and then a *whoosh* as earth, rocks and mud rose into the sky, spread out and showered down to the ground. Cheering and clapping broke out; every car and charabanc tooted its horn. A few fish and an eel were found wriggling on the grass to be quickly scooped up by the staff and later preserved and exhibited in the farm's museum. The crater had been checked; a bulldozer pushed the earth back in, leaving a depression that would hopefully fill with rain and aquifer-fed water. Quiet returned.

Hugh was a Scottish Highlander, the youngest of seven children of a gamekeeper on the Black Isle. He was sent to Royal Edinburgh High School, where he excelled before qualifying as a veterinary surgeon at Edinburgh University. He first practised as a vet in the Highlands. The pay was low, the board and lodging basic. He was meant to be a profit-sharing partner in the practice, but never enjoyed any of the profit. Then he spotted an advert in his professional journal for the position of 'Veterinary Officer for the Hong Kong Dairy Farm'. A few months later, he arrived. Although it was the thirties, there was no recession in Hong Kong. The farm had been established in the late 1800s and soon began producing dairy products from its own herd. At the time, it was widely believed that Europeans could not be healthy without a regular diet of dairy products. Pigs followed. The Europeans were suspicious of Chinese-raised pigs, believing them to be disease carriers. Chickens were then introduced and the same logic applied. To produce and distribute milk, sterile conditions and refrigeration were necessary and so the farm branched out into ice cream production, ice and the cold storage of marine products.

The management of the farm believed in investing heavily in new technologies. The labs had all the latest German and Japanese equipment. Hugh particularly enjoyed this aspect of his job – it took him back to his university days.

Life was easy. He had met and married Elizabeth, a midwife working at the new Queen Mary Hospital. She was a Cornish woman who had come out in the 'fishing fleet' and she had netted her catch. They lived in a spacious Art Deco villa. Their personal staff included a chauffeur, a gardener, an 'amah' for their new baby girl, and a houseboy named Chan, who looked after all the domestic arrangements and was an amazing cook. Professionally, Hugh was supported by a number of assistants, all at various levels of qualification. His role was largely supervisory, although he did like to don his 'dirty mac' and literally get stuck in with any difficult bovine delivery.

During the week, a full cooked breakfast would be served at five thirty in the morning along with a pint of 'bloody Mary'. Lunch would be a light curry tiffin. Gin and tonic for Elizabeth, India Pale Ale for Hugh. At sunset, they both would drink whisky without water, but as the evening lengthened, more water would be added to the new whisky measures, so eventually they would be drinking water, flavoured with whisky.

They loved to entertain. There would be English, Scottish, French and Spanish themed nights, but of course, the speciality was Chinese food cooked by Chan, eaten from shared bowls with chopsticks. Hugh was an accomplished Highland bagpiper and often would play at various dinners in the evenings. His terms were: a generous allowance for his chauffeur (who did not drink), 'hospitality' for both of them, and half a guinea to be donated to the RSPCA. For Hugh, this was a great way to meet many indigenous people from the colony. He also played frequently at Chinese functions, which meant he had entry to where few Europeans would be invited.

At weekends, his capable staff took over and this freed him and Elizabeth up for golf and sailing. He was a good shot and would join a shooting party for snipe shooting, occasionally with Chiang Kai-shek, who gave him an inscribed gold tie-clip of a retriever. Apparently, Chiang handed these out like sweeties. Once a month, Hugh undertook veterinary duties at the Happy Valley Racecourse. He would also venture further afield as a vet supervising horse racing meetings, travelling in flying boats to Singapore and Bangkok, and even making several visits to Japan. It was indeed a charmed life of comfort and ease; so different to the harsh realities of the Highlands. But, dark clouds were gathering...

In 1931, the Japanese had invaded Manchuria, and then, in 1937, China. Most European strategists seriously under-estimated what the Japanese could and were doing to build up their armed forces. Their naval expansion, particularly aircraft carriers, was extraordinarily rapid, their technicians first copying and then vastly improving on what was being produced elsewhere. But, it was their resilience, their determination and their total loyalty to the Emperor that were being under-estimated. Also, as Hugh had observed, the Japanese were *everywhere*. Throughout the whole region, they had established shops, factories and other businesses, some of which had a truly global reach, including their banks. They belonged to golf and sailing clubs, attended the universities, the medical and even the veterinary faculties. What a clever (and completely legal) way to build up an intelligence network! In Japan, Hugh had been met with nothing but courtesy and kindness; however, he had seen the factories and shipyards working twenty-four hours a day, building the Imperial war machine, and had drawn his conclusions.

Of course, after 1937, residents in the colony had their concerns. It was like a fog that comes in from nowhere and spreads so quickly that it seeps under doors, through windows and walls with an omnipresent deadliness, even into the children's nurseries. In private parties, in the clubs and hotels, people talked about little else. Then, on 3<sup>rd</sup> September 1939, war was declared by Great Britain on Germany. As the months rolled by, more Forces' chaps would appear at social and formal functions. It began to emerge that it was very much a WORLD WAR and that Hong Kong was vulnerable.

And once it became known that Churchill decided to deploy what slender resources he had in the East to Singapore and effectively leave Hong Kong undefended, the consensus – in fact, the official advice – was that women and children be evacuated. This process actually speeded up once stories abounded that the Japanese were sinking the ships carrying these women and children. Elizabeth and her daughter caught one of the few remaining steamships that was prepared to 'run the gauntlet' to South Africa.

A few days later, Hugh presented himself at the Royal Hong Kong Regiment ('volunteers') recruiting office. He recognised the sergeant, a senior clerk in one of the banks. The sergeant also recognised him. The man's uniform was new and rather tight. He looked down his list and stated blandly, "I'm afraid not you, doctor, you're in a listed occupation."

"Look here, sergeant, you know, don't you, that I won the Gold Cup for marksmanship in the colony?"

"With respect, sir, it is not rifles that *they* will be using, but heavy machine guns, armoured cars and cannon. You will receive a formal letter from us giving our reason for your rejection as well as our thanks for volunteering."

That was the close of the matter.

Hugh made his plans well. He had stockpiled crates of whisky, cartons of cigarettes and tinned foods, hidden all over the farm. Veterinary supplies that could be stored without deterioration were laid down too.

On 8th December 1941, the British element of the farm staff enacted the 'Plan', which was to billet at Queen Mary's Hospital. They heard the bangs, thuds and crump of artillery and the fast, unmistakable ticking of machine-gun fire. They knew that a fierce and terrible battle was raging. At night, the sky was infused by the savage flames erupting from burning buildings and warehouses. Bright lights flashed and strobed until dawn. On the blackest of Christmas Days, the fighting abated and Hong Kong was surrounded. The British staff had now heard about the appalling atrocities that had been committed during that month by the Japanese forces. They were all fearful, but their orders were to stay put, despite seeing and hearing the cattle who were suffering from lack of food and water; many had been turned out to pick what they could get on the hillsides, which at that time of the year was precious little. Reports came in that the pigs were being extensively killed, and only a few of the chickens were left. Staff were in discussion with their management and they all without exception offered to return to the farm and look after the animals. Again, the order was: "stay put".

It appeared that before or during the Japanese attack on Hong Kong, the Japanese powers had decided the farm was to come under the auspices of the Nippon Suisan Kaisha; the NSK had been using the cold store at East Point in connection with their marine products – another example illustrating the amount of infiltration and planning that the Japanese had undertaken as part of their war plans. However, as Hugh was quick to discover, there were many rival factions within the Japanese hierarchy, and it was the Army Investigating Bureau (AIB) that took original possession of the farm. This department was also known as the 'Department of Loot', its purpose being to seize every possible asset that could be of use to the Japanese forces.

Finally, on 12th January 1942, the British staff of the farm were summonsed by the AIB to appear at the Farm. The senior brigand amongst this collection of bandits was one Lieutenant Hideki, a portly, grizzled, bespectacled autocratic type who looked, and most likely was, a civilian in army uniform. He insisted on being called 'Captain'. In the same vein, it amused Hugh that the colony had suddenly become awash with counts, lords and knights, all self-styled, all believing that some form of ennoblement would protect them from the wrath of their invaders. Earlier in the year, at one dinner party, attending were Sirs Arthur, Lancelot and Percival; this coterie of charlatans was inevitably known, disdainfully, as 'King Arthur and the Knights of the Round Table'. After the Occupation, these jumped up mountebanks went on to milk their 'titles' for all they could. Strangely, as the Occupation drew to a close, a number of high ranking Japanese would convert to Christianity in an attempt to protect themselves from likely prosecution.

Hideki's right-hand man was a little fellow called Ikeda, who was an official with the Bank of Canton. Together, they looked like Laurel and Hardy, but, in reality, there was nothing funny about these two.

When Hugh returned to the villa from the farm, he found nothing more than a shell: all artefacts and furniture had been removed, windows and mirrors smashed. It stank of urine and of the faeces that had been smeared over the walls. Most of the Chinese staff had disappeared and now the farm hands were Russians. The new Masters were knowledgeable about pigs, but had no idea about cattle. Apparently, the Emperor had decreed that his forces must eat beef to build up their strength, but the herd comprised only dairy cattle. Ikeda asked Hugh if cows produced litters or gave birth like humans, whereupon Hugh demonstrated a live delivery to him for which Ikeda was very appreciative.

Hugh needed various stock medicines and Hideki invited him to join 'the party'. They assembled at A.S. Watson's in the Alexandra Building, and after passing round a looted bottle of whisky, it was a free-for-all. Almost all the spirits, cigarettes and tinned goods had already been emptied, but shaving cream and *Bay Rum* hair tonic filled Hugh's bag. After the Occupation, guilt overtook him and he made a payment to A.S. Watson.

In March 1942, the brigands suddenly departed and the hand over to the NSK was effected. *These* Masters were pleasant, well-educated professional men, most of whom had lived in the Colony before the war. The only requirement was that the stock of animals be built up and properly looked after. The secret stocks of whisky, cigarettes and tinned goods had been exhausted or found and looted. 'Tobacco' was made from dried leaves and grass. The Russians were distilling 'vodka' from vegetable peelings, soiled cattle fodder and rice water. Drunk with a generous pinch of red pepper it was passable. Ominously, veterinary medicines and materials were already running critically low.

Towards the middle of 1944, food was in extremely short supply and malaria was rife. The five foot eight inches Hugh, who had weighed eleven stone before hostilities now weighed just nine. The Europeans craved sugar, and a can of peaches would be traded for half a bottle of whisky. The British staff were free to *walk* anywhere they wished. But it was not safe to go out at night or to stray far from urban areas. The Masters now began to insist on the export of cattle to other occupied territories. Of course, Hugh and his staff chose the weakest ones. Surprisingly, but probably because no cattle were imported, there were no outbreaks of rinderpest, only one case of anthrax and one record of tuberculosis. There were no cases of 'foot rot'. Supplies of fodder were initially intermittent, but slowly improved.

Later that year, human flesh began to appear in some Chinese butchers' shops. Corpses would be found lying in the road with their buttocks removed. Packs of wild dogs roamed the hills. Hugh did join the Japanese on several 'shooting parties' – incredibly, all members were dressed in plus-fours and Norfolk jackets. Attempting to poison the dogs with laced meat was too dangerous simply because humans would seize the meat and eat it themselves.

Then, on 15th August 1945, it was suddenly over. A herd of nearly 2,000 cattle had been depleted to 315, of which, according to Hugh's records, at least 220 were in very poor condition, although they did pick up quickly once adequate rations could recommence.

Hugh could recall the detail all too easily – was it because he tried so hard to forget it? The Rock was perhaps too good a place on which to reflect – and drink. Good Lord, he had consumed *five* fingers of whisky! Time to secure the bottle and go home; besides, the wind was up and the rain starting to wet his shirt. But something was obstructing the smooth passage of the bottle back into the crevice. Maybe the detonation had dislodged some rocks? The unexpected difficulty brought a frown to Hugh's face. No, there was definitely some 'chunky' material down there. As a vet, he was not afraid of any of God's creatures; reptiles and insects did not bother him. He was used to sticking his hands into unusual places. So, now he felt the obstruction with his fingertips. It was soft, cold and leathery, slightly similar to the distended abdominals of a dead creature.

However, in the same moment, he detected there were some sharp, inorganic objects in its belly. His fingertips moved along; now, some tendrils were tickling the back of his hands. He clasped the neck of the object and with a swift movement, yanked it out of its lair. It was a leather bag, about the size of a small pillow case. Now he could see that the 'tendrils' were a leather thong that tied the neck of the bag, but, so engrossed had he been in his discovery that he had completely forgotten about the gathering clouds; in an instant, the typhoon dumped a torrent of water on him and the sunlight disappeared, as if extinguished by the unyielding might of competitor elements. He undid the thong and poured some of the contents onto the rock 'table', half expecting some serpent to wriggle out.

He could not believe what he saw... twelve gold ingots,

each hallmarked and with a weight of what must be eight ounces – enough to keep a man 'in the style to which he had become accustomed' for many years. Hugh could now see there were some sealed manila envelopes and four leather pouches, also tied with leather thongs, and about the size of a man's distended scrotum. These intrigued him and he opened one of them. Diamonds spilled out: cut and polished, others uncut. Some had been hacked from their settings, but still in their mounts. Carefully, but quickly, he scooped these back into the pouch and moved onto the next bag. Giant, exquisite rubies, this time all cut and polished, most hacked from their settings. The third bag spilled out emeralds and the fourth sapphires. By now on The Rock, the only light was that of the lightning itself. Despite being soaked to the skin, Hugh couldn't help but excitedly open the largest of the envelopes.

His hands were slightly trembling from the shockwaves going through his mind at the impossibility of what was happening. Surely, this discovery was not real... would this end with his awakening from a dream that was of course too good to be true? Now, ropes of pearls ran out. Like most well-to-do men in the Far East he had had to endure many hours in jewellers' shops while his wife would choose her pearls. "Pearls before swine," he would mutter. Consequently, he knew a thing or two about pearls and these were the finest!

The last package he opened contained jade. This jade was nonpareil; the tissue paper in which it was wrapped had turned to mash, such was the rain and wind that were now upon him. Time to go! He stashed his whisky away in its time-honoured place, and in what was now total darkness strode quickly across those so-familiar fields to the villa, clutching the leather bag closely to his person.

His wife was startled at his sodden appearance and ordered him to have a hot bath immediately. She knew the cold and the wet would bring on his malaria. She did not question the leather bag, which he placed in the desk drawer in his study. Once showered and changed, he told her he was not to be disturbed and made a list of the bag's contents which, once catalogued, he locked securely in the filing cabinet.

The next day he telephoned Chief Superintendent 'Mac' of the Hong Kong Police, requesting a meeting 'on a police matter'. Mac was extremely busy, but could see him at four thirty that afternoon at HQ. Hugh hardly ever ventured into town at that hour and was surprised to see how busy it had become. He presented himself at HQ at four twenty-five and was met by Senior Superintendent Ng, who handed him an envelope. It was a brief note from Mac stating that he had been called away on urgent business. The note went on to state that Ng was an extremely trusted and competent officer who could handle the matter or, failing that, Mac could see Hugh at four thirty the next day. But next day was when Hugh was flying off to Bangkok.

"If you wish, doctor, I can be of assistance to you," offered Ng, rather plaintively.

"Yes... Mac speaks very highly of you," Hugh conceded.

"It is our great honour to serve him."

"Could we go somewhere private?"

Ng raised the counter flap. "Follow me, doctor."

They went down a brightly lit corridor. Ng unlocked a door that led into a room containing no more than a table, a few chairs and a filing cabinet. He unlocked the cabinet and produced a bottle of whisky, water and a tumbler.

"Would you care for a snifter?"

"Snifters are for brandy, but yes, I will have one. What about you?"

"I'm on duty, but thanks all the same." The man spoke good English.

Hugh offered Ng a cigarette which was politely refused. "On duty."

He asked Ng about his history. Ng had been a young teacher in mainland China until 1937 and had then come over to Hong Kong to join the police force, mainly because of his fluency in English, Mandarin and Cantonese. He had detested the Japanese, but had somehow survived and was promoted quickly through the ranks after the Occupation. Hugh liked this man and decided to trust him. He showed him the contents of the bag.

"Loot." Hugh's eyes blazed, his mind still charged with the electricity of his find. "Obviously, and as an honest citizen, I'm handing it in."

Ng did not react in the way Hugh had expected. Instead, he leant back in his chair and told him this was happening almost weekly and that there was a procedure. The contents would be catalogued and photographed. A detailed receipt would be given to the finder and a few days later, the finder would receive the photographs. Regular advertisements in the English and Chinese papers were being run, inviting claimants to come forward. Sessions were held for the claimants, and Hong Kong's jewellers were present. The claimants had to produce itemised receipts, photographs or at least give detailed descriptions of the goods. Their interest would be noted and, if after three months no other claims were received, then it was theirs. A charge of twelve per cent of the estimated value was made: two per cent to the police fund, ten per cent to the finder. Ng told him the cataloguing and photographing would take a couple of hours.

"I'll go to my club and have a snifter if that's all right with you."

Two hours later, he returned and was handed the detailed manifest. He noticed that Ng smelt strongly of tobacco overlain with a whiff of whisky; well, perhaps his shift had finished...?

The next day he duly took the dawn flying boat to Bangkok as planned and spent two weeks there. Arriving back at Hong Kong, he went that same evening to a Caledonian Club function where he bumped into Mac and naturally enquired after his loot. To his consternation, Mac looked very concerned and guided him into a quiet area of the function room.

"Ng suddenly left the force – the day you flew to Bangkok, in fact. We don't know where he is and have heard nothing from him. Let me make a call to HQ."

A few minutes later, Mac came back, ashen-faced. "No record AT ALL of your loot, I'm sorry to say." Mac swallowed hard.

"It appears that the bugger has filched it."

Not a trace of Ng or the loot ever emerged.

Hugh was my father and on my twelfth birthday he called me into his study at our home in South Africa. Apart from a generous haul of presents that I had already opened, he now gave me a small but stout envelope. He bade me open it. It contained eight pieces of jade, mainly green, but some almost white and others a pink or rose. All were exquisitely carved and expertly worked.

"If I go 'up there', and perhaps your Mom and sister fall on hard times, show them this. It is worth a great deal of money." He then told me about the loot and said these pieces were so beautiful that he had not been able to resist keeping them. Two months later he was dead.

Events then unfurled quickly. I was 'pulled' from my boarding school in Port Elizabeth and strangely, instead of going back to our house, we went to a seaside cottage that we used to rent. A week later, everything that was inside our house was brought out onto the lawn and sold by auction, there and then. My die-cast metal toy cars (Dinky toys), my air rifle, my bicycle, books, models and, saddest of all, my canoe that had been made specially for me... this was purchased by the next-door neighbour for his son Paul, who kindly allowed me to use it for a few more weeks. My Pekingese, Snowy, was put down. After a few more weeks, my mother and I were on the *RMMV Stirling Castle* sailing for Southampton. My mother travelled first class as a companion to an old lady and I travelled 'tourist'. It was on this ship that I first came across queuing, and the oddity of being served by *white* men and women.

England was cold and grey. We stayed above a shoe shop in Oxford Street, where my sister, who had previously travelled over, worked as a sales assistant.

I overheard them talking one night. All the money my mother had in the world was ten pounds. My sister had nothing. As for me, I was to be 'put into care'. It was then that I produced the jade. They were naturally very excited, and the next day we went to an auction house for the valuation. It was all so strange to me: people in this uninspiring land queued for meals, for buses and now they were queuing in an auction house. I saw a young woman in a brown dress remove her gold necklace and receive sixty pounds in cash. Our pieces would go to auction.

The jade expert was a tall, slender woman with carefully coiffured white hair yet very black eyebrows and eyelashes. She wore a simple black dress, and around her neck a gold chain with a large jade pendant. She arranged the pieces expertly on a black velvet cushion. Suddenly, she threw the pieces a foot into the air, catching them all neatly in one hand. I will always remember how she tapped them together, held them to her cheek, and examined them with a jeweller's glass under a very bright light. They were scratched with her nail, touched with a pin and finally weighed and plunged into water.

She sat back and looked my anxious mother, that look going straight into her eyes. "Oh dear," she said.

We waited for the verdict like orphans in a railway station hoping for the train to salvation. Yes, they were lovely pieces, decorative; those that been shaped were beautifully carved, but they were not jade. Some were from the Transvaal, some from Australia and others were New Zealand Greenstone. She picked up several pink and white pieces. "Beautiful in their own right," the clinical voice said, "but not jade. A similar type of stone, but chemically died. This one is a man-made polymer. It has been made in a factory."

My mother became angry, shouting that these were from the Far East, and all were genuine. How could they be anything else? What qualifications did the woman have?

The lady was calm. "I'm the senior jade expert here. I have many years' experience. This House will not be accepting these pieces for auction; furthermore, we will not certify them. I know it is disappointing for you." She scribbled some details on her business card and gave the card to my mother. "Try these people, they're only around the corner and they'll give you a decent price – maybe as much as five pounds."

Dejectedly, we naturally grieved our circumstance. Yet, my sister went on to become a successful shoe designer; my mother the warden of a hostel for young women in Aberdeen, and I was enrolled in the Foundlings Hospital in Edinburgh. Some years later, we met Mac in Aberdeen where he had become an extremely successful (and wealthy) businessman. He was most generous to us and enjoyed an extremely lavish lifestyle. After he died, a rumour persisted that his wealth was ill-gotten from war loot that he had stolen from its finders. We will never know.

I still have those pieces, along with some worthless Tang Dynasty bowls, a 'priceless' stamp collection that I can't even give away and hundreds of share certificates for a diamond mine, except there are no diamonds in that 'mine'.

# Chapter Two: Nobody's Child

As always, things happened to me that do not happen to other people. This is not simply a tale about my formative years, but some events that will also stay with me forever. I am sure what happened then will never happen in this day and age.

My first boarding school was Grey's College in Port Elizabeth, South Africa. I was sent there at ten years old. At one point Grey's supplied a fair number of the Springboks Rugby team. It was more English, than England. But there were no midnight feasts or songs round the campfire. It was a harsh, brutal place. First you had to go through the 'Induction Ceremony'. Stage One – 'Walk the Plank'. The plank in question was a diving board thirty-three foot above the water. You were blind folded and had to walk the length and then fall into the water below in the pool. It was not a pleasant experience for a blind folded non-swimmer. Stage Two – 'The Gauntlet'. Here twenty older boys stood in Indian file with their legs outstretched. You had to crawl between their legs whilst they beat your bare back with wet knotted towels. Anyone who crawled too fast received 'a kicking' which forced them to slow down. Stage Three – 'Flickers'. Here the new boys were stripped naked, their hands tied to shower heads and the 'old boys' would flick their genitals with wet towels. It was in this school that I perfected the art of 'towel flicking', so much so that it became my party trick. I would build a pyramid canned beans/soups, place a half size can on top, then 'flick' a beach towel (with wettened tip) at the tin. The wet piece would curl round the small can; I would then yank the towel backwards and then, faster than a speeding bullet, the tin would fly to me. I would catch and place it on the table behind me. This would be done the moment my assistant switched the lights off for a quarter second. Kids loved it; in particular when the tin would appear in my trousers. Grown-ups hated it, particularly when mirrors and porcelain pieces were smashed by flying cans of beans. No wonder your genitals hurt for days after the 'The Ceremony'.

We played rugby four afternoons a week and on a Saturday night, by way of some gentle relief, it was Boxing Night. I was never any good at boxing. I would always be buffttd hard on the nose in the first round. I was so bad in fact, that I was excused from the bouts and 'promoted' to time keeper. I must say, this pugilistic entertainment did serve me well in later life. I was able 'to give as good as I got'.

The food was absolutely disgusting. Scrag end of mutton was served at least three times a week. None of the boys could leave the table until everyone of them had finished his stew. Certainly Oliver Twist would never have 'asked for more'. We found a way round this. New pairs of socks would come packaged in long wide plastic 'sleeves' open at one end and sealed at the other. These bags fitted perfectly into your shorts pocket. When The Master was not looking, we would scoop the filth up with our hands and stuff it into the bags. We were never found out. That reminds me of a true story.

A former colleague, of mine was an engineer. Roland was sent to Pakistan to lecture the military there on the latest development in flow meters. He arrived at the 'camp' in the early evening and was billeted in a comfortable room just of the main hall. At seven thirty he met the officers in their mess. Beer, gin and whisky flowed like the River of Babylon. This was followed by a veritable feast of curries. When he eventually located his bed it was not only rotating but also swaying from side to side. The next morning his 'boy' Ali woke him with a mug of hot sweet tea. "I have something very special for you Sahib, I bring." He brought a plate which he placed on the small table and pulled up a chair. On the plate was a red ball bigger than a large grapefruit. It was covered in a bright red sauce that stank sometimes of dried fish, sometimes like a billy goat's ejaculating urethra. It looked hot and fiery.

"What is it?" he questioned Ali.

"Wife made it. Goat. Very special for you." Ali laid out a knife and fork. "Enjoy most great." With that Ali retreated and closed the door.

Roland tried the windows. He would throw it into the bushes, Ali would never know. Locked and barred. Maybe to stop marauders, more likely for the Air Con. The toilet. Yes flush it down the toilet. He opened the door, to find Ali cleaning the WC. He would go to the hall, it was big enough; there must be somewhere to hide this monstrosity. Nowhere in the hall. Windows locked and barred. But, there was a ventilation grill. Out came the Swiss Army Knife. Seconds later 'the ball' along with the sauce was stuffed into the cavity. A quick flick of the screw driver blade and the job was done.

The door opened and Ali appeared. He looked at the empty plate and smiled. "Bit stuffy in there. Excellent dish," said Roland.

"I get you more," beamed Ali.

Roland said (most emphatically) that it was bad luck before a lecture to have two helpings. Somehow, Ali accepted this.

Roland went back to his bedroom and drank two bottles of coke. It is renowned as a stomach settler. After a mango and two dry biscuits he felt slightly better, but decided to rest until just before eleven, when there was a reception before his brief lecture. A quarter to eleven he entered the hall, now thronged with about thirty officers, all smartly turned out. Now, just under the vent, was a table with a white tablecloth. The table was groaning with beers and spirits. Apparently it was OK to drink alcohol, as long as it was not made from 'the juice of the grape', which of course included brandy. Roland's first gin and tonic took him back to the early evening last night; he was beginning to feel better. The group was jolly, relaxed. Better this than being shot at.

A very fat Colonel in a dazzling white uniform

announced, "God, it is hot in here. Dammed heat." He threw a switch on the wall. There was a strange clicking and whirling noise as the fan picked up speed to its max. Suddenly, with a great clattering noise and incredible fury, a giant red cone sprung out of the vent and literally sprayed most of the white, brown and blue uniforms with a deep vermilion. Revolvers were drawn and several fired. Everybody hit the floor. In the panic the white table cloth was dragged down with the bottles, glasses and ice. Everything made of glass shattered, further drenching the uniforms. Alarmingly, there was a loud BANG followed by a blinding blue flash. The fan had shorted out. More pistols were fired. Roland gave his lecture the next day – in a tent, which was considered far safer. Unofficially the enquiry had established that the cause of the damage was a rat's nest. Officially it was 'a simulated practise drill'.

My parents had their hands full with me. They would have in one hand a glass, in the other a cigarette. There were other problems too. At that time prescription medicines would be dispersed by physicians like sweeties. As a vet, father also had a ready access to opiates, the abuse of which led to some bizarre episodes. Too desperate to narrate here, or anywhere. But I do remember on one occasion, he flew into a rage and chased me out of the house and into the garden screaming, "I'm going to thrash you within an inch of your life!" We reached a large flowerbed, he at one end, I at the other. He removed his leather belt. He meant business! The chase continued. His trousers fell down. He kicked them aside. As a Scot, he believed in: "Wherever you be, let your bollickies swing free." He wore no underpants, even when attired in a kilt. What the neighbours made of a grown man chasing around the garden, naked from the waist down, I never will know. Then there was the time he tried to push my mother out of the car (it was doing fifty miles per hour at the time, with me in the back), or when he threw her down the stairs. On other occasion she went for him with a knife. So, Grey's College was not such a bad place to be after all. I settled in and became 'Top of The Class'. I was happy.

My parents decided I was old enough to travel home on my own by Lock's Bus. The distance from Port Elizabeth to George is about two hundred miles. Of course, the roads were not as good then as they are now. I took a bus from the school to the bus station. I was just about able to carry my trunk it had a handle on it, so it was 'portable'. I boarded Lock's Bus at four in the afternoon. It was a really old rickety bus, with hard seats. It was dirty and smelt of everything under the sun. I sat at the back, on top of the very noisy engine cover. All the passengers were adults. Every single one of them smoked cigarettes. Once we were on the highway, hip bottles of Oom Tas were drunk straight from the bottle by both men and women. Yet another smell to the noxious mixture swirling around. Reading made me sick, so I stared out of the window until it became dark. The bus would stop every forty-five minutes or so to pick up passengers or drop them off. Every few hours, the bus would pause at a petrol station so we could have a pee. At one of these I bought a small melon, a chocolate bar and a bottle of cold Cocoa Cola. The bus was now nearly full. An old smelly man sat next to me and offered me a Texan. We used to chant, "Texan is what the Qafas puff, Texan is what makes the Qafas tough." Well, this cigarette just made me feel sick. But I smoked it nevertheless.

It was not a pleasant night. At times we would be thundering along straight roads, at others labouring up winding mountain passes. A new fragrance was layered into the pot pourri of odours – vomit. Then, at about one in the morning, the engine conked out. Everyone piled out and stood by the roadside. Finally to everybody's amazement, the driver pulled a very fat, long, but dead snake from the engine. Another two hours followed whilst he extracted more bits of snake. Then the engine coughed into life, we boarded and set off again. Shortly afterwards, we arrived at a small farm house. The driver left the door of the bus open. He switched off the engine and went into the house. We were in a field. There were two decrepit shacks, one with a 'Woman' sign and one with a 'Man' sign on the door. Inside the shack, I found a pit and a stack of old damp newspapers. The stench was almost as bad as the bus. You washed your hands at a stand pipe.

At the first glimmer of dawn, the driver emerged from the house and off we went. Although I was now eleven years old – shortly to be twelve – I had a reasonable sense of direction and knew for sure, that we were literally zig-zagging across the country, picking up and depositing parcels and people. We entered a flat, featureless landscape. Many shades of brown. It was hot. The air shimmered and 'pools of water' could be seen in the distance, to suddenly disappear as you approached them. This stretch of the journey was very long indeed. One passenger produced a guitar, another a banjo and a third accompanied them on a mouth organ. The atmosphere became light hearted and jolly.

We stopped at a small 'dorp', one street, flanked by clap board buildings. The bus parked in a garage where the engine needed attention. The passengers drifted into a small coffee shop. My money was nearly gone. My travelling companion bought me a boerewors sausage sandwich. Boerewors literally means 'farmer's sausage'. Once tasted, never forgotten, meaty, fatty and spicy. The spices are usually toasted coriander seed, black pepper, cloves, nutmeg and allspice. My particular sausage was smoothed in fried onions and tomato sauce. Yummy. For several hours, we sat on the kerbside, watching the occasional traffic pass. Castle Larger had now replaced Oom Tas. My companion also bought me a bottle of Castle. It was cold, very cold. When the bus had been fixed, we set off again. All of us became sleepy and I fell into a deep doze. When I awoke, my companion had departed, he had stuffed a box of matches and three cigarettes in their packet into my top pocket. The landscape was becoming greener, cattle and sheep were grazing in the fields, tractors could be seen at work.

Darkness fell. I recognised some of the small towns that we passed through – soon I would be home.

The bus stopped outside my house. The driver retrieved my trunk from the hold. Father appeared and was very angry with the driver, but not as angry as my mother. She was screaming, using very bad words and trying to punch the driver. He kept stating, "Madame, this is not a luxury bus, it's an Economy Coach." To settle the argument, he threw down a handful of notes, the 'refund'. Father tossed the trunk onto his shoulder, took my hand and led me into the house. Apparently, my arrival was scheduled for eight o'clock in the morning, not eight o'clock at night. The school was meant to provide me with a packed food box. I told my parents that if it had, I would have eaten the bananas and biscuits and thrown the rest away. My return journey was by steam train. Father waved me off at the station. That was the last time I saw him before he died in somewhat mysterious circumstances. Was it accidental death through an overdose of drink and drugs? Was it the fire? A heart attack? Suicide? I will never know.

The Foundlings Hospital in Edinburgh was a bed of rose petals compared to Greys. The boys were all very friendly and there were GIRLS! Of course, the girls slept in a separate house to our building; the one exception was when they contracted an 'infectious disease'. No, not one of 'those diseases', these was measles and chicken pox. Then they were placed in quarantine in the 'infirmary' on the same floor as us boys. The infirmary was next to where Matron slept. Matron was partial to a tipple or ten and was normally 'out' in her bed by eleven. Many boys contracted 'infectious diseases', including me. Heavy petting and kissing was enough to contract the disease from the sickly girls. The food was divine, pies and chips, haggis and turnips, macaroni cheese and on Sundays, a roast dinner. Because of my rugby playing skills, I was held in high regard by my peers. Sadly, I lagged behind academically. There were a great deal of new subjects – Latin, French, Geometry and Mathematics, all of which I found horribly difficult. I went from 'First in the Class' at Greys to last. I was sent into the 'B' Stream. Woodwork, Arithmetic and Bible Studies – a promising career beckoned as an – Undertaker! One of the masters, joked that I was 'God's Gift to Mathematics'; well, at least I eventually proved him wrong.

This was the era of The Beatles. Most the 'cool' boys acquired guitars and formed bands. I was learning the Highland Bagpipes, however, the House Master bought me a recorder so I could keep up with these budding pop bands. Apart from struggling academically, I was relativity happy. During the long summer holidays I worked on a grouse shooting estate beating, that is to directing the grouse to the guns. In subsequent seasons I looked after and led the ponies that would carry the fat ladies and gentlemen up and down the glens. These ponies would also be employed in bringing down basketfuls of felled grouse. I lived in a bothy with young male medical students. It was basic, but it was fun! At Christmas and Easter I went to an uncle; my mother would occasionally join us – cigarette in one hand, glass in another.

The problem was mid-term. For this, my mother would send me four ten shillings notes. To put this in perspective, just under two shillings would buy you a pint of beer. I was told to find another boarder to spend mid-term with. Nobody would take on that responsibility, so I slept rough. I spent my nights in woods by the river, broke into boats to shelter there. The school boiler house was pleasant, sleeping on coal sacks. After several mid-terms I found the solution. The swimming baths that we used on Monday afternoons had a double life. From nine o'clock at night until the next morning it was for 'Adults Only'. During that time you could swim, enjoy the Turkish baths, the Swedish sauna, the Jet Room, and have a massage. There was a small coffee counter there, where you could have a snack. Then, exhausted, you could sleep it off in a private cubicle. It was very popular with jockeys, long distant lorry drivers, dancers and late night revellers. The management turned a blind eye to my age, after all, there were lots of 'young boys' there.

I was fascinated by the Turkish bath. The rule was that you had to wear towel at all times. Users wore towels going in and coming out, but these were discarded whilst in The Room. Here I saw naked men and women. Both sexes sprouted enormous hair bushes between their legs, however, some of the ladies had trimmed, or even shaved theirs. The men had big dangly willies, sometimes that were not that dangly, but firm and erect. Their bodies (by and large) were lean and well muscled. Some of the ladies were also lean, but generally plump and wobbly. This was an era when most ladies wore corsets – 'The Playtex 24-Hour Living Girdle', to control those rolls of fat. After the swimming, steam and sauna, I would have a cup of tea and then retire to my cubicle. During all my overnight visits there, I was never molested or propositioned.

So the terms progressed. In my fourth year I decided to run away. I wanted to escape to Paris and become a sculptor. Like Brancusi. I decided to do this one November night. I simply walked out into Edinburgh and took a bus to the outskirts. It was a bright, cloudless night and bitterly cold. I started hitching, however, after several hours of walking without a lift I decided to sleep in a haystack. It was cold and I shared it with lots of little fury rodents, but I slept well. Two weeks later I arrived at Marble Arch in London. My days were spent wandering around, the nights sleeping on building sites. Always cold, always hungry. The small stock of money that I had was running out. I then found that I needed a passport to go to Paris, so I decided to return to Scotland. Here, I was caught by The Housemaster in his car on the Forth Road Bridge. I had been sighted and reported. He took me to me his house, and made a few telephone calls. In one of them he said, "The laddie isn't going anywhere until he has a good breakfast." A 'good breakfast'. It was cooked and served by The Housemaster's wife. I was then taken to the infirmary where I had to take a bath and then was put to bed. Eventually, a doctor arrived, examined me and asked a lot of questions – a lot of questions.

For two days I was confined to bed. My only visitor was Matron. A couple of the lads sneaked in to visit me in the dead of night, finally, in the early evening The Housemaster came to see me. He sat awkwardly on the edge of the edge of the bed and kindly asked me about my adventures. He finally stood up and gazed out of the window. He was a former SAS man who eventually settled as a PE Instructor in the regiment. "All the boarders here are Foundlings – from one parent families whose mothers, or sometimes, fathers have difficulties." He paused and tugged at his moustache. "We're all a family here." He turned and looked at me. His Adam's Apple was moving up and down rapidly. He blurted out: "We all love you." He sat on the bed and looked at the floor. "You're a tough bugger, Guy – well done. Do you want to come back?"

I replied that I did and that I was sorry for the fuss that I caused.

"Good man!" he exclaimed and patted my shoulder. "Tomorrow you will go in front of the whole school. You will apologise. Then you will be tawsed." He sucked in his breath. "Six on each hand. No one has ever had that. Are you up for it?"

"Yes, Sir."

"Good man! You are a tough old bugger!"

Next day I stood in front of the whole school. Apologised. The History Master, another SAS man, known as 'Mr Tawser', squared up to me. "Ready?"

"Yes, Sir." I squeaked.

I removed my jacket and rolled up both sleeves. The procedure required that the arm to be tawsed had to be held palm upwards and supported by the other hand. The History Master removed the tawse from his shoulder, where he would habitually keep it under his jacket: 'The execution's sword is always well hidden'. He looked me straight in the eye – and winked. Then the blows came. Sharp, stinging and very painful. I wanted to cry out, to scream in agony. My eyes were watering. I stared straight ahead. "Other hand now," he whispered. The process was repeated. He nodded his head. "Jacket on," he whispered. Spontaneously all the pupils, boys and girls broke into cheers and began clapping furiously. On and on.

The Headmaster shouted for "Order" and then Mrs Macrae began playing on the piano fortissimo – 'All Things Bright and Beautiful' – as loud as possible. The Housemaster put his hand on my shoulder and whispered, "Well done, trouper – it's all over. Rejoin the school!" Nobody ever raised any questions about my episode. Forgotten.

My uncle was Deputy Keeper of The Signet and Chairman of the Hospital's Board of Directors. The Governors had an Extraordinary General Meeting. Motion – to expel me or not. The Board voted, and the result was right down the middle. My uncle had the casting vote. Being the honourable man he was, he decided to vote: "Expel!" However, just before the motion was passed, a leading legal light stood up and pleaded that the whole thing had been "a boyish prank" and he urged for a re-vote. It turned to be: "Not Expel." On Leavers' Day, I was given, like all the other Foundling Leavers, a ten pound note and a copy of the bible and wearing my new donated suit, the kind man came up to me and offered me a place in his law firm. I turned it down; a decision I regret to this day.

In my last year I was promoted to a prefect and made huge strides academically. One day The Housemaster called me into his study. Tommy, who was in the year before me had 'a problem'. Could I help? Normally, such help was given by one Foundling to another on academic matters or some form of sports coaching. It could only be that Tommy required rugby coaching; this puzzled me, as he was good at the game. It appeared that Tommy had a 'crossed wire'. He was attracted to other boys, rather than girls. He had been reported doing "vulgar and inappropriate" things with a Day Boy (non-Foundling). Could I talk to Tommy? Tommy had agreed. I met Tommy alone in the Housemaster's study. We talked. He liked girls, but was attracted to boys. He had 'done it' many times with other boys. He liked it. He liked it a lot. He found girls' bottoms too big. He disliked their breasts. I told him 'doing it' with another boy was illegal and if discovered, he would go to prison.

"I won't be discovered," he retorted.

"But you already have been," I stated flatly. Tommy asked if I had ever 'done it' with a girl.

"Not yet, but I am looking forward to it when it happens."

I reported back to The Housemaster. "Thank you. Nothing we can do. He might grow out of it."

Tommy went on to become a famous surgeon. Changed sex and was known as Tomasin. He was a scratch golfer and his change created problems when he still insisted on playing golf with 'the boys'. Today, The hospital is a 'chi chi' Gallery of Modern Art. The refractory where we ate our Scotch pies and chips now serves deep fried smoked goat's cheese and elderflower wine. The dormitories are offices. The gallery officials' eyes glaze over when you tell them you spent five years of your life in this very building. Most of the former pupils became doctors, lawyers, accountants and engineers. Sadly, quite a few are dead now.

I finished my fifth year and went on to achieve better grades at Napier Technical College (now known as Napier University). So I could say I read French and Geography at Napier University. All I need now is to purchase a fake title, so I can call myself Sir Guy Gundle MA.

It was in the spring on that year I went for the Duke of Edinburgh's Silver Award. The Duke is one of my heroes. "Seldom explain, never complain, just get on with it." I already had the Bronze Award, the Silver was obviously tougher. It involved travelling with three others by bus to a Youth Hostel in the Kielder Forest, staying overnight, then at the crack of dawn going orienteering in the forest. This involved charging around the forest using a map and compass to find and be clocked in at various points. Pilots would call these 'waypoints'. It rained heavily, was bitterly cold and the course went on forever. We finished at two in the afternoon, walked six miles to a bus stop and travelled to Cumbria where we camped in a valley next to a raging river.

The next day, we travelled by bus to Lochgilphead, where we camped by the ruins of a derelict castle. It was cold and wet. The following morning, we were picked up in a Land Rover and were taken to the shores of the loch. Here we donned wet suits and plunged into the loch. These rubber/neoprene suits are very hot – until you plunge into the cold water. That water seeps between the suit and you. It is not a pleasant sensation, however, within a minute it warms up. Standing in waist deep water, we were instructed in how to use an aqualung. Three hours later we were 'qualified' to dive. We now boarded a rubber dingy that took us into the slightly deeper waters of the loch and dived. My lasting impression of the loch bottom was that of thousands of huge crabs scuttling along the loch floor. I thought these creatures could be turned into 'crab cakes' and go a fair way to solving the world's hunger problems. "Let them Eat Cake." That night we stayed on a one ton yacht where we were given a static sailing lesson.

At the crack of dawn, the engine was fired up and we joined almost fifty similar such craft. We were to race to Tarbet! The gun fired and we were off. The wind driving the boat fast forward. We reached open water and now waves began breaking over the prow. I felt slightly queasy. Movement was difficult. Constantly adjusting the sails was hard work. Cold and wet, but thrilling, as the sun was setting when we sailed into Tarbet Harbour, moored and made good. At a quayside hotel we had a slap up dinner consisting of Prawn cocktail, steak and chips and double cream whipped with whisky. There was wine and beer too. I think the skipper paid for us. We had come third in our class, whatever 'class' meant. The skipper was extremely pleased. Next day we sailed back to Lochgilphead. What fun, what an adventure. Thank you, Duke.

Three further days were spent hiking and camping in the Highlands of Scotland. A great deal of drizzle, freezing cold nights. A diet of canned soup, baked beans and fried eggs. Our water came from burns, cold, brown and peaty. This test completed our outdoor stage. My companions travelled back to Edinburgh and I went to visit my Aunt Grete. She lived in a Highland hamlet on the hillside overlooking the loch. She spent twenty-five years of her adult life running a hotel, latterly with her husband in a suburb of Aberdeen. They did not have any children and when her husband died she sold the hotel for a 'tidy' sum and settled in the remote hamlet. A couple of years later, my Aunt Christina left Grete a substantial sum and left me, a teapot! I had never met Grete and did not know what to expect.

The bus arrived at two in the afternoon in the one street hamlet. I found an old teuchar (Gaelic Speaking Highlander, usually male) coming out of the pub and asked him where my aunt's house was. "You're looking at it." It was a large Victorian stone house, halfway up the hillside. He directed me to the road that wound pass it. It was large edifice with a magnificent view over the loch. There was no one in. I sat down on the bench that had a plaque fixed to it. *Enjoy your retirement Murry, you have done roamin.* The plaque was old and rusting, obviously belonged to a previous owner. I sat on the bench and ate my last bar of chocolate.

It was a fine sunny day, but I felt cold. My throat was sore, as if a wire bristled bottle brush was being rubbed up and down my throat linings. My nose was running and I had a persistent cough. I dozed a little. I was woken by a bicycle bell ringing loudly. A trim woman was riding an old-fashioned bicycle with a wicker work basket in the front. The basket was filled with bread and milk and some other groceries. She wore a tweed jacket and corduroy trousers, she propped up the bicycle and came over to me:

"You must be Guy! I'm Grete." We shook hands. She apologised for not leaving a note on the door. The house faced north. Despite the number of tall windows, it was dark and gloomy and rather chilly. She took me up to large bedroom and then into the bathroom. She suggested I should have a bath. I welcomed this idea, as I had not bathed for a week and I was cold. I bathed and changed into less dirty clothes. There was now a peat fire glowing in the lounge. Shortly, she brought in a pot of tea and a plate of warm Scottish flapjacks. There is nothing better in the world than warm Scottish flapjacks spread with butter, home-made berry jam and a dollop of double cream. She had one, I finished the rest.

There was something I could not place about Grete. She moved stiffly and was reluctant to make eye contact. Despite her mannish clothes, she was feminine and must have been very attractive in her younger days. She was squatting in front of the fire, adjusting the burning peat. She asked me to hand her the poker. I walked round and passed the poker to her. Then I saw the reason for her awkwardness. Her entire left cheek was a mass of scars, bumps and old lacerations. It was also motley coloured – red, brown and purple in places. It really looked like a visage out of The Phantom of the Opera. It shocked me. "Sorry, to have startled you." Grete looked at me now full face. "It's my childhood disease, don't worry, it is not infectious."

I smiled. "Don't worry, it does not bother me." I felt awkward, I wanted to touch her shoulder, but sat down instead.

We were sitting by the fire. She had two companions, Golden Labradors, Holmes and Watson. Lovely dogs. Grete did not have a television. She did have a huge old-fashioned wireless with a booming sonorous tone. One of the backlit dials was inscribed with cities like Bombay, Calcutta. Lucknow, Rangoon, Colombo, Baghdad, Tehran, Cape Town and Lourenco Marques. It hissed and squeaked as you turned the dial. I expected the plummy tones of a young David

Jacobs to announce: "Good Evening, this is David Jacobs of Radio SEAC in Ceylon..." Her library was comprehensive. Just before dark she took me on a tour of her garden, which at the rear of the house was south facing and protected by the hill and tall pine trees. Her glass house was her pride and joy. She claimed she never bought any fruit or vegetables, other than bananas and oranges. She even grew her own lemons. She played bridge, shot, made jam and fished for trout in the loch. Tomorrow we would go fishing. After running a hotel for thirty-five years (never a holiday), she relished the quiet life.

She told me her story. Not all the Gundles were academically gifted. One became a butcher, another a shop-keeper and Grete went into catering. Today it would be called the 'hospitality trade'. She was employed by The Rest Inn. Initially, a trainee, she started helping cook prepare breakfasts and then serving them. Next she commenced chambermaid duties, cleaning the bedrooms, making the beds up with fresh linen. This was followed by a few hours in reception, taking bookings and some basic book keeping. After that it was a couple of hours behind the bar, cleaning the bars and bottling up for the next session. She enjoyed three hours on her own in the afternoon; not really enough time to go Aberdeen proper. From six till closing time, she was behind the bar again. The dining room was open only for breakfast, otherwise you could have bar snacks: Scotch eggs, pickled eggs, sandwiches, deep fried things 'in the basket'. The inn was really a public house with a dozen rooms upstairs, whose main trade was travelling salesmen. There were two bars, one was rather plush and catered for the 'passing trade' and one for the locals. The owner manager was a small round man called Willie. He managed a tight ship. War was coming. He reasoned that drink and victuals would be in short supply. War, or no war, beer would be brewed. The quality would suffer, but there would always be beer. Whisky would be produced and exported for valuable foreign exchange. Whisky would be in short supply.

Whisky keeps – forever. Willie extended his downstairs cellar lengthwise, but also created another, deeper cellar. He laid down all the quality whisky he could afford. Not only whisky, but fine wines, port and bottles of old ale. He knew gin, on the other hand, would not keep. He also stockpiled tins of ham, bully beef, oysters and sardines. Hams from Italy were hung from the rafters of the cellar. War was declared. Aberdeen, which was already a major fishing and ship repairing centre now was an important harbour to The Royal Navy and The Rest Inn, effectively became an officers' billet and mess. When the war in Europe ended, there were four bottles of whisky left to celebrate with.

Grete continued to live and work at the inn throughout the war. She also worked in a naval repair yard, threading the fine wires in electronic equipment. This activity was seen as 'women's work', Of course, she met, and no doubt, flirted with many men. How much her disfigurement affected her, or them, she did not say.

It was in the local, at precisely six o'clock every week day evening that a certain Ian Grant would appear. He was a young, local bank manager. He had done his wartime service on a destroyer and achieved the rank of lieutenant. You might think that being young AND a bank manager was an oxymoron, but he was actually the Deputy Bank Manager. Good looking and sharp suited, he drove a Jaguar. Not many people knew he was the only son of a poor farm worker. When his parents died, he was left nothing. They had lived in a tied cottage. So, despite the smart suits and expensive car, he rented a room in a house where he lodged with an elderly spinster. Ian would stop for a couple (or six) 'wee' drams of Grants of course, washer down with 'heavy' beer chasers. Some people become maudlin when they become drunk, others aggressive or morose. Ian became 'exuberant'. He would behave like a pissed newt on steroids. At best he could be amusing; at his worst, offensive. There would be several 'shoving' episodes. On one occasion a fist fight ensued in the car park. Willie, said "enough was enough". Ian was banned for three months. Upon his return, the bad behaviour repeated itself and a six-month ban was imposed. This hit Ian hard as there were no other watering holes within walking distance of his lodgings.

Despite his errant bar room behaviour, he was an exceptionally good Deputy Bank Manager. Most of the wealthy clients of the bank were 'little old ladies'. Wealthy widows in fact. If a man did not succumb to fags n' booze, or arteries blocked with fat, then he would retire at sixty-five. Within a few years, he would be 'pushing up daisies'. Of course, the ladies just went on and on. This was also in a banking age when there were no 'fire walls' limiting what a Bank Manager could do with regard to investing on behalf of clients. Ian advised his clients well and they appreciated it. One of his 'little old ladies' was a Mrs Day. Her husband was a successful potato merchant who was killed in a car accident at the age of fifty. Their only son died of leukaemia at the age of twenty-four. Despite these misfortunes Mrs Day was a cheerful lady. Ian built her a balanced portfolio of 'blue chip' shares. Household names that rendered a high yield and long-term capital growth. He persuaded Mrs Day to take her ample private pension and re-invest her dividend proceeds. "Compounding makes you rich, there's no hitch," he would chant.

One day Mrs Day came to see him at the bank. As usual, she brought him a box of his favourite Havanas and a bottle of Grants Special Reserve. Ian conducted a quick review of the portfolio, which as always was simply grand. Mrs Day listened abstractedly. "Aren't you pleased?" queried Ian.

"Oh yes I am, but I have had some bad news." The poor lady was suffering from an inoperable brain tumour. She stated this as a matter of fact. "You see, with both husband and son gone, I have no one to leave my money to. The house will go to my housekeeper, along with a small legacy. The gardener and my driver (she never used the word chauffeur) are also in line for something, but there is an awful lot left over."

Ian laughed. "You could give it to me. Sorry, everyone thinks I am rich, because I dress well and drive an expensive car, but I rent from an elderly spinster. I'm sorry, I'm being very unprofessional. Do you have no old friends or acquaintances?"

She had not. She preferred the company of her Pekingese, Chow Chow to that of other human beings. No decision was reached. They shook hands and Ian slipped the cigars and whisky into his briefcase.

Two months later, Mrs Day was dead; a month after that, Ian Grant received a substantial part of her fortune. The first thing he did was make several enquiries as to who exactly owned The Rest Inn. It was a large hotel group and they were willing to sell, because The Rest Inn "no longer fitted their profile". The deal was done. Ian immediately sacked Willie the manager and several other staff. He promoted Grete to Manageress. Then he moved into Willie's quarters above the pub. This created some problems as to where the new Assistant Manager would live. The problem was solved. Willie's flat had two bedrooms, a kitchen, a bathroom and a large lounge. Grete would have the spare bedroom. The Assistant Manager would have Grete's old room. Of course, one thing led to another and Ian and Grete were married six months later.

Ian resigned from the bank, cut down on his nocturnal nips and concentrated on building up the business. The dining room was extended and opened for lunch and dinner, seven days a week. A large annex was built with twenty-four bedrooms. This was followed by a banqueting suite (weddings, funerals, corporate events). They were favoured by the Aberdeen Oil Boom. The City became 'The Texas of Scotland'. Then Ian dropped dead and Grete commenced her new life.

Tea (really supper in Scottish) was ham, egg and chipped potatoes, rather than chips. I washed it down with a bottle of India Pale Ale. She consumed several large whiskies. The next morning, after a full cooked breakfast we went down to the loch and along a jetty to which was tied a clinker built boat. It was covered with a canvas tarpaulin under which were fishing rods, all the fishing paraphernalia and a seagull engine. We boarded – along with Holmes and Watson – and she quickly fastened the engine and started it. It was very noisy and puffed clouds of white smoke. It took us into the middle of the loch. Here we fly fished, also using spinners and worm bait. Unfortunately no fish. At lunchtime went put putted to a large house on the other side of the loch. We tied up and rang the doorbell. Dogs barked within which set off Holmes and Watson. A lady in a tweed skirt and blue blouse appeared welcoming us in. I was feeling faint and glad to sit down. We ate a simple lunch. I was taken on another garden tour, then we crossed the loch again, I was glad when we made it to the house.

I retired to bed for a few hours and managed lamb chops and vegetables, and an excellent jam roly poly pudding and custard. At eight o'clock that evening aunty gave me a glass of whisky and a couple of aspirin. I went to bed and experienced an uncomfortable night. The next day I was distinctly unwell. I sat in front of the fire and drunk a little soup with bread dunked in it. She took my temperature. She called the doctor. He was a young man with a large black bag. He gave me 'a shot' in my bottom and some pills. I was told to rest. Another troubled night, sometimes I was hot and dry, sometimes shivering cold, but sweating copiously.

Aunty appeared several times during the night. When daylight broke she brought in a young plump woman, who had strawberry blonde hair and intense blue eyes, she had big white teeth and smelt of fresh mown hay. Her name was Morag and she was going to be my 'nurse'. Grete commented: "Wet nurse." They both found this extremely funny. I did not know what the term "wet nurse" meant.

Morag made up a fire, changed the sheets and placed several hot water bottles in the bed 'to air it'. She sat me by the fire. She lived in the glen and her ambition was to study domestic science at Edinburgh. Her ambition was to be the greatest pastry chef in the world. I must have dozed off for several hours, for when I woke it was snowing heavily outside. Grete joined us. "We have no doctor. He's gone skiing. Tonight, Guy, you will have your crisis." I did not like the sound of that. Apart from a painful throat and earache, it felt as if my lungs were stuck together. Well, I was a tough lad and I would handle my 'crisis' like a man.

Morag returned. She had changed into corduroys and a chunky sweater. I went to bed. The main lights were switched off. Morag sat by the fire, reading with the light on. She was drinking a cup of soup. I dozed intermittently. My aunt gave a 'hot toddy' and some more pills. I drifted off. Something disturbed me. Someone was lying next to me in the bed. Someone soft, plump and female. It was warm and pleasant. The nicest experience I had ever had. It was Morag, she rolled around, wrestling with her garments. Despite my sodden T-shirt and underpants, I could feel her naked body. She whispered "Do you know what a wet nurse does?" I had no idea. "I'll show you." The next thing I found a stiff nipple being thrust into my mouth. Not just the nipple, but the large part of a large beast too. They say the Bluebirds live in Heaven, making occasional trips to Earth to bring good, but always unexpected news. When they are in Heaven, they feast on ambrosia and nectar. On Earth they live only on fallen nuts and fruit. Now I feasted on ambrosia and nectar. I was in Heaven. My crisis came, the evil left my body. I woke to a fairy tale landscape of virgin snow. I was weak, but I was well again.

I returned to Edinburgh. I met Morag a few times. We had a few drinks in various bars. She had lost her freshness; s the no longer smelt of hay, but tobacco, liquor and cheap deodorant. She went to finish her course in Switzerland. As for Grete, we exchanged Christmas cards, then the cards stopped. I learnt from a distant relation that she had passed away and the house had become a bed and breakfast place.

# Chapter Three: The Three Persimmons

I had just turned eighteen. I was as fit and lean as a Tour de France competitor, having cycled round most of France in six weeks: thighs of woven steel whip cord, stomach flat as a board, brown as a berry.

It was mid-July and I had a place at Edinburgh University. I was to move into a Hall of Residence at the start of September, but The Hall was being refurbished and the move was postponed to the first week in December. I had to find lodgings from mid-July until then.

I telephoned regarding a 'Room to Let' on the outskirts of Edinburgh. The door was answered by a pleasant, plump middle-aged lady. I had already explained it was for a limited period only.

"Share the kitchen." I was allowed a cupboard of my own and the lower two shelves of the refrigerator. "But, please clean up after you." The bathroom/toilet was to be shared, and again the exhortation to "clean up after you". I was allowed to share the lounge with her, but not when she was entertaining. My room upstairs was large, light and airy. There was another WC on this floor.

"Oh, I nearly forgot, the roof terrace." She led me up a steep, narrow staircase which emerged into a kind of cabin cluttered with deck chairs, a sun umbrella and small tables. "Feel free to use this area. Nobody overlooks us and yet we can see the whole of Edinburgh. It is not locked and when up here I leave the cabin door open to ventilate the house."

I paid the deposit, signed the agreement and moved in. Mrs Grey quickly realised I was not up to cooking, so kindly allowed me to share her meals provided I washed up and occasionally mopped the kitchen floor. This was the late sixties and her meals were way ahead of the time. Spaghetti bolognaise, lasagne, cannelloni, stuffed baked peppers, artichokes and a very strange vegetable – avocado.

All meals were accompanied by wine. For a lady who took in a lodger, her taste in wine was unusual and expensive. She had an account with a venerable Edinburgh wine merchant, and together we took a virtual journey around France. Over the evenings, we started in the Champagne region with the eponymous product of that region. Then we moved to the Loire Valley for the crisp, fragrant wines of that area. Over to Burgundy next – deep, rich, full bodied reds. For a while, we travelled down the Rhone and then basked in the south. Finally, of course, it was Bordeaux. Great old boys, mainly *Cru Bourgeois*, but the odd something a bit special. It was an educational journey that stood me in good stead for the rest of my life and I will always remember her for that, the fact that she shared these wines with me. Some were undoubtedly expensive, but most represented value for money.

A heat wave had broken over Edinburgh. It was hot and, for once, no wind from any direction. I took my easel onto the roof and began to paint. My subject was 'Persimmons'. Persimmons were hard to find in Edinburgh then (and probably now as well). I did find three – wax ones. It was so hot that I had to shield them from the sun. I brought my tape recorder up and played all the great hits of the sixties endlessly, over and over again. I had to wear gym shoes to protect my feet from the hot roof. The only other thing I wore was a pair of cut-down denims.

At four o'clock, Mrs Grey emerged from the cabin. "So, you're here then. Mind if I join you?"

She laid out a deck chair and small table, then disappeared into the cabin. Ten minutes later, she emerged with a large jug of pinkish liquid in which were floating ice cubes, fruit and green vegetables. She poured me a glass.

"What is it?" I asked.

"*Pimms*, a kind of alcoholic cordial to which you add you gin, lemonade and fruity bits; lots of ice of course."

It was cold, wet and tasted good. Mrs Grey lay back and pushed her dress up to expose her thighs to catch the strong sun.

The next day, about the same time, the ritual was repeated. More *Pimms*. She offered me a cigarette, but I told her I could not paint and smoke at the same time.

"What are you painting?"

"Fruit."

"Oh, from imagination." She could not see my shielded persimmons. "Can I look?"

"No. Please. I do not like anyone to see what I am painting until it is finished. Never!"

"OK, OK. I won't look – never."

The hot, sultry afternoons continued. She now appeared in a 'bikini', or rather a two-piece bathing costume: boxer-like trunks, just ending above the knee, her top finishing on the upper ribs. A matronly outfit. She produced a large bottle of sun cream.

"Let me apply it to you."

I declined – no need, I was tanned enough. Then I was invited to oil her up. This gave me a strange, sensual pleasure – gently massaging the oil into her soft white flesh.

"The soles of the feet are particularly important." So, I obliged.

Then one afternoon, she suddenly sat next to me in the deck chair. "Do you mind if I take my top off?"

"Of course not."

I had seen paintings of bare breasts in all the national galleries and art books, but never in the flesh, as it were. They were large and pendulous with huge erect nipples, which reminded me of those rubber extensions at the end of pencils.

"C'mon, oil them," she commanded. This was a new experience. I have to say it was not unpleasant.

As the days passed, the skies became hot and angry. The forecast predicted only a few more days of the heat wave.

"Would you like to paint me in the all?"

The question stunned me. "This is oil paint, it is hard to clean off the skin."

"No. I mean, paint me posing in the nude?"

"OK then."

The trunks came off. First time I had ever seen a naked woman.

"Aren't you going to use a fresh canvas?"

"Oh yes."

The skies turned a grey-brown colour, a sharp wind sprung up. There were drops of moisture in the air.

"I'm cold." She threw on her towelling robe. She came over to me to look at the painting. I tried to stop her, but she pushed past.

What she saw was a painting of three persimmons.

# Chapter Four: Teapot

Objects have always been important in my life. Bicycles, motor bikes, nice motors, aircraft, even pens. In fact, I am something of a pen fetishist. But one object changed my life forever. It brought me fame, honour, riches and love of women. What was it? An old, chipped, cracked teapot. But what a story!

*And here is that story.*

Aunt Christina was a relative of our family. In fact, I never knew she even existed until I received a letter from her one day inviting me for afternoon tea. I was in my first year at Edinburgh University. She lived in Morningside - a posh part of Edinburgh, where the music hall joke was, "they carry coal in *sex,* not *sacks*". I arrived exactly at the time specified: three forty-five on a Sunday afternoon. Her first-floor apartment, was in one of those old stone tenements, it was large and spacious. The windows on the left looked out onto the street, the windows on the right onto green parkland.

We shook hands. The drawing room was indeed well-appointed. Antique furniture, paintings, objects of art. A maid in a black woollen dress and white lace apron brought in the 'tea'. This was in a different league to what I had ever experienced. Tiny sandwiches (with the crusts cut off) of dressed crab, wild Scottish smoked salmon, smoked ham, beef (sliced paper thin) and egg and cress. Then, mini cream puffs, warm buttered dropped scones with blackberry jam and clotted cream, brandy snaps and filo pastry cups filled with *Chantilly* cream with strawberries peeping out. All this came off a three-tiered plate. The tea was a delicious *Darjeeling*, accompanied by just a drop of milk.

Aunt Christina was very interested in me. I told her that

I was reading Sino studies. The time flew. Finally, she rang a small bell, and the maid cleared way. Aunt Christina went over to the sideboard and poured two large whiskies, each with a splash of water.

"*Slàinte mhath.*"

"*Slàinte mhath.*"

I raised my glass. Of course, I had drunk whisky before, but this was different to anything I had ever tasted. Smokey, peaty, with a hint of iodine and… oh, so smooth! We agreed to meet next week, same place, same time.

The following visits followed the same pattern. I had time now to observe my aunt. She was probably in her late sixties. Trim, elegantly dressed. White hair, or as they now say, 'ash blond'. Piercing grey eyes. She was a lady who never missed a trick. During term time, the Sunday visits became a regular fixture. Slowly, Aunt Christina's past life started to unravel and what a story it was! She had read Oriental Studies at Oxford. Not bad for an impoverished gamekeeper's daughter with six other siblings. My father invited her out to Hong Kong, where he worked, to stay as long as she liked. She had already secured a post there as an English teacher. Once in Hong Kong, though, something went wrong between her and my mother. Old Chinese proverb says: "The symbol for 'Trouble' is two women under the same roof". How true. Well, she met and married a rich banker, George Sanderson. In Hong Kong, you *really* had to be rich to have the sobriquet 'rich' in Hong Kong. And George was indeed rich. He had an expensive mansion on the Peak, a string of horses in training, and a fleet of motor cars, yachts, motor launches and speedboats. He was a keen rival of father's as a shot and on the golf course.

Then the Clouds of War began to gather. George was a 'larger than life' character. He worked hard, played hard and lived hard. Unfortunately, whilst everyone was making their 'just in case' preparations, George dropped dead from a heart attack. There were no children, and this left aunt having to put George's affairs 'in order', and she really did not have time for any detailed 'just in case' preparations. Then, on 8 December 1941, it happened – the Invasion of Hong Kong, followed by the Surrender on 'Black Christmas'. Like everybody else, she had heard of the atrocities being committed by the Japanese troops, and she decided to activate Plan B...

Plan B was a motor launch built by the British Power Boat Company, capable of 29 knots. The craft had extra fuel tanks added and the very latest wireless and navigation aids. The Plan included stocking the craft with adequate water and provisions. It was kept moored in a derelict-looking boathouse conveniently located away from prying eyes. Christina and four trusted Chinese hands launched the craft on a foggy, moonless night and motored at speed towards a small fishing settlement on the mainland. Their journey was fortunately uneventful. The launch was concealed amongst all the other marine paraphernalia clustered together. Christina made for a small missionary settlement that she financially supported and visited regularly. Here, she was able to blend in with the other missionaries.

It is difficult to imagine now how extensive the Japanese hold already was at that time, and how it was rapidly becoming even larger, conquering huge chunks of mainland China, Burma, Siam, Malaya, French Indo-China, Korea, Formosa and the Dutch East Indies. There was no place to hide. For a while, she felt relatively safe with the missionaries. But then rumours and reports circulated. It was too dangerous to stay, she had to move on. She dyed her strawberry blonde hair black. My family were originally Viking invaders who had settled in northern Scotland, so she had Scandinavian features such as almond eyes – but she could not disguise her *grey* eyes.

On the plus side, she spoke fluent Cantonese and Mandarin. She travelled west, using whatever means of transport were available, but often on foot. Finally, she settled in a small town which afforded relative safety. She taught and also worked in the local hospital. Her travails were not over, however, because China itself was gripped in a brutal civil war. After many adventures, she reached India and eventually returned to a peacetime Hong Kong in the autumn of 1945. Like father, she found it a changed place and difficult to adapt to. She salvaged what she could – mainly investments and numerous titles to land. Small, valuable items had been well hidden and escaped the mass looting that had taken place. George had invested a great deal of money in solid companies in Great Britain, so most of the fortune was safe, if not battered. To her horror, however, her beloved string of racehorses had all been eaten! She founded a school to promote British culture to the ever- increasing influx of mainland Chinese immigrants. She never remarried, although she enjoyed the company of many friends. In 1960, she decided to 'retire' to Edinburgh. From what I gathered, she played golf, bridge and travelled extensively.

I really enjoyed my visits to aunt. Always so civilised, refined and cultured. She also had a wonderful sense of humour. Her facial expressions would convey moods and nuances that mere words could not. Her apartment was a calm island in the mad sea of my life. The long summer holiday arrived again and I went to Thailand for a study trip. When I returned and took tea, I was shocked at aunt's appearance. Always a trim lady, she was skin and bone. Her stylish dress hung loosely on her. Her facial bones were pronounced, the skin thin and translucent. The gorgeous grey eyes were sunken in dark, deep sockets. The maid had 'gone home'. The sandwiches were stale and purchased from a bakery several days ago. The tea was bitter and strong, but the whisky was the same. I noticed the glasses were none too clean.

"I've not been well. Problems inside." She patted her stomach.

When I took my leave, she came close to me and kissed me affectionately, something she had never done.

"You're a good boy, er, I mean man. Your father would have been proud of you."

Tea next week was postponed. Unfortunately, there was never to be any more tea. She passed away peacefully three weeks later. I was sitting an important exam on the same day as her funeral and was therefore unable to attend, to my everlasting regret.

Some weeks later, I received a letter from a firm of solicitors inviting me to attend the reading of the Will at aunt's Morningside residence on Tuesday afternoon at two-thirty. I dressed in my only suit and wore a white shirt and dark tie. I arrived at two-fifteen and found thirty or so people in the drawing room. At one end were two sombre-looking gentlemen sitting at a rosewood table. Running alongside the wall was a table covered with a white cloth and a spread of sandwiches, jugs of coffee and milk and a tea urn. There were also bottles of wine and whisky and glasses. The air was heavy with cigarette smoke and liquor fumes. An awful lot of furniture and artefacts had been brought into that room; everything was labelled. Most of the doors in the apartment were open and each doorway was guarded by a stout gentleman. It seemed so invasive from the beautifully furnished, airy, elegant place that I used to visit. I noticed that, unlike all my previous visits, there were no cut flowers. I poured myself a glass of throat-wrenching whisky and ate a very bland ham sandwich.

At exactly two-thirty, one of the sombre-looking gentlemen bashed his glass with a spoon and silence descended. He read out the will, slowly and carefully. More cigarettes were lit. Glasses were topped up, glances exchanged. I never appreciated the old girl was so wealthy. Bequests included Agnes the maid, aunt's hairdresser, the local butcher, a seamstress, a steward on a cruise ship, and her golf club – with very specific instructions as to how it was to be spent, mainly on improving the ladies' changing rooms. Other benefitting organisations included a donkey sanctuary, another animal sanctuary, an old people's home, Oxford University and the bridge club. More cigarettes were lit, the same glasses refreshed. Again, I looked around at the assembled throng: I did not recognise any of them; all middle class, mostly middle aged, well dressed. No children, thank goodness.

The Sombre Man now took a long drink from his weak whisky. The serious stuff was coming. The throng sensed it too. He read out the names of the beneficiaries who would receive certain investments. Even I recognised the famous names of British companies: stalwart, blue-chip, copper-bottomed entities that had been around for years and for that matter, are still around, although some have changed names to protect the innocent. He moved on to the paintings, furniture, Chinese and Persian rugs, crockery, cutlery, ornaments and jewellery. It was this last item that caused a stir amongst the crowd. Suddenly, conversations simultaneously broke out all around.

The Sombre Man tapped his glass vigorously with the spoon. "Quiet please! I will take questions later."

The Morningside apartment itself was to go to a certain Miss Gundle, which was met with all round approval. More names, more objects. Then I heard my name! I was to be left the Ming Teapot, Exhibit 448d. I had admired a certain teapot which aunt told me was Ming. It had a certain charm, but was chipped and cracked and looked rather sorry. It could not have been worth much. A couple of quid maybe in a flea market? Sombre Man now read some instructions regarding this teapot. I was to INSIST on an X-ray examination as part of the valuation. Sombre Man cleared his throat and took another pull at his whisky and read from the will.

"From the stench of corruption comes forth sweetness. From the humble clay comes forth wealth. Sometimes we must destroy what we loved in order to build again."

The Sombre Man smiled. "Well, thus it is written." He suggested a short break, then he would take questions and, like a judge, rose, bowed and disappeared from the room.

So, I had inherited a broken teapot. Aunt always served tea in a heavy, round gold teapot, which was only coloured gold of course, but it made a lovely cup of tea.

I tried to work the room, introduce myself, but nobody was interested in me. They were all rather smug, insular types, yet some of these people were my blood relations! Well, you can choose your friends, but not your relations, as they say.

Sombre Man returned, tapped his long-suffering (refreshed) glass again and started to take questions. There was a lot of bitterness about who got what and why, but the will was the Will of Aunt Christina, who was of sound mind etc. Finally, with some impatience and bad temper, he moved on to the 'Disposal Instructions'. These were complicated for some of the items, but in my case, it was simple. I would be shown the teapot and a photograph of the same. I had to sign a statement with my name and address and certify the photograph was a 'true likeness'. Then it was mine. Cardboard boxes of various sizes and packing materials were to hand. I could pack it and go. This I did as I was not comfortable with this pack of lounge lizards. Once, aunt may have been one of them, but no, she was in a completely different strata to them, and in a very different place too now.

I made an appointment with a venerable firm of antique dealers to have the teapot valued. The office I was shown into was more like an attorney's office than a dealer's. A sprightly man sat behind a large, red, Moroccan tooled desk.

"Sale or insurance?" he asked.

I wanted to sell. He looked at the pot that I had placed before him. "It's in the style of Ming, whether it is Ming or not we will soon decide. The poor thing has been in the wars."

He sprayed something onto the pot. "Don't worry, it's only distilled water." He polished a section of the pot. "A lovely *Zisha* clay purple hue. Lovely curved spout. It was said of an Imperial Chinese eunuch once that he had a huge sprout on his teapot." I had to sit there as Sprightly laughed at his own joke.

"The handle is thinner at the top than at the bottom, a

classic indication of the real article. Ha! Look, here is the maker's mark – a Master Craftsman." He reeled off the man's name and the emperor in which dynasty the craftsman had worked. "Can you see here... some very light fingerprints? Another sign of authenticity."

I marvelled at Sprightly – the knowledge that he must have acquired over years of study, travel and handling these pieces. Things were beginning to look up. He picked up the pot and a puzzled expression came over his face. "Very strange, very odd. It is unnaturally heavy – and thick. Sir, I have handled hundreds, if not thousands of such teapots, and none have been as heavy as this, or with such thick walls. Teapots of this era were called *Yixing*. It marked a revolution in tea making. Previously, tea leaves had been dried, pounded in a mortar and pestle until in powder form, mixed in the pot with boiling water and then poured into a ewer for serving.

"With *Yixing* teapots, leaves were placed directly into the pot and boiling water added, then the tea was poured straight into the cup. This opened a whole new range of tea making opportunities. Also, at that time teapots became lighter and thinner as production techniques improved. Obviously, nobody wants to pour tea from a pot weighing several pounds."

He sat back and lit his pipe. Scented clouds of Latakia and Perique swirled round the room. "All right. It is far too thick and heavy to be genuine, I'm afraid. Way off. It has been badly bashed up, poorly repaired. No attempt whatsoever has been made at a cosmetic repair. The fingerprints, the maker's mark look genuine, but the piece isn't. I would say it is an imitation, one of thousands that were churned out on the thirties in the Far East. It's been badly smashed and clumsily repaired. Sorry, sir. Try the flea market, if I were you."

I asked him about X-ray.

"Never heard of it for porcelain... besides it would cost a fortune for something that will probably fetch five shillings or so – at most."

I took the pot back to my lodgings, glared at it and started drinking cheap sherry. I had thought that Aunt Christina and I had had a special bond, yet the Anglicised Scots took the top off the cream, whilst I was left with a teapot worth probably 'five shillings at most'. Then I thought of those words in the will: *From the stench of corruption comes forth sweetness. From the humble clay comes forth wealth. Sometimes we must destroy what we loved in order to build again.*

Strange... *destroy what we loved in order to build again*? I drank more sherry. Whisky made me mellow, whereas cider and sherry made me aggressive. I was aggressive now. I spent my adolescence in a Foundlings Hospital; I lived on my university grant supplemented by odd jobs. And here was this Anglo-Scottish rabble rubbing their hands at the Bluebirds that had descended on them from Heaven, showering them with life-changing wealth. I saw red and, in a fury that surprised even me, I flung the teapot at the fire grate, shattering it into dozens of pieces.

But amongst those pieces, I now realised, were various small, and not so small, objects. Fortunately, there was no fire in the grate at the time. I crouched down – my God! Some gold coins, pearls and pieces of jewellery heavily encrusted with diamonds, emeralds and rubies. My pulse racing, I rushed into the kitchen and picked up a heavy chopper. Using the back of it, I carefully fragmented all the pieces of that now-sacred teapot on the hearth stone. More and more precious objects emerged. The world could have stopped turning and I wouldn't have noticed. I continued my work into the night until every single object had been retrieved and all that was left of the teapot was dust.

The next day, I visited that 'five shillings at most' dealer again. My haul was valued at more than thirty times what my annual grant was worth! So, what to do now? Well, slowly, over the years, I would sell a piece or two. And, every year the value of the remaining pieces increased. It literally changed my life.

I have thought about this a lot, and can only think the precious objects were embedded in a crude, specially made fake teapot that was broken on purpose and then deliberately so badly repaired that it would be extremely unattractive to looters. Obviously, and I am sure of this to this day, Aunt Christina did not want that 'lizard pack' to know what I was receiving, particularly having so accurately predicted their behaviour over the other jewellery she had bequeathed, and which I had witnessed at so grotesque a spectacle.

No wonder why aunt had insisted on an X-ray! The lesson – if there is one? Well, listen to aunty, she knows best.

# Chapter Five: The Puckle

He was not a stepfather, not even a real uncle, but I called him 'uncle'. A small, precise man who had been a senior partner in a major firm of Chartered Accountants in Hong Kong.

"So, your results will be out soon. What sort of career do you have in mind?"

"Poet. Uncle – I am going to be a poet."

"Most poets go to university and have a day job. What sort of day job are you considering?"

"Sculptor – that's my second string."

He blew great clouds of blue smoke from his Burmese cheroot. Being a sculptor demanded a workshop, raw materials, equipment, tools and, most of all – commissions.

"Any other day job?"

"Travel writer."

"What about being a Chartered Accountant?"

It was now *my* turn to express surprise. I explained that maths had not been my strong point at school. I had needed extra coaching just to pass the basic exam. He replied that I had had a Scottish education and, armed with such and the Bible, a ten-pound note and a new suit – all provided by the Foundlings Hospital – I could do anything, or be anything, I wanted.

"Just continue your homework, four nights a week."

Thus it was that I left the dull, grey-brown of Edinburgh with its little old ladies in tweed coats and pillbox hats to come down to London. It was a hugely exciting time. The sixties were in full flow and the place was on fire: Carnaby Street, free love, mini-skirts, The Beatles, The Stones, Pink Floyd.

So it was that I arrived for an interview with a firm of Chartered Accountants in the city of London. It was pretty much a formality; I was offered the position, subject to a 'skill test'. For the skill test, I was led into the records office and given a copy of the London telephone directory. The directory had been opened at a certain page and I was instructed to add up all the numbers on two particular pages. Office computers had not been invented then, nor, indeed, had calculators. I was given a blunt pencil. I began my task. I had just reached the foot of the first page whereupon the door was flung open and an urchin in ill-fitting clothes burst in.

"So, they have given you 'The Test'! You'll find the answers on the last page." With that, he dumped a pile of papers on a nearby desk and sauntered out, whistling. This urchin went by the name of Barry and was the office junior and tea boy, who hailed from Romford in Essex. Subsequently, he eventually rose to be the Chief Executive Officer of a global, Hong Kong-based PLC, hugely eclipsing all of us, whether qualified or unqualified as accountants.

But now, he had disturbed my concentration. I turned to the last page of the directory and yes, there was indeed a number written in pencil. What to do? Replicate the number? Two – obviously conflicting – emotions swirled around in my mind, and I felt my heart start to thump as I wrestled with this dilemma. Eventually, self-confidence and pride won, and I decided to continue my own addition, and... low and behold, reached the same number! A week later I received my formal offer letter.

For the first two weeks, I spent my time filing massive piles of papers. Then a young, extremely good-looking man came up to me in the records office. He introduced himself. "Sebastian Don. You must be Guy Uisdean Gundle."

I confirmed I was. He went on to tell me that we would be going for a preliminary 'Client Meeting'... that is, with clients who were apparently not 'conventional'. He then asked if I was broad-minded. I didn't give it much thought at the time and instead just confirmed that I was 'very relaxed' about anything.

"Excellent," he replied, emphatically. He looked

straight at me. "You will need to be." He winked and was gone.

It wasn't long before I got to learn what he had meant.

We had taken the bus to Carnaby Street and had entered a boutique that was selling kaftans, beads, joss sticks, hubble-bubble pipes and other such essentials of life. A svelte, seductively attractive woman met us and led us up a flight of stairs into a dimly lit room with shuttered windows. Most of the space here was taken up by a huge brass bedstead covered with a patchwork quilt, with bedside lockers either side. Apart from a single chair, there was no other furniture in the room at all. Without saying a word, Sebastian took off his jacket and waistcoat, folding them up neatly; he removed his tie and shirt, hanging them on the back of a chair swiftly followed by his unbuckled belt and trousers. He was wearing a pair of underpants that were somewhere between Y-fronts and those sort of shorts that runners wore in those days. I remember they were in candy-pink stripes.

Only now did he glance at me. "C'mon, strip!" he commanded, clearly intolerant of any refusal on my part to ask the obvious question of *why*, or such like. So, I obediently followed his example, all the time thinking this was some weird dream from which I was about to awake. Removal of my outer garments unfortunately and inevitably revealed my Y-fronts, which, once white in colour, had over the years deteriorated to an unwelcoming grey and which also unfavourably sported several large holes.

Sebastian was now under the quilt and was beckoning impatiently for me to do the same. Oh no, I had heard of this kind of stuff and it was not for me! The look on my face must have given my thoughts away and I could guess resistance would meet with Sebastian's disapproval. Ludicrously, it went through my mind how my dismissal notice from the firm surely could not be justified on the grounds of "refusal to get into bed with scantily-clad male colleague…" What Sebastian would have thought of that I will never know because at that point the door opened and a winsome redhead in a kaftan wafted in as if on a summer breeze.

"Hello, darling, you must be Guy." She gave me a wet kiss on my cheek and then peeled off her kaftan. She was as naked as the day she was born! She swayed over to the bed, all her wobbly bits wobbling, and she climbed in next to Sebastian, kissing him full on the mouth. Gingerly, I climbed under the coverlet on the other side of the bed, apprehensively awaiting the next move. The door then opened again, and another kaftan entered, her black hair cut in a tight bob. She, too, flung off her kaftan; her bits were smaller and there was less to wobble. She snuggled up close to me. Her body was so hot that it felt she was on fire!

The first kaftan opened the top drawer of the bedside locker, which seemed to be brimming with a fragrant, dark tobacco. She took an extra-long cigarette paper and rolled up a 'big one'. She lit it, inhaled deeply and then passed the wet, lipstick-stained joint to Sebastian, who also inhaled it deeply before passing it to the second kaftan. After taking a heavy pull, she handed it to me. I took a drag, then another and rested whilst a wave of euphoria overwhelmed me.

"Hey man, don't bogart that joint!" Sebastian snarled. I immediately passed it back to the second kaftan. Eventually, when the joint had been passed to and fro and was half gone (not to say the least about us), Sebastian declared the 'meeting' formally open. Incredibly, consumed with the joint and with the naked young redhead lying virtually on top of him, he launched into a merciless monologue about stock obsolescence, working capital, return on capital employed, and the perils of overtrading. Then, just when I thought he would cease this farce, and taking no notice of the girls, who were clearly not the slightest bit interested, he started up again, this time banging on about the importance of the audit trail, how imperative it was to safeguard the assets, pension schemes and that he would now begin producing schedules from the files we had brought with us, to back up his statements – which he started to do there and then – reaching for them on the floor whilst simultaneously continuing to maintain contact with the redhead.

In the midst of all this expert rambling, and with my mind otherwise happily overwhelmed by the euphoric wave of the tobacco, I became aware of a hot hand plucking at the tired elastic of my Y-fronts. With great relief, I ruled out Sebastian as I could see both of his hands above the quilt. And it was not the first kaftan, as both her hands were playing with Sebastian's nipples. I glanced at the second kaftan; she wore a vacant expression on her face and was dreamily gazing at the ceiling. Now, that same hand was removing my underpants and decisively gripping my manhood.

Well, when that happens to a man, *his* hands will also start to wander and what those hands found was a wet, moist, verdant coppice. Sebastian had now stopped talking, the files had slid to the floor and the first kaftan was on top of him, pumping her bottom up and down rhythmically. He started to groan. The second kaftan had guided my willing manhood to a place where it was very happy. Soon, I was flying through the clouds and the rain – and what soft, gentle, fragrant-scented rain it was. Again and again, I flew. Finally, my engine gave out and I glided to Earth with the first kaftan atop of me. When the storm had ceased, she extricated herself from me and lay flat on her back.

"Tea, anyone?" she plaintively offered. All Sebastian and the second kaftan could do was to mutter their assent. The first kaftan reached for a stout stick on the floor by the bed and banged three times with it. By the time another joint had been lit, a third kaftan had appeared with a tray bearing an ornate tea pot and tiny, silver tea cups. I remember it being wonderfully refreshing and cleansing.

That ended my first 'client meeting'. The formal minutes did not reflect the meeting, but then, do they ever?

What would I have written? Perhaps Sebastian's business lecture would have sufficed for most of the official agenda items, with all parties being in unanimous agreement. And they would surely have provided an effective camouflage for the activities that really did go on that day. I had begun to look forward to more of the same such meetings, but, sadly, a year later the shop went bust, and what happened to those girls I have no idea. Perhaps their talents were utilised elsewhere? Nevertheless, to this day I still have a wonderful 'thing' about cheesecloth kaftans.

As I write these events, it is with some effort that I have to put memories of those kaftans aside, and bring things back to Earth because, strictly speaking, in this firm I was but one of thirty articled clerks in the organisation. All young men, most living at home. Only two of us, Tarquil and myself, lived in bedsits so it was not unreasonable that we should combine forces and rent a flat.

Tarquil was a gifted accountant and sailed through his exams, whereas I was a plodder and struggled. We both smoked for Britain and certainly, Tarquil seemed to drink for his country as well.

Eventually, the amber stuff blighted Tarquil's brilliance and at the grand age of twenty-one he left the firm and went to work as a book-keeper for a small retail group. It was there that he met Arrowminta.

Arrowminta Bradger was the daughter of a wealthy brewer; she was young and attractive. She lived just off Sloane Square and would drive her old British racing green MG Sports down to 'Mater and Pater' every weekend. Tarquil, Minty and I became firm friends.

Then came the time when Tarquil had to spend a fortnight in Milan on business and it was at that time Minty invited me to join her at 'home'.

At exactly 15.40 on that first Friday of Tarquil's absence, we sped down the M4 to Minty's home. Home was a Georgian manor house which had been bolted on to a much earlier farmhouse. Not bad at all. My jaw dropped as we got out of the car – hopefully, Minty didn't notice.

As soon as I settled into my room, there was a knock on the door and a gentleman carrying a silver tankard of ale appeared and placed same on the sideboard.

"I am Bernard," he announced with much dignity. "Sir must be thirsty." Then he retreated.

I went downstairs to the large kitchen area, which seemed to be the hub of the house: flagstone flooring, a long oak table and chairs, wood-burning Aga cooker. Minty was seated at one end of the table reading *Country Life*. The door leading from the yard opened and a petite, mature yet very lithe and supple woman in jodhpurs, riding boots and hacking jacket entered.

"Hello, I'm Annie, Arrowroot's Mum," was her confident, self-assured introduction. I shook her hand without having a chance to get up. She stood over me, preferring it that way, so it seemed, as she removed her hard hat to reveal a mass of shiny, incredibly silky, jet-black hair – all done up so neatly in a tight bun. She said no more as she walked over to the stove to stir the simmering contents of a large copper pot. She seemed to be nonchalantly dealing with this as if having contentedly done so for many years, and momentarily I felt a deep-rooted longing for such warm, secure homeliness – and oh, how this woman made such a thing seem so naturally possible!

I was dreamily reflecting on this when suddenly, and with the speed of a fork of lightning, she grabbed a heavy saucepan off the shelf and flung it with a force of such violence that can only emanate from raw instinct through the open window. In disbelief, I saw her yank another saucepan off the shelf and Annie had shot through the open door. There was a loud clanging noise. A minute later she emerged with a dead rook in the pan.

"Got him!" she exclaimed, triumphantly. I was shocked beyond words.

I think I said something like: "That's incredible." Seeming to take no notice of my astonishment, she quickly and efficiently began to pluck the bird and then over the sink slit it open, prising out its innards. Soon it was reduced to a tiny meaty fowl. A couple more downward strokes with a cleaver and the pieces were thrown into the pot that earlier she had been stirring. She then removed some bloody stuff from the offal, chopped it roughly and consigned that too to the pot. "The heart," she said.

"That'll be delicious." She smiled at me. "It'll be ready in an hour, then we can eat." I felt sick.

There was no need for me to change as I had come straight from work and wore my city suit. About twelve of us were gathered in the drawing room, sipping dry sherry: the ladies in pretty, floral frocks; gentlemen in cavalry twirls and tweed jackets; inevitably, I felt slightly out of place.

Dinner, as I remember it, was rich and gamey. Crystal glasses, Wedgwood crockery and silver cutlery with ivory handles. The ladies withdrew as if by instinct, and us 'gentlemen' drank port and a very excellent old brandy. We reconvened in the drawing room and the conversation seems to have concentrated mainly on country matters. It was after midnight when I finally and wearily made it to my bedroom. My jeans and T-shirt had been pressed and laid out; the lidded ale tankard replenished.

I had bought, especially for this occasion, a pair of expensive black silk pyjamas. I changed into them and was just finishing off the last of my ale, when I heard a soft knock on the door. Secretly, I had been hoping for that truly wonderful sound at something like this hour because, surely, it could mean only one thing: that this was my moment. After all these months of longing, I had finally conquered Minty! The tortoise had triumphed over that hare, Tarquil. All I had to do now was 'bite and hold' my territory. Just to think about what this would mean: Minty had no siblings, so some of this wealth would be mine… the brewery, the pubs, the manor itself; the horses – what a dandy life would surely open up for me now. Rich, monied ease at last.

Confidently, and with a feeling of elation that I hadn't

experienced for a very long time, I opened the door a little.

"It's me," came the soft female voice.

I opened it wider. Although the corridor was dark, I could make out a female form – wonderful... but no, this was not Minty, but her mother!

"Minty is not too well, poor darling; so, *I'm* the substitute!" she announced. Her black hair, now released from the confines of the tight bun, hung down to her waist. She wore nothing more than what I can only call a 'cutty-sark': it was sleeveless, short and transparent. Under her armpit was a small, purple clutch bag. I had expected Minty, but was going to end up with Annie, so it seemed! Well, often it is the substitute that scores the goals. I must have relented my grip on the door because now she breezily entered the room, quietly closing the door behind her. I gazed at her with some incredulity: yes, the garment was completely transparent. It revealed a pair of stupendous breasts, nipples erect. Between her legs was a blur of darkness. She pressed her softness against me.

"What will Mr Bradger say?" I almost squeaked, breathlessly.

"No problems. We exchange hospitality with our guests. It's a country house custom."

I was beginning to like this country life stuff; this I could adapt to. She took my hand and led me over to the four-poster. Now, in a moment, the cutty-sark was off and two seconds later, the lights were out, my silk pyjamas gone and we under the covers. The clipper was on the tide and picking up speed.

Well, they say, "the lower classes do *it* more often, the upper classes do *it* less, but with more verve and imagination". I could now certainly verify that. The sleeping Naga sprung to his full height, the ocean of milk churned and churned and finally gouts of Amrita burst forth. This time, not so much clouds and rain, but 'thunder and forked lightning'.

I marvelled at the woman's dexterity and staying power. I suppose all those hours in the saddle must strengthen the pelvic floor. Of course, I had read about 'The Singapore Grip', but did not expect to experience it in rural Gloucestershire. My judo coach had told me to never do the same exercises back to back; certainly, we did not perform the same exercise twice in a row in that bed.

Finally, we rested. After a few minutes, Annie switched on the bedside table light and took her clutch bag over to a small table. I stared at a painting, which if not a Stubbs, was certainly in the school of. Maybe she was doing something that ladies needed to do after coitus?

"Come," she insisted, pulling up a chair. Somewhat sheepishly I walked over to the table and sat on the chair. On the table, there was a small mirror, some lines of white powder and a couple of straws.

"What is it?" I asked.

"Angel Dust. Do as I do." She placed a straw up her right nostril, pressed her left nostril with her thumb and then inhaled through the nostril. "Don't snort too hard, slowly and gently."

I replicated her action. It was a little like taking snuff. I switched to the left nostril and then followed her back to bed. A rush of pleasure descended upon me. I was riding with her on a Magic Carpet, we were flying over the Euphrates and Tigris and then over the Plains of Araby. Where and when it ended, I cannot say, but the next thing I knew, Bernard was placing a cup of tea by the bedside.

"Breakfast is being served in twenty minutes, sir." His gaze upon me gave nothing of his thoughts away. Perhaps he knew all too well about these 'country-house customs'. "I have taken the liberty of providing sir with a Puffa. It's rather chilly on those gallops." The garment in question was one of those quilted jackets, much favoured by the 'Country Set'. It was a dark green colour and smelt a little of stale perfume and tobacco.

When we arrived on The Gallops that morning, it was misty. The air hung with a curious aroma of whisky, coffee and wet dog. Then I heard the rumble of hooves. Suddenly, through the mist, burst a magnificent black horse, head down and snorting vapour. A full two seconds later, the pack appeared, lathered in sweat.

"Unbelievable," I said to the man standing next to me.

"Yes, and we are going to have a puckle on him next Saturday at Newbury."

"Absolutely," I replied, for want of anything else to say.

It turned out that the man was the Royal trainer and the horse in question *The Digger*.

After the gallops, we all travelled back in the shooting break to the manor for brunch. Minty was in fine form and demonstrated no ill effects of her apparent condition. Annie, on the other hand, completely ignored me, which began to trouble me as it was starting to occur to me that something was going seriously wrong with my plans of conquering Minty and getting rich quick and easy. I then travelled with her to a 'point to point' on some lord's estate and finally she dropped me off at Wandsworth and made her own way back in the mini and parked at Sloane Square. We talked on the long way back but I couldn't seem to get the conversation 'right' – we were clearly not on the same page in our lives nor going to the next chapter together either.

That Friday, and still trying to put such thoughts aside, I attempted to re-focus on wealth acquisition and went to the bank to draw out my entire month's salary in cash. With what may have been more ambition than judgement, I drove my old banger to Newbury and placed the lot on *The Digger* at 12 to 1. He was running in a hot Novice Hurdle and hit the front almost immediately, streaming over the hurdles like liquid mercury. He led for three flights but then was 'reeled in' by the pack. You certainly could not fault his jumping, but there were others that seemed be more in command. With two flights left in the final straight he was sixth and I was beginning to wonder how I could survive financially the next month.

Then, suddenly, he began to accelerate – it was almost as if he left the others standing still. He flowed over the last, gave himself a shake like a dog emerging from a pond, and literally shot into an ever-increasing lead to finish ten lengths ahead of the next runner.

A year's salary won. It was only in the press reports later that I learned the term 'puckle' meant a restraining nose band. *The Digger* had been 'a puller' and it was this device that did the trick.

Tarquil returned from Milan. He begged, borrowed and stole funds, and bought a baby BMW *Roadster* – canary yellow. He had it parked outside Minty's flat on the morning of her birthday. It was tied with a giant pink ribbon. He phoned her to "look out the window". Well, they married, had two children and he lived a life of comfort and ease thereafter, the brewery, the pubs, the manor, the horses – all his.

I saw Annie at Tarquil's and Minty's wedding. Again, she was cold and distant towards me. I told myself I had done nothing wrong, but the feeling of being disliked so much by someone stayed with me for some time, much as I tried to remove myself from its vice-like clutches. Two months after the wedding, Annie eloped with a wildlife correspondent from a cheesy newspaper. I learnt soon afterwards that the trauma of it all was simply too much for Mr Bradger to bear and that he 'sucked off' his Purdey – both barrels discharged for good measure.

Sometimes, I regret things but sometimes *time* offers clarification on what *life* is really all about, and it is certainly not always what it seems at the time. I wonder? But, for once, this was a case of 'fast horses and fast woman'.

# Chapter Six: Big Bertha and the Garden Party

I had a sixties summer affair with her. (Big) Bertha. She was BIG, black, round, hot and fiery. A lot of adjectives, I know, but she was a lot of woman. I would go down to her place at five thirty in the morning, crossing from Hampton Wick to Kingston over Kingston Bridge. A wonderful time of day. Scullers on the river, joggers along the tow path. Little traffic. I would open up Bertha and rake her out with my long iron rod. She was on fire and I would break out into a sweat. My next task was to check the clockwork temperature chart recorder. This was an instrument of beauty. It was kept in a glass case that had to be polished every day. It consisted of a brass cylinder driven by a clockwork mechanism, which also had to be wound every day. On the cylinder was graph paper with a blue line showing the desired water temperature in various storage tanks hourly. A red stylograph traced the actual temperature. My job was to exactly track the red line to the blue line. 'Chase The Blue Vein' as it were. I would be awarded a weekly bonus if I 'more or less' achieved the requisite result. The bonus could be as much as half a day's wages, so worth going the extra mile.

My next job would be to hurl shovelfuls of small coal right up to the and work back all the way to the orifice. I would now pull out the ash pan and shovel the dead coals into a large metal bin with wheels which I would have to push all the way to the bin yard. After consulting the cylinder, I would shovel larger lumps of coal into Bertha, again commencing at the rear and working to the front. These jobs done, I would close Bertha's door and make a cup of tea. Bertha's function in life was to provide hot water as well as heating, for the eighty flats in the three blocks. Before finishing with Bertha, I had to thoroughly clean the boiler house. Coal dust and fire can be an explosive mixture, not to say what coal dust can do your lungs.

Tuesday was bin day. The garbage for the flats was thrown down shutes that ended up in huge wheeled bins in the bin areas. The refuse collectors would come mid-morning and empty the bins. My job was to wash and disinfect these bins, a horrible dirty task it was too. Then I switched hats and became a gardener. Cutting grass, trimming lawns, weeding, planting, and pruning, all in a day's work. I would leave the best job to the end of the day – watering. For this I would strip down to my shorts and simply water everything that grew. Apart from strapping horses, stoking a coal fired boiler is the best way I know of building a superbly sculptured torso. The outdoor work also gave me a deep tan; then, of course, youth was on my side. Oh, how I wish I could have that body now.

Working in the flats produced a surprising pleasant by-product. A number of the flats were rented/owned by young professional ladies. Occasionally, some of these ladies would return home in the late afternoon. It was not long before I was invited to tea; tea led on to drinks, drinks to supper and eventually, so to bed. It certainly cut down on my travel time to work.

One day, the former Sergeant Major who ran the place told me that the following day arrangements had been made so I could join the other assistant caretakers to go to one of the properties within the group for a spot of gardening, which would make a pleasant change. The next day I joined the other assistant caretakers in a van which drove us to a much smaller block of flats overlooking Ham Common. Our job was to give the gardens a once over. As a treat, lunch and liquid refreshment would be provided for us at the local pub. We had brought our own garden tools and a push lawn mower. It was a hot sunny day and we worked like demons. True to his word, the Sergeant Major stood the lunch and liquid refreshments bill. Fuelled by Ram and Special we worked even harder and faster. The sun beat down, the sweat poured off us The SM was beaming with pride. "Well done, lads!" We were all lads in the group. "Let's pack up now."

A tall elderly gentleman had been watching us for the last half-hour. I noticed he was smoking a Dunhill half apple, expensive. He now strode over to the SM. "Colonel Ayr, that is A-Y-R. I am the Secretary of the Residents' Association here. May I ask you who ordered you to do this?" At the mention of 'Colonel' the SM stiffened involuntary and almost stood to attention.

"Head Office Instructions," he replied. "It gives the lads a chance to look at other properties."

"Head Office? We don't have a Head Office. I am the Secretary here and the office is my flat there."

Now very flustered, the SM took out a piece of paper and showed it to the Colonel. "You better come inside; you can use my telephone." The rest of us continued to pack away the tools.

Ten minutes later the SM emerged and told us all to get inside the van. He drove home in complete silence. Back at the flats, he turned round to us and said, "Wrong bloody flats."

A couple of us started giggling, then, to his credit. He burst out laughing. "Wrong bloody flats, but the Colonel said we did an excellent job."

# Chapter Seven: Common People

Initially, moving from St. John's Wood to Wandsworth Common was a quite a downgrade, but a huge savings in rent. St. John's Wood had been a small dark, one-bedroomed basement flat, but Wandsworth Common was a spacious house. Downstairs, three reception rooms, the largest, was oak panelled and served as my bedroom, the back lounge was in fact our lounge and a smaller room was Claud's bedroom. There was also a bathroom and kitchen. Upstairs consisted of three bedrooms, one was used as a lounge and of course, kitchen and bathroom. The upstairs flat had its own entrance and was rented by two cigar lesbians. My job was to collect the rent from Claud and the upstairs tenants. The back lounge had French doors that led into a long, but wide garden. Lawn with flowers on each side and a kind of 'wild' area at the foot of the plot.

After a hot hard day in the city, followed by a sweaty commute, there was nothing I liked better in the summer than watering, pruning and dead-heading the dozens of rose bushes, particularly the climbing roses. By way of a change, I would also cut and water the grass. Under my inexperienced care the garden the garden blossomed. I bought all sorts of plants and sowed poppies, foxgloves, hollyhocks, delphiniums, pansies and carnations. Claud and I would spend many pleasant summer evenings on the 'crazy paved' patio playing backgammon, smoking French cigarettes and drinking strong, dry cider.

The landlady, a Mrs Humphries, would inspect the property every six months. She was impressed, particularly with the garden. She liked me and made me an offer. She found owning the property irksome, and she wanted to sell it to me for a serious discount. I thanked her, but as an articled clerk could not afford the mortgage. That was not a problem she said. I had to have somewhere to live and therefore pay rent. I was already collecting three other rents. I had a prosperous future ahead. Her brother was a solicitor and he would 'fix it' for me. I turned it down and instead, one year later, moved into a mortgaged poky Victorian conversion that was eventually demolished. Today, Mrs Humphries' house would be worth a million plus. I suppose we all make mistakes.

Claud was French, very good looking, full of charm. He spent most nights 'staying with friends' – mainly female friends, from what I could gather.

One evening after work, my colleague Sam and myself, went for a quick half after work. It was a small, quiet pub, just east of Ludgate. Sam was tall, dark and athletic. Women were attracted to him. I was short and fat and did not have much success with the ladies. Going out with Sam usually meant getting one of his 'cast offs'.

We had settled down to our ale, when a small, attractive, Japanese woman asked me for a light. Japanese women at that time were not common or garden. She started chatting to me; actually she seemed more interested in me than Sam. The three of us consumed more pints and finally closing time loomed. She was staying in a hostel, not very nice. Fuelled up by alcohol I invited her to stay. Sam was also included as he would miss the last train. We took a taxi to Wandsworth Common. Unusually, Claud was at home, watching TV. Yumi would like a bath, so whilst she bathed, Sam and I took a walk.

I argued that she had the hots for me. It was me, who she chatted up. It was me that she had come home with. She had no interest in Sam. She was mine. He argued to the contrary. She had given him 'signals'. She was on for him. So we tossed a coin and I won, Yumi would sleep with me in my bedroom, Sam would sleep on the couch. Decided.

We returned. The house was in darkness. There were groaning, creaking noises coming from Claud's bedroom. One did not have to be Philip Marlowe to work out what had happened.

The next day Sam and I went to work. When I came back in the evening, Claud was there, smoking and reading a French newspaper. He smiled at me: "Sorry, it all happened very quickly, she came out of the bath and that was that."

"What was she like?"

His eyes missed over. "Man, she chased The Blue Vein all night long."

I went into my bedroom to change and there, on the bedside locker, was a bottle of whisky. Under it was a note. "Thanks for the accommodation – please phone me." A phone number. I phoned and after several attempts got through the next day. She came over at the weekend, we talked a great deal about The Meaning of Life and the Cosmos. She was not well. She had a lousy cold. No Blue Vein, or anything else for me, except a rotten cold and she never returned our backgammon set.

Claud was the 'personal assistant' to a lady who owned a Public Relation company in Fleet Street. She lived in a large house in Draycott Avenue in Chelsea. Claud's main duty was that of a chauffeur. For that function he had to wear a smart grey suit, white shirt, black tie and grey peaked cap. The vehicle he drove was a four-door Lincoln Continental Convertible 1969. It was the size of a tennis court and was powered by a 7.6 litre engine. This particular car had been owned by a former West African president and equipped with bullet resistant windows and was bomb proof. The hood could come down or retract electronically. The leather seats (more like a sofa than seats) were of Connelly hide and the carpets Wilton. The fittings included a fridge, cocktail cabinet, retractable tables, footrests, a radio, a music player (both stereophonic) and a radio phone. There was nowhere to park it in Draycott Avenue, so it lived outside the Wandsworth common house. We used to party in it and when the house was too full, make love on the back seat. Ladies found it irresistible. Claud would drive up to Fleet Street every week day in his uniform with me riding in the back. I always got a kick out of phoning the office on the radio phone to say we were struck in traffic and my driver was doing the best he could. There were no mobile phones at that time – only radio phones, which added an extra sweetness to the pleasure.

At weekends we would cruise down the King's Road, top retracted, Claud in his uniform and me wearing a black shirt, white kipper tie, white suit, dark glasses and a fedora. We were unlucky if 'chicks' did not jump in the back when we stopped at traffic lights. My patter was always the same. I was a film director (Polish) and I was having a break from the stuffiness of Claridges. I wanted to meet real people and go into real homes and have some fun. Did we have fun! It was my own personal 'Summer of Love'. It gave me a newfound confidence in my dealings with women. Sadly, like summer, it had to end. Claud was recalled to Paris to help his father in the family restaurant and I never saw him again.

Claud's place in the house was taken Tarquil, my work colleague. He was a small man, who did not have a big car, but a big bike. A Honda 750 to be precise. In the days when the pubs opened between twelve and two on a Sunday lunchtime, traditionally they would place some free snacks on the counter. Usually only crisps and peanuts, but some of them would stretch to chipolatas on sticks, or pineapple chunks and cheddar. Unfortunately this practise was banned by the EU, by Brussels sprouting its bureaucrats on the grounds that it was unhygienic. Well, it never harmed me!

Despite having a wide selection of Wandsworth hostelries that Tarquil and I could frequent on a Sunday, we chose The Stag in a mews in Belgravia, because the beer was good and its snacks were to die for. The snacks were made by Sally, a plump, red-faced woman, with black piggy eyes and a small piggy snout, but a great generous smile and generous laugh. Sally ran a party catering business – serving mainly the private residents of Mayfair and Belgravia, but also some Investment Houses and a few embassies. The Stag was where she showcased her products and Sunday lunch time was when she did it.

I do not have a sweet tooth, but cannot resist savoury things, particularly vol au vents. Sally's vol au vent pastry cases were made on the premises and then filled with ingredients that she made at home and brought in. The main medium was béchamel sauce; this of course, can be flavoured so, we had with the cubes of chicken breast béchamel with chicken stock, white wine and tarragon or Coronation style (lightly curried). There was also chicken in aspic with tarragon. For the mushroom vol au vents it was béchamel with truffle oil. The prawns were with Coronation béchamel or a fragrant fish stock; some bathed in a lemony tartar sauce. Strips of smoked salmon would be embedded in a creamy crab pate. Baby white asparagus tips wrapped in anchovy fillets would peep out of herbed mayonnaise. For the sweet toothed, ripe plump strawberries would squat in a bed of Chantilly cream thickened with almond paste. There were mini quiches and mini pork pies, quail scotch eggs. But what they really came for were her 'Baby Yorkies' table tennis ball sized Yorkshire puddings, crammed with rare roast beef and horseradish sauce. With this dish, she was way ahead of her time.

The routine was always the same. An enormous metal platter the size of a wagon wheel of finger food would be brought out by Sally at exactly fourteen minutes past twelve. It was sealed in clingflim and placed on the counter. Sally would disappear in the kitchen and re-emerge with another identical dish. The Sloanes and Hooray Henrys would gather round. Nobody would make a move. Her assistant would appear with several beer jugs of forks. The Sloanes and Henrys placed several forks into their top pockets along with the paper serviettes provided. The assistant would then place several piles of small plates on the counter. The circling wolves would clutch half a dozen or so plates in one hand. Sally then appeared and ripped off the clingflim from the first salver. The scrummage began – handfuls of finger food would be piled on plates which would be passed back in a line to the inner depths of the pub. What disgusted me most was the sight of Henriettas wrapping the food in serviettes and then stuffing the parcels into their expensive leather handbags. The whole process would then repeat itself with the second salver.

I have often wondered how I would behave in a concentration camp. Would I too exhibit such animal behaviour? Perhaps I would if my survival depended upon it. But to see such behaviour in this apparent well bred, well fed crowd was revolting.

Tarquil agreed with me. We hatched a plan. The following hot sunny Sunday at ten minutes past twelve we arrived outside The Stag on Tarquil's bike. He kept the engine running. I placed a folded rug on the pillion seat, kept my helmet and goggles on and strolled to the counter where the finger food was placed. At fourteen minutes past twelve Sally came out the kitchen and placed the giant salver on the counter. She went back into the kitchen. I picked up the dish and walked calmly to the door. A Henrietta rose and opened the door for me. I thanked her then clambered on the back of Tarquil's bike, covered the dish with the rug and we set off bumping along the Mew's cobbles. We turned into Eaton Square and picked up speed. The traffic was light. We were two young men on a motorbike transporting a rugged round mirror. Round Sloane Square, then he opened up crossing Chelsea Bridge. He quickly and expertly threaded his bike through the 'back doubles'. We nearly lost our precious cargo on the Wandsworth Roundabout and then thundered along the Trinity Road, diving into several side streets before arriving at The House. The party was already in full swing. The oven full of sausage rolls, chipolatas, meat loaf and quiche. The fridge full of beer, wine and cider. The Dansett stacked with Ray Charles LPs. We received a standing ovation as we paraded our booty. Later that night, the back seat of the Lincoln was once again pressed into service. I still cannot resist vol au vents.

# Chapter Eight: Never Write a Man off until He is Dead

Today Rotherhithe Street is all about huge glass riverside condominiums (gym and swimming pool in the basement). These are interspersed with gastro pubs, boutiques, bistros and artisan's ateliers. Nursery schools and play spaces abound. Transport links to Canary Wharf and the city of London are convenient. A pleasant place with sweeping river vistas.

In 1977 it was quite different. Rotherhithe Street was then flanked by deserted warehouses, bomb sites, derelict docks, areas of land piled high with sea dredged aggregates. Towards the east there were still some active warehouses on the banks of the Thames. A number of council blocks built in the thirties squatted along the other side of the street. It was a desolate location. Unloved and barren, even tramps and vagabonds gave it a wide berth. You could hear the tumble weed in the wind.

We used to say "Rotherhithe Street was the arsehole of the world and Barney Brothers was two hundred yards up it".

Barney Brothers was a lard refinery. Barges brimming with grassy green liquid pig fat would tie up alongside the refinery and pump their cargo into giant tanks; it would then be refined and packed for sale to supermarkets, grocery shops and butchers. Some of it went to the big biscuit companies and bakeries.

You smelt Barney Brothers long before you saw it. A foul odour of rotten eggs, spiced with gagging chemicals hung over the site. Even in the Accounts Department, those who worked there, had a greyish pallor with an unnatural sheen. All the invoices were blotched with specks of grease. The wind blew fiercely from the east carrying with it dust from the gravel mountains. All surfaces were greasy and grainy. Even on the windiest of days, a cloud of toxic stench would hang over the buildings.

Eyes would water, skin would itch and burn.

On my first day working there I wore a smart pair of grey trousers and an electric blue velvet jacket. That evening I had a date with a girl. Simple meal at Nick's, couple of drinks in The Bottle and then... I did not have time to change, but why should I? I was smartly turned out. The meal was fine.

We clicked like a house on fire. She sat close next to me in the pub – then the fire went out.

"You smell as if you have been cooking fish and chips for months in your clothes."

I had absorbed the fragrance of the refinery. We never met again.

I was 'The Accounts Office Manager' and reported to 'The Chief Accountant', Freddy, a pleasant man in his thirties who chain smoked. Apart from him and small rotund man from Sri Lanka called King Colombo, the remaining nine staff were female.

This was a time when inflation ran into double figures. Entities were hugely focused on debt collection. Freddy's predecessor, George, would visit the smaller customers and collect – cash. Needless to say, a great deal of that cash never reached the company's bank account and stayed with George.

What I have observed in life is that where envy and necessity met an opportunity, fraud follows, as night follows day. Here at Barney Brothers the Financial Director had had a serious stroke and the controls that once were in place were no longer being exercised. The other directors enjoyed the trappings of power – lavish expense accounts, big motors, golf days, Fat Cat pensions. So there was the opportunity for George. Not only was cash being syphoned off, but he set up a number of Supplier Accounts with bank accounts. Prompt, regular and large payments were made to these suppliers. The funds were filtered back to holding company. The holding company, purchased a large ocean going yacht and that yacht was sold to a Bolivian national – for cash of course.

Today with all the Money Laundering Regulations etc. it would not be possible, but then it was taking candy from a baby. George was never seen again.

So, that was the state of the ledgers that was inherited by Freddy and myself.

Inflation was still high and we hung onto our cash for dear life. When a supplier telephoned chasing money, the initial response was, "Can we please have proof of delivery?" This was noted on his record and until the POD arrived, nothing else happened. When it did arrive (of course we had the original already) we gave out that it had to be processed – two more weeks delay. Then it was included on the fortnightly cheque run. After that, it had to be signed and counter signed, before being sent second-class post.

From an old dart board we made a wheel with an arrow which we spun to give us a suitable excuse for payment delay; some of these would be:

"Books with the auditors."
"Mr So and So is on holiday."
"He can't sign, he has broken his wrist."
"We have had a fire."
"We have had a flood."
"Mice have eaten the records."
"The Accounting Machine is broken."
"Need a second signature."
And so on and so on...

On the other hand, I also had to chase money. Two excuses I will remember always are:

"May I speak to the Accountant?"
"No, she has run away."
"Oh. The Financial Director then?"
"He has run ways with her."
Or phoning a customer in Ireland:
"He has gone fishing."

"When will he return?"

"Depends on the fish; if they are biting, he will stay, if they are not biting, he will wait until they are."

Freddy and I decided to drive over to Ireland to collect. It was Easter and our hotel had packed us a lunch. We decided to stop at another hotel at lunch time for a drink. We were told it was Easter and the bar was closed, but we could buy a bottle of wine to drink off site. We ordered the wine and a barman was despatched to locate it in the cellar. Time went by, we remonstrated with the other barman.

"Sorry. Would you like a drink whilst you are waiting?"

We left after three pints of Guinness and several hours later arrived at a small village with what seemed to be a road block in our way.

"You can't come here. Turn around and take the other road," a large gruff man ordered us.

Freddy told them he could go anywhere he wanted. They shook their heads, but let us through. Within minutes we were in the middle of an IRA march, many men in balaclavas and firearms. Not a good place to be in a vehicle with English number plates. We took the first turn we came to and thundered down the back streets and eventually onto the open road passing the other way through the road block.

That evening we arrived at our inn and went to the small village pub. It was empty. An attractive colleen was behind the bar. Almost as soon as we had perched ourselves on our barstools, nearly a hundred young revellers arrived within minutes. The colleen was unflappable, she lined up a continuous stream of pints. Every one was served quickly. Then, as fast as the pub had filled, it was empty.

"Puck Fair," she said.

I presume it was some sort of festival, but I tell you if we could import colleens of that ilk into our English boozers, we would never have to wait to be served.

Later that evening we went swimming in the freezing

Atlantic and Freddy lost his gold medallion and chain. This upset him because it was a wedding present from his wife. The next morning, at low tide, we miraculously found it in the sand. Rusted to bits. *All that glistens is not gold.*

We made it to the customer. We got our money. We declined his offer of fishing, but we did buy a racing greyhound from the local priest. We named the pup "Starburst Rupture". He came over to England a few weeks later and then spent four months in a kind of doggy training camp.

The big day came. Slough Greyhound Track. The trainer told us, "Do not put your shirts on him; it's a pipe opener." He led from start to finish – 6 to 1. Next time, we were to put our shirts on him. He broke cleanly and quickly took the lead. Coming into the final straight he was three lengths clear, then he began to go backwards until he was last. Just before the finishing line, he dropped dead. We did at least receive an insurance payout.

Freddy was a good, long suffering guy, but he had an obsession. He wanted a company car. He had been promised a company car. All the other senior personnel had big swanky motors. There was always some excuse for the car to be postponed. Then the day came.

The Managing Director's secretary called me into her office. "Could you give this envelope to Freddy please?" There were keys inside the envelope. She knew, I knew. "Tell him it's parked in the yard."

"There's lots of cars parked in the yard, Gwen."

"The reg. number is on the envelope."

I handed Freddy the envelope. "For you, from Gwen."

His eyes lit up. He ripped open the envelope. Everyone fell silent. They also knew.

He stood up and went out to the yard.

Suddenly, everyone was quizzing me about 'the car'. "What sort was it?" This, I honestly did not know.

"He's coming back."

Everyone rushed to their desks.

Freddy calmly walked in, opened his briefcase, and placed a few personal effects from the drawer into the case. He came up to me and gave me his bunch of office keys and the car keys.

"Bye, everyone." With that he walked out and was never heard of again.

The car in question was a two-door, five-year-old DAF 600cc Varomatic, with fifty thousand on the clock. It had belonged to a pig dealer and certainly smelt that way. It had no gears, but a continuously variable transmission. It actually went at the same speed backwards as forwards and had won all the World Backwards Driving Competitions.

Companies spend millions developing a new vehicle, the name is vital. Ford were going to call one of their models 'Caprino', which can be Sicilian for 'goat shit'. No wonder they changed it to 'Capri'. Granada is another evocative name.

They were going to launch a people's car in China called Pinyin si, which means 'Four'. Four gears? Four occupants? However, when they discovered the word was homophonous with the word 'Death', the name was dropped.

Names like Mustang, Sirocco, and Spider, all convey a message. Rolls Royce use Carmargue, Silver Cloud, Ghost, Phantom, Wraith and Corniche.

But the name Daf? Somewhere between a Daffodil, Daphne, Daffy Duck and Daft.

The fellow they replaced Freddy with was not a patch on him, but he was given a brand new Ford Granada 2.8 Automatic Saloon. Alloy wheels, black leather interior, tilt and slide sun roof.

Throughout my career I have worked all over London. The city of London. Euston, in Dover Street opposite The Ritz, the fleshpots of Soho and the sedate plushness of Holland Park. I always find something to attract me. In Rotherhithe in 1977? Yes, I found a swimming pool about fifteen minutes' walk away from the refinery. It was of Victorian origin and often, at lunch time, I would be the only customer.

The first time I attended, there was one other swimmer, a man. He swam down the pool, stopped halfway, stood up and then swam to the end, turned around and swam without stopping back again. This intrigued me. I swam halfway, stopped and then saw the attraction. An unrestricted view straight into the female shower area. This certainly added a new dimension to my lunch time swim.

The Managing Director of Barney Brothers was a Cedric Bricks. In order to have urgent cheques signed I often had to track him down (with the help of Gwen) to his various daytime lairs, usually in the city, but sometimes, into the West End. His favourite refuge was 'The Black Cockerel', deep in the bowels of a city office block. It had the most novel of features for that time – air conditioning. Mr Bricks spent a great deal of his time there, drinking champagne and smoking Havana cigars. It featured a private cinema, a ticker tape machine that gave the latest share prices and a 'blower' that provided horse racing commentaries and prices. "An essential venue for business," Mr Bricks used to say.

There were a number of young ladies in pink uniforms that gave the gentlemen members massages.

"Lots of chaps here with war wounds, bad backs and groin injuries, they come to seek relief."

Mr Bricks always gave me a great welcome. I think the other members felt he was very important to have his clerk come all the way just to have a cheque signed.

I would be served champagne (sometimes, two flutes), smoked salmon sandwiches and chicken and mushroom vol au vents. The ladies were particularly charming to me. I liked the way they sat close to me, their hands on my thigh – nice.

Back at the office, Mr Bricks would often come up to the Records Room upstairs where I was on my own filing confidential documents.

I felt this was the place and the time to bring up an issue that had been troubling me for ages. A bill for dinner for five at a riverside city pub, put down on one of the manager's expenses. That bill came to more than my entire month's salary. I showed it to him.

"That's John and Trevor (two of BB's managers). Christmas lunch. What about it?"

"A great deal of money, sir."

The other three gentlemen were the lard buyers for the country's biggest supermarket. Mr Bricks explained to me that the supermarket's policy was never to receive gifts, other than one hospitality event at Christmas time. This was the event. One third of BB's turnover went to this supermarket chain. "It's a 'Thank You'."

"At least we are all right when it comes to lard, it's not whisky," I said knowingly.

"You are right to bring these things to me, Gundle, but come and look out of this window."

A transporter had pulled in to the yard to take delivery.

"Look, Gundle." The driver opened the doors and emerged with two lamb carcasses.

"What are two nice lambs doing in a lard refinery? Watch what happens next."

Instead of the ten double pallets that were scheduled, eleven were placed in the container.

"Those carcasses will be sold for CASH. The lard will go back to the butcher that supplied the lambs and he will sell that lard for more than the lambs cost him. The lambs were probably nicked from the slaughter house anyway."

"It's disgusting. Are you going to call the police?"

"Of course not, it's only lard. As long as they thieve only what is honest."

I liked Mr Bricks. It was shame that he suffered a fatal heart attack at 'The Black Cockerel' a year later.

Everybody has heard of the The Truck Acts of 1887; in fact, they talk of little else down at The Flag.

Basically, these Acts stipulated that employees be paid in CASH. They were eventually repealed. But nobody told Barney Brothers.

So every Wednesday, the weekly wages were calculated for some hundred employees. The bank was given a figure of the necessary notes and coin. On Thursday morning we emptied all the vending machines on site, bagged up the Copper and Silver and then two of us would drive down to the bank in Rotherhithe, carrying sacks of metal. Always at the same time, always in the same car, always me and The Chief Accountant. We would march into the bank with our sacks of cash, hand over a cheque and receive several bulging sacks of notes and coin, the entire weekly wages for nearly one hundred employees.

We would drive back, lock all the doors and windows of the Accounts Department and fill the wage packets, just before two o'clock men and women would start to mill round the pay window. Exactly at two, the window would be open. The ritual was always the same.

Wives and girlfriends knew only the person named on the packet could receive the packet, after signature. They would then snatch the packet from their men, rip it open and dole out a weekly allowance to the man. A good quantity of that would be immediately spent at the pub opposite.

The females would query the hours, the pay rates, almost everything. Of course, we could only talk to the "name on the packet". Often it would be discovered that men were not where they said they were, particularly on the night shift. Tricky situations.

Anyway, I protested about this high risk method of cash movement and a security firm was hired. They would arrive on Thursday morning, passwords were exchanged, then the cheque given. Half an hour later they would re-appear with sacks of cash and the wage packets would be made up. Two security guards would be stationed outside, mainly to maintain order amongst the men and their partners. It worked well and we all felt safe.

Finally, I obtained a great job in an exciting company opposite the Ritz Hotel. Goodbye Rotherhithe.

Two weeks after I left, there was a knock on my door in the evening. A uniformed policeman and a pass flashing detective.

Of course, I let them in. They were investigating the wages snatch at Barney Brothers. Did I know about it? Had I been in touch with any of my former colleagues there?

I told them King Colombo and I had become good friends, but he had left six months ago.

Yes, they were going to pay him a visit after me.

It turned out that the security chaps arrived on Thursday morning. Passwords were exchanged. The cheque handed over. One of the staff went to the bakery to buy our sandwich lunches. Then the security firm turned up, same uniforms, same helmets, same passwords.

The bank was phoned. Yes the cash had been handed over.

For years after that every time I made or received a phone call, I heard a strange and ominous 'click' followed by a whirling, hissing noise. No one was ever arrested, the money never recovered.

This time *they* stole more than was honest.


King Colombo lived in the next street to me in a large three-storey terraced Victorian house. He and his Chinese wife had bought it to run as a house of bed-sits. King, his wife, Lily and three young children lived on the ground floor. The rest of the house was rented out. As time went by and King became more prosperous he slowly reclaimed the rooms for his own use.

But when I knew him then, the family lived downstairs, not just the family but several guests from many nations. Lily was a fantastic cook and every night eight to ten courses would be laid out for all and sundry – Chinese, Malay and Indian dishes.

In the basement, King displayed an impressive cellar. His booze cabinet would groan with XO brandy and an eclectic array of malts. A most generous host.

One evening he invited me over for drinks. Lily was out for the night and this would be "just a few drinks for a few close friends".

The usual ship of nations had docked. Somalis, Ethiopians, Sri Lankans, Chinese and a few West Africans. The air was thick with joviality and cigar smoke. A large West African called 'Happy Monday' dominated the scene. In a deep and booming voice he gave forth on the world economic situation, hunger, the ecology and almost any subject you cared to name. A man of huge charm. The gleam of his white teeth could be seen from outer space, but his clothes were shabby and cheap; his suit could have done with a clean and press. He could have done with a bath.

As the evening wore on, it was decided by all that we drive in two cars down to 'The Purple Rayah', one of very few Malaysian restaurants at the time around in Great Britain.

Ten of us sat down. The food was astonishing. Fish Curries, Beef Rendang, Nash Goring, Nasi Lemak, noodles with a Sambal Oelek (a past of shrimps, fermented fish, ginger, garlic, shallots, rice vinegar, lime juice and palm sugar), Dosais to die for, fermented rice flour pancakes, crisp on the outside, slightly gooey on the inside, filled with waxy potato and all the usual suspects – split black gam, ginger, fresh curry leaves chillies, coriander, mustard seeds and enough turmeric to stop Type Two Diabetes in its tracks. Prawn Puri, Green Banana Bhaji and various vegetarian Thalis, hot, herby and spicy, cooked with the minimum of oil.

All this was washed down by vast quantities of Tiger beer. Happy now did a deal on an entire bottle of Remy XO. Some sipped, some downed it in one. Several had it with ice, or with Coca Cola. A couple mixed it with Ginger Ale.

Now Happy demanded cigars all round, nothing would do except Bolivar Bonitas. Coffee made with the droppings of rats from Vietnam who live on the coffee berries.

There comes a point in a restaurant when no matter how good it is, I feel hot and need the cool night air. I suggested to Happy that we ask for the bill. The proprietor waltzed up and placed the bill in front of me. It represented almost a month's net pay.

The table feel silent. I did my sums. "Probably better for us each to pay one tenth, then we can give cash for the tip." The silence continued. One or two pattered their jacket pockets.

"Hey, Happy, you told us this was going to be your shout."

"Yeah, I won't have come otherwise," the Somali moaned.

"Me, too," said one of the West Africans.

King looked embarrassed. "I did think you told us this would be on you, Happy. I would have brought my cards otherwise."

I felt sorry for Happy, who seemed to have shrunk several feet.

"I'll settle it, give me what you can." I placed my new credit card over the bill.

A few threw some cash on the plate. The Chinese man gave me a cheque, another his visiting card with IOU written and signed on the back. We were too drunk to drive back, so we piled into taxis. My taxi dropped me off at my flat.

I have dined many times since at King's house, but never saw any of the crowd. Not until a year later. King phoned me at work in the late afternoon.

"Happy's in town, he wants us to join him for diner."

"Not on your life. I've still not paid off the bill."

"He's in a suite at The Ritz, two minutes' walk where you work. It will all go on his bill."

The Ritz has fond memories for me. I had just started

dating a lady. She was tall and angular, with bony hips, small (but perfectly formed breasts), and a long swan like neck. She wore her jet black hair in bob. On the other hand I was short and fat. But she liked me. Unfortunately, she lived in Kent and on the wrong side of the tracks. The edges were a little rough, you might say.

I took her to the Champagne Bar (at The Ritz).

"What's your poison?"

"Baby Cham." This was a cheap nasty cider perry in a small bottle that looked like a Baby Champagne bottle. Karl the barman roared with laughter. "Madame has such a wicked sense of humour."

I roared with laughter too. "A bottle of Bolly, please, Karl."

Unfortunately, those bubbles never did the job of seduction. Unfortunately many years later I heard the lady had died, a spinster.

On another occasion when I worked for an American company, my female boss insisted on arriving in the UK on a Bank Holiday Monday. The company was in serious financial difficulties.

"Meet me at my hotel." I knew it would be The Ritz. I declined.

On this occasion a butler opened the door to Happy's suite. Happy rushed out to meet us. He seemed to have grown taller, bigger and was wearing tribal costume.

He put his arms around us and led us into a vast reception room, where six of his wives were in attendance.

After a number of glasses of Krug we sat down to a very elegant dinner. One of those meals that have nuances in flavours but leave only a faint pleasant after taste, a wisp, a memory.

It was a fabulous evening. King and I were driven home by Happy's chauffeur. King told me

Happy was now the Finance Minister of one of those long thin West Africa States.

King took a deep draw on his Bonita, "Never write off a man until he is dead."

# Chapter Nine: Juice

I have a tall apple tree in my garden. It produces an amazing amount of blossom, but not many apples. In autumn, the best apples were at the top of the tree – bright red, big and juicy. You could climb up a ladder to retrieve them, but Mrs 'Health and Safety' would not approve. You could wrap the prongs of a rake around the stalks and pull them down, or shake the branches with the rake. Alternatively, you could just wait and eventually they would fall onto the soft lawn. If picked up within twelve hours, they would be worm free. I have found when all else fails – DO NOTHING! The Mountain will come to Mohamed.

I had worked for several years in the seventies in the derelict and desolate Rotherhithe and now my workplace suddenly changed to a posh office in Dover Street, just opposite the Ritz hotel. My contract stated I "could claim lunch everyday upon the production of a receipt". So for the first week I bought hot salt beef on rye and submitted the receipts to Fiona, the Managing Director's personal assistant. She flushed up angrily and rebuked me by saying: "'Lunch means lunch, and not a beef sandwich." So I lunched very well for free thereafter – if there is ever such a thing as a 'free lunch'.

My employer imported 'fresh frozen fruit juice'. In particular, orange juice from Florida. Grade 'A' Valencia orange juice. This would be picked at the height of its ripeness, squeezed and then the juice would be frozen and vacuumed, the process would reduce the juice to a gloopy syrup which would be canned and frozen. The product would be then emptied into a dispensing machine, which would chill the syrup. When ready for dispensing it would be re-mixed with filtered, cold water and poured into precise measured quantities. Ideal if you are operating a large hotel and have to deliver a thousand servings in two hours.

This concept took off rapidly and before long there were seven hundred dispensers in operation. The Managing Director, Algy, was a gentleman of huge charm and energy. He lived during the week in a luxurious apartment in Pimlico and then every Friday at two o'clock, drove down to his country cottage in Hampshire. Fiona and I would be left to man the office. When Fiona came back from lunch I would stroll down to the cigar shop and literally be taken by the hand into the walk-in humidor by an attractive young Swiss lady. Together we would chose a Havana, which I would take back to the Managing Director's office. I would sit in his chair and light up. I would help myself to a tot or four of the Armagnac that the company imported and some coffee that they also imported. I would reflect on life and reflect some more if I had the energy.

Well, on a particular Friday, Fiona telephoned me on the internal telephone: "Gino Mincuzzi is coming upstairs – he has an appointment with Algy. It must have slipped Algy's mind. *You* have to see him."

"OK – show him in."

Gino was the son of a famous hotelier who owned a chain of seventy hotels in Britain. The company had been touting for his business, unsuccessfully, for ages. Fiona showed him into my, or rather, Algy's cigar fumed office. Tall, extremely good looking sharp suited with a smile that could melt entire icebergs, he shook my hand warmly. "Juice?" I enquired, taking down clean glass.

"No thank you. The product is excellent, I know that. I'm here to talk numbers."

"Excellent, I'm the Numbers Man."

"Great!" he beamed at me.

I went through the numbers, volume discounts and so on. He listened and made notes on a pad with his Mount Blanc pen and then shook his head: "The numbers, almost work, but not quite."

"What brix are you working on?"

He told me it was a high concentrate. Brix is the

correlation of water to sugar. "Well if you lowered it by a mere ten percentage, this will be your gross profit, also we could pass on our Citrus Board subsidy to you."

I now reworked the numbers.

"Wonderful! Can you get me out a contract on Monday?"

I affirmed I could. As he headed out to the door, he said, "It's for one hundred and twenty machines." That was the biggest single order that the company had ever taken.

On Monday morning I was waiting for Algy when he arrived at ten that morning. He could not believe what I told him. "All things come to he who waits."

"Yes, I agree, as will be the case with your commission cheque."

# Chapter Ten: The Rat who Adored Chocolate

CTN stands for Confectioner Tobacconist Newsagent. It is difficult for me to write a true account about my time as a CTN owner. To create a story that will grab the reader's bits and squeeze their lemons so tightly that juice runs down their legs. But things happen to me that do not happen to other people. Running a CTN is like flying an airliner – long periods of inactivity interspersed with action.

The shop was really a concrete hut, no store room or WC. It was based at the foot of a suburban railway concourse in South London. It was adjacent to a famous boys' school and opposite to a popular park with public tennis courts. I arrived every day at five thirty, laid out the newspapers and magazines. At six a trickle of commutes would start buying their tobacco and newspapers. By seven this had become a raging torrent. It was all over by eight fifteen, then the schoolboys would enter in droves. I displayed a selection of twenty or so glass jars with boiled sweets. I would weigh these out by the ounce into paper packets. At fifty per cent profit, this was a nice earner.

At ten thirty Nadine would arrive. She was a sexy French housewife and the 'turn on' of the day was for her, with me, to leaf through the newly delivered 'dirty nags'. *Oh la la*. At ten thirty I went to my squash club and would play as many as three matches before coming back at quarter to three. Half an hour later, the schoolboys would be back; as they melted away, the commuters would return. This was the week day pattern. At weekends it was the weather that drove sales. In the hot weather the customers would come in droves from across the park for fizzy drinks and ice cream.

As I have mentioned, there was no WC in the hut. If one needed a comfort break, I had to lock the door and go up to the station. So I would pee into an empty glass pop bottle behind the counter then empty the contents of same behind the hut in the bushes. On one occasion I had performed my act, but the telephone rang. I placed the full bottle with cap screwed tight on the counter. I had just finished the call, when a tough looking man walked in. He looked at the counter and then to my horror, grabbed the aforementioned bottle. "Hmm cream soda, my favourite. I'll have this." This had been the last bottle in the shop. I told him *that* bottle was not for sale and pointed to all the other flavours that were available. "Nah. I want this one." He looked at me menacingly. This was a man who was used to getting his way.

I had nowhere to go. Then the brain went into overdrive. "Could you pass it to me please, sir. I need to ring it up."

Reluctantly, he passed it to me. I did the only thing that I could. I 'accidentally' dropped it hard on the concrete floor behind the counter. These were good quality glass bottles; over engineered for purpose, you might say. For a split second I thought it was not going to shatter, but then it did, showering everything within a large radius behind the counter with urine. This particular specimen was dark yellow and malodorous. I apologised profusely. "You did that deliberately," he hissed angrily. I offered him any bottle in the shop free of charge. He let go a stream of obscenities at me finishing finally with, "You and your efing shop stink." As soon as he walked out, I locked up, mopped up and disinfected. In future it was the long walk to the station WC.

My next adventure was with Ratty. The Council would not allow me to keep refuse bins or bags outside 'The Hut' in the evening. I imagine this was because the numerous urban foxes would scatter the contents everywhere. So, every evening I had to bring in my black rubbish bag and then take it out next morning. One evening as I was bringing in the bag and about to lock up, something brown leapt out of the bag. It was a large rat. It ran under the counter in a gap about half its size. It would have to be ejected. I locked the hut and engaged the help of the two young park keepers. I offered them a couple of packets of cigarettes of their choice. We entered the shop, left the door open and systematically began to move every counter, every refrigerator and all the lower shelves. No rat. We repeated the exercise. No rat. There were no holes in the concrete walls. We checked the upper shelves. No rat. No gaps where pipes and cables came in. We decided to call it a day. I locked up and went home.

The next morning after the rush, I noticed the silver paper tops wrapping the big bars of chocolate had been gnawed. Rat Attack! I called on the assistance again of the two young park keepers. We repeated the exercise. No rat. There was only one solution – get a cat. I went to the Cat Rescue Centre and chose a giant ginger tom. There was a twenty-four-hour cooling off period. I (sensibly) reflected in that period that I could not keep a cat in 'The Hut'. That evening, or rather morning, at three o'clock my telephone rang. The Police – my alarm was ringing. I arrived at the scene. No sign of an intruder. I switched the alarm off, but the moment I switched it on it went off again. A ballast train had set it off once before, but once re-set it worked. Not this time. The next day more of the big bars of chocolate had been nibbled. I broke these up into pieces and sold them from the glass jar as 'chocolate delights', actually making more profit from them in that form than entire bars. The alarm man simply said, "Rats." Ratty had gnawed through the wire. He replaced the cable with a special (and expensive) covering. The next day more chocolate damage occurred. I also noticed a fishy ammonia like smell. I telephoned a pest control company. They would cure the problem, but the whole process may take several days. I was now desperate. One of the young park keepers suggested 'Ransoms', the iron mongers up the road. "They sell rat traps." Ransoms was an old-fashioned ironmongers set in a time warp. If you could not wear it, eat it, or make love to it, they sold it. A rat trap was produced, a mean horrible looking thing. A bear trap in miniature. That evening I baited it – with chocolate.

The following morning I arrived at 'The Hut' at five in the morning, half an hour earlier than normal. I did not know what to expect. An untouched bait and trap? Partly nibbled bait in an unsprung trap? Trap sprung, no rat. Trap sprung, no bait. Dead rat in sprung trap? What I found was a rat caught in a trap by its leg. It appeared to have made an attempt to gnaw through its leg in order to escape. There was some blood on the floor around its leg. *What do I do?* It was too early to seek assistance from the park keepers. I would find a brick or a stone and despatch him. Then I heard a low, soft melancholy voice. "So, you're going to despatch me then?" Funny the radio was off, there was nobody around. No commuters. Even the traffic was light. "I'm talking to you. I'm the rat – Ruttus Novegicus, otherwise known as vermin."

I looked at the rat. It was looking at me directly with its little eyes. "You're caught in a trap, can't walk out," I sang.

Now the rat sang:

"Please release me let me go. To waste my life would be a sin. Release me and let me love again."

It was Clifton Chenier, The Black Cajun. Clearly he was playing his 24lb piano accordion and the ivories in the background were being tinkled, all in true Zydeco fashion, loud and clear.

"What have I ever done to you?" demanded Ratty.

"You have eaten all my expensive bars of chocolate," I replied.

"Eaten? Ah com'on just nibbled a little here and there. The silver covering is good for my teeth and I adore, but absolutely adore chocolate. The smell just drives me wild. I can't resist it. I promise I won't do it again."

"You also ate through my alarm cables."

"I'm so sorry. I can't help it. The phenol formaldehyde give me such a high, partly when blended with polyoxymethylene. Oh, man, it takes me to another place; that combined with sex – chem sex. Have you tried it?"

"Not recently."

"You mustn't treat me as vermin, we're all God's creatures. All born equal."

"Yeah, some more than others," I quipped. Ratty laughed.

I needed to sit down. Here was a rat that could read minds, that talked, sang. Knew about chemistry and could laugh! His meta cognitive thought processes were amazing, for a rat. Perhaps I should not have tried that 'whaccy baccy' last night? Was my mind in a fever funk?

"Well, do whatever you want me, get it over with. I've had a good life. I'm great grandfather, you know." He began to grind his teeth.

I love animals. My father loved animals, he was a vet. I felt a huge remorse at my past cruelty. As a boy I had fashioned a catapult out of a forked piece of wood, and old shoe tongue and a strip of inner tube. I was 'dead eyed Dick'. My mother and some of her friends were sitting under a tree in the garden taking tea. A robin was perched above them. I fired my catty and hit the robin, who fell dead into my mother's friend's tea. Boy! Did I receive hiding for that. Then I tortured my cat because he ate my pet mice. I did not reason that is what cats do. My son kept a rabbit that died alone and unloved. I was close to tears now. I looked at Ratty. "I'm going to take you to hospital to get you better."

"Oh no! Hospital is where sick people go to die. Please NO!" he pleaded.

"This is a *private* hospital," I emphasised.

"Private? That's OK then. Thanks. I feel I have been too much of a burden on you already." He ground his teeth. I subsequently learnt this was a kind of a self-comfort action.

There was only one other time that an animal talked to me. That was many years later when my Cavalier King Charles Spaniel was dying. "Help me! Help me please!" she cried in her pain and confusion. Not only did I hear it, but the wife did too. There is a great deal that we mere mortals do not understand.

"Would you like some milk and a small piece of chocolate before we go?"

"Oh yes please. Never say no." Ratty nodded his head. After his meal, I loaded Ratty, still attached to the trap and placed him in a cardboard box into which I pierced a number of holes. I locked the shop, placed the box in the front foot well of the car and drove to a local veterinary practise. We sat there until eight o'clock when the doors opened.

"Patient's name?" asked the forbidding receptionist.

"Guy Uisdean Gundle."

"Funny name for a pet," snapped the receptionist.

"Oh, sorry. Ratty." I lifted the lid. The Gorgon melted into butter. "You poor thing. Come."

She knocked on a door and without waiting strode in. "An emergency, Claire," she said to a corpulent lady with big teeth and a white coat.

Claire examined Ratty. "A wild rat. Ruttus Novegicus. Where did you find him?" I told her briefly. "All right. Kindest thing is to put him to sleep." Ratty's body stiffened, his tail swirled rapidly.

The answer was obviously *no*. "Ratty wants to live." Ratty nodded his head.

"OK, I will give him a shot of antibiotics, saline and painkiller. In half an hour or so nurse will clean his wound and bind it. We will have to put a collar on him to stop him biting his leg. He is best left here overnight. Then you could take him home."

"Could he stay here until he is fit?"

"Of course." She told me the 'boarding rate' – the same as a three-star Bed and Breakfast. I agreed. She gave Ratty the shot. Ten minutes later she lifted a drowsy Ratty out of the box, released him from the trap and placed him on a bed of straw in a large plastic cage that nurse had brought in.

"Nurse will take care of him now. Telephone tomorrow about eleven. Could you now go to reception?" I did and paid a large sum on account. My atonement for my bestial sins was starting. I could see robin, the cat and rabbit, nodding their heads in approval at St. Peter's Gate.

My telephone call generated a good outcome. Ratty was eating well and walking a little, but obviously sore. Life is a strange business. There is a cult that believes in 'seeding'. *Give your money or time away to those less fortunate and it will come back tenfold.*

Suddenly, the nascent wet summer burst into hot, I mean hot, sunny days. That meant HUGE ice cream sales. Like most CTN owners I had a Walls Ice Cream chest freezer in my establishment. Walls would deliver once a week, when the weather was exceptionally hot they might stretch to twice weekly – if you were lucky. Somewhat like small town French restaurants that do not open at lunchtimes. When the weather was hot and I mean hot I could sell the entire contents of the freezer by lunchtime. So I used a company called Rossi, just down the road. They supplied me a second-hand chest freezer and their products were GOOD. Their margins were better and, of course, I would mark them up considerably over the normal selling price. But one of the strongest points was that they could deliver every morning at six o'clock. Goodness, did I cream it double big time Arizona City? There were several occasions when Rossi would make a double delivery at lunch time as well. They also delivered seven days a week. Incidentally, one of their most famous products was Francis Rossi, co-founder of Status Quo band which are still going strong. Within a day I had recouped my private hospital bills.

"What you shall sow, you will reap."

Five days later I collected Ratty in his (borrowed) plastic box. He was smiling and pleased, but not talking any more. I told him that every evening in a certain place I would leave some grains and saucer of milk. Very occasionally I would also place a tiny treat of chocolate there too. I let him free. He walked with a slight limp, but otherwise was in excellent shape. I'm sure he gave me a wink. Robin, the cat and rabbit were now nodding in approval again. I found Ratty's 'secret' entrance. It was right under the front door. A two-inch gap between floor and door. A little cement fixed that permanently. The summer dragged on, day after day of soaring temperatures, water shortages, a drought in fact. Day after day I stocked up my freezers. The till rang out sweet music to my ears. Thank you, Ratty, thank you Lord.

Well, when you deal with a tide of humanity every day, you become hard bitten and cynical. One of my favourite customers (also my most profitable), was Georges. A swarthy Mediterranean type who purchased the Financial Times and five Swiss cigars everyday. Most evenings it was also an expansive box of chocolates. On Saturday it was a polished box of twenty-five Monte Christo 'A'. These were the absolute 'dog's bollocks' as far as Havana cigars went. Today Cohiba is now in pole position. Wholesaling cigars to the club and restaurant trade was a profitable side line for me. Georges was the biggest spending customer and the most profitable one too. One Saturday morning he came in and said he needed cash. This was before the days of the 'the hole in the wall' or Saturday opening for banks. Of course, he could. How much did he want? He wanted four hundred quid. A large sum, approximately two days of takings. I just had enough as I was planning to go to the night safe that evening.

"It's a lot of cash, Georges. Could I have a post-dated cheque?"

He did not have his cheque book, but he removed his gold Rolex. "This will cover it. It's only for a month." Well, we are all faced with making judgements. I would take a punt. I counted out the cash. He thanked me. I placed the Rolex where everybody places valuable things – in the underwear drawer at home.

The weeks went by. No Georges. Well he did say "a month". The month went by. Then I had a brainwave. I would take the timepiece to a pawnbroker. I might not get back four hundred, but I would receive, say, three hundred.

I decided to give it another week, then I took the watch to the pawnbroker that afternoon. On that Saturday morning Georges walked in. White suit, white tie, black shirt. Face tanned brown as a berry. He bought his usual box of Monties and was about to go, when I reminded him of his obligation.

"Oh yes. I completely forgot." He peeled off four centies and handed them to me. He turned on his heel.

"Your Rolex," I called after him.

"Keep it. It is fake. Cost a fiver, worth nothing." Funnily, that evening it stopped completely, never to go again. Just like 'My Old Grandfather's Clock'.

As suddenly as that glorious summer had come, it departed. The carrion crows descended on me. I suffered three burglaries in a row. First, they came in from the front, then the roof. I re-enforced the front. Laid steel plates on the roof and smeared them with sticky 'burglar proof' tar. On the third occasion they came through the roof again. For weeks afterwards shifty characters from the estate would offer to sell me tarry black cartons of cigarettes. It was too much to bear. I disposed of the business, lock, stock and barrel. As I drove off the apron for the last time, I saw a brown rat sitting on the wall. He raised what was his injured from leg to me in salute. "God Bless You, Ratty!" I shouted. The two young park keepers looked at me oddly.

I now concentrated on wholesaling cigarettes to CTNs. What a hard slog that was. Trundling up and down the hard congested steers of South London. Clinching a deal delivering from the van. The Asian shopkeepers were very friendly and hospitable, but they drove a hard bargain. The white British ones would not give me the time of day. One morning I walked into a large but empty newsagent. Behind the counter was a small miserable white British reading a children's comic. The only memorable feature about him was his large moustache. I went into my brief sales pitch. Without looking up from his comic, he told me in a flat voice to "Suck off" or words to that effect.

"Look, just because you've got hair growing round it, there's no need to speak like a runt," or words to that effect. With the speed of greased lighting, the man jumped over the counter, baseball bat in his hand. He obviously was not going to play a game. Fortunately, he slipped and fell with his face straight into my upward ascending fist. I felt his nose implode at the same moment as my knee went into his groin, popping his nuts. He went face down. I kicked him in the ribs three times. Thank goodness, in those days CTNs did not have CCTV. I was out in a flash, and strolled nonchalantly down the street and round the corner to my van. The local radio news that early evening was all about a robbery of a newsagent. They were looking for a short fat man, smartly dressed. My wholesaling days were done.

"Give me in due time, I beseech out, a little tobacco shop. With little bright boxes, piled neatly upon the shelves."

I now had a problem. No income and lots of debt to the tobacco companies. I sold all the stock in one job lot, but still had a mountain of debt. Eventually I landed a job as an accountant, but it would take years to shift that mountain. I decided to file for bankruptcy. I arranged to see a lawyer.

Their office was on the first floor, up a narrow dingy corridor. The room was piled high with documents from floor to ceiling, every nook, every cranny. A gnome like man peered behind a desk with just a gap big enough between the documents to see me. He chain smoked and the room reeked of stale tobacco. I showed him a list of what I owed in descending order.

"You don't need to file for file for bankruptcy." He did some calculations. "In two and a half years you will be free of this."

"Impossible," I replied.

"Possible!" he barked. "You have a very powerful ally on your side. Inflation. Currently sixteen per cent. Your salary will go up, but the debt will stay frozen. Secondly *they* won't bankrupt you, more trouble than its worth. You're small fry. Make them an offer, so much a month. They'll go for it. Follow it up in writing and tell them you will do it. Good Luck."

He shook my hand, still sitting down. He never billed me. I took his advice. I had been told not to give preference to any supplier. Surprisingly, every single suppler accepted my terms. It was a struggle, often I was late, but I would always tell them. They were all paid off within two years. In the following years I have done many such deals for clients. If the debtor trusts you and you can build on that trust, you can recover.

# Chapter Eleven: The Consultant

The reasons I moved to the area and I am still there after forty five years are:

Richmond Park, the River Thames, the racecourses, the golf courses and The Flag.

The Flag has been through many makeovers, but in the early nineties still retained a great deal of its original character. It maintained its four separate bars – The Eponymous Jenny's Bar downstairs (for the over twenty-fives), the Saloon Bar, The Snug and The Public Bar., the last three divided by etched and bezeled glass partitions.

From Wednesday nights onwards it would be heaving, but The Public Bar would be empty. To be served in The Public you pressed a bell push and the service was instant.

I was intrigued by The Snug. From seven to nine in the evenings it was thronged with 'The Surrey Blazers', middle-aged gentlemen with brass buttoned blue blazers, club ties, cavalry twirls and expensive loafers. Their ladies were of the blue-rinse variety, lots of 'slap' and ''lippy'. It was draught pink gin and tonic (Vera Lynn and Super Sonic in bowl glasses, ice and a slice) all round.

This particular evening, The Public was full with a visiting darts team. The Saloon, packed as usual,

The Snug, however, empty, except for a lone 'blazer'. I entered and ordered a pint. He nodded in my direction. "Quiet tonight."

He mentioned the Chinese restaurant down the road that had just opened. This led on with our conversation. He had just come back from Hong Kong. He was planning to export Loch Fyne langoustines to Hong Kong. He introduced himself as Harry Harris.

"What business are you in?" he queried.

I told him I was starting up as a Management Consultant.

How did I operate? I told him it was on a flat fee basis, with a Success Bonus built in.

He hired me to start the next week, for one week, but with one strange request.

His company did not have a computer. He was not going to have a computer. He did not understand computers.

I arrived on Monday morning at the agreed time of ten o'clock. I handed him my contract which he placed in a desk drawer. "Later." Clearly he was not a man to be rushed.

Claire, his plump Scottish assistant sat down with us and with a pile of invoices. She extracted a small bundle and went through them.

Harry sounded off. "Ten per cent of these invoices have errors. Ten per cent. We deal in quantity, quality, weight and currency – plenty of margin for error. I am a small fish in a big pond swimming with the large fish. The big fish make six per cent, I make ten. The big fish don't care about these details. All they're interested in is their golf, their company car, their pension. Is it any wonder their foreign workers on substance wages don't give a stuff?"

If an error was in his favour, he keep quiet about it, but for tax purposes reserved for it. If the other way round, the entire invoice would not be paid until the appropriate credit was received. This approach run through his entire business. His credit control and debt collection was ruthless. He practised every tax reduction trick in the book. His manual systems were fail safe and would instantly throw up any shortfalls in a contract.

Instinctively he could weigh up and assess risk. "Risk is wild, but *she* can be tamed," was Mr Harry Harris' catchphrase.

The office itself was a large room with four dealing staff and smaller room with two back office workers. The WC was outside. Upstairs was a kitchen, lounge and accounts office. Of course, no computers, just an Imperial manual typewriter, an old electric typewriter, a telex and a fax. Yet he was making millions.

Harry told me that he had left school with no particular ambition or qualifications, back packed around Europe for six months then joined the business – his uncle's business. His uncle and his business partner would come in about ten, work till one, liquid lunch at the pub, returning at three to sign a few letters. The office would close at five.

It did not take Harry long to spot his chance; he bought the gentlemen out on a profit share basis and after a couple of years, the business became his. No other directors or shareholders. No external funding or bank borrowing.

Before I knew it, it was Friday. Harry appeared after lunch. "Finished your report then?"

I had finished. He suggested we go to his house at about five thirty and that I present my report to him there.

I followed his Aston Martin in my 2CV (with difficulty) after we left the office at six thirty, an hour later than agreed. His house was a Surrey mansion, flanked on three sides by a members' only golf course. The garage had six tilt doors. It housed his collection of classic cars which were used by the company "for promotional purposes" and therefore, tax allowable.

The drawing room was the size of a tennis court. His girlfriend appeared with a tray of canopies and large tumblers of whisky. We drank.

"Your report?" he asked.

I took a hard backed folder from my briefcase and handed it to him. He drew a long draught from his tumbler, smiled at me with his long nicotined teeth and then began to thumb urgently through it.

"You've made a mistake. There's no report here, unless it is written in invisible ink," he guffawed.

"No. No mistake, there is no report, nothing to recommend, other than, of course, computerisation which is not part of my brief. Harry, I cannot fault your business, it functions with a hundred per cent efficiency and efficient businesses are profitable businesses."

Based on my conclusions, he offered me a full-time

105

job. With little work in the pipeline and a hefty mortgage to meet (yes, The Mortgage never sleeps). I accepted.

Harry had absolute power over his staff; as we know, absolute power corrupts absolutely. He was a bully and a tyrant. He approbated in public and praised in private. The goalposts were moved on a whim, when it suited him. There was a "No Smoking" rule in the office for everyone, except him.

By and large I was left on my own. However, everyday, when he was in the office, he would come stomping up the stairs at exactly five thirty. He would throw himself into a chair and then begin a minute post mortem of the working day. I seldom left the office until seven. I resented these involuntary 'free' sessions. When I arrived home, my clothes would stink, having been kippered in nicotine.

He had a young sidekick named Jonquil. Jonquil was no flower, no shrinking violet. He had cast himself in the image of Harry and always appeared to me to be a single dimensioned young man.

The office was located on the main road that slices through Tooting. Harry and Jonquil's motors were parked in a gravel surfaced area behind the building, my 2CV on a public road. A lap fence separated the car park from a large private lawned garden. In the middle of this garden was a substantial pound and from time to time, a man in full scuba gear would disappear into its depths.

I learned that his name was Carlo and that the pond was stocked with Koi Carp. Carlo would spend hours 'below the waves' filming and feeding his carp.

The tension between Harry and myself began to grow. One hot summer's day I appeared in a cream suit that I had specially tailored for me in Cambodia. It concealed my corpulence well. This day happened to be Harry's birthday and his girlfriend had given him an extremely natty waistcoat from Liberty's. It sported brass buttons, small lapels and was in blue with dove grey horizontal stripes. He was proudly wearing this when I came down the stairs.

"Anyone for cricket?" he guffawed.

"Ah, the thwack of leather on willow," trilled Jonquil.

I looked at Harry, something went inside me. "At least I don't dress like a bouncing bell hop."

Harry jumped up, he came towards me with menace. "Back off, Harry!" shouted Jonquil.

Harry stopped within six inches of me. I could smell his rancid breath. A rat, must have crawled into his lungs and died last week.

After a few seconds, he turned round: "First and final formal warning. Jonquil, write out a statement of what you witnessed this morning."

Needless to say, things went from worse to worse; but, I now had to ask Harry a favour. My niece was getting married and I had to attend the wedding rehearsal in Bournemouth on a Friday afternoon. I requested that I leave work at twelve thirty on the Friday.

Harry raised every possible objection. It was the day of the Expo. They had a stall at Earl's Court. I was back office support. I replied that on this particular Friday, it was a public holiday for most of Europe and all the British traders would be at the Expo.

He offered me four thirty. I told him I could not make Tooting to Bournemouth in a 2CV in that time. I stressed the importance of the event for me, but he would give no quarter, so we left it in the air.

The Friday in question came round. It was an eventual morning. Harry arrived in his new pride and joy, a 1955 Daimler Drophead Convertible Coupe. Silver and chrome bodywork, red leather and polished wood grain and an enormous cream Bakelite spoked steering wheel. Harry told us proudly that it had a 'preselector gear box'.

Having viewed Harry's new toy, I then had to go to the bank and pick up £20,000 in case to pay a Polish supplier at the Expo. Upon my return, I counted the money out in front of Harry and Jonquil, who then re-counted it. It was then placed in a brand new Maxwell Scott attaché case.

Twelve thirty arrived. I cleared my desk and came

downstairs. I met Harry and Jonquil, leaving for the Expo.

"Where are you going?" Harry asked.

"The rehearsal."

Harry's face flushed a dark purple, the veins in his temple popped. He strode into the vehicle with Jonquil struggling to match his speed. The engine roared into life. There was loud clunk as the preselector was forced into slot. With gravel shooting in every direction the beast shot *backwards* demolishing the flimsy lap fence and tearing across the lawn at easily twenty-five miles per hour. With a huge splash its rear entered the pond, the beast's rear tilted downwards with the radiator grill pointing upwards at thirty degrees.

Still the engine roared, louder and louder. The beast crept backwards. Foot by foot, deeper and deeper. Water rushed into the compartment and both Harry and Jonquil were left with the water up to their necks. The engine coughed and died. The beast continued to sink. Harry began to shout hysterically that he could not release his seat belt and furthermore, he could not swim. Jonquil freed himself, swam round the back of the beast, opened Harry's door and just managed to undo the seat belt before Harry was about to slip below the waves.

Heroically, Jonquil began to kick towards the shore supporting Harry.

By now, all employees were out watching.

"Harry is now a Big Fish swimming with the Little Fish," I quipped.

Harry obviously heard my remark and began vigorously kicking out.

I jumped into my 2CV and gunned it down the back streets roughly in the direction of Bournemouth.

They called the RAC, but they could not move the beast.

A tractor from the local golf course was pressed into service, but to no avail. Finally a crane was hired: £250 for the initial survey, £1,500 per day thereafter. They could not place the webbing under the beast. Divers were then hired.

They were not allowed to use hoses, but did eventually manage to secure the webbing.

A week later, the beast was lowered onto a flatbed truck. It was decided it was beyond repair or restoration and sold for parts.

The bill from the Koi Carp Carlo was in thousands. The insurance refused to pay. Most of the twenty thousand in the attach case was Papier-mâché.

Jonquil set up in business on his own, stealing Harry's customers. Harry died of lung cancer seven months later.

# Chapter Twelve: Sinthea

Over the years, I have 'serviced' many clients. No two were – or indeed ever are – the same. Of all of them, Sinthea is the one I remember most. Certainly the sexiest one! It is strange how often a series of random events can conspire to come together to become 'a congruence' of events. This is the story of Sinthea, a *femme fatale*. *Fatale* in the literal sense.

I was in The Albert with Colonel Win Ward. An early winter evening; log fire crackling. We were seated in front of the fire in comfortable, buttoned down armchairs. He was cradling a pint of *Winter Warmer* – that strong, sweet dark ale that is served there in the winter months. I nursed a pint of my favourite *Young's Ordinary*; ordinary in name, but not in taste or its refreshment quotient. The Colonel had been sent over from Boston Mass. to sort out *The Big Boss*, the management consultancy where I worked. A tall, lanky Yank, he had obtained his rank in the US Air Force. With *Big Boss,* he did the usual hatchet job: some top dogs were put down; problem children given some stick and some carrot; cash cows fed well, producing more cash, and the stars obligingly stroked. The long-standing fish tank in reception went. Several car parking spaces cancelled. Half the office space rented out. The worse thing was the removal of the plants, which had been watered, fed and talked to every week. Some underlings fired, including my old mate Hughie, but I survived and received a pay rise! The Colonel clearly liked my practical, common sense attitude.

We were relaxed and musing, mainly about work.

"How well did you know Charles?" he asked.

Charles Crabbe was the former Managing Director (deceased). I told him I had little to do with him. He had interviewed me.

"What I do remember was that he was completely bald."

"Chemo," interjected the Colonel.

I mentioned the enormous bushes of hair sprouting from his nose and ears. I had wanted to pull it out by the clump. Win leaned forward towards me.

"He was very ill then. But, you know what? Before his illness he was a brilliant man. Completely in control."

Win went on to give me the man's history. Crabbe (Crabbie) had received a first-class honours degree from Oxford in Arabic Studies. He worked for many years in the oil industry, mainly in Libya. He was a BIG wheeler dealer. He returned to England, married and had three children. Set up his own consultancy advising all the oil majors at one time or another. He met our founder (of *Big Boss*) and was tasked with setting up the UK arm of the company. A couple of years later, his wife died of breast cancer. The kids were teenagers by then, but the poor fella hit the skids.

"Have you ever been in his house?"

I had not, but I knew the place. I told Win one of the things I would do with my young son on a Sunday afternoon was to cycle around the local Richmond Park and Kingston Hill. Crabbie's house was indeed huge, a beacon amongst others that were in fact large houses by the standards of most.

"It's big!" exclaimed Win. "The gravelled area in front can park a dozen autos. Then, you go up the stairs into what you English call a 'vestibule'; that, in turn, leads into an enormous hall. Black and white tiles, paintings the size of pool tables, a chandelier and a marble carved staircase. Magnificent! And all in the best of taste. His study and reception room look out onto the avenue, but the real view is from the rear of the house."

The Colonel was clearly warming to his subject on this cold, grey winter's evening.

"He's got – or rather, had – a large lounge and dining room which overlooked his croquet lawn. At the bottom of the garden is a squash court, and running along the right-hand side is an 'orangery', which really does produce oranges, figs, avocados and grapes. All this on the ground floor. The basement leads directly onto the garden at the back. In the basement is a pool table, gym, sauna, library and the butler Stephen's personal quarters. Stephen was his butler. Crabbie liked his autos too, you know. Rolls Royce Silver Cloud 11, Bugatti something or other and a classic Morgan – all parked in the treble garage."

Win looked at me closely. "Do you know how he died?"

I replied I had no idea.

"In bed."

"Most people do," I remarked, all too casually.

"No, I mean on the job, with a nineteen-year old – a woman – a 'lady of the night'. She woke up in the morning and found herself lying next to a stiff."

My blood ran cold. "I know that lady…"

He raised his eyebrow. "A client of yours?"

"Yes, but not, unfortunately, in the carnal sense… I'm going to refresh our glasses, then I will tell *you* the story of it."

My best friend, Hughie, by the way, had been the book despatch manager: one of the men fired by Win. I took a long swig at my drink, looked at the Colonel and started the tale.

"Every single day, Hughie and I went at precisely twelve o'clock to The Postillion. It was a free-house owned by a German lady, who served German food, and only German food, at lunch time: deep fried knuckle of pork, bratwurst and sauerkraut, *schnitzel* with red cabbage and, for two, stuffed pig's stomach, to mention just a few. We would wash this down with two pints of Old Rasper, a strong dry cider, which unfortunately is now no longer on the market."

"So, good tack, good liquor... I can guess what you have left out," quipped Win.

"Yeah, the girl, the barmaid – Sinthea," I conceded. Then, after a pause, I asked him: "Did you know Princess Diana?"

"You're playing me with me now! Yes, I – and millions of others – did, but not intimately."

I went on to describe Sinthea. She had indeed been a Di lookalike. She knew it too and cultivated it, particularly the hair style. She wore the same powder blue jeans every day. Well, maybe she had several pairs of the same; it would be unthinkable for her to wear the *same* jeans all the time! They were so tight they seemed to have been sprayed on. You could even read the serial number of her house key in her back pocket – I should know!

"And no knickers," I informed Win.

"Knickers? You mean… panties?"

Well, Win was of a generation when women still wore panties. He seemed slightly repulsed by the idea a woman would not wearing any pants.

"Yes," I confirmed. "And a white blouse knotted just above the navel. A dish even tastier than stuffed pig's stomach. She was the most delicious dish I ever contemplated."

I then embarked on the story proper of Sinthea.

"She was a good, professional barmaid; friendly and accommodating too. She told me her name was Sinthea and not Cynthia. That took me back to exactly what she had confessed to me: 'My Dad was drunk when he registered my name, and shortly after that he buggered off. Never knew him, he and my mother weren't married.'"

I paused, thinking of her. "For six months, Hughie and I lunched in The Postillion, every working day. One Monday I went to order the drinks. The barflies were buzzing around Sinthea as flies around the honeypot as usual. I was single at the time. 'Guy, are you free in the evenings this week?' she suddenly asked me.

"The barflies stopped buzzing. '

Oh, every evening,' I quickly replied.

"'I've a tax problem, could you come round to my place, say tomorrow evening, seven thirty?'

"The barflies were now fireflies, glowing a bright emerald green and resentfully silent.

"'Of course,' I agreed.

"Sinthea let me in. This time she was not wearing the jeans and blouse, but a really stylish floral frock – and I know a good frock when I see one. Her apartment was in a small modern block in a particularly smart part of Surbiton. I was taken aback by the classy style of her place. Parquet floors, Persian rugs, silver, porcelain and some very expensive paintings. Good quality chairs and sofas. No sign of her infant 'toddler'. She went to a large yew wood cabinet. Inside was a glass-fronted fridge well stocked with lager and champagne. Without asking, she poured me a large malt, added lots of ice and a splash of water.

"Then she told me her story. She had lived with her mother in a council flat. At the age of nineteen she met a man, fell in love – then fell pregnant. The chap bunked off, apparently to Thailand to become a dive instructor. She did not get on with her mother and insisted on being re-housed. The council offered her various flats, all of which she turned down. Finally, a housing association found her the flat in which we were sitting. She received generous state benefits, and was allowed to take in a lodger. The lodger was a female English student, who spent most of her time reading."

"Yes," interjected Win. "My daughter is one of those."

"Well, Sinthea eventually became bored and started working down at The Postillion. Everything was fine. Childcare was managed by the student and a child minder. The Postillion gave her stimulation. Then, the Department of Health and Social Security struck. She was caught up in one of their trawls. Now she had to attend an enquiry. Could I help, she wanted to know?

"She replenished my glass and produced a plate of prawn crackers. Yes, I could help her, get her off the hook. But I had a question. Where did all this wealth come from? It certainly did not come from state benefits or rent or wages at The Postillion. I asked her to level with me.

"Then out came another story. After six months, when

114

things had settled down, Sinthea decided to 'have a night out' with two of her girlfriends. They travelled to a disco in Mayfair and were having a great time doing girlie things. A swarthy, good looking gentleman appeared and started chatting to them. After a few minutes he asked them if they would like to have cocktails with him at the Park Lane Hilton. Well, nothing ventured, nothing gained, and – safety in numbers. They accompanied him into a waiting chauffeur-driven Mercedes and were whisked to The Hilton. Champagne cocktails followed. He was a funny, entertaining man with buckets of easy charm. He then suggested that they meet his boss in his boss's suite and have a light supper. The suite was sumptuous. The 'boss' was a Sheik dressed in flowing white robes. More champagne flowed. Finally, they, plus some other men and women sat down to a five-course meal.

"Everybody spoke English. The whole affair was extremely jolly. At one o'clock the party broke up. The Sheik took Sinthea out onto the balcony overlooking Park Lane. He came straight to the point. His bones were old and cold, he needed a warm nubile body to warm them. Would she oblige? A maid would be sleeping at the foot of the bed. There was also a panic button in case she needed it. *He will probably need it more than me,* thought Sinthea. He showed her the room and introduced her to the maid. Sinthea agreed. The other girls were sent home in a limo, each with a Rolex, a string of pearls and two hundred pounds.

"So, she spent the night with 'Sheikey'. With him, he gave what was written on the label. She warmed his old, cold bones. The next morning she breakfasted with him. He gave her a Rolex, a string of pearls and five hundred pounds. The limo took her home. Warming Sheikey's bones became a regular event – in fact, whenever he was in town, which was often because he required a great deal of medical treatment, including injections of liquid gold. Then, one of Sheikey's brothers arrived; he also required his (not so old) bones warmed. He also required a few other bits warmed too. She did not mind. He was handsome, the gifts and the thousand pounds a night came in handy too. She was also, quite frankly, becoming horny. This induced a bit of 'hysteria', which needed a release. More brothers arrived on the scene; her warming qualities were now in great demand.

"She did not want to bank the money because the Department of Health and Social Security could and did inspect bank accounts regularly. So she bought 'nice things', some of which I could see before me. The supply of brothers seemed to have become unending. Some tried to bargain with her, but she would not have it. One thousand pounds or no warmth. Sheikey passed away and the brothers were beginning to cut up rough."

I leaned over to Win. "Dirty stuff. Kinky, not what nice girls do, not over here, anyway."

"Hey, fella, at least we don't go for spanking and all that nursery business," he retorted angrily.

I continued: "Anyway, the rough trade became rougher and it was starting to play havoc with her body, she picked up several doses. Also Aids was beginning to make the headlines. She was getting scared. She wanted to spend more time with her little girl. So she packed it in. Before I go on to the next 'episode' I will get you another glass."

Win bought the drinks. He was disgruntled. The barman had refused to continue serving him Winter Warmer by the pint, so he mixed his half pint with Special, much stronger than my Ordinary.

"So, now she had retired from working 'night duty', she collected her benefits, rent and worked at The Postillion. All quiet on the Western Front. Then she receives a call from a smooth-talking gentleman called 'Stephen'.

"Oh-oh. Not a certain butler by any chance?"

"Yes, the very same. A 'nice English gentleman' would like his old bones warmed; furthermore, this nice English gentleman lives at the foot of Kingston Hill, nice and local, but not too local. Well, Sinthea had become a little bored. She told him if it was only to be 'bone warming' then she was interested. OK, so the Rolls driven by Stephen picks her up at seven thirty in the evening and takes her to Crabbie's place. They sit by the fire and drink fine wine. It turns out he was an old friend of Sheikey and some of the brothers. Small world! Then they dine. You would have experienced Crabbie's fare. More sitting by the fire. They go upstairs and Crabbie asks her to take a shower and liberally apply Blue Grass perfume by Elizabeth Arden."

"For Christ's sake, that's an old girl's fragrance!" blurted out Win.

"She then has to wear a certain night dress. They get into bed. She warms his bones, nothing else. Next day they tuck into a full English and she is driven home by Stephen. Four hundred quid. Not quite West End rates, but then good food, good wine and no rough or kinky.

"This becomes a twice-weekly fixture. The perfume was his wife's, as well as the night dress. Comfort for a lonely, bereaved man."

"I could do with some of this bone warming too," commented Win, wistfully.

"This went on for months. A nice little earner. They became friends. One night, maybe a little too much old brandy? Maybe Sildenafil for the old man's, er... problem, who knows? They go upstairs, Crabbie starts to scuttle around; now it is more than his bones that need warming, or to be more precise, the Main Bone! Afterwards, they fall asleep. Next morning she wakes up to a cold stiff Crabbie and, well, you know the rest."

Win did indeed. But he let me conclude the tale.

"I managed to get her off the hook with the Department. We did not mention the 'night duty' to them. I said she was lonely and she enjoyed company and being bought the occasional drink. The Postillion paid her in cash and they did not keep proper records, nor did she, so we put in an 'estimate' for her earnings there... let's say, a 'low estimate'. She received a caution, that's all. She was anxious to settle my fee. I asked for it to be paid 'in kind'. She said that would spoil our relationship. I did meet her one Saturday morning at the pub. She was waiting for her boyfriend... 'Boy' friend? He was sixty if a day, a balding ginge with a wispy beard, a paunch on legs wearing a sheepskin coat, driving a Jag. Whoever wears sheepskin these days? Anyway, a few months after that, The Postillion was closed and would shortly become a block of flats. Never saw Sinthea again."

# Chapter Thirteen: The Photograph

My Accounts assistant boxed for the county. She sported shortly-cut, spiky hair and a broken nose. She always dressed the same: black leather trousers, white T-shirt and a shiny black leather biker's jacket with an abundance of silver zips.

On this particular day, we were to travel from the Hounslow Office to the Gloucester Depot.

Jeremiah Fox, the Gloucester General Manager, telephoned me.

"Guy, there's snow on the Welsh Hills and it is coming in fast towards us. You could postpone, or I could book you and Ingrid into The Candlewick to overnight. The forecast is bad. Your decision."

I conferred with Ingrid. To stay overnight was fine with her, if we could stop off at her flat on the way out so she could collect some 'overnight things'.

I told Jeremiah to book the rooms.

All the way down, the weather was excellent: bright and sunny. At the depot, we despatched the task in hand by four thirty. It had begun to snow. We were almost the last to leave the building. In a blizzard that was getting worse by the minute, we turned off the motorway and down the 'B' road. The car was difficult to handle on the fresh snow.

Ingrid could tell I was struggling to keep the car on the road. "See that little button with the symbol of an icicle? Push it and you will have snow traction control."

I did. The response was instant.

We arrived at The Candlewick in darkness, yet in a complete white-out. It was built in Tudor times from solid blocks of Cotswold stone. In the Great Hall were two enormous log fires which crackled and spat as if in competition with each other.

After check-in, we climbed the carved stone staircase that led to The Minstrel's Gallery with its mullioned windows.

"Foxy has booked me into The Honeymoon Suite," I said.

"Oh. Let me have a peep."

The 'suite' consisted of an oak-panelled vestibule, leading into a large, furnished drawing room, elegantly populated with period pieces. On the sideboard was a large cornucopia of fresh tropical fruit and a decanter of white port.

A huge four-poster dominated the bedroom. There were 'His' and 'Hers' dressing rooms. The bathroom was in black marble, flecked with amber. Showerheads the size of dinner plates, a bidet and a whirlpool bath completed the arrangements.

By contrast, Ingrid's accommodation was little more than a box room.

We met in the bar at seven thirty. For the first time ever, Ingrid was wearing a dress – an expensive floral number. We drank the local ale and then went in for dinner.

It was retro style: prawn cocktail, steak Diane, Black Forest Gateau, and a deep, mature Cotes du Rhone.

We returned to the bar and had several Remy XO. Finally, the barman pulled down the shutters. He placed the brandy on our table, along with a small tin. "Help yourselves... put the money in the 'Honesty Box'."

Eventually, the fires lost their aggression and when the empty bottle clattered to the floor we swayed up the staircase. Outside my room, Ingrid kissed me wetly and clumsily on the mouth.

"See you at breakfast." She tottered along on her high heels.

I had a shower and donned the towelling robe provided. I poured a nightcap. Then I heard the most exciting and evocative sound in the whole world – the quiet, but firm, knock on a locked door.

It was not Room Service, for sure. I opened the door, but kept the chain on.

"May I come in?" whispered Ingrid, hoarsely.

I let her in. She pushed herself against the door, which shut with a resounding click. She was wearing a kind of transparent sleeping garment. Nothing else.

"My room is freezing."

For two years, this woman had worked opposite me – leather trousers, sometimes jeans and chunky hand-knits, but never had I seen her like this.

She moved towards me. She placed her hand on my forearm and stood so close that I could feel the heat radiating through the flimsy material. She leaned her head on my shoulder. "I just want a tiny piece of that big bed," she murmured.

I knew within seconds we would be naked; we might not even make it to the four-poster. It would be a hard landing, gear down, flaps fully extended. Then I caught sight on the sideboard of the picture taken when my baby was newly born.

Instantly I wrenched the key fob from her hand. "I'll sleep in your room – far too *hot* in here!"

She blocked me, but I pushed past her into the corridor, walking briskly towards her bedroom.

Her box room was as hot as a baker's oven.

So, Managers beware: always carry a photograph of your baby when travelling.

# Chapter Fourteen: The Problem

They had placed my desk by the fax machine. Was this a promotion or a demotion? All the windows in the office opened out onto the main road and therefore, because of the noise and traffic fumes, remained firmly closed. The only other window was by the fax machine. It looked out onto a quiet courtyard and was always open allowing welcome fresh air into the stifling room. I was the only one who had my own desk; all the others, British and Japanese, sat eight to a table – on tables designed for six.

Max, one of the engineers, came up to me and said, "You are so lucky, you have no idea what it is like to have a horse with colic farting in your face every few minutes – at least where *you* sit, the air is sweet."

My Masters regarded me as 'confidential'; therefore, I was allowed to arrange the faxes that came from, and went to, Tokyo. The faxes in English were written in big block capitals with no punctuation. The confidential ones were in Japanese. None of the Brits in the Hounslow office could read or write Japanese, none, that is, except for I, who had secretly been attending Japanese classes at evening college. I had told everyone that I had to leave on time on Tuesdays because I was attending a 'Public Speaking Course'. Amazing how quickly you can learn to read and write Japanese when you have the will.

This fax, in Japanese, was from the Chairman; it praised Aki, The Japanese Managing Director, for the achievements of Amber Company Ltd. Aki was ordered to take the top six employees and their partners out to dinner at the best restaurant in London as a 'Thank You'. But *not* a Japanese restaurant, it stressed. This was to happen in six weeks' time, on Founder's Day. Of course, the best restaurant in town was The Red Berry. Bookings had to be made many months in advance and they seated no more than ten to a table. I immediately telephoned them from the meeting room. They were fully booked and could not, or would not, reserve more than ten to a table. However, they sponsored a charity: *The All Seeing I*, a Third World eye charity.

"I will donate ten per cent of our spend to the 'I'," I said. They took my credit card in my own name, Guy Gundle, and the deal was done. *Twelve* persons.

Six weeks later we were seated at The Red Berry. Louise was next to Max. I heard her question him: "How on earth did Guy get us into this place? You have to be a celeb and they never allow more than ten to a table."

"Guy knows where to find the keys to locked doors," stated Max, glancing at me.

Max was now looking at Archibald, Louise's husband. God, Archie was fat! He had a jaw like a Staffordshire bull terrier; a slab of fat under-slung it. Short tufts of red hair sprouted on his glistening pate. From where Max sat, Archie's hair looked like it was weeping nodules of rust. How could she have married him? He turned to Louise. He had fancied her at the Christmas party: the little black number she had worn had shown off her ample assets to their best effect. Now, after her diet, they were shriveled like prunes. No, he definitely preferred his women built for comfort rather than speed.

I felt a sharp dig in my ribs. "You haven't listened to a word I've been saying," Louise hissed. "I said, did you speak to Aki about *the problem*?"

"No, not yet."

"No? Guy, you have got to do something about it. I can't cope with it anymore. It's disgusting, quite the most revolting thing I've ever experienced. No one should have to put up with it. I get nauseous. I have a headache at the end of the day. I feel defiled. The others all feel the same. If you don't do something – then I will!"

She tossed back her fifth glass of Chateau Louden, that golden blend of Semillon and Chardonnay from the predominantly red Bordeaux area. *Pearls before swine*, I thought.

"You BETTER!" She banged her fist down on the table with such violence that all the diners fell silent. Mrs Aki looked questioningly at me.

"Louise – too much vino. She'll fall asleep shortly." I shrugged.

I never believed Mrs Aki was forty with two teenage boys. She was as dainty as a china doll, shining jet-black hair, immaculate in a Gharani Strok bias cut dress. That dress had cost the equivalent of one month of my yearly salary. I knew that; I had seen the invoice on Aki's desk. From her elegant clutch bag, Mrs Aki produced a small, red lacquered box. She snapped it open and extracted a silver egg-shaped object encrusted with brightly coloured gemstones. Her long crimson thumbnail turned a small stone and then she placed the egg on the table.

There was a whirring sound, the egg rolled upright and two little panels opened at its base; tiny, flat duck-like feet emerged followed by bright green, scaly plastic legs. The egg rose up onto its legs. Two more panels opened at the top of the egg and claws on the end of spindly green arms wriggled out. Then the top of the egg sprung open and a reptilian head rose from the apex, a long tongue flickering monstrously.

Now the gemstones lit up and strobed, and 'The Egg' began to walk towards me. It shrieked in Japanese: "I am The Egg Monster – I eat naughty children!"

The diners, not only on our table, but on all the other tables, were instantly quiet. The waiting staff stopped their duties, mesmerised.

The Egg Monster advanced towards me and the edge of the table; I instinctively placed a folded linen napkin in its path.

"SHIT!" it trilled in English. "SHIT! SHIT! SHIT!" The Egg Monster rolled over on its side; its arms, legs and head retracted, the lights switched off and it fell silent.

"For your little boy, Gundle-San," said Mrs Aki, placing The Egg Monster back in its box and handing it to me.

"Thank you very much, Mrs Aki – it's extremely kind of you."

I did not know whether to kiss her, shake her hand, or touch her shoulder. I ended up, rather ridiculously, patting her bag on the table and bowing.

"Gundle-San, how do you and the men, er, women too, of course, find Mr Aki?"

"He is a very fair man – a good boss. He has a sense of humour."

"Unusual for a Japanese, *neh*? How do you cope with…" she paused and took a sip of her Chateau Yquem. "Er, with his problem?"

"His *problem*, Mrs Aki?"

"You know what I mean." Her eyes levelled with mine.

"Well, if it is *the* problem I think you mean, then he should stay off the garlic, raw fish, durian and pickled cabbage – at least during the week."

"I am the one who eats those. Mr Aki eats very plain food – baby food in fact. You see, Gunder-San, he has cancer; half his stomach has been removed, he does not have too long to live. That is why he has so much…" she wrinkled her nose, "GAS."

# Chapter Fifteen: The Christmas Party

It was difficult to explain the importance of 'The Christmas Party' to my Japanese boss.

"It is a time when hatchets are buried, grievances forgotten – a time for bonding, seeing the other party's point of view. People eat and drink more than they should; they let their guard down, and they get to know each other. It is the time that employers thank their employees for their efforts over the year."

"What sort of budget does it attract?" Aki-san asked.

I explained the Tax Allowance and said most companies would spend up to that.

"That, then, is your budget, Mr Gundle."

Our problem was that the administrative office was in Hounslow and the depot was in Gloucester.

The Hounslow employees were known as 'The Hounds' and those in Gloucester were known as 'The Foxes', named after their General Manager, Jeremiah Fox (Fox by name, fox by nature).

The Foxes had already booked their Christmas party at an old coaching inn in Gloucester. The Hounds were invited, but none of us fancied either the long journey or the overnight stay with its prospect of the next morning in Gloucester.

I was instructed to organise a combined party. But where? Then the idea came. Using my ancient national A-Z, I drew a line between Gloucester and Hounslow and bisected it. It fell roughly at Oxford, so, with The Judgement of Solomon, I announced the party would be in a modern hotel on the outskirts of Oxford. Partners were also invited, as were their young children. All invitees would be taken to the venue by coach and brought back by coach. Dress informal, plus bathing attire... yes, bathing attire.

There was a long-lasting and deep schism between the Foxes and the Hounds. The Foxes had been taken over by the Japanese company and were reluctant to change. The Hounds were an eclectic bunch of various nationalities representative of a newly formed, foreign-controlled company.

I lost count of the hours I had to sit in meetings with the Foxes, arguing about company cars and pension schemes. The Christmas party, therefore, had to bring us all together – that was *my* brief.

I drove to the Oxford hotel and met the General Manager, a charming Swedish woman. The dining area ran along the indoor swimming pool and, with all its exotic foliage, looked more like a scene from South Pacific rather than a hotel in Bicester. There was a bar, a lounge area and a dance floor.

"Will the guests have complimentary drinks?" I had ventured earlier. I now told Olga the bar was to be free all night.

"Free? All night? Can they order anything?"

"Anything." My reply was unequivocal. "Now to the wine with the meal."

I instructed that the white was to be strong, cheap and fairly sweet. We settled on an Italian *Pinot Grigio* – 14.5%. The red was of the same strength, from Corsica. Port and brandy to be served at the end of the dinner. Each guest was to have a bottle of local ale – 8.5%. But my particular pleasure came in selecting the disco music: all the old Rock 'n' Roll greats.

I also opted for a Table Top Magician. If that combination did not succeed in persuading the Foxes to lie down with the Hounds, then there would never be 'Peace in The Valley'.

The evening came, and so did the moment of truth. The Foxes arrived, smartly attired in lounge suits, their Vixens dressed to the nines. The Hounds were laid back in their version of 'smart casual'. The two groups sat separately, painfully sipping their drinks and nibbling canapés. This was desperate, absolutely desperate.

I appealed to Olga for help.

"We could bring on Thelma," she suggested.

"Who is Thelma?" I asked nervously.

"He is behind the bar at the moment."

"What does he... or she, er, do?"

"Sing."

"Give it a go then." I couldn't see anything to lose at this stage.

Olga took me to the bar. "Simon," she addressed one of the barmen. "Tonight you are Thelma – this is Mr Gundle, The Chief Financial Officer of Amber. Work your magic, darling."

He minced over to me, took me by the hand and then led me to a door by the side of the bar, which when opened led into a long corridor; he opened a door at the end and we entered a small dingy room. He unlocked a filing cabinet, produced two glasses, a bottle of brandy and a bottle of water.

"Drink," he commanded.

What instruments did I play? Could I sing? I told him I was very much a country music fan, particularly of The Carter family, but could only play five of their pieces on the guitar, nothing else. He handed me a resonator guitar: "Play," he demanded.

The guitar was in tune. I played 'The Sea of Galilee' and sung in the reedy voice of June Carter.

Thelma (aka Simon) burst into a paroxysm of wild excitement: "That's perfect! What else can you sing?" I reeled off the other four numbers.

"Fantastic – that's enough!" He opened a large wickerwork basket and threw me a heavy black barathea pinafore, a white blouse with frilly cuffs and soft collared neck, a huge pair of gaudy red and white polka dot bloomers, a huge blond wig and fleshy woollen tights.

"I'm game for it; but I can't wear the tights."

"OK. We'll go for your hairy legs – should get a laugh."

In the meantime, Simon had stripped down to his very brief satin briefs, little more than a posing pouch and now was struggling into a corset like contraption. He inflated his 'boobs' with a hand rubber pump, slipped on an outrageous dress and was already finishing of his makeup and adjusting his wig.

"Just the makeup for you, darling. I'll do it for you, sit still pout your lips. Oh yes, listen, you will be wired, so don't sing or play to too loudly, the system will do it for you."

Simon and I walked down the corridor to another door which led to the small stage.

"OK. I will get them going, then when I am ready – I will call you on, Miss June Carter."

He went on stage, just leaving the door slightly open so I could see and hear what was going to happen. He was a real pro. He tried to recruit a drummer – of course, no takers. He played 'Waltzing Matilda' on the system and bashed the bass and kettle drum to demonstrate.

"It's so easy, easier than patting your head AND rubbing your gut. You, sir, in that tie that spelled 'Bullshit', come." He had selected one of the grumpiest Foxes, who, nevertheless came up on stage.

Then he recruited a couple of maracas shakers, two tambourine thumpers, a washboard player and a kazoo blower and three fat 'Ya Ya' ladies to sing the chorus and shake their bits in time.

"Our first act, in fact, our only act, comes all the way from Tennessee – Miss June Carter!" he roared. The lights went up and I walked on. For a second there was a stunned silence, then the crowd burst into a wild uproar. Here was their straight laced, pinstriped Chief Financial Officer in a black pinny, flashing her giant bloomers and patting an outrageous blond wig. I ignored it all. I was back in my study playing for myself and no one else. I mellowed my girlie voice for this one – it brought the house down. I don't know why, but it is the only way I can sing. 'The Sea of Galilee' has a great chorus: 'On the sea, the sea, the sea of Galilee, my Jesus is walking on the sea'.

The Ya Yas gave it their all and shook their bits absolutely in time, so hard in fact that they nearly fell off; in fact, they sang along in perfect pitch and harmony. When they reached the phrase 'The bloody sea', they really belted it out – BLOODY! Grumpy was actually a natural drummer, in fact I learnt later that he had once played drums in a skiffle group. So much for hiding your light under a bushel.

Thelma thumped the piano with great gusto. Next I moved on to 'When the World's on Fire', and here the Ya Yas really excelled themselves – unbelievable what three drunk ladies can sing when they are in the rhythm. I had picked up a bottleneck from the top of the piano and with that and vibrato effect from the sound system the piece really got them swaying. I then switched to a capo and thumb pick and moved into the much faster 'Wildwood Flower'. For this Thelma reached for a banjo, which she picked with the most amazing dexterity. I noted the washboard had gone into overdrive. This is really a 'ladies' song and had to climb a whole octave to pitch it right, but I got there. Everyone now was singing along heartily. The stage now began to fill with dancing couples, men and women, men and men, women and women. Suddenly, everyone was singing in 'American'. Finally, I finished off with 'The Church in The Wild Wood'. For this I had to take my voice down a few tones; a slower number. I had done my numbers, now it was Thelma's turn.

She took over, absolutely stunning in a slinky black dress, not over-camp at all. She gave the most wonderful renditions of the big band twenties' and thirties' music. It happened that I was also a fan of Al Bowlly and involuntarily found myself crooning with Thelma, much to the merriment of all the assembled guests.

And thus, the ice was broken, the wine flowed, the feasting commenced, the crackers were pulled, and on went the silly hats. The Hounds had agreed to wear their swimming gear under their 'smart casual' and after the brandies, on an agreed signal, stripped down and plunged into the pool. Soon, almost all the guests, swimwear or not, were frolicking in the water.

Then the disco began. Towelling robes were produced and the drunken revellers slid around the wet floor. Unspeakable activities were being performed on and under the tables.

I woke in my hotel bedroom, with a somnolent form next to me. To my horror I realised it was Thelma! I grabbed my clothes and bounded down the corridor to the toilets in the lobby, where I changed. Although it was eight thirty, there were only a few of our group having breakfast. I went through the card, Continental, Full English. Fortunately, my room was empty when I returned. To this day, I cannot remember what happened, but there was no lasting harm. Not for the first time I have fallen into a barrel of tits and ended up sucking my thumb!

All I can say is this: from that day on, co-operation between the two units was first class. The Lion did lie down with The Lamb, The Fox with The Hound. There was Peace in the Valley.

So, Managers beware: think carefully before you mess with 'The Christmas Party'.

# Chapter Sixteen: Tastevin

Food was important to me. I used to live to eat, now, sadly, I eat to live. My first job in the restaurant business, was as a kind of kitchen porter in a Greek (Cypriot) restaurant, called The Kouzina – The Kitchen. I worked there on Fridays and Saturday nights. My primary task was to wash up. No fancy dishwater then. I loved it; it had a rhythm to it. I was also responsible for the coffees and desserts. On Saturday evening when the establishment closed, we all sat down to a meal of chargrilled steak, salad and wine.

My next assignment was as a 'commis' waiter in forty cover establishment above a pub in Brompton Road, West London. My task was to take customers coats and then, upon their departure, help them into their garments. The coat hooks ran up a flight of stairs. Each hook corresponded to a table number. Easy and fool proof. I instinctively knew which coat belonged to each wearer. Large ladies wore large coats and so on. But, also, smell helped. I could have literally done that job blind, by merely relying on my sense of smell. The tips I received were extremely generous, double what I earned in my clerical day job. I declared this to the owner, who waved her plump hand and said, "They're yours. You're only a commis, you don't share in the tronc." In addition, I was now promoted to taking the dessert orders and serving as well. My trick here was not to use a pen and pad. I would remember what everybody ordered and where they all sat. It was a simple technique of memory association. If a woman with almond eyes ordered Chinese Chow Chow (Ice cream and lycees), that made the Chinese connection. A fat, effeminate man ordering cream puffs, he was a 'puff' Easy. Never failed and brought me even more tips.

My final employment was as a 'short order' chef in the evenings in a wine bar. The chief tool of the trade in the kitchen was the microwave. Chips and steak were the only thing I needed to really cook. This bar was actually a pick up joint. The punters bought very expensive wines to impress their 'chicks', but most of the bottles were never finished. I was under strict instructions to 'recycle' the wine. White into the white jar, red into the red. It was then poured into carafes and sold as 'house'. Normally, I would finish off any decent bottle before it was recycled. Needless to say, this took its eventual toll on me and I gave up this employment.

Subsequently, my new wife and I only had one ambition – to open and run a restaurant. We found a small twenty-nine cover licensed establishment in Battersea and put in an offer which was accepted. For several nights we parked outside the place and counted forty or so diners in and eventually out. So, it was trading at full plus capacity.

The license was transferred and we became the proud owners. We decided to run it pretty much along the same lines – Rustic French. This was the mid-eighties and the days of rickety tables and chairs and red and white gingham were rapidly disappearing along with Salad Nicoise and Pepper Steak. It was a new game now.

The chef came with the restaurant. Unfortunately, she had a problem, anti-depressants washed down with a huge quantity of wine rendered Jeanette incapable on most evenings. Her replacement was good, but an alarming quantity of expensive wine began to disappear. With his permission, I searched his rucksack. No evidence.

We closed on Sundays and one Sunday morning I pulled up opposite the restaurant with the intention of giving the place a good clean. I saw Stephan, the chef, with a large dog. I sat in the car and watched. He went to the bin locker and unlocked the panel. A chute led directly from the kitchen into the bins. He pulled out one of the bins and from its depths produced several bottles of wine and a few packages wrapped in Bacofoil. At this stage I approached him. The wines were our very best, old Bordeaux and mighty burgundies. In the foil were pounds of fillet steak. I fired him there and then. I became the chef.

Customer numbers began to dwindle. There would be evenings with no customers at all. Finally, we decided on a makeover. My wife was from Malaysia and the plan was to re-launch as a 'Franco Malaysian' restaurant with a thirties style theme. We imported a chef from Malaysia who arrived with two metal choppers, a large one and a small one. We purchased a chopping block from Soho. He banished all the kitchen knives.

It worked. A new type of customers began to appear. One evening Suzy de Sousa, the TV documentary presenter turned up. In a quiet moment she convinced that what we needed was 'PR' or Public Relations and for five thousand pounds (three thousand in cash, two on the invoice) she would turn around the business. I agreed to pay her the in stage payments.

The result was dramatic. Reviews appeared in the local and national newspapers, the glossy magazines, even local radio. Our little eaterie became the haunt of minor celebs. You had to wait three weeks for a booking. We opened all day Sunday.

The previous owner had been a former banqueting manager and knew his wines. We inherited a fantastic stock of French wines. I was careful to maintain this and soon was selling wines by the case to customers.

I was invited to enter a French wine competition, open only to professional sommeliers. The first part was easy, multiple choices questions. I made it through. The next round was a two-thousand word essay (in English) describing certain French wine producing regions. This was easy for me and I passed through to the final round, which was to be held at a top London hotel in three months' time.

For those months I read and studied all I could about French wine. I went to every possible tasting and expanded the cellar.

Finally, the day came. Twenty of us in a series of 'practical' tests. We had to serve wine, describe the ideal cellar conditions, talk about different types of serving glasses, and so on.

Then the 'Taste Off'. In a room with a window facing the north, there was a single glass of red wine in a Paris goblet on a white tablecloth. The three judges invited me to taste, while previous contestants sat in rows watching.

I held the glass to the light, swirled, sniffed, tasted and spat.

"Beaujolais," I pronounced.

"We all know that," said one of the judges tiredly.

"Morgon."

"Yes we know that too. Shipper?"

"Dubeouf," I was confident. We stocked Beaujolais from all the regions. Our shipper was Dubeouf 'The King of Beaujolais'. The wine was fairly cheap and easy drinking. Popular amongst our clientele.

"Year?" I took a guess. I was right.

"Anything else?"

No there was not. "Well done," you may sit.

Two more contestants came in and to my relief got it all horribly wrong. One nominated Boozy, the red wine from Northern France. Another a gamay variety from the South of France.

"Finally, Madame Du-Barry." The name was familiar to me.

A woman entered. White shirt, black trousers and waistcoat. It was none other than our former chef, Jeanette.

She strode up to the table, sampled and then not only pronounced that it was Dubeouf's Morgan and the exact year but went on to describe the particular field it was grown in, that it had only been partially chaptalized, but not undergone a full malolactic fermentation, resulting in the micro bubbles. Neither had it been fully macerated. It had been a good year, but this particular wine in this glass, had been poorly finished, badly stored and had had some 'horrid' top notes. She proceeded at length to describe these notes and the 'mouth-feel'.

"I do not commend this wine to The House." She sat to loud applause from the judges.

"Madame Du-Barry is the only one of all of you to have picked up on our slightly doggy glass of plonk." He looked at his fellow judges and then pronounced her the winner.

Of course, I congratulated her. A few weeks later, we found a buyer and sold the establishment.

# Chapter Seventeen: Waterboarding

It was mid-August in the city: hot and humid. I was booted and suited and a whole two hours early for my interview just off The Strand. I could easily have killed time in a coffee shop, or maybe have gone to one of the many cosmopolitan restaurants in the area and sat there in comfort, enjoying the air conditioning; otherwise, it was straight to the agency and see if they might see me early. I decided on the latter.

"Guy," said a young, well-upholstered man suddenly appearing in reception and greeting me cordially. "I'm Gordon."

*That's odd?* I thought. *Surely the interview is with Tommy?*

Putting this tricky feeling to one side, I said nothing about it and instead apologised for my over-punctuality. "I'm crazily early, but it is cooler here than the street."

He seemed to understand in a curiously non-committal sort of way and led me into the interview room. We sat facing each other over a low-level rosewood table, a file – about me, presumably – open in front of him. He wore a pair of pin-striped trousers and an expensive, pink *Sea Island* cotton shirt complemented with cufflinks, but no tie. I felt overdressed in my three-piece and silk tie.

I had expected an offer of a glass of water or something similar, given the almost unbearable heat and humidity, but instead it was straight into battle. "It's all about leadership. Where are you coming from on that?"

The question threw me.

"Leadership starts with The Mandate," I opined. "If you don't have The Mandate, no point in coming through the front door."

"The successful candidate will have The Mandate," he stated flatly, clearly unimpressed at my response.

His piercing blue eyes were doing exactly that – going straight through me. Perhaps this was all part of the test?

So, I stuck to my guns and elaborated that in my (considerable) experience, what appeared to be The Mandate often was not. There were secret agendas; those who were the apparent decision makers often were not. The axis of power could unexpectedly shift and change – stars would rise and fall. The external environment could change. To be a successful leader, you needed to have a real, functioning Mandate. Once you had that, then it was 'Cometh the hour, cometh the man'. Coco the Clown could do the job... if The Mandate had been successfully negotiated.

Again, Gordon – if he was in agreement with my very general 'opener' – kept it well-hidden. The Executioner's Sword is always well hidden.

"OK, so you have The Mandate sorted, what next?" A strong whiff of exasperation had crept into his voice. "How would *you* lead?"

"Gordon, I don't want to trot out all the old clichés..." I paused momentarily to consider a different approach. This hadn't been a great start. And I could feel those eyes again. "But you have to be whiter than white. Purer than the driven snow. Lead by example. Your vision must their vision. You need to know when to stick to your guns and when to cut loose. In the army, it's simple: Queen and Country, the Regiment, yourself far down the list."

"How did you lead in the Sudan?"

That was a strange one. I had never been to the Sudan or anywhere in Africa other than Tunisia and South Africa. He really was coming from all angles.

"Well, I aligned my vision with all stakeholders. That meant giving and taking – 'The Power of Alignment' – then I lived 'The Brand'. Where I led, others followed. Of course, you praised in public and approbated in private. Fair remuneration, incentive schemes – all of that helped. Targets had to be achievable. Once achieved, effort could be rewarded. Simple things: luxury food parcels, designer sunglasses with the Corporate Logo, free use of the Company jeeps, golf lessons..."

"Golf? In the Sudan?" He was listening, after all.

"Very popular," I heard myself reply, thinking *this is sheer madness – whoever heard of golf in the southern Sahara?* Nevertheless, I went on: "You only have to worry about the 'greens', which aren't 'green' at all but brown, rolled sand. Golf's a big thing out there. Those are the practical things, the Reward Tools. But, you know, even body language is important." I knew it was time to get well away from a conversation denigrating into desert golf, and a digression on body language seemed as good an option as any right now. "The old thing: get your body language right and the right attitude will follow. A leader must be fearful, but *show* no fear."

As my subject unfolded, and the temperature in the room increased despite the air-conditioning, I unbuttoned my jacket and threw it, executive-style, over my chair. I then undid my waistcoat. This was getting more like it now. There was a flip chart on the walls with a few pens. I gleefully drew Gordon my version of the 'Satisfaction Cycle'. I had seen all this stuff dozens of times when working as an accountant for a management consultancy. It all bubbled gaily to the surface now. I couldn't stop. I was on fire.

Finally, Gordon held up his hand. Without making any direct comments about my excellent display of business and commercial expertise, he rather witheringly commanded: "Let's move on now. Scenario One: You have two identical companies: one with an all-female board, one with an all-male board. How do you think they reach decisions?"

I had worked with both. Apart from the question being 'so yesterday', I had in fact written several articles about this very subject. There was the soft, female approach: always changing, always flexible; then the hard, male approach: rigid, unbending. After laying out both with examples, the conclusion was obvious – combine the best of both worlds. He seemed to like this.

"Now, to the Sudan." His manner had changed – more

upbeat, almost human, to my relief. "Operationally, what were the difficulties you had in bringing fresh water to the people?"

The penny was dropping… Gordon was interviewing the *wrong* candidate. This was nothing less than lunacy. *I* had applied for a job with a young fabric company that had just launched on the Stock Market, a company with global ambitions which drew its inspiration from Africa. Who did he think he was interviewing? Another 'Guy'… one who did have the appointment that I was now trapped in. Was the real Guy waiting patiently outside for an interview that would never come?

I could have sat there and worried. No. I decided to relax and have some fun. One of the chaps in my creative writing class had been a water engineer in the Sudan. In fact, he talked and wrote about nothing else.

I opened up. I described the geology of the region, trying not to sound like my fellow writer: a rookie geologist simply had to put an 'X' on the spot, you drilled down and up would come pure, fresh water. I even described the taste of the water. The only issue was that once the villagers became used to pure water, their immunity to 'dirty' water disappeared, so when they went to visit a village with dirty water, they all fell ill. I went from generalisation to daredevil economising with the truth. "As a result," I stated, "we developed a 'quick roll-out' programme, enrolling the help of all the villagers."

I described how we set up 'fast-drill' trucks that were fully equipped with all manner of machinery. "From 'drill to fill' could take as little as a week. We beat all targets, all budgets. A real 'win/win,'" I eventually concluded.

I knew I had him. As his restlessness at my extensive knowledge and sudden upsurge in confidence increased, damp stains started appearing on the pink shirt under his armpits. Despite the air conditioning, tiny beads of sweat had broken out on his forehead. He licked his lips frequently and twirled his Mont Blanc pen. Gone was the façade of aloof superiority of just an hour ago.

"Great!" he managed to blurt out finally. "Thanks. You're definitely on a very short shortlist. In my book, I make you the favourite." He stood up to indicate the end of the interview and shook my hand with a firm grip that was most definitely moist and damp with perspiration. I walked out feeling pretty good about myself in a curious sort of a way, fundamentally very pleased with my 'ad-hoc performance' in there, but as the sunshine hit me, I knew I needed a pint of decent ale. Ruminating over the experience in the nearest pub, I had downed three before I felt ready to leave.

About a month later, I read in the *Financial Times* that a Mr *Guy Gunthorpe* had been appointed as CEO of a certain Water Board at a salary of £750,000 pa. Not myself, Mr *Guy Gundle*. Right Place, Wrong Man. But on reflection maybe Coco the Clown could have fared better after all?

Fate is a curious thing. As Fate would have it I had been shortlisted for another design company job at the *same* agency one month later. So, there I was, different suit and tie.

"Charlie will see you soon," said the receptionist. I perched myself on the edge of the sofa, scared that if I sat back, I would never be able to stand up.

"Guy. Charlie, come."

I know my frocks, this was a Dosa, raw wild silk from the 'Africa' range. Simple and stunning. It was low cut and I caught glimpse of Charlie's chlorine bleached white bra. She smelt of an expensive faded scent which barely disguised the fetid odour of stale tobacco. Her slate grey eyes pieced mine. I looked at her, she looked at me, I looked at her, she looked at me.

"This isn't going to work, is it?" I said flatly.

"Your choice."

"No, it's not – thank you for your time."

I left the agency and wandered down to Gordon's Wine Bar and ordered a bottle of something cold, crisp, white and full of citrus.

This male/female clash has happened not once to me in my career, but *three* times. I suppose I'm a 'bloke's bloke'.

Beware of employment agencies, they are even lower of the 'scumbag scale' than estate agencies.

# Chapter Eighteen: Lady in Red

Humans form relationships with other humans. Love, hate and all the emotions in between. Most of us have some kinds of feelings towards animals. They are all God's creatures – even snakes, spiders and scorpions. People who mistreat animals tend to mistreat humans. We also have affections for *things*. When I was even poorer than now, I wanted three *things*. A decent pair of shoes that did not let in water. A Cashmere coat. And a nice motor, not the old bangers that I have risked life and limb in.

Late in middle age, I had all three and together. Nice. Step out on a cold, wet winter's night in a pair of smart, warm, dry shoes with a decent coat on your back, and slip behind the heavy, polished *Bakelite* steering wheel. The engine purrs into life at the turn of a key, first time. The dials glowing in the walnut dash, the de-mister on. Soft leather, deep pile carpet. Warm, filtered air circulates in the cabin. Windscreen wipers actually wipe the windscreen clean and clear. A heated wash/wipe finishes the job.

'Boys Toys'. My first motorised convenience was a bicycle that I purchased in Holland. It had a tiny engine mounted on the handlebars. You pedalled along and then, using a lever, dropped the engine onto the front wheel. A small rubber wheel sat on the front tyre embedded in the engine and with this spinning around (big wheel driving small wheel) the engine kick- started and the small wheel then drove the big wheel. When you needed to stop, you simply pulled the engine up off the tyre with the lever. To stop the engine, you cut the petrol supply.

With this device, I travelled all over Holland. Holland is, of course, a small, flat country. I finally 'lent' my bike to a Dutch girl. I never saw it again. A lesson I should have learned.

My next bicycle was a moped. A second-hand *Norman Nippy* with a small Sachs engine. It never really worked and I sold it for the same price I bought it for.

Then came the Honda 50cc. I do not know how many millions of these have been made. They are the 'workhorse' of the East, transporting enormous loads and sometimes entire families. It gave me independence from public transport. You switched on the ignition and off you went. It had indicators, reliable brakes, excellent headlights and was a comfortable ride. It could cruise all day at a steady 50mph. After well over half a century, variants of this machine are still being made. Perhaps they will eventually be replaced by an electric version?

Then it was a real motorbike. A single cylinder Honda 125cc. This was a motorbike that looked like a motorbike. Big handlebars with mirrors. A large petrol tank. Dials housed in two black cylinders. A seat for a passenger. The engine was responsive and it would cruise at just over 75mph. I took her all around Scotland, France and Spain. She was easy to service and maintain and never gave me any trouble. When I see one parked today, I have to resist the temptation not to sit on it.

It was at this time that I had agreed to take a girl out for a meal and a drink one evening. She came to the door wearing a short and very tight skirt.

"Ready?"

"Yes, where's your car?"

I indicated my steed.

"Oh no! I am not going on THAT."

So, we went by bus and came back by taxi in which she was sick all over me. Some girls just cannot handle a *Bangalore Phal* and four pints of lager.

However, I was determined to continue my relationship with her. I had a brainwave and traded in my steed for a *Reliant Robin* three-wheeler. Although they were cars, they had only three wheels and were classed as 'motorised tricycles' and therefore could be driven on a motorbike licence.

I picked up the keys from a second-hand car lot in Stockwell.

"How do I drive it?" I asked.

The salesman gave me a funny look, then climbed into the driver's seat.

"From right to left, ABC – Accelerator, Brake, Clutch. Four gears and this is how you operate reverse. Here's the handbrake: handbrake on, handbrake off. Simple."

He had done the deal – no longer interested, but he did push me across the road into a large space.

I made sure the engine was in neutral and then switched on. I depressed the accelerator several times and measured the engine pitch. Clutch in, first gear selected. Clutch released. Accelerator depressed. The vehicle shot backwards and smashed into the car behind. Panicking, I selected neutral, tried another gear and off we went… straight into horn-blaring traffic. If I pushed the accelerator down, the car speeded up; if I eased back, it slowed. Easy. Then I had to stop suddenly. The car stalled.

I was now going up a small hill, so when I put it into neutral, it ran backwards; fortunately, I braked and then applied the handbrake. So… neutral, restart engine, into gear… and very slowly, with a howling engine, it climbed up the traffic-laden hill. A smell of burning reminded me that the handbrake was still on.

I released it and we bunny hopped forward alarmingly. Amidst a maniacal cacophony of blazing horns, I swung into a quiet side street and parked in a generous space. I switched the engine off and smoked two cigarettes in a row.

The street was quiet. I restarted and gingerly drove down it. I mastered the technique of traversing from first gear into second and then back again. I learned how to stop, go into neutral and then proceed. I worked out how to use the indicators and turned left into another deserted street. Hey, this was fun! Slowly down the back doubles, I worked my way towards Brixton, changing between neutral, first and second.

The streets were becoming narrower, cars parked on each side. Steering needed to be more precise. A hundred yards ahead of me was a large classic *Chevrolet* with those gigantic tail fins. A real monster of lights and chrome. Several men were proudly polishing her. As I approached the Monster, a man sauntered over from the other side of the street with a six pack of beer. I swerved to avoid him and smacked the Monster, then scraped along its side. All Hell broke loose. I hit the accelerator hard, bumped into another car, managed second gear and then miraculously found third gear. After a few more back doubles at a very dangerous speed and a few glancing blows to other parked cars, I ducked into an industrial estate. At the far end, I pulled up and smoked three cigarettes in a row.

Arriving here probably saved my life. It was a Saturday so the estate was deserted. Slowly and thoroughly, I practised gear changing, using the indicators, performing emergency stops, hill starts and even reversing. It was much later that afternoon that I drove home to Wandsworth Common, this time without incident.

A week later, in the early evening, I arrived at my Diva's doorstep. She appeared. The dress was even shorter and tighter than the last one.

"My car," I announced proudly.

"I wouldn't be seen dead in that thing." So it was bus and taxi home. She was sick again, even though we had a Chinese this time. It must have been the four lagers...

I, however, loved that old banger. I turned it over several times. You simply stuck the bits together with special glue.

But, later that year when travelling up to Scotland along the M1, I began to feel that I was sinking. Strange, I was actually peering *under* the steering wheel to try and see over the dash. There was a CRACK of plastic and all I could see was dashboard. Sparks were flying everywhere. My (driver's) seat had fallen through the floor-well and was scraping along the surface of the motorway at 55mph. How I managed to pull over safely onto the hard shoulder I still do not know. My unlucky (or was it lucky?) passengers got out, smoked several cigarettes and then helped me to glue it all back together. Incredibly, it got us to Scotland and back.

Finally, I passed my Driving Test and bought a brand new *Mini* for just under one thousand pounds. Two years and twenty thousand miles later, I sold it for one thousand, two hundred and fifty pounds. That's inflation for you.

The Diva did consent in coming with me in the *Mini* and happily she was not sick this time. I lost touch with her; however, after many years I came across her in my local Off-Licence. Years of heavy smoking and many barrels of sweet sherry had taken their toll. She was wrinkled and immensely fat. We exchanged phone numbers, but never did meet up. I learned that a year after that meeting she had passed away, single, lonely and unloved.

Continuing relationships with *things*, a thing that I have had a relationship with for over forty years is my bicycle, a Falcon Tourer. It was a Special (Queen's) Jubilee edition (1977). What made it 'Special' was the painted-on Union flag on the frame. The frame was a Reynolds 571, a great, Birmingham-made grade of tubing. The gears were Shimano (Japanese), other bits Italian, Indian and Chinese. I estimate that I must have done nearly two hundred thousand miles on my *Black Falcon*. In the course of that, only the frame, handlebars and the *Falcon* badge remain; everything else has been replaced once and probably then again. The second time was a major refurbishment. The wheels were no longer made and slightly larger ones had to be found. Then the tyres and tubes were difficult to source. The front forks needed to be specially treated and re-chromed and so it went on. By the time the whole job was complete, I could have purchased a decent new road racer.

But it was great to have the *Black Falcon* back. His eye was sharp, his black feathers glistening, the silver chrome sparkling. It was a Saturday morning in June. A lovely sunny day with a gentle breeze. I took him from my apartment on the Thames, over Kingston Bridge and then along the towpath to the riverside entrance of Hampton Court Palace, a gentle seven-mile round trip. I set off at eight-thirty before the buggies, the pole walkers or the family hordes had time to rise. I was determined to smile at everybody. It is fun doing that. Sometimes they smile back, sometimes they wave, occasionally they look embarrassed.

The *Black Falcon* was soaring beautifully. He refrained from his habit of trying to pluck babies from their buggies and dash their brains out on the jagged rocks. Naughty Falkie! Then I saw her. Lady in Red. Red jogging pants, matching red top, red trainers with pink flashes. Her long black hair flowing in the wind. A smidgen of make-up and, of course, red matching lipstick. I smiled, she smiled, then she waved. I carried on, then just before the Palace, my chain came off. I up-ended the bike and began the process of re-siting the chain. Now The Lady in Red was coming back the other way. She stopped. "Do you want any help? I have got some tissues. I know about bikes."

Now, nothing *really* scares me – snakes, spiders, rats, scorpions, charging rhinos, the Great White Shark. Nothing at all. Except TISSUES.

"I'm fine, thanks, I carry an old rag just for the purpose." Which, indeed, I was using.

"Hmm. That's a vintage bike, isn't it?"

I gave her a run down on the *Black Falcon*, talked her through the gearing arrangements. The *Black Falcon* positively glowed with pride.

"He's amazing. Do you mind if I sit on him?"

Naturally, *he* did not object. Neither did I.

"Perfect fit, but then we are about the same height," she announced.

I told her that I had been specially measured for him. I did not tell her that that since then, I had shrunk two inches. Old age, I presume.

"Could I take him for a spin?"

The *Black Falcon* was keen; after all, it is not every day

that a beautiful woman gets to ride on your back.

I asked her to be no more than ten minutes. The big Saturday Handicap was on in less than three hours and I had not done my homework.

I sat down and watched the river flow by. I walked up and down the bank. Sat down, got up, walked some more. Twenty minutes gone. Did some bending and stretching. Blew my nose on a clean linen handkerchief. Picked my teeth with a blade of grass. Now a full forty minutes had gone by. It then struck me. I had just given my beautiful *Black Falcon* to a completely unknown woman and she was not going to come back. She was probably in Chiswick by now. I had only my apartment key on me and nothing else – no money, no mobile, nothing.

I thought about what to do now. I could jog to the Hampton Court Ticket Office and ask to use their phone. I would report the theft to the Police. What an idiot. Had I not learnt from the first time in Holland? I began to jog, then I saw her pedalling towards me at enormous speed.

She was perspiring and breathless. "So sorry, so sorry, but the chain came off. Not easy to put back."

The *Black Falcon* had gone into a sulk.

"Bet you thought I had run off with him?"

I smiled. "Oh no. I was just a little concerned."

"Here's my card. We must go together for a nice long cycle, say to Windsor and back, a few pit stops on the way. I am free most Saturdays."

She was a Senior Corporate Lawyer with a really top, swanky city law firm. The reverse of her card showed her credentials in Spanish; that may have explained the flowing black hair and flashing dark eyes.

As I cycled slowly home, deep in thought, it occurred to me: *Why did these things never happen to me when I was young and single?*

# Chapter Nineteen: The Throwback

The square was surrounded on three sides by rather drab, characterless five-storey council flats built in the thirties. The fourth side comprised railway arches. To the south, Elephant and Castle; to the north, Southwark and London Bridge. In the square sat an area of grass, bushes and flowerbeds optimistically put there by a well-meaning, local voluntary organisation but whose weeds, however, seemed to be faring better than the drought-tolerant perennials. It was a pleasant Thursday in late July, its warm sunshine under a soothing blue sky would usually lift up, even a little, the most dispirited soul from the depths of despair. Children were playing on the swings and slides, shouting and screaming, rushing around. If only I could bottle and sell their energy, I would be a millionaire. On a bench, a little further away, sat two sad men, smoking and drinking strong lager from cans. "How do children progress from their joyful, energetic state to being hobos?" I wondered.

A jet droned overhead, a train rumbled by. A man from an upper window could be seen pleasuring himself in full view, dreaming of his muse. A young man in designer jeans and top was doing something furtively in the bushes. Snorting perhaps? And my unease returned.

Beyond this square, somewhere, lay a green and pleasant land: parish churches, the peel of bells, the thwack of leather on willow, and of course the village pub with its low beams, horse brasses and decent jugs of ale. But here was the metropolis: a melting pot of nations and cultures; yet another city of broken dreams; everyone going to and from it, all hopes and roots left elsewhere.

I checked the time yet again and looked at the grey door in the arches to where Mrs Robertson could be seen, and heard, bickering with a younger man who evidently could also bicker, argue and, like her, live a life of penny-pinching and conspiring. I knew who they were; their engineering company had been established here decades ago, and at this very moment I felt a lump in my throat as I contemplated a highly unwelcome thought: was this where I was going to end up? I anxiously phoned the agency and got straight through to Clarice, my contact.

"I can't go through with it," I blurted out. "It's all too miserable. I promised myself I would only work in nice, smart locations. In the few minutes I have been here, I've seen one guy committing a lewd act, another snorting coke, two drunk hobos – and it's only eleven in the morning…" My head was in my hands, my stomach in my boots. It wasn't in my nature to let people down, but this…

She could be very persuasive. The position had enormous potential, they desperately needed someone like me, a 'turnaround' specialist. Essentially, they were lovely people, and I would fit in well. There was only one true candidate – me. She begged me not to let her down. Then, with some menace, came the not-so-subtle hint that, if I did not show for this one, other opportunities might not be forthcoming.

I managed to convince myself that I would probably benefit from the interview experience and minutes later found myself pushing the buzzer next to the grey door. It opened, I walked up the stairs and stood in front of a plump woman in a bright yellow dress. I was to follow her. We proceeded down a long corridor at right angles to the arches. She knocked and I was shown into a large office lined with books. Behind a large, tooled leather table sat an elderly but nonetheless elegant woman. She rose to shake my hand, and bade me to sit on the straight-backed chair on the visitor's side of the desk. I noticed a small, grey-haired man also sitting at the table.

"Gerald Robertson," she said. "My son."

She smiled at me. "We make pumps. Have been doing so since the late thirties. Small, specialised rotary pumps. Originally, they were in steel, British racing green and post box red with brass fittings, but then we switched to plastic in the seventies… plastic is easy to shape and mould. It is hard-wearing and can be made soft."

"It's cheap!" squeaked the Grey Man, his deep-set, dark brown eyes bulging in their sockets. He clearly wanted to say a lot more but for some reason accepted that he could not. I remember it going through my mind as to whether he had been involved in some sort of an accident years before – his demeanour was so odd – but for now I had to concentrate on what the agency had sent me here for.

I learnt that the pumps were made in southern Spain, in Cadiz. I commented that it was a strange place to have a European manufacturing business. Mrs Robertson told me that they had a sherry-importing business there. The original metal pumps had been made in the local foundry, and it was logical to use the inherited expertise for the plastic product.

"Do you drink sherry, Mr Gundle?" asked Mrs Robertson, standing up before I could answer.

"I do. It's the 'new' whisky."

"It's not too early," was her verdict on the acceptability of having alcohol with a job interview at eleven in the morning. She poured me a very small measure into an extremely large glass. The liquid was a light golden colour, but I could immediately taste that it was of a great age.

"Nutty, balsamic, dry, oaked… and vanilla top notes."

Both of them smiled.

"We're teetotal," piped the Grey Man.

Suddenly, the 'interview' was over and I was hired. Initially, it would be through the Agency, then they would consider a contract.

On the way out, the plump woman congratulated me. "You passed the Sherry Test then."

"Seems so."

"Nutty." She winked at me.

I quickly picked up that I was dealing with a real 'basket case' here. Despite all the security, the File Server had been stolen. All back-ups failed. Six months' data lost. My task was to restore the records from any prime data and occasional printouts that could be found. The previous accountant had retired just before the theft to run a 'beach goods' business. Nothing would bring him back.

After a two-week probation, I was placed on a contract which I ended up drafting myself. I worked from eight in the morning to seven at night, Monday to Friday. Those were the hours that the offices were open and manned by daytime security. At night, a different security team took over. Lunch was brought to me by the Italian *Travattoria* across the road: a large plate of pasta, a pudding and a bottle of mineral water. I could not afford to take time out from my task. It was long, hard work, but probably the most lucrative contract I had ever undertaken. The Grey Man would hasten and pester me to do just about every task under the sun – except the one I was appointed to do – but I stuck to my mission.

Hamish McClintock was a tall, craggy Scot with a lantern chin and unkempt eyebrows. He had served as a captain in the Royal Engineers and then, in civil life, had retrained as an accountant. His role was that of 'advisor'. He invited me to lunch at the *Travattoria* – we sat down to pasta, pudding and a bottle of mineral water over which Hamish was very frank and open about what had gone on. He looked straight at me with an uncompromising air.

"Under the Old Man's guidance," he began, and I could immediately tell this was going to be a long discourse, "that is, Mrs Robertson's husband and the father of Gerald, the company grew and prospered. 'In wars, profit soars' had been the business approach. There have been a lot of wars – a big demand for pumps. Then, at seventy, the Old Man dropped dead at his desk. Gerald took over. Gerald had been repressed and now came his chance. His university project in Madrid had been to develop a moped. He decided to resume this at the earliest opportunity. Strong, lightweight bicycles were made to his own design in Spain and a lightweight petrol engine bolted on – *The Robertson Rocket* had been born. A little motor drove a rotary pump, which, using air pressure, drove the bicycle. It was air cooled and could chug along all day at 35mph on a spit of petrol. Problem was: the bicycle was a bastard to pedal and then, as a motor bike, you were competing with the *Honda 50*. No contest. Although it was cheap to manufacture and the margins good, a dealer network had to be built up from scratch."

Hamish paused to take a sip of water.

"The Robertsons pumped millions into it. It sold like a lead balloon in the UK, where it was regarded as a 'fair weather' fun bike. They then differentiated into a folding bike. Even worse: there were several bad accidents and a huge bill for compensation claims.

"Undeterred by *The Rocket's* failure, Gerald launched into electric golf buggies. These were no ordinary golf buggies. You walked along the fairway and the buggy would follow, five yards behind you, like a faithful Fido. You stopped, it stopped. You started, it started. It was radio-controlled by a gizmo that the golfer carried in his pocket. Very neat. Here, the issue was it needed four wheels and what was an extremely heavy battery that was difficult to load into the boot of your car. It was also expensive to make and difficult to market. Another flop.

"Drivable electric cars for young children followed. Nothing new in that, but these were luxury, top-end replicas. There were serious health and safety issues. Eventually, they were withdrawn, but I can to this day still see a hundred or so of them in the warehouse."

He again paused, but this time to allow me time for all these revelations to properly sink in.

"These three ventures bled millions out of the family's coffers. In mid-December of one fateful year, the Accountants were called in, followed by the Liquidators. The properties were all owned as family trusts and completely fire walled. Everything else was liquidated, except the pumps business. The Family bought that back. And part of the deal with the Board of Trade was that an experienced accountant with engineering knowledge be brought in to 'supervise' Gerald and rein him in from his worst excesses.

"On Christmas Eve, about a hundred workers were summonsed to the main warehouse and given their cards and I not talking Christmas cards. The tyres of the Robertson's Roller were slashed and a few weeks later Gerald was badly beaten up... hospitalised for several weeks, in fact. He's not a 'bad lad' but unfortunately now is just a shadow of his former self. No sense of blame or remorse whatsoever, though." Hamish paused and stared mournfully into his pasta.

*Well, that's that,* I thought, *at least I know it all now.* I relaxed slightly. "Thank you, Hamish," I said, "if only I'd known this three weeks ago. Quite incredible."

But, Hamish wasn't finished. "He's back to his old ways, though. Over the far side, there are five Spanish guys working on a new pump. They have been at it for nearly two years now. They practise 'Spanish customs', that is: start at ten, lunch at twelve, back at three, knock off at five. All Spanish holidays plus the English ones. The much-vaunted pump is 'almost there' apparently, but never quite seems able to work. When do you stop? When do you pull up the stumps?"

I again thanked Hamish for his frankness. I had partly recovered from what I had just heard and now it was my turn to be frank.

I told him I was puzzled by the fact that despite full order books, stonking great profits and controlled costs, the Company was always short of cash. Slowly it began to dawn on me that there was a 'hole', and a big black one at that. I looked straight at Hamish and told him two things.

Firstly, the sum missing was £1.6m. Secondly, it had been extracted by Julian Withers, the previous accountant.

His jaw dropped.

"You know what? I had my suspicions. Julian was the son of Jack Withers, John's Number One Man. An old family retainer and friend. Julian was beyond reproach and above suspicion. A loyal, hard-working servant. He was extremely long-suffering, a veritable saint. He was also a decent chap, but he had had enough and now runs a 'beach goods' shop on the south coast. You would have to have cast iron, bomb-resistant proof to convince the Robertsons."

"I've got it. I need to catalogue and tabulate, but it's all there. It would have emerged eventually, I just got there first."

We decided I would complete my documentation, then a Board meeting would be held and I would present my case. Hamish gave me his one hundred per cent support.

The plump woman in the yellow dress was called Catherine, and, whatever she knew about the firm, she really did keep to herself. She seemed to have survived life at the Company by having learnt to adapt. Maybe her motto was 'Change or Die'? Either that or she would have had to have been more than a little idiosyncratic before she started in order to regard daily working life at the Robertsons as either normal or perhaps even bearable. "They're ready for you now," she advised me, again with that wink of hers. "They're all in the Board Room."

I gathered up my four bulky files, knocked and entered. At the head of one of the largest tables I have ever seen sat Mrs Robertson. On her left, Hamish, and on her right a younger version of the Grey Man, a confident and good-looking businessman with dark hair.

"Paul Robertson, my other son," announced Mrs Robertson. He shook my hand; the handshake was dry and firm. I understood he had very little to do with the business. He was a 'Fund Manager' and by the look of his immaculate clothes, very successful at it too.

Standing to the right of the table was a large cardboard box. *Must be some top-secret product to end up here rather than the warehouse*, I thought. But, my mind was focused on what I was obliged to inform them of – and of how they would react.

Hamish smiled at me. "You have the floor, sir."

I told them that for nearly two years order books had been bulging, everything at full capacity. Gross profit margins were huge and government contracts paid sixty per cent up front. The Company, on the other hand, took ninety days' credit with its suppliers. Overhead costs were cut to the bone. R&D had been fully expensed and manufacturing drew on materials that had already been paid for, in some cases, years ago. No dividends had been paid for years and directors' salaries were nominal. How could the Company be sucking up so much cash from the Family?

"That's indeed what I want to know!" bellowed Paul.

"Well, I am going to show you where the cash has gone and has been going for over a year now."

Slowly, I built up my case. I had come to the scene with an open but inquiring mind. But the clues were there for all and everyone to see. Only a matter of time before they would out. I told them that, whilst I took no Company information home (which was strictly against policy) I did a lot of my investigative work in my own time, mainly at weekends.

I had reached the point where I had allowed the hounds to sniff the hare… I now had to let the hare out of the sack.

"The sum is £1.6m and the miscreant is Julian Withers."

"Impossible!" shrieked a voice. "Absolutely Impossible!" It was Gerald's voice. When a banging sound came from the large cardboard box, I knew it was him. *He was in the box.*

Gerald screeched on from the box that Julian was the most loyal, the most trusted servant. He would never commit such an act. I was mistaken and had taken them all for a ride spending thousands of pounds of their money on a wild goose chase.

The box was now being banged so violently that it began to rock wildly yet the others around the table paid it no notice.

"Let Mr Gundle finish!" commanded Hamish.

"Three of you are here." I could not resist it: "And one in the box. I am going to leave you four files, one for each of you. Read them at your leisure. Bearing in mind the magnitude of the sum, a note will have to be entered in the published accounts. That's all I have to say". I gathered my pen and pad and left the room.

Two weeks later, I was back in the same room with the same people and the same box. Hamish stated they had read the contents of the files and had done their own due diligence... and reluctantly they concurred with my evidence.

"It's a classic case of opportunity meeting need and greed. A betrayal of trust, a lack of control."

The cardboard box started banging and rocking again; unperturbed, Hamish said they would be calling in the police and an officer would be coming next week.

What followed were many hours and days spent with 'plain-clothes' officers; hardly 'plain' at all – jeans, T-shirts and trainers – mostly failed Accountants, but they knew their brief; they were 'The Light Brigade' preparing a case for 'The Heavy Brigade' – the Prosecutor.

Finally, they concluded there was a 'strong' case, but the one big 'fishbone' – Julian Withers – was in Rio. He was also suffering from Aids and did not have too long to live.

I had become used to our so-called Board meetings, with Cardboard Box in attendance. We all looked at each other, including cardboard box, then we looked at Mr Plain-Clothes officer. The silence was as thick as the foetid city air.

"We've got to do a deal with him, let him steal what's honest, but return most of it," someone ventured.

"That's an option," said Plain-Clothes. "Our Brazilians are used to that sort of thing."

"Will you go there and sort something out, Mr Gundle?"

"No! Do it by telephone call!" shouted the Cardboard

Box.

"Oh, shut up, Gerald," barked his mother.

And, so it was. I telephoned Julian Withers. He said he was prepared to talk to me in person in Rio. He had already been declared a suspect by the local police. He could only draw three thousand pounds a week from his bank accounts.

There was a long argument between Cardboard Box and his mother about whether I was to fly Club Class or Economy and what sort of hotel I was to stay in. What sort of salary would they pay me? Finally, I flew out Club Class, but with Air France.

When I arrived in Rio, I was greeted by Captain Concalves, a detective in the city's police force, a charming and dashing young man. He drove me to my hotel, a decent establishment catering mainly for business users. We then walked a few blocks to a beach front cafe.

As we sat down at a table far enough away to guarantee not being overheard, Concalves spoke: "This is informal. This is Rio! How do you say? Ah, yes, no names or pack drill!"

Concalves and I were going to get on.

Mr Withers lived on the eighth floor of an apartment block, which we could easily see. He lived there with his partner, Derrick. They were known to wine and dine a lot, and kept a speedboat at the Marina; to all intents and purposes, they were law-abiding citizens, though immensely wealthier than most of Rio's poor.

After pasta, pudding and espresso, Concalves drove me to my base in Rio – the Robertson distributor for Brazil. A private office was made available for us. He produced some wires and headphones, fiddled around with a Swiss Army Knife and then gave me the thumbs up.

"He is expecting you to call."

I dialled the number. It was answered by Julian. He named a café for us to meet in. Concalves gave me the thumbs-up. I was to arrive alone and wear nothing but a pair of shorts and a T-shirt. I finished the call with Julian at six o'clock that evening.

Concalves nodded in broad approval of how it had gone. "Don't worry, we will be sitting very close to you and we will be, how do you say... tooled up?"

"Hey, do you read Raymond Chandler?"

He looked perplexed.

Julian Withers could have passed for a male model – a superbly sculptured body, tanned to a dark gold – he wore tailored shorts and a designer T-shirt. He sat down and removed his expensive, mirrored sunglasses. His eyes were chips of blue ice, soft and kind. He flipped back his long blond hair as we browsed the menu.

"The *Spaghetti Zeppelin* here is renowned, it is cooked in a grease-proof bag, which seals in all the flavour." Then he ordered a bottled of sparkling wine.

I decided to open the batting. I told him how, after just a couple of weeks into my assignment, I had easily found the clues – they were all there. I related how we prepared the files for the Police and how the Prosecutor ruled there was a strong case.

Julian took a deep breath. "I knew it would be found out eventually, but I didn't expect they would track me down so quickly. I went to great lengths to conceal my identity; to cover my tracks. I suppose, looking back, they would have known I had been here several times before – setting up the distribution business. The world really is a small place. So, what are you after, Mr Gundle?"

"A deal. I understand you are not... too well? You probably won't be able to spend it all, and the Robertsons will agree to taking just some of it back. Agree a deal and all charges will be dropped. You will be a free man."

Julian looked pained. The game was up and, indeed, he must have realised his life was going to end very badly, very prematurely. "It's not just me. It's my partner, Derrick. I want a pension for him..."

"I'll level with you, Julian. This is all about saving face. The Robertsons get back most of their dosh, you get to live a life of luxury for the rest of your days. And yes, Derrick receives a pension."

"And what do you get?"

"Do you know, I hadn't thought of that. An expenses-paid holiday in the sun, I suppose? Restoring stolen goods to their rightful owner...?" For a moment, it seemed a shame to me to have to tell those kind, blue eyes such bad news, and to remind him of his killer illness.

The seafood pasta arrived. It was excellent. He ordered another bottle of the crisp, citrus wine, and I re-focused on my mission – justice for people who had been swindled.

"You have not asked me why I did it." He stared at me, waiting for me to say something, but it had reached the point where I was no longer interested – I had had enough of this already. Eventually, he broke the silence between us. "John Robertson and my father Jack Withers went to school together. John's family were loaded: landowners who branched out into agricultural equipment, an ocean-going yacht, racehorses, a sherry-importing business and olive groves in southern Spain. My Dad, Jack, won a scholarship. John went to university to read engineering, Dad did an engineering apprenticeship. The Robertsons bought property in Kensington, Dad lived in a two-down, two-up in Wandsworth. The two of them combined forces and rented a railway arch to develop the rotary pump. Not a new idea, but the way they put it together, it was a revelation, or you might say, a Revolution! Jack provided the cash, Dad provided the brawn, the muscle, the expertise.

"Five days a week he travelled the country in an old and unreliable Austin flogging those pumps. At weekends, he was in the workshop. John, on the other hand, arrived after lunch on Monday from the country and left just after lunch on Friday. When the final version of the pump was to be patented, it was in the Robertson name. Dad was always promised a share in the company, but it never happened, never. The Old Man loved the Good Life: fast cars, racehorses, yachts, fine cigars, champagne and foreign travel. But Dad was the worker, the man who created the wealth.

"When the war came, they both went into the Tank Regiment, John Robertson as a commissioned officer, and Dad as a non-commissioned officer. Although they saw action, it was the business of fitting Robertsons' rotary pumps into tank engines by which they achieved fame – and the Robertsons' fortune. After the war, the Robertsons gobbled up all the surrounding property for a song. The pump company went from strength to strength. Gerald went to Madrid to read engineering, I went to technical college. History repeating itself.

"Dad died, and then John died three months later. The 'Throwback' took over – mopeds, golf buggies, kids' cars. I was there when, on Christmas Eve, Gerald and his mother gave us all our cards. Off to *The Savoy* for their family meal. Of course, there was the Opportunity. Can you blame me?"

I avoided answering directly as I had no intention of appearing to sympathise with his crime. But I did tell him that he hadn't had to stay with the firm. He could have gone and worked anywhere, done anything.

It was now dark, but still hot and humid. "How much can you give them back?" I desperately needed to know. To encourage a more positive response, I added, "The deal also will include Derrick's freedom."

He looked offended and lit what seemed like his tenth cigarette of the evening. "Five hundred thousand," he stated, flatly.

"No deal then."

We spent another tortuous hour in discussion. My argument was that he deserved something from the Robertsons, not just for his service, but for his father's too. But, on the other hand, he was a criminal, a thief. His partner was also involved and therefore liable to prosecution – and imprisonment. A deal could be done quickly and easily and they both would be free men. By the time we were on the brandy, we had agreed. He would return eight hundred thousand pounds. We shook hands. The deal was done, so I thought.

A great weariness suddenly overtook me. I returned to the hotel and slept for a straight twelve hours, it was two o'clock in the afternoon when I arrived at the Distributor. I sent news of the deal to London by fax and agreed to meet Concalves at the same establishment where we had first met. An agreement had to be drawn up, witnessed and signed by both parties and then filed with the Brazilian authorities. The Robertsons would also have to agree to formally drop all charges. The funds would have to be transferred.

The Distributor provided me with a firm of lawyers and I spent most of the following day in their offices. But a fax then arrived from Gerald: Was I mad? I had just given away eight hundred thousand pounds of their money. I had to re-negotiate. He was prepared to sacrifice only four hundred thousand, and so on and so on. He ordered me to find a cheaper hotel, and insisted that I report every day to The Distributor, who would find me some work to do and they would be re-charged for my time. This pettiness from Gerald made me angry; I wrote an angry reply, calmed down and rewrote it. I pictured Gerald and that cardboard box.

I obediently moved into a budget hotel. Fans, but no air con; a shower and toilet en suite. It did have a fridge and a small balcony, so I could sip a cold beer and watch the sun setting. I had the distinct impression that a number of the rooms in the block were being rented by the hour. But it did the job. During the day, I shuttled between The Distributor and The Lawyer. I enjoyed being with The Distributor: the staff were young and sparky; everything was laid back and relaxed.

It was on one of these relatively enjoyable working days that I was asked to review an insurance policy (in English). It was then that I had my 'light bulb' moment. I politely asked Gerald to fax me the Company's Insurance

Policy. He replied by return stating that it was over one hundred and twenty pages long.

"Fax me the damn thing in its entirety NOW otherwise you can stuff your job where the sun don't shine!" was the gist of my response. The full document came through. I examined it all. Yes! They were covered for three hundred thousand pounds' losses through theft. My hours at The Distributor went from ten until five to eight until seven. Lunch was taken at the desk. The Insurance Company was playing 'hard ball'. Their official reply stated: *We had not been informed of this immediately after the event as should have been the case... furthermore, the circumstances surrounding this particular situation are highly unusual... any recovery, if undertaken, would have to be scaled down proportionally to what you have already recovered... we also note, with concern, that proper control measures are, in our view, not in place to safeguard the company's assets.*

I then received a phone call from Hamish. This was 'part of the course'. "Don't let the bastards grind you down, keep at them, water will wear down stone in the end." He also ordered me to move back into a decent hotel. I told him I was all right where I was.

It was on a Friday that I received the telephone call from Julian Withers. Would I like to join them both for some motor-boating on Sunday? Concalves freaked at this, but agreed to offer covert surveillance.

Sunday arrived and the sun shone, the ocean was bright blue and the boat was fast and luxurious. We were joined by several young men and women. *How can they all look so gorgeous?* I attempted to water-ski, but failed. At three o'clock we tied up at a little beach bar that served the freshest shellfish, simply chargrilled. Julian and Derrick were absolutely charming. This was light years away from Southwark.

The weeks extended to over a month. Every time we thought we were near an agreement, some new obstacle reared its head. The Insurance Company finally caved in and offered two hundred thousand; that, plus the eight hundred thousand from Julian meant the Robertsons were out of pocket by only six hundred thousand – blood money really for the value of both the Withers.

Mrs Robertson was grateful, Gerald was not. I had the eventual pleasure of telling Gerald to climb back into his box, stop throwing his toys out and to stick his job where the sun doesn't shine.

Julian passed away a few months after my return. Derrick slipped into obscurity and the Robertsons are still going strong – their newly developed pump is a world-beating best-seller.

I still cannot quite believe I experienced all this.

# Chapter Twenty: The Iron Buddha

I don't expect an accountant to wear a pinstripe suit, and carry a briefcase these days, but neither do I expect him to dress like Rupert Bear and present a vestmental challenge!

Mr Xenophon MacFluffer or 'Fluffy'as he was universally known was the chief and only accountant of the fabled IRON BUDDHA PR Ltd. He sported a curly white beard, crimson sweater, Nike trainers (more Pat Pong Road, than Covent Garden) and mustard coloured trousers with brown cross stripes.

"Sorry to have kept you waiting – running late." He was an hour late. A sufficient time for me to soak in the detail of the fabled IRON BUDDHA PR's reception.

The fabled IRON BUDDHA PR (IB) was on the top floor of an old hat factory, just north of Oxford Street – a few minutes from the fleshpots of Soho.

The plain white washed brick walls were festooned with framed awards; these awards and other indicators reminded me of the Cork/Gully Indices of Corporate Failure, namely:

Awards for achievements in China, Ghana, Best Employer Award, Investors in People – Yes.

Fish Tank – the size of the Saragossa Sea – Yes.

Company Flags – Yes.

Corporate Car Park, spaces marked out with replica personalised number plates to match those on the BMWs – Yes.

Elderly unqualified accountant – Yes.

Same Auditor for decades – well, no. They had opted for an audit exemption.

Then I add to my own tick box – pictures of staff in tight cycle shorts and T-shirts leaning on mountain bikes – Yes.

Naturally, reception was dominated by a huge iron Buddha. How on earth did they get this up here I wondered? I walked over to the Buddha and tapped it for 'good luck'. It was not iron, but plastic! Plastic pieces that had been glued together. Oh dear, all at the fabled Iron Buddha PR was not what it seemed.

Fluffy led me into the main office. This was the size of a tennis court; with a glass roof. At one end was a 'chill' area – button-down leather sofas, a pool table, flat screen TV and a glass fronted refrigerator filled with bottled lager, champagne and Mars bars.

The right-hand side of the office was composed of smoked glass partitioned meeting rooms of various dimensions. At the far end was Ami's office (large) and Fluffy's office (small). The worker bees were contained in landscaped cells surrounded by acoustic panels and plants, which no doubt dissipated the negative *chi*.

On Fluffy's desk was a large plastic model of a Frisian cow, whose transparent udder was filled with plastic 'gold' dollars. The proverbial 'Cash Cow'. Everywhere there were pictures of Fluffy, Fluffy in tight cycle shorts and stretched T-shirt. Fluffy at the controls of a light aircraft and Fluffy at the helm of a yacht At least, the iron Buddha behind his desk was made of metal.

"Well, did you find any skeletons in the cupboard?" he asked.

"A few – but not a mass burial."

He made me an espresso from his desk side machine.

"Shoot! I'm all yours," he boomed.

"Give me a bit of history about yourself, Fluffy, and the company."

Fluffy sat back and sipped his espresso. "I was an articled clerk with a firm of City Chartered Accountants and then when I started failing exams that I had already passed I decided to give up my studies. I applied to the fabled IRON BUDDHA PR as an Assistant Accountant; the chief was a qualified guy who eventually left.

Ami had this whole operation funded by a venture capital firm – that meant a massive interest bearing loan and then they took fifty-five per cent of the equity. Well, being funded by a venture capitalist is like a little boy wetting his pants – it's all warm and nice when it happens, but then soon it becomes cold and smelly."

"A bit like invoice discounting," I interjected.

"Exactly! We had to resort to those buggers, the invoice discounters, at that time. It added an extra half day's admin to the workload and was horribly expensive. We have an excellent credit policy in place now, so we don't need those bandits.

"Anyway, Ami and the capitalists soon came to blows and it became an obsession with her to buy the rodents out. Gawd, what a business! We had to borrow money and go through a 'White Wash Procedure'. Do know what that is?"

"Sure. A due diligence when you borrow money to buy back your own shares."

Fluffy continued: "Yeah. Having done that Ami then decided to buy the building from the landlord, who was, of course, the venture capitalist. The mortgage never sleeps, you know. Months of budgets, cash-flows, due diligence. We were audited in those days – what a pain that was. The only function of auditors is to go in after the battle and bayonet the dead!"

I asked him about the relationship with the bank.

"Totally unhelpful. They will always lend you an umbrella when the sun is shining. Hey, here's a joke – man phones his bank and asks to speak to the manager (in those days you had a manager) – telephonist replies: 'Mr Western died last night.' Two minutes later man phones bank again and is told the same thing. Then man phones again and the telephonist says: 'I've already told you twice, Mr Western died last night.'

"'I know,' says man, 'I just want to hear it again, it's *so, so* good!'"

Fluffy guffawed loudly at his own joke. "Can't live with them, can't live without them. *R*ags make paper, paper makes money, money is lent by banks, loans bring destitution, which reduces us to beggars, beggars wear rags, rags make paper etc."

I decided not to pursue the subject of banks and let Fluffy continue.

"Well we succeeded in the battle of the building – the building is ours. Then I had to cope with the corporate aspects of her three divorces, two of her former husbands were directors and shareholders of IB. Buddha *says* 'you can't have two tigers on the same hill'. You know, it is like being the captain of an ocean liner steaming from Southampton to New York, a difficult task at the best of times, but when you have to deal with a hurricane, a hijacking, food poisoning and mutiny, it's tough. Life's a bitch, then there's death! Oh the lawyers. If you find a good lawyer, shoot him before he goes bad on you. Oh then were the lawyers – lawyers can seriously damage your health. It is easier to find a good plumber than a good lawyer. We paid £50k to those legal rent boys to frank our White Wash. The same again for each of Ami's divorces – £150k in all, just for the divorces.

"A year ago we tried to sue four errant debtors. Ami insisted in using this cheesy firm just off Fleet Street. All I wanted was for the turkeys to send a 'Seven Day Letter' £50k latter and a month of *my* time – no letters sent! We now use a firm in the Midlands who charge us just one pound for the letter – no questions asked. Now some of these legal rent boys are on 'success fees', a multiplier kicks in and costs go through the roof! A new development is an 'After the Event' insurance premium. Can you imagine paying the insurance premium *after* your house has burnt down! Recently we won a little case and decided to thank the lawyer by inviting him to a lunch at 'The Ivy'. Unusually Ami picked up the tab. The entire conversation was about boats and schools. The turkey sent us a one grand bill for his time! We did a little PR for him later and screwed him back, good and proper."

I responded to Fluffy by telling him the best strategy was to ensure that company processes were well documented and an active policy of risk reduction was practised.

"Risk! Risk is wild. Whilst all this was going on, we still had to run a business. Now I believe she is trying to sell out?"

"Probably," I replied.

Fluffy leaned over his desk: "What you get with me is what is written on the tin. I believe handsome is handsome does and if it ain't broke, don't fix it."

I retorted, "If you always do what you always did, you'll always get what you always got."

"Hah"! roared Fluffy. "Been there, done that, worn the T-shirt."

"Yes I can see that from all these photographs."

Before my meeting with Fluffy, I had arranged to meet Perequentia Amelia Ferrous (Ami) at the Goring. Two pots of tea and an hour later, she breezed in – all Chloe. No apologies. We briefly discussed our mutual connection, Mauve, of Sunburst Rupture Communications Ltd.

"I want to sell. I've had enough. I'm over fifty you know." She banged the low table.

The rings around her neck confirmed that.

"When you get to my age, things start to go south." She paused.

"I don't think you've even reached the Equator," I quipped. I was going to add that she didn't look a day over forty (with the gaslight behind her) but plopped a sugar lump into my tea – which was surprising, because I don't take sugar.

"I'm tired. Three husbands, five children, managing twenty-eight girls and Fluffy. The tedium of mediocrity is killing me. It's all too much!" She laid back on the sofa and spread her legs wide.

"Tell me about Fluffy."

"Loyal servant, but he's past his 'sell by date'. He practises husbandry, he is a safe pair of hands. He has built and flies an aeroplane, sails a boat, does the Iron Man, but when he swipes his pass in the door, all the energy gets left behind, I don't think he is up to the due diligence. He can't stand change and he might even sabotage the due diligence process."

"Who's the proposed buyer?" I questioned.

"Fiscal Dymatrix." She lowered her voice and glanced around.

"No – not them!" I shrieked. "They are the biggest shits that walked the earth. Or rather, that slithered down a porcelain tube."

"Are they going down the tubes?" She was startled.

"No. There are just totally anal. They will screw you."

She placed her hand on my forearm. "Honey, nobody screws me without paying a premium for that pleasure."

For the next twenty minutes we bartered about my fee. I finally accepted a very one sided arrangement (her side).

Ami informed me that Fluffy was to take three weeks off to sail round the Aegean and she would indicate to him that I would be doing 'a review' of the business.

We shook hands and I paid the bill.

*** 

"I will start with VAT, Fluffy."

"No problem, we had an inspection two years ago."

"Well there is a problem, Fluffy, big expensive problems that have built up over a period of time."

"I leave the VAT to Baybee."

"Who's Baybee?"

"The bookkeeper. Anyway, what kind of figures are we talking about?"

"Big figures, Fluffy – fifty grand at least, there are many other things that are wrong, like VAT payments have been put to the input account and therefore claimed twice."

VAT is not a simple tax. I had just completed an exercise on pet food supplements. First HMRC defines what it is a pet. Dogs (but not working dogs), cats, caged birds and tropical fish (but not coarse fish) are all classed as pets. Rabbits, reptiles and horses are not. Where's the logic?

"Did you know that kangaroo meat carries VAT?"

Fluffy appeared perplexed. "Didn't know that – why is it relevant?"

"Just illustrating how contrary VAT can be. Let's move on to Payroll Tax."

"What can go wrong with payroll? We run it on Sage and always pay by the nineteenth."

He was beginning to squirm, like a live roasted scorpion on a stick. I was now sure of my ground, and continued:

"There is a whole raft of expensive issues with your payroll operation. Did Ami give you a copy of 'The Shining Path', which highlights some of the obvious and expensive pitfalls?"

His eyes narrowed: "The Shining Path… do you mean 'sendero luminoso', the Peruvian Maoist guerrilla group?"

I laughed: "No, it is a risk template that my firm has devised, a kind of checklist."

"Look, I just can't keep up to date with all this. I haven't time. Time is the medium in which we all burn."

"But you have time to build an aeroplane. It's not the time, but the timing."

Fluffy opened a drawer in his desk and produced a couple of mini Mars bars. "Let's change the subject."

"We're not finished yet, Fluffy."

There were tax issues on the extensive staff entertaining interns, mobile phones, staff loans, taxis home, client overpayments and more that were hidden in the general expenses.

By way of some light relief I told him about my experience with the Revenue on Christmas Hampers. The Revenue suggested to me what would be 'reasonable' would be "a turkey and a bottle wine". On their scale you might receive a couple of Turkey Twizzlers from Lidl for the turkey component. I had argued with Taxman that a bottle of Cru Bourgeois was the absolute minimum, but at sixty pounds a bottle of Chase Spleen this was rejected. Certainly IB's The Fortnam hampers at one hundred and fifty pounds that IB provided for their staff would be completely disallowed.

I continued to state that I had examined all the insurance policies and IB was either doubly insured, or not insured at all No risk analysis had been done.

The Purchase Ledger was in a mess, with invoices not being paid, or paid twice. Many supplier credit notes were not been taken.

Fluffy looked at me. "Ami runs this organisation with fear, anger, greed and self-interest; I know it is an unfortunate acronym, but there it is. A little is actually good, too much becomes destructive.

Ami is tight – tight as a duck's arse – water tight. But she is generous on some things. Though…"

Fluffy's voice had dropped a fraction. "For instance, every Tuesday in the new month we have a guest speaker; there are twenty-eight employees here, so amongst them they know people. We have had accountants, lawyers, bankers, insurance and pension people, hairdressers, lifestyle gurus and even a dentist. The seminars start at five and we lay on a buffet. Not bad yuh? A great chance for extra-mural bonding, but within these walls, so to speak. Then on the second Thursday of every month, we nominate three staff to make a presentation on any subject they wish. We encourage them to use presentational aids. Refreshments are provided."

Fluffy paused and bit into a mini Mars bar. "OK. What do you think of the 'Gents' toilet?"

"Lovely," I replied. "I couldn't believe it. Trouser press, ironing board, steam iron, giveaway hair brushes and combs, hair driers, disposable toothbrushes and toothpaste, moisturisers and even a shower with fluffy (pardon me) white towels."

"Well, the 'Ladies' goes even further than that. Most important. No bromihidrosis allowed here; we like the employees to look good and smell nice. We also believe that 'Happy Hens' lay more eggs. We follow the Fedex model – happy employees equal happy customers, happy customers equal bigger profits, bigger profits equal happy shareholders, happy shareholders equal a happy CEO, a happy CEO equals a happy CEO's wife and *she*, after all, is the one that wears the trousers!

"Well, a variation on the Fedex model. Now, you've noticed the showers, well they are there because of our bicycle scheme. Very tax efficient as you well know. You're never too old to cycle. Incidentally, we have had a huge amount of spin off from this idea; we are considered a 'green company', big on CSR and as a result, we have acquired a number of new clients. We've gotta think out of the box. Cycling is fun and keeps you fit after all! On the other extreme, we actively encourage our employees to engage in business entertaining. Of course it is not tax allowable, but then it is not a taxable benefit to the employee either.

"I know the days of the three-hour lunch are long gone, but we feel it so important 'to press the flesh', to make one-to-one contact. Here we positively encourage employees to entertain, to network. We honestly believe it is easier to develop and expand existing business than to win new business. Putting the bullshit aside, we aim to 'delight our customers'. Do you know we had as a client, a tin pot little mobile phone account, five hundred a month; it got taken over by the Amber Corp. Our Account Director worked on their PR Director, created needs that she didn't even know she required. Eventually, she give him an Amber mobile – it could only receive one number – hers! Needless to say he could only dial out one number – hers! That account is now thirty-five thousand a month!

Here we listen! That doesn't means we can't stop sowing the seed to create crops the client never even knew he wanted!"

\*\*\*

"Cigarette – I need a cigarette; and get me some wine!" yelled Ami. A girl was despatched to obtain a packet of Marlboro Lights and a bottle of pink Grenache. Now a lighter had to be found – this was not a major obstacle considering nearly all the girls were smokers. Then the ashtray was smudged and had to be washed and polished. It took three girls to light the cigarette and pour the wine. I was not offered a glass, but then pink Grenache is hardly my tipple. I was now gagging on tobacco smoke. I noticed that the smoke detector had been disconnected.

Her voice came to me through the clouds. "What do you think of the deal?"

IB had turned over three million pounds a year for the last ten years and made one million after all salaries and bonuses which included Ami's out-take. Fiscal was prepared to pay a straight five million; I thought this was astonishingly generous.

"Tell them six million." Barked Ami. "And they've got to pay for the fixed assets."

Fiscal was also up for grabs. It needed a complete set of clubs in its bag and IB was the sand wedge as it were, thus the five million pounds offer, six million was over the top.

Ami had the concentration span of a gnat on steroids and clearly the medication was now wearing off. I tried to explain about the benefits to key staff of a share option scheme.

"It's *me* they want, not the  staff – I'm worth at least six million pounds."

A long argument followed about valuing the fixed assets. I explained that Fiscal was simply not going to sit down and argue the toss about the price of a footstool and furthermore, the newest computer in the office was four years old – a boat anchor by today's standards. She was talking about 'removing' some of the assets until I told her that the fixed asset schedule had already been sent to Fiscal.

"Ami, this really is a once in a lifetime opportunity for you. Take it and cash in your chips."

I slowly began to realise that IB was Ami's whole life; she lived for the company and in fact, lived *off* the company. She relished the political intrigues but she was smart enough to know that this was all going to change.

I stood up and walked over to an iron Buddha. I placed my hand on his head. Metal.

"Buddha preaches that we live in a constant state of change, nothing stays the same. Change gives rise to opportunity, opportunity can be good or bad, it depends what you make of it. Your time has come; it is time to embrace change. Take Fiscal's offer, work out your year's notice and then do something completely different with your life."

I reflected how difficult it can sometimes be to communicate. I remembered when I was pitching for a quality programme to a brewery where the boardroom was alongside the River Wandle. I removed my Rolex watch and was banging on about the 'fitness of purpose' of my watch. We had had a good lunch and a couple of the directors were nodding off. Suddenly, I fling the Rolex out of the window straight into the Wandle. It woke the buggers up – little did they know it was a five-pound fake!

But how to communicate to Ms Perequentia Amelia Ferrous that she was about to jeopardise this fantastic offer?

"Ten per cent tax on five million pounds means you will walk away with four and half million pounds. Fluffy told me you dream of owning a baby Bentley and flying a Lear Jet. Well, that would be within your grasp; this really is payback time. I will take care of all the details."

"Six million pounds and they have to pay for the fixed assets."

"Five and half million pounds and you throw in the fixed assets."

I gathered up my papers. "You don't realise that the heyday of IB is over. There are newer, younger smarter kids on the block. Soon you will be a C-lister, an also ran, a has-been. It is but a short step from the limo to the gutter. You spend your whole life rushing here, rushing there, people to see, places to go. What quality of life do you have? You are driven by your Blackberry. When did you last read a book? Sit on a beach and throw pebbles at a tin can? You have so much, yet so little."

***

Baybee was a Sino Bolivian. What parts came from China and what parts came from Bolivia it was difficult to say, but certainly all the parts were finely engineered and in the right places. The sum of the parts was quite exquisite. Well upholstered, but not fat, she was built for comfort, rather than speed – more of a Rolls Royce Silver Cloud than a Maserati Grancubrio.

Hard boiled, smooth skinned and seeped in sin, she had a penchant for Shantung shot wild silk dresses, in bright primrose or deep electric blue. They say *Age is the Great Gelder*. At my age, I am more interested in the dress, rather than what's underneath it... but, for Baybee I could make an exception. She had come to England to study English, married, had two children (now grown up), then she divorced. Currently she was 'in a relationship' with an Australian float plane jockey, who doubled as a ski instructor in Austria in the winter.

Baybee played squash three times a week, appreciated fine wine and was rumoured to smoke a pipe (Dunhill Half Apple). She was now presenting her non-financial measurement methodologies to me. "If you can't measure it, you can't manage it!"

Sales Invoices were raised in Excel, a macro converted them into Word, and they were then approved by the

177

Account Directors and of course, Ami, before being posted into Sage. I pointed out that this was a complicated three-step process, prone to error and omission and suggested that the invoices be raised as draughts straight into Sage. To be fair to her, she considered this. Next she moved on to the 'Efficiency Reports', these measured retainer, project and staff efficiency as well as a pointer to the more economic deployment of staff. Staff completed weekly timesheets that were studded with macros and drop downs. To be late with your time-sheet was a P45 offence; surprisingly, even Ami submitted her timesheets on time. A macro was run which converted the data into Access, but other macros then converted the Access data back into Excel reports.

My comments were that only Baybee knew how the whole thing worked and although it did the job wonderfully well, it was fiendishly complicated.

The timesheets also formed the basis of a 'Linear Tracking' programme. This ensured that all billable time and expenses were captured and accounted for. This was a simple programme written in Excel and wonderfully effective. She then demonstrated the 'Traffic Lights'. Baybee learnt this when she worked for John Lewis – there they felt that the floor walkers were too stupid to understand profit and loss accounts. The Traffic Lights coded profitably into green (good), amber (OK) and red (bad). Leading on from the Traffic Lights, she then had developed the Carcinogram .This was a 3D graphics programme that resembled a Venn diagram tracked over quarters. The red area was shown as a cancer, which hopefully would shrink over time. Smiley, straight and frowning faces symbols were used to as a method of appraising various performances. I had almost been sacked by Inchcape Motors Retail plc. when I tried to introduce them there. Expense mark-ups, although aggressive, were transparent and almost all clients were happy with a) a ten per cent generic handling charge on the fee b) a seventeen and a half per cent mark up on rechargeables and c) a two and a half per cent charge for preparing third party invoice bundles.

Baybee was now in full flow: "My mantra is *filing is next to Godliness, a place for everything and everything in its place. The willing horse does all the work* and I'm that willing horse, I don't do service with a snarl."

Lord Rank once said to me that "a man is either paid half of what he is worth, or double". I knew which category Baybee fell into.

Two weeks later the due diligence started with KGMP. VAT, Payroll, Benefits and National Insurance, Corporation Tax, Health and Safety, Employee Relations, Insurances and all Contracts were reviewed. A full documented six-year company history, cash flow projections and five-year forecasts were provided. An entity like IB was not selling cans of beans; last year an old bear in stripy pyjamas may have gone to bed, this year a sleek black panther sprung out, but with retained clients it is easier to forecast what is going to come in against a relatively fixed run rate.

The KGMP man was a twenty-eight-year-old Swede who seemed to exist on no sleep at all judging by the times of his e-mails. Boxes of Lever Arch files were compiled. The game plan was that Fluffy and Baybee would handle the operational side of the business and I would deal with the 'Blonde Bomber' as we called the Swede. Matters progressed in fits and starts and we all could see the finishing line looming into sight, when, suddenly a letter arrived from HMRC requesting a 'routine' inspection.

Well, it was hardly 'routine'. No stone was left unturned. IB's dilemma was did they declare the untaxed benefits or not? I turned to two highly regarded firms of accountants and received no definitive answer. Finally, I decided to come clean and discovered that at least we escaped the HMRC penalties.

The Revenue Johnny was a guy who had been a Quantity Surveyor and this was first case as an Inspector.

Oh dear – he was the cat that had found the cream (and no doubt fast track promotion). The Determination was for three hundred thousand pounds, but by chipping away initially by me and then by Fluffy it was finally reduced to sixty thousand pounds. Certainly, IB had drawn the short straw with Tax Johnny. I have noticed the trend is for HMRC these days is to make a perfunctory enquiry or else 'The Full Monty'. Here we had the 'Full Monty'. Obviously a prime dictate of HMRC is that they must not waste Taxpayers money. In accountancy parlance the benefit must exceed the cost and certainly at IB that was the case.

Eventually Fluffy, working under my guidance wore down the Johnny and the settlement was reached.

***

I had agreed to meet Ami at The Shree Krisna, the oldest Indian restaurant in South London. It is in that long drag that runs from the A3 right up to Clapham Common, winding through the underbelly of Tooting. I knew it when The Shree was little more than the front room of someone's house. It was then decorated with garish bright blue elephant gods and multi-limbed goddesses. It used to have no liquor license and if you wanted a drink the pub across the road allowed you to take your pint over. The premises, the menu and the prices have all expanded, but the old favourites are still on the list.

The agreed time was seven thirty, so if her past form was anything to go on, she would not be there till eight fifteen, therefore, I arrived at eight o'clock. She was there, a bottle of pink Grenache, more half-empty than half-full and lipstick speared over her teeth.

"You're late! I've already ordered – some chicken and a salad."

In between making and taking mobile calls she munched her way through *my* Dosai, *my* Iddly and most of *my* Lemon Rice whilst leaving her chicken salad. On her second bottle, she began to expand that she believed accountants were generally anal retentives, who became bogged down with too much detail.

"We are a tight outfit. Have you heard of the 'Law of Molecular Attrition'?"

I confessed I had not.

"Well, the more employees you have, the more employees you need to have. A few molecules in a closed vessel do not collide – many molecules will collide and create heat, but not much else. Godammit, if the Ford Motor Company has done away with Purchase Orders for brake assemblies, why do *we* need 'em? We had this Management Johnny who came and told us we had to have Purchase Orders. We had to practise risk management, disaster recovery, engage in strategic planning – Gawd!"

I interjected IB seems to suffer from *inherent dysfunctionality*. It is like every morning you put on your cowboy boots and then wonder why you can't pull up your Chloe drains?

At some point in the game, you've *got to stop making bread and repair those machines that make the bread.* You have been extremely successful at IB, but there is no measurement for how successful you *could* have been... it is like so many outfits in this trade, they are almost there, but not quite. It is that extra couple of per cent that makes the difference between an also ran and a winner."

She shook her head, "Here we eat what we kill. We travel light, like the Boers – a horse, a rifle and some biltong."

"But the Redcoats won in the end."

She ignored me: "I can't read a balance sheet, the KPIs tell me everything. Fluffy used to have a KPI to measure the number of times the boardroom door squeaked, because that room was only ever used for pitches. We look at client efficiency, employee efficiency, and non-fiscal measurements, churn rates, every three months we unveil the carcinogram to all staff, I believe in absolute transparency. We also do a climate analysis every quarter to gauge staff perception about IB. That programme was developed by Bjorn Borg's tennis coach, you know."

People were the biggest asset of her enterprise; she explained how she would leverage on their creative energy, and even the most junior of employees had something to contribute. She believed in creating plenipotentiary powers for her team. *Mistakes were treasures when you learned from them* and that it was her policy *to praise in public and approbate in private. Say it enough times and you will believe it,* I thought

At that moment her taxi arrived and I was left to settle the bill. I departed feeling a little drunk and strangely hungry.

***

About a year later, I was in 'The Hole in the Wall' opposite Waterloo Station, that 'Last Chance Saloon' where desperate commuters go to top up their alcohol levels before facing the long evening ahead.

Blow me down! There was Fluffy, Hugo Boss suit, crisp white silk shirt and a classic tie.

Ravel loafers had replaced the trainers. He was clean shaven and tanned, his crooked teeth had been fixed and he looked about ten years younger.

The story he told was entirely predictable. A cheque for five and a half million pounds had been handed over to Ami and the whole company moved 'lock stock and barrel' to Fiscal's offices in mid-town (that grey area between The West End and The City). For three months everything remained unchanged and profitable. Then Future Financials Inc. made a bid for Fiscal; at that point, *everything* changed!

The CEO of Fiscal was Mike Hunt, an erudite aloof individual, completely dominated by his venture capital company board, the financial director, Guy Humboldt, his

Director of Human Resources, Sally Lightfoot and his legal advisor, Temperance Day.

IB's excellent reporting systems were replaced by a 'Dead Sea Scrolls' statutory accounting format. All new clients had to have contracts approved by 'The Credit and Ethical Committee'. IB had few bad debts in its history. Ethical Committee? Fiscal had no morals or ethics.

One by one the staff benefits were eroded. The bicycle scheme went out the door. Business entertaining over forty pounds had to be approved in advance. Out went the Friday night champagne busts. No more duvet days. No taxis or pizzas after working late, therefore, no more working late.

Then there was the 'great rock cake incident'. Guy Humboldt disallowed a claim for a rock cake served with a latte.

Future Financials set up their Sarbanes Oxley department. I am all in favour of SOX, but those dummies at FF used it as an aggrandisement exercise. There was also 'The Money Laundering Committee'.

Now we had a situation where FF was dictating to Fiscal and was Fiscal dictating to IB.

Subsidiaries invoiced subsidiaries at inflated rates.

Ami's wings were savagely clipped and soon revenues went south.

After a year, Ami left "to pursue her charitable interests".

What employees were left were either made redundant or walked. Fiscal had paid five and a half million pounds for nothing – the sand wedge in a set of clubs.

Fluffy leaned over me, spilling his beer in the process.

"Ami is in her element. Lives in Vietnam, runs a spa there which finances an orphanage.

"I visited her when I had to fly an old DC3 back here. She is just *so* happy! She's taken up with a monk! The relationship is purely platonic, not tantric; they do yoga, meditate, eat mungbeans, lentils etc. The kids come over regularly and do 'Turtle Watch'. She is also the president of a hardwood replanting programme. This is a programme where it is recognised that the West needs, or rather wants, hardwood and will pay a premium for the product. You can just imagine the tax breaks! You want to go there man, Apart from anything else. She has a beautiful all teak built schooner and a Cessna float plane. It is such a far cry from Oxford Street."

He beamed with pride: "I work for Aero Classics – we provide trips in classic aircraft. We also hire out the aircraft for filming – very profitable. So, *never write off a man until he's dead.*"

"What about Baybee?" I enquired.

Now he smiled: "Here's a tale. When we were taken over by Fiscal, we were left alone, as I have said. Suddenly Ami, Baybee and I were stripped of our bank mandates, but the buggers didn't realise that Baybee was still on 'fax pay'. You know, that funny form that you manually fill in with employees' bank details and pay, and then you simply attach a pre-numbered form and fax it over to the bank. The only limit is the amount of cash in the bank.

"Like us all, Baybee was treated badly; we were *mushrooms,* fed on shit and kept in the dark. Baybee started to skim a grand or ten at a time, she only took what was honest. She was instrumental in getting the Bolivian Tourist account, so the dosh flowed into IB, the work was done by Fiscal, recharged. But, no intercompany cash changed hands.

"Baybee set up a string of dummy supplier accounts, most of them based in Bolivia. She also, by the way, set up some Bolivian customers! When the cash balance topped eight million, Baybee cleaned out – the whole darned lot, just done on a piece of faxed paper with a sticky label. She now owns a massive estate in Bolivia which makes the most wonderful cigars and wine. She's set up a string of youth squash clubs and a youth orchestra."

The old adage held true again. "Most crime is committed by decent people when opportunity meets desperation, envy and resentment."

What a game! I decided I would book a flight to Vietnam for some R&R.

# Chapter Twenty-One: Sunset Watcher

My interview for the Big Boss (Mass) Corporation Inc. was strange indeed, to say the least. I was interviewed by ten different associates (employees), each interview lasting exactly seven and a half minutes. Questions varied from: When did you last cry? What did you think of the last movie you saw? What makes you really angry? But nothing was asked about my experience or abilities. The company had been founded by a former US fighter pilot who had become a professor at Harvard. He started with Quality Programmes at a time when the Japanese ran circles around the American automobile industry with their Quality Circles. By the nineties, it had branched out into Process Improvement and then Leadership to become a truly global entity of wholly-owned companies and franchises. I got the UK job and started work on the eighteenth floor of a multi-occupied tower block.

The views were spectacular. To the north, London. To the south, The South Downs. To the west, Richmond Park and the Thames and to the east, the suburban sprawl of the London boroughs, stretching along to Kent. The main office was an open plan area with views to the west. Nine associates in a landscaped area. The work cells were characterised by the curved lines that constrained them and their occupants, and green foliage abounded. Every Monday, a team of green-uniformed operatives turned up to feed, wash, water, polish, and talk to the plants. At the head of the area was the 'break out' or 'chill' space. Soft leather couches, TV, pool table, mini-kitchen and a glass-fronted fridge – well stocked with lager and champagne.

*I* was the Accounts Department and found myself situated in a cell, which distinguished itself from the others by having two filing cabinets, the only such cabinets on the whole floor. There were seven females in the area, myself and the only other male   Geronimo 'Gerry', whom I sat next to. Access was from a corridor that ran down the side of the open space. Several small, east-facing offices led off this corridor, each office occupied by a male consultant.

Gerry was in his early forties; he never turned up before ten thirty. Immediately upon arrival, he would clamp his headphones on and then promptly fall asleep until twelve thirty, when he would awake to consume a huge 'full English' breakfast and a pint of black coffee delivered to his desk by the local 'Greasy Spoon'. After several loud burps, he would fall asleep again, stirring at three to take, and make, a number of telephone calls in excellent French, Italian, Spanish and German. His Russian was not so good. He would either wear lime-green or pink chinos, 'posh' lumberjack woollen shirts in garish squares of Lovat green, rusty red and puce. He was always tie-less and I never saw him with a jacket on.

This was early autumn and the sunsets to the west were unbelievable, coloured by the heavily polluted air. Gerry would issue a general e-mail to all staff rating the quality of the sunset, scoring each one with marks out of ten. Thus, he became known as 'The Sunset Watcher'. Unless there was a beer or champagne bust, he would slope off at six whilst the rest of us toiled till six thirty and then hit the bars.

I did ask Gerry once, "Where is the stationery cupboard?"

He looked at me, screwed up his face and said, "Hey, dude, please don't disturb me ever again – I'm very busy and cannot tolerate having my flow of Chi interrupted." That was that. Apart from his flatulence and booming voice in polyglot tongues after three in the afternoon, he did not bother me. Anyway, I had plenty to do. I was finding thousands of pounds of unbilled time and materials. It was as if nobody 'gave a damn'.

Three months flashed by and the sunsets were now happening at four fifteen… four, even earlier. Leaving me to ponder: would Gerry have time to make his phone calls or would the sunsets interrupt his 'work' for the day?

In any event, I was finally 'summonsed' to the MD's

office for my probationary review.

They did a '360 degree' review on me. If you have ever had this pleasure, you will know that this is where every associate has to assess both you and your interaction with them. My review was not particularly glowing. It seemed I 'did not fit in with our culture here'.

My answer was that I did not know what the 'culture here' was and furthermore, the longest serving associate had only served eighteen months, too little for a 'culture' of any kind to become embedded. I was to be 're-educated', which meant having lunch once a week in the local Italian restaurant with the Personnel Officer (or perhaps I should say 'Head of Human Resources'), a fat, cheery woman. This was not a particularly onerous admonishment, especially when I knew she liked a bottle or three of *Chianti* with her lunch.

She asked me if there was any associate that I had a problem with. I told her of my experience of Gerry and added that I could not see how someone like him, who did so little work, should receive such a huge salary.

She smiled and recited a story, which I recalled having read somewhere before, of a particular whaling boat where a crew member did no work, had his own private cabin, ate gourmet meals off fine bone china and drank the finest claret. "But when the whale was sighted," she concluded triumphantly, "he would fire his harpoon with deadly accuracy, never missing. Always successful."

And so it was that the Sunset Watcher's job was to write copy, and this he did with enormous talent and panache, giving Boss the leading edge over all its competitors. He provided quality over quantity. I had to learn, apparently, to accept the culture and break out of my Protestant Work Ethic.

Boss was the only company I had ever worked for where bonuses were increased directly *as the losses increased*. Two years later, it was sold for a pound and a few months after that all associates were out of a job. The Sunset Watcher never worked again.

# Chapter Twenty-Two: Ealing Comedy

Ealing is west of London and north of the Thames. It is not that far from Kew, which is not that far from Richmond, but to me it is definitely North London. Now it is very much a Polish enclave, but embedded with little clusters of other ethnic groups, particularly Lebanese and peoples from the 'Stans" – Pakistan, Afghanistan, Uzbekistan and Kurdistan.

The offices were serviced and all of them in the block were let by the week, but a number of the tenants had been there for several years. Kalos Health Restore was one of those longer term tenants. It existed to bring accident victims back to health thereby mitigating insurance claims. Some fifteen staff (almost all female). Only a couple of retired surgeons and the Chief Accountant were male. I was brought in 'to beef up' the accounting operation. The Chief Accountant was very friendly to me at the interview and I was offered the job on the stop. "Start on Monday, through the agency and let's see how things go."

So I started. I was given a desk in the open plan office and a laptop connected to the main system, except the connection did not work. The IT woman, Candice, was rude and abrupt. I would have to have to wait until she was free. I busied myself with various printouts and looked at the sales brochures. Nobody spoke to me. Five thirty came and I went home – end of Day One. Day Two was very much the same, as was Day Three. Halfway through Day Four, I telephoned the Chief Accountant, Hugo Aurelius Brown, to state that, unless I was connected there was no point in me continuing to attend and be paid. On Day Five, I was connected, but asked by the very grumpy IT woman to 'Google' something to establish the connection. I put in the name of Hugo Aurelius Brown and up he came with a photograph of the very same. An extremely detailed summary of the Criminal Court Case wherein Mr Hugo Aurelius Brown had been charged with embezzling funds from an Employee Pension Scheme. He had been tried, convicted and sent to prison for a year. He had been debarred from being a Company Director for ten years and expelled from his Accounting Association. The same Mr Hugo Aurelius Brown. At this point the Head of Human Resources, a fat ugly roly poly woman called me over. I was all fingers and thumbs trying to shut down my system. "Now!" she shouted. "Now!" I walked smartly over to her desk and was given a dressing down for using my mobile phone in the office. It was against the house rules. I apologised, I did not know the house rules. It was my agency that kept telephoning me.

When I arrived back at my desk, my screen had mysteriously come back into life at the same detailed Court Judgement which Mr Hugo Aurelius Brown seemed to be reading. What could I do? I smiled: "Hullo, Hugo, I'm now connected, thanks." He sat opposite me and launched into a diatribe about the long overdue debtors' list. Why had I not done anything about it? He would not accept that I had only just been connected. He did need very thick reading glasses. He did not have his reading glasses on. Was he able to see what was on the screen? It had also scrolled pretty far down. Who knew? Thus ended my fifth day.

Apart from Hugo and myself, there were two 'ladies' in the Accounts Department; a White South African called Kerena who ran the Purchase Ledger and a New Zealander (Estelle) who ran the Sales Ledger. The White South African, was very white. The whitest person I have ever seen. 'A whiter shade of pale' could not describe that colour, not even a 'ghostly white'. Is the purest alabaster that shade of white? It has been said that the artist Lucian Freud bought up hundreds of tubes of white paint because they were being taken off the market due to their toxic content. This paint gave him the desired fleshy whiteness that he needed for his Notting Hill Nudes. I wonder what he would have made of her? She was well larded, but like most fat women, had a decent pair of legs. Smooth, blemish free, perfect white legs that went all the way up. Unlike most fat women, her arms were firm, well-muscled and extraordinarily white. Her face was pretty and her teeth dazzling white. All this whiteness was set off by a shining cap of black, lustrous hair. She only ever wore a black, sleeve-less mini dress which displayed her ample bosom to perfect effect.

I spent a few years in South Africa I can speak passable Afrikaans. I said "Hullo" to her in Afrikaans.

"I do not speak that filthy language," she retorted angrily. But it was clear that she was of Afrikaner stock.

After a few minutes of polite conversation, she confided in me that she had had a 'breast reduction'. "They were just far too big, too heavy, gave me back pain." What prompted this disclosure, I did not know. Maybe, I was staring at those awesome alabaster mounds?

Estelle was the complete opposite; thin, almost gaunt with angular bits of bone sticking out. She was tanned a golden brown with yellow teeth to match. She told me she had had a breast argumentation.

You might think I am making all this up, but it is absolutely true. The world is unequal. Go to a serious nudist beach, not Brighton or Bournemouth, but one of those in the South of France, where they really do 'let it all hang out.' Those beaches where the gendarmes tell Muslin ladies that 'burkinis' are not appropriate. You will see females with breasts the size of giant melons that really need to be supported on a trolley. Then you will sight breasts that are like two fried eggs in a pan 'sunny side up'. It really is an unequal distribution of assets. I gave myself a mental slap for thinking these thoughts; I had a 'department' to run.

Both females were smokers. Every hour, on the hour, they disappeared for ten minutes for a smoke in the car park. How come Estelle's teeth were yellow and Kerena's were so white? Another mystery. They would arrive late, leave early and have long lunch hours. I did not mind if the job was being done, which it was not. Hugo had told me I was 'in charge' of them; their line manager.

But they completely ignored me. I needed a formal Mandate from Hugo and asked him for a meeting.

The Meeting Room was hot and airless. No windows. Just big enough for a round table and six chairs. You did not want to go in there with anyone who had just had a Lebanese lunch.

He was cordial. "How are you settling in?" I said I was OK now I was connected. "Oh, Candice is doing a lot of work for Arthur (The Managing Director) at home. Extra Mural bonding you might say." He winked.

I did not really want to know that. It happens wherever I work. *Don't get your pussy where you get your pay check,* I thought.

I mentioned that I had experienced great difficulties with the payroll system and the quarterly staff bonuses. I copped a great deal of abuse from the staff; I was really being 'thrown into the deep end'.

He brushed this aside, but confided in me with great pride how he paid the senior consultant surgeons. Their remuneration was calculated, then the gross sum was paid to a company in Lichtenstein. The Lichtenstein outfit granted the consultant a loan equal to the gross sum and then charged Kalos Health Restore two per cent 'admin fee'. When the consultant eventually died, the loan was written off.

"Brilliant eh," Hugo beamed.

A light bulb began to glow dimly in my brain. My (mature) student days – Case Law 'Substance Over Form'.

"Substance Over Form. Do you have Revenue clearance for such a Scheme"? I queried.

"Not exactly, but they have accepted a similar scheme operating out of the Isle of Man." He was angry now.

"Oh yes. I remember that. The Isle of Man has not been formally approved and entities operating have been advised to provide for full tax and National Insurance. Bollocks, listen, Guy, when I need your tax advice, I will ask for it. What is the issue you want to discuss with me?"

I explained my position with Kerena and Estelle. "If I am to be in charge, I want *you* to tell them that in no uncertain terms."

"Listen, Guy, I already have. Surely, a big boy like you can manage two nice young females, without me having to wet nurse you? If you have to fuck 'em to get the desired result, do it. That's your Mandate!"

"I don't think having sexual intercourse with subordinate staff is an appropriate method of management."

"Fuck you, man! Stop wasting my time! If you are not up to the job, find another one." He stood up, and opened the door. "Meeting over."

Well, I tried hard with the two. I felt I was fair, but firm. I went to endless lengths to try and agree objectives that were achievable and how we would satisfy these requirements. I granted them all sorts of little privileges and favours to facilitate their tasks. I even offered to take them out to lunch (offer refused). Finally, I decided I had to 'man up' and came down on them heavy and hard. The Caveman approached seemed to work, but I had underestimated the cards that they held. They brought The Head of Human Resources into play.

The twenty-minute meeting with her in the meeting was a cruel and personal attack on me. I was a power crazed male chauvinist pig, with a phobia against Antipodeans. I was cold, harsh and unfeeling. I rode rough shod over everybody's sensitivities. Finally, having inflicted her thousand cuts she added: "You also smelt strongly of garlic – cut out the Lebanese lunches."

I did remark that the ladies smelt strongly of stale tobacco. I would take her comments on board. Then I asked her if she had any complaints against me professionally.

"You will have to ask Hugo that."

So I continued week after week. I was becoming aware that all was not well with the organisation. Lots of impromptu meetings with staff; whisperings, strange looks, absences. Mysterious forces were at work. Forces that were tearing the entity apart. I could not work it out. They were very well paid, they received decent pensions, generous allowances and expenses. Nobody was over worked. Then it hit me. There was no leadership. The Managing Director was never there. He was screwing his IT Director. The Chief Accountant only made guest appearances. The operational staff were always out 'on assignments'. In short, everybody, from the top down to the office junior was on the make. Actually, I will exclude the office junior. She was a sweet girl, called Mandy that could not do enough for her colleagues. I think I can say, she was the only person who showed me any friendliness. After three months it came. Sony from the agency telephoned me. I went into the vacant meeting room. "They've advertised your job," he blurted out.

He was right. It was in the local paper. The advert accurately described my job and all the necessary qualifications. "Immediate Start".

A week later I was called into the meeting room by Hugo.

"We have eventually found your replacement," he stated flatly. "She starts on Monday. You will, of course, train her in all aspects of the job for the next three days. So next Wednesday will be your last day." Once again he stood up and opened the door. Christmas Day was the following Wednesday week and I was scheduled for a major eye operation.

Lucy was an attractive woman, in fact, I would say, extremely attractive and pleasant. She had come from Ireland where she had worked as hotel receptionist. She had little accountancy experience and no qualifications. She was a single mother who confided in me she was unable to work late. I taught her all I could in the limited time. At five on Wednesday afternoon I shook her hand and wished her well. I stopped off at a Lebanese coffee shop and phoned Hugo from my mobile.

"Guy, it was never a permanent job. Anyway, you never

got on well with the girls or with Personnel, so, please don't waste any more of my time," he barked.

"That's fine, Hugo. Prepare yourself for a return to Ford Open Prison, you fraudster." I clicked the phone off. My hands were shaking. Was it anger or was the treble espresso a bit on the strong side?

I was careful. I wore surgical gloves and posted the letter from Newbury to Her Majesty's Revenue and Customs. The inspection came six weeks later. Seven months later I had a call from Mandy asking to meet me in a local pub. She looked absolutely radiant, as if a huge weight had been lifted from her.

She gave me the low down on events. The Revenue levied a charge of seven million for back taxes on payroll. A group of staff had taken the customer list and set up a rival business. Kalos sued and lost and then went into Liquidation. The Serious Fraud Office were called. Hugo and others were charged with fraud and sentenced to varying lengths of prison sentences. Hugo received two years. Everybody lost their jobs. Mandy retrained as a Traffic Warden and loved the 'outdoor life'. She had become engaged to a fellow Traffic Warden. We promised we would keep in touch, but of course, never did.

# Chapter Twenty-Three: Fury

"Her name was Julie, we called her the office bicycle. Everyone rode her, except for me, that is." The Court laughed.

"Silence!" Roared Lord Justice Quinlan-Pratt. "This is not vaudeville." The judge turned to our barrister. "Is this testimony really necessary?"

"Absolutely, my Lord." The judge sighed weakly." Pray continue…"

I recounted that Mr Michael, the Chairman had asked me to get rid of her and replace her, but not a man, as a man would not get the lunches, make the coffee. He had told me to hire a woman – a fat, old, ugly, dog. So I hired Mrs Frossdike.

"A fat, old, ugly, dog!" repeated the defending barrister. "From where I stand I am looking at Mrs Frossdike. A stylish designer outfit. She's not fat, old, ugly or canine. She's demure and fragrant, if one's eyes could smell, that is."

"I agree that she is not old. I failed Mr Michael on that one. But when she weighed in at Tiger Tech she was eighteen stone and certainly not fragrant or demure. She would smoke forty a day. Drink four pints of sweet cider at lunchtime and never stopped eating – deep fried triple cheeseburgers fried in batter. Chocolate bars, sweets, crisps, sausage sandwiches. In fact there was never a moment when she didn't have something in her mouth."

A female juror burst into giggles.

"What's so funny?" demanded the judger. Now the entire Court erupted.

"Quiet!" shouted the judge.

The Clerk whispered something into the Judge's ear.

"Disgusting." The judge shook his head.

I continued: "What we didn't know is that Mr Plumbstead, the Commercial Director had a passion, for, shall we say, larger ladies, his wife being small and scrawny. Soon Mrs Frossdike and he became 'an item'."

"An item?" queried the judge.

"Yes, lovers. Mrs Frossdike would go every night to Mr Plumbstead's rowing club. She took to the sport. Soon the pounds fell off. She stopped smoking. Diet drinks replaced the cider, celery sticks instead of burgers. She began to look good, dress well. Her skin developed a healthy tone and texture, her breasts..."

"Enough! Enough! This is all too subjective and in fact irrelevant to the case. 'Beauty is in the eye of the beholder'."

The Judge thumped his table.

"It is relevant, my Lord. She became an anorexic and therefore, unattractive to Mr Plumbstead. It was now Mr Armstrong, the Managing Director, who became attracted to her."

"Don't tell me, Mr Armstrong's wife is a large lady and therefore, there was an attraction of opposites," quipped the defence barrister.

"That's exactly what happened," I replied. "In fact Mrs Frossdike fell pregnant. She went to Mr Plumbstead and demanded fifty grand for a termination."

"You have proof of this?" asked the Defence.

"Yes. You see we are wholesale. We don't work at weekends. Stock began to suddenly go missing. So Mr Brown, the warehouse manager and myself went up to the mezzanine floor and rigged up a video camera. At eleven on a Saturday morning a truck owned by Mr Wellbeloved, Mr Plumbstead's brother-in-law, pulled in. Mr Wellbeloved and Mr Plumbstead loaded up the van with stock. Mr Wellbeloved handed Mr Plumbstead a huge wad of cash. Mr Wellbeloved said, 'No need to count it, Ron, it's all there, fifty grand. It's all on the video.' Mr Plumbstead said, 'That will shut the bitch up and is more than enough for the end job.'"

The Court adjourned and then returned to watch the video which was as I had recounted, despite the grainy quality and bad sound.

I was now confident, sweating less and leaning on the brass rail. "She then went to Mr Armstrong and asked the same. He bolted. Gone for three weeks. AWOL. It was only when the Company Credit Card arrived that I realised he had been staying at The Rolling Hills Golf and Country Club. I tracked him down and had a man to man with him. Told him to come back and face the music. He did."

"I can't see where all this going?" whined the Defence.

"I'll tell you where it is going... Mrs Frossdike went to Tiger Tech and erased all the backup tapes. The evidence is all there, traced back to her password and her pc. She went to the bank and withdrew all the other backups. Again, the Court has all the evidence. She then destroyed all our bespoke operating systems. All data gone. Everything. Our cash flow went south. She spilled the beans to Tecky Toad, our largest creditor and they put the company into liquidation."

# Chapter Twenty-Four: Bricks

Let's be sexist. If you are a female and do not have much in the brain box, then fashion is a trade, for the hard-working, that can reap rich rewards. If you are a male with a similarly geared brainbox and you want to swerve the motor trade, try the construction industry. All you need as your point of entry is a paintbrush and, hey presto, you are a painter/decorator. Work hard, be reliable and do a good job and you will never be out of work. In the boom times, skilled men (and woman) and materials are at an absolute premium, in a recession the market is flooded with these commodities and the consumer can then pick and choose.

Jack Brompton suffered as a child from dyslexia at a time when not many people could even spell the condition. Brompton senior recognised this and using his 'rolled trouser' connections obtained a plumbing apprenticeship for Jack. Plumbing is not seen as the most glamorous of trades, crawling into small dusty spaces, unblocking drains and toilets is not everybody's bowl of cherries; however, we all have to spend our time in the bathroom and that *particular* room can be turned into a really exciting place. Marble, hand crafted Italian tiles grouted with gold flakes, toilets that gently shower your personal waste disposal area and blow dry it softly with warm air. Gold plated dolphin taps, whirlpool baths, jet sprays, mood lighting and whale music, can make these rooms exciting, particularly if you share your lavage and ablutions with a friend.

Kitchens are also a place where, some of us, also spend a lot time. The humble kitchen sink has now become a work of art. Heavy ceramic, chrome, stainless steel, control consoles that could drive a space ship. 'His and hers' sinks. Ingenuous use of every conceivable space. Lighting to match every mood and task and of, the 'must have' central island which would double as a breakfast bar.

Jack was working in the boom time, the mid-eighties.

He enjoyed plenty of work, but not really, the sort of work that he felt was really his forte. It was a Friday afternoon and he was finishing installing three men's urinals in a small distribution centre. His mobile rang. He was extremely proud of his mobile. It cost him a small monthly fortune, but he could take calls at work and that was valuable to him. Now came the call that would change his life. It was Bertram Clancy of Clancy's models. Bertram's models were not the two legged kind. They were model trains, ships, cars and aircraft. Bertram would go berserk if you mentioned the words 'toy models', these were scale models. His shop was in Noel Street, a street that was north of Soho and ran parallel to Oxford Street. Through the 'rolled trouser brigade', Jack had quoted for a complete refurbishment of the shop. It was not really 'up his street', but together with his school friends, Jason and Barry, they had enough trades between them to pull it off. Some months back they had formed JJB West Pimlico Refurbishments Ltd. Just for this event. Now Bertram offered him the contract. He would pay twenty-five per cent up front, a further twenty-five per cent at the two-week stage and a further forty-five per cent upon completion, two weeks later. There were onerous penalties for late completion. The start was due a week on Monday. Jack accepted immediately.

Jason and Barry were contacted: "All systems are GO!" There was a mountain of work ahead in that week – parking suspensions to be organised from the Council, contractors to be hired, materials purchased and planning to be done. On Sunday all the stock was packed away and put into storage by Bertram and his staff. On Monday, The Boys moved in. Everybody called the three of them The Boys, because they were all in their early thirties. The basement and ground floor were gutted. Flooring sanded and painted in white. Who had ever seen white painted floors before? Pipes and ducts ran on the outside of the walls and were clearly visible. The shelving was old reclaimed timber. Display areas varied from using traditional oak to stainless steel. The children's area was pained in bright, glossy primary colours. A model rail track ran right round the interior of the ground floor and in the basement was a similar track for model racing cars. Model kits were displayed in heavy transparent bins. The lighting was spectacular. It was able to turn bright daylight into the darkest night over the railway track. Above thousands of stars twinkled. An astronomer had been called in to advise on the constellations. Heating and air conditioning was installed. The end result was magical.

Jack made sure a photographer was present at the champagne re-launch. He also had several hundred quality walking umbrellas made up with the JJB logo. These were given away as promos, and as the gods would have it, it rained heavily on the day. Several more retail commissions followed quickly. The Boys took a suite of offices above a builder's yard in suburbia. Business expanded rapidly. Some tasty domestic refurbishment projects followed in the West End, namely Holland Park and Camden Hill. They formally launched their new business at The Ritz. Every guest received a glossy catalogue and a walking umbrella. Again it rained heavily. Through 'contacts' Jack began a member of The Ritz Casino. You may think this was an extravagance, but the casino is full of rich people consumed by fears. Fears such as, where can I find a reliable marble fitter? I need a cabinet maker, not just a joiner. I simply cannot find a mural painter. Does anyone know a good French polisher? Of course, Jack knew all the answers to these vexing questions and, furthermore, was able to provide practical solutions. It was in the casino that I met him. Horses are my game, but, frankly, I am a snob. I like to mix with rich people who dress well and smell nice. I enjoy nibbling canapés and sipping champagne. Most of the clientele were not UK citizens, so on certain tax and legal matters I was able to assist them, for a fee, of course. With Jack, I was able to relax, no need to put on a show. He needed someone to steer the ship financially, could I help? Of course I could. Actually I had no work at that time to speak of. I reported to the offices on Monday morning.

Things looked good. They had almost more work than they could handle. Mark ups were enormous. They worked exclusively indoors. The workforce wore slippers, or overshoes, white track suit bottoms and corporate blue polo shirts with matching zip up jerkins. Smoking was not allowed on or off the site. They had to talk softly and not use bad language. Most of their workforce had the security of a regular weekly wage. The Boys' reputation spread quickly, their services were in enormous demand. Yes they all had BMWs and there was a company flagpole. The Company flag was hoisted at every site if possible. A PR company promoted their abilities and every week there was a feature in Homes and Gardens, Country Life, even Vogue. They lapped it up and not only attracted a top drawer clientele, but a terrific clutch of artists, artisans and master craftsmen.

Collecting debts, however, was a problem. This was my job. I found the best way to go about it was to visit the owners on site. Usually, I would take tea with them. We would talk about all manner of things. I suppose, I am a good listener. Often, they would require some kind of small service, which, usually. I could provide. When you dig deep, it is surprising what you can find and what you can deliver. I would never mention that filthy word 'money'. But accounts would be settled, the next day. I now faced a tough assignment. A Greek ship owner, who liked to be known simply as Phil was holding back on his ten per cent retention, nearly seventy-five thousand pounds. The issue was a screw in his shower tray. It kept galvanising. I appeared with my uniformed plumber. He had found the problem and he knew how to fix it. He bought a rubber tube from a local cycle shop and cut out a washer, which was inserted between the screw head and the shower tray. This would stop the electrolysis galvanising the screw head. It did not work and Phil did not pay. I then had idea, I took an identical screw to a very posh jeweller and had them cast it gold with a tiny diamond on top. Again, I arrived with my uniformed plumber and presented the screw to Phil in its cushioned satin lined box. The piece was screwed in and Phil signed me a cheque on the spot for his outstanding debt.

I suppose it was fair to say that The Boys were three working-class lads who had made good. Soon they learned to relax and mix with their masters. Now there was a very well-known construction company in the area and twice a year The Chief held a golf day. An entire Surrey club was taken over by him. The boys were invited, but none of them had ever been on a golf course or even swung a club. I coached them in the basics of golf etiquette and we spent many concentrated hours on the driving range. Of course, they kitted themselves out with all the very most expensive gear. Actually, when the big day came, they did not do too badly. Interestingly, the next golf day was cancelled and six months later that construction company went into liquidation. Some said it was as a direct result of the cancellation. Others, more sagely, muttered about the end of the good times.

I was becoming alarmed at the amount of overtime being claimed by, what was now, a regular workforce. The Boys were not interested. Brompton senior condescended to drive round the West End with me to visit all the sites after five on a Friday afternoon. Every single site was deserted. Yet on Monday, all the time sheets came in showing the entire workforce had left at eight in the evening! Was this a wakeup call? I delivered the first of many lectures. The recession is coming, cut back, cut back. Reduce costs, reduce fees, slim down. The response was: "The rich are not affected by the recession."

My response was: "Skilled men (and women) and materials will flood the market and then the rich will call the tune, they will shop around."

Despite the ominous storm clouds that gathered, JJB won a contract to refurbish a mansion in Bishop's Avenue. This place was gross. You could drive a London double-decker bus in through the front door, it could do a full circle turn and exit. There was a moat with Koi carp at a thousand pounds a throw. The obligatory gold plated taps, a hairdressers, a karaoke room, cinema and indoor and outdoor swimming pools. The dolls' house cost twenty-five grand. Yet, despite all this opulence, the servants slept in the loft on the unfinished bare rafters.

Projects were being truncated or cancelled. There was no comfortable backlog anymore. The cash was not flowing. Slowly the light began to glow with The Boys. The BMWs went. Some of the office space and parts of the yard were let out. Pension contributions cancelled. Overtime banned. Staff laid off. We decided on a plan, rather a naughty plan. A plan I certainly would not subscribe to today. But for all that, it happened frequently then and it still does now. We would form another company, with a completely different name. The remaining 'good' contracts would be transferred to it. The 'bad' contracts would be left in the old company, which would be allowed to be liquidated. I was to front the old company. Why I did this, I do not know. Sure, I had been paid well, but I did a good job and gave good advice – largely ignored.

Being the 'front man' was the most awful job I ever did in my life. The phone would start ringing at half past eight in the morning and would be still ringing when I left at six in the evening. Angry people who were owed a great deal of money. One day a woman strode into the office. She was holding a baby. She thrust a statement under my nose. Her husband had worked for JJB as a tiler and she wanted paying. There and then. She knew I had a 'wad of cash'. This was true, but it was for 'essential services'. I explained quietly to her all about fraudulent preference and as a result could not pay her. "I ain't leaving until yer do!" she exclaimed, undid her shirt and began to breast feed the baby.

This was fine with me, but when she started to change the baby on my desk, I pulled out a wad of notes. "It's not

the full sum, but that's all I can do. Others, get nothing."
She took the money and left.

My next visitor was a huge man. He had the words 'love' and 'hate' tattooed across his knuckles. He introduced himself as a High Court Sheriff. He had come to collect the bricks in the yard as a result of non-payment. Outside was a large lorry, their folk lift had already been unloaded. I looked at him and smiled. "No problem. I actually have your statement to hand." The figures agreed. "Good, so we can load?" he smiled back, but none too sweetly.

"Of course, you can. You have naturally identified which of the bricks have been paid for, and which have not?" He looked at me blankly. I explained the workings of the Romolpa Clause to him. Namely, he could take only *those bricks that had not been paid for.* I passed him my law text book. "I presume you can read? There it is." He read it. He made a call on his mobile. He then departed.

It was decided to liquidate the old company. A meeting of creditors was called. We met in a hall in Croydon. I drove The Boys there in my ancient 2CV. It was unnerving to face all those angry suppliers. We had always paid them on the due day, bang on the nail. A few of them had done very well out their association with The Boys. Now they were here for blood. The Liquidator polished his spectacles and formally called the meeting open. Immediately he was handed a note by one of his assistants. "Oh dear. I'm afraid a Winding Up Petition Hearing has been granted in the Kingston Crown Court. So there is no point in having this meeting. Meeting adjourned."

There was one last card to play. If we could obtain a majority of creditors' support by debt value, we could restructure the company, basically, by employing the creditors in the new company and allowing them to recover their outstanding debt. Excluding the Statutory Creditors, six creditors accounted for seventy per cent of the debt by value. They all pledged their support for the plan.

We turned up at court an hour beforehand. We met our barrister, a Spanish women who spoke good English, in the 'robing room'. This was fifteen minutes before we were called. I knew the retirement age for a judge was seventy years of age, but I must say, our 'boy' appeared to be eighty, if he was a day. This guy certainly had got out of the wrong side of bed that morning. It was also clear to me, that he had little detailed knowledge of company law. Our barrister had even less knowledge of the subject. At one point the judge referred to our barrister as a 'young woman', at another, he spoke to her in Spanish. Then there was a great deal of whispering. Now the judge addressed me: "Mr Gundle, do you know the meaning of Shadow Director?" I replied I did. He then went on to explain that a Shadow Director had to bear the same responsibilities as a full board Director.

Was I a Shadow Director? I now had my moment. "Sir, a Shadow Director is not a formally elected Board Director. He is one that gives advice to the Board and therefore influences them. However, I can categorically state I did give plenty of advice to the Directors, but almost all of it was ignored, therefore, *de facto* I am *not* a Shadow Director." I had no idea what *de facto* meant, but it sounded good in the context. I now continued that the company had over seventy per cent support of the creditors by value and, furthermore, there was a viable plan to turn the business round. He now threw his toys out of his pram, or rather, his chair against the wall. He ranted that the whole proceeding should never have happened, a complete waste of taxpayers' money and the court's time. From what we could make out, we were free to continue trading with both the old and the new company.

Somehow or other, we pulled through. Gradually the creditors were satisfied, new contracts flowed in, but smaller and less grand. The operation was scaled down, but became more profitable. It survived and eventually thrived. It is still around today, doing very well indeed. Yet a few years ago I asked Jack for a small favour. "Why should I do this for you?" he growled at me. I told him to jump in the lake, or words to that effect.

# Chapter Twenty-Five: Rock Wraith

I was over the moon landing an interview with the mighty Rock Wraith plc. Here was a two hundred year old *Scottish* company that had its roots in the Far East. A real *Hong* company, extending into South East Asia and India and then growing worldwide, originally into the furthest corners of the British Empire, but in the United States, Continental Europe and finally into Russia.

Rock did not actually make anything. It imported and exported. It distributed. It was the darling of the stock exchange, either holding or increasing its dividend through good years and bad. As a consequence its share price also steadily rose over the years. It was the share choice of widows and orphans' investments. My interview was with the Motor Division, based at the biggest multi franchise in Europe. It suited me well as it was located in a large provincial town in Surrey, fifteen miles from my home.

The interview was with the General Manager, Tim Whitehawk. It started at nine in the morning and was in full swing at two in the afternoon. "Oh, lunch, I forgot. I'll ask Sandra my PA to bring us a couple of pot noodles." I always think it is a good sign to be offered lunch at an interview. I suppose pot noodles could be considered lunch. Finally, the interview terminated at three. "I'll be in touch," Tim called after me.

I drove straight to my local and over a couple of pints considered events. Rock were looking for 'new blood'; someone *not* from the Motor Trade. Tim left school at sixteen and went straight into the trade. "Yes at just seventeen I was a junior salesman at this very site. Sheepskin coat, cavalry twirls, hush puppies. I rose quickly and became the youngest ever General Manager at thirty." He confessed to being fifty-eight years old – forty-one years working on the same site at the same trade. No wonder they were looking for 'new blood'.

Two days later I received the call. Another interview,

this time with the Area Accountant. That was a breeze. I ticked all the boxes. I started my new job a month later. I walked through the sparkling clean showroom – gleaming white ceramic floors, all glass and chrome. The new models polished to a soft glow under the spotlights. That peculiar new car smell, part leather, part plastic. Metal? Metal does smell, well, it does have a unique smell to me at least. I shook hands with Tim and he led me upstairs. This was a different scene. The last time this office had enjoyed a lick of paint was in Harold Macmillan's day. The walls were still coated with nicotine. The windows were firmly shut. "Keep out the traffic noise – and fumes," explained Tim. The sixteen staff sat in four rows, four across. The younger more junior at the front, the older at the back. I was introduced to each staff member. Three men, thirteen woman. The oldest member of the team had served for seventy years. He sat at the back by the window. The youngest was only seventeen, she sat in the front, far from the window. They all faced to glass boxes. The smaller box was for my No. Two, George, I had been allocated the larger box. The staff were all allocated to one of the four motor franchises. That meant four separate computer systems, four sets of management statements. In addition there was a large parts franchise. This was going to be fun!

George proved to be a helpful young man. Considered too young to take command. For some reason he reminded me of a young ostrich. He 'marked my card' as best he could. My predecessor had experienced mental problems. His predecessor suffered a fatal heart attack in the office. I clearly had two problems to deal with. Firstly, tensions amongst the staff, secondly, coming to grips with four different computer systems.

My first staff problem occurred on the very first hot day of the year. Freddie decided to discard his tie. At eleven that morning Tim telephoned me. "Freddie isn't wearing a tie, that's contrary to the Staff Handbook, Section 126 – Gentlemen's attire (Office Staff)."

I replied I had already spoken to Freddie about it and he had reminded me of Section 179 – Office Temperature. We were well out of the ambient range. "Deal with him as you think fit, you're the bloody expert, but deal with him pronto quick!" he barked down the phone at me.

This was my first test of leadership. Freddie was not going to budge. "You poor thing – you know what I think the best course of action is for you? You need to go home, the heat is too much for you. Hopefully you will feel better tomorrow and able to wear your tie."

He knew when he was beat. "Yes, that's a good idea, a rest, and a cold beer will revive me." The moment he was out of the door, all the rest of the staff began to feign the ill effects of heat.

"Quiet!" I bellowed. "It is darn hot, but tomorrow we will have some electric fans."

"Tim won't allow them, no budget," grumbled the seventy-year lifer.

"Well, I'll buy them myself." I was as good as my word. I purchased three powerful fans the next day. Up to then, the only fan was the one in my glass box.

The next morning the day promised to be even hotter. Freddie arrived tie-less. I called him into my box. Pointed to my throat and raised my eyebrows. He smiled and produced a piece of paper – a doctor's note saying that Freddie was suffering from *milaria rubra* and that he must allow air to circulate around the inflamed area, namely his lower neck. "OK, Freddie, you take care now. We don't want you to overheat, do we?"

I phoned Tim with the news. He uttered two words in reply: "The bugger!"

My next staff challenge two days later. Bob was a big, fat bald man. A fifty-year lifer. Mary was a five foot nothing slip of a lady. She liked to hum when she was working. Bob did not like her to hum. He came to see me about 'the problem'. I asked Marie to come in separately and discussed the issue. The only concession she was prepared to make was "hum more quietly". Neither of them would change desks. I was sitting in my box, with the door open as usual, when I heard Bob swearing in a loud voice. Swearing was contrary to Section 112 of The Staff Handbook. Bob would know that. Marie squeaked and squawked and then started screaming at Bob. Time for me to intervene. There was a loud crack, followed by furniture being toppled. Several female screams broke out, there was a commotion. Marie was flat on her back, Bob standing over her, glowering. It turned out that Bob had punched her, punched her hard. When the paramedics arrived, she had come round and her jaw was swelling rapidly. She spent a week in hospital and had to have her jaw wired up. In the court case that followed, Bob was found guilty of grievous bodily harm and was sentenced to sixty hours of community service, being of previous good character. He resigned from Rock Wraith. In the internal enquiry that followed at work, I was giving a formal written warning for "failing to ensure the safety of the staff entrusted to me".

I did make one friend in my time at Rock Wraith. He was the Service Manager, Andrew. He ran a tight shop, but went out of his way to give me every assistance, unlike most of the managers who took the attitude, "No one showed us, why should we show anyone else?" Andrew was one of the privileged few who had been awarded the accolade of being awarded two weeks' holiday in the company villa in Marbella. He had been recruiting trainee vehicle service technicians and out of the CVs picked a certain Charlie Johnson. "He's just the man for us – hire him," he ordered and then went off for his long deserved holiday. 'Charlie' Johnson was in fact 'Charlotte' Johnson, a petite svelte little number, but she knew about engines. Andrew returned, sun bronzed from his holiday and the first thing he saw on the service floor was Charlie's perfectly formed little bottom as she bent deep into the engine compartment. He could not have a female in *his* service department. It was a danger and a distraction, a threat to Mr and Mrs Health and Safety. He called her in and in front of me and his Assistant Manager explained to her that she had been hired in error. There were no toilet facilities for ladies in the department. I protested that Charlie could use the customers' toilets. "Out of the question." Charlie was summarily dismissed. Well, Charlie had pluck, perhaps the fact that her mother was an employment lawyer may have helped, but Rock Wraith was taken to court and fined thirty thousand pounds for Sex Discrimination. Charlie was re-instated and eventually became a Service Manager herself.

Sir Des O' Donoghue was the Chief Executive Office of Rock Wraith. Like a dictator of a banana republic, his picture was everywhere on the premises. Like some of his contemporaries, he espoused the mantra "We are a NOW Company". Predictable dividends and a rising share price was all that mattered. Des had joined Rock as an apprentice mechanic straight from school at the age of sixteen. Fifteen years ago, he was appointed as Chief Executive Office of the Motor Retail Division. He inherited eighty sites throughout Britain; now there were twenty-nine, but twenty-nine profitable sites. Tim related this information to me in his poky office facing the main showroom. This was a privileged meeting, Tim had produced the chocolate biscuits from his desk drawer, not an honour bestowed upon anyone. "His Highness is coming here tomorrow, so Guy make sure the Accounts Department is absolutely ship shape. Nothing on top of the filing cabinets, waste paper bins to be empty, no photos of children, babies or pets. Sir Des hates animals. Desks to be uncluttered and polished. The carpet to be hoovered. Absolutely no clutter. Do you read me, Guy?" I assured him that his instructions would be carried out to the letter.

At eleven the next morning, I had a quiet call from Tim: "Can you come down now." As forewarned, I took a notepad and my trusty old add lister. This piece of old battery driven Bakelite had been with me for many years. It was so old and worn that the numbers on the keys had been worn away many years ago, but it worked even though employed a different computing logic to the modern calculator. Sir Des was big, fat and bald. He wore cheap chain store clothing, his trousers were pulled up well over his substantial paunch. His spectacles were untinted and reflected the neon lights back to you, making it had to see his eyes. He reeked of stale tobacco. His handshake was soft and plump.

"You've a problem with your oil!" he barked at me. He had written some figures on a small notepad. He grabbed my add lister and began to punch the keys, again and again. "This damned thing is broke." He thrust it back at me.

"If it ain't broke, don't fix it," I quipped.

"Good God, if we adopted that philosophy, the Service Departments would not make Siamese groat.

It's preventative maintenance, man." Tim rapidly produced a slim modern calculator. Sir Des reworked the figures. "*Your* figures show we are using an *extra litre of oil* for every single service we undertake on this site, so either your figures are a load of bollocks, or the oil is being nicked wholesale." A long discussion followed about the logistics of 'nicking' the oil in wholesale quantities, or how to verify the accuracy of the figures. It was decided that I would report the oil consumption on a weekly basis directly to Sir Des.

Back in my box, George was keen to know how I progressed. He agreed to help me to compile the figures to ensure greater accuracy. Our informal conversation expanded now to the subject of 'Provisions'. A Provision is a figure that is made against an unknown future cost. The Monthly Management Statements logged some thirty different Provisions, provisions for event that had not happened, or were likely not to happen – training costs, dilapidations, legal actions, terrorism, floods, fire and pestilence, even political changes. "The name of the game is to match the actual figures as close as we can to the budget. We do this by increasing or releasing the

Provisions, even the Profit Reserves. They're the brakes and accelerator of the results, deployed to give us a nice smooth ride. There are so many of them, it's like a squirrel and his nuts, he forgets where he has hidden them and, in fact, what they are." Now it fell into place, the last few months had shown spectacular profits, yet Tim had banged on about increasing the Provisions, for the drains. The drains were Victorian, they had stood for over a hundred years. Tim argued that they were about to collapse. I argued that if they had stood for that long, they were stand for another hundred years. There were moves afoot in the accountancy profession to ban 'big bath provisioning', but nobody had told Rock.

The oil problem was eventually solved – a mix up between metric and imperial measures. But now Tim had summoned me to deal with another issue. A team of Management Consultants had descended on the company. It was ordered that every department was to have Staff Meetings. These meetings had been banned by Tim as a 'waste of time'. "Just do it! The instruction comes from up high."

I called the meeting at lunchtime, brought in pizzas at my own cost. It would be free form, no agenda. It was a jolly affair. The staff car park was a problem – easily solved. It was agreed we would have a new carpet, an air conditioning for next summer. Then, we grasped the real issue – the female toilets. We entered these toilets. They looked all right to me. Places where you performed your bodily functions, then washed your hands. Job done. But no, this is not what the females wanted. In the end, I appointed the Spokeswoman as leader of the project. "Your budget is no more than two thousand." It seemed to please them. For us blokes, The Gents was simply there for bodily functions, being sick after a hangover and reading 'The Racing Post'.

No sooner had the meeting finished when Tim called me to his office. He was delighted with the outcome. The chocolate biscuits were produced. Most items could be postponed to the next financial year. The toilet project would be undertaken by the site's 'odd job men'. Well, at least I was doing something right.

The payroll for the two hundred employees of the multi franchised site was run by a capable lady called June. Every single week she had to calculate the gross and net pay and then ensure they were paid correctly. After a while she began to trust and confide in me. It appeared that certain managers had certain 'favourites' in their departments and awarded them accordingly. I suppose we were call this 'flexibility' granted to those managers as a motional tool. However, June was now concerned. The wages paid to the delivery drivers of the Parts Department was now exceeding fifty-five hours per week. There were forty of these ladies; surprisingly, they were all ladies. They delivered engine parts, not engines. I did a number of checks. Gathered my evidence and presented it to Tim. "Where have you been all these years?" he scoffed at me. "We've done dozens, no, hundreds of stock checks on the drivers. Everything is absolutely kosher. So, they adjust their time sheets a little. For Christ sakes, man, get real. Leave it!" he shouted at me. So I left it.

The next episode, I could not leave. It had come to my attention that the debtors' ledger in a department was extending, yet this was a *cash only d*epartment. Something was untoward. I prepared my case and finally had a one-to-one with the manager. He fired a broadside at me. "What did I know about business? Had I ever had to face customers?" He promised he would 'reel in the debt'. Several months went by and the debt extended. The term 'teeming and lading' sprung into my mind from my student days. This is where a perpetrator takes payment from a customer, spends it himself and then uses other funds collected to eventually clear the original debt. After another meeting with the cove, I decided to telephone some of debtors. They went berserk, they had all paid and could produce evidence as such.

I now brought my evidence to Tim. "I trust you. You are probably right. But listen, Bert is a forty-year-old lifer. He is a church elder, a scout leader and his son is about to enter The Royal Air force." Tim opened his drawer and extracted two chocolate biscuits, one of which he kindly offered to me. "Bert has done this before, many years ago. Let me talk to him."

I replied, "You probably have a provision for this kind of thing. I'll leave it to you."

Two weeks later I called down to see Tim. He stood up and shut the door. No chocolate biscuits this time. "He's confessed." He sat down and thrust his thumbs behind his braces. "It's only forty thousand, you can find a way of... getting rid of it."

I looked at Tim. "I will refer you to The Staff Handbook. In these circumstances, I must report my findings to The General Manager. As you have frequently reminded me Tim – that's YOU. I have done so. The next step is report to Internal Audit. Internal Audit were the KGB of Rock, nobody survived their investigation. Nobody."

"Do what you jolly well like, but if you do, you're finished here!" he growled at me. I left the room and reported to Internal Audit.

The Auditor arrived the next day. A stick-like man with shakes. He brought a flash of Cola with him. At one point I mistook his cup of Cola for my black coffee. It was whisky flavoured Cola, stronger than even I was used to. Notwithstanding, the man knew what he was about. His enquiries took two weeks. The police were called. Bert confessed formally, received seventy-five hours community service and was sacked. I was effectively sent to 'Coventry' by most of my co-workers. My car refused to start or mysteriously ran out petrol. My tires were always flat. The battery usually flat. Time passed.

A new Internal Auditor appeared on the scene. It was clear that he was 'out to get me'. No stone was left under turned. I found him odd. He never sat down. His lunch, eaten standing up, was a white bread sandwich and a chocolate biscuit. He only drunk water, no coffee or tea. Another lifer. I could not connect to him. He found a 'hole' in the Vehicle License System. This was his own particularly speciality, a 'tool' that he had developed, all by himself! Eventually I lost it with him; here he was worrying about a few refundable quid of Vehicle Licenses when vehicles worth thirty thousand quid were simply disappearing off the forecourt!

We were now going into our financial year end. An instruction came from 'on high'. All Provisions were to be released. Any accountant disregarding this instruction would be dismissed. I discussed this with George. "Goodness me! Do you not know what The Big Event is? Des is retiring, his final bonus AND pension is going to be geared to this result!" I was shocked. I did as I was I told. Forty million pounds of profit was released into the results. Des and his managers all went off to an extended week of golf in Marbella.

A few days later my mother passed away. She did it just in a critical time that we all had to write a critical review of all the departments' results. I was told 'bereavement' was no excuse to prevent the production of the reports. So I did mine. A smiley face for good, a straight face for average and frowney face for bad. I could have dropped a nucleus bomb on the organisation! The moment I walked into the showroom, I was escorted into Tim's office and fired. I was escorted upstairs to my 'box' with a black plastic bag to fill with personal effects. "There's not enough shit in me to fill this  bag," I announced loudly. The only thing I took was trusty add lister.

I found another job quickly. I phoned Tim to clear the ground for a reference. He refused. I let rip. I would havoc and destruction upon him and his company. "Go ahead, do what you want." I did.

For some weeks I had been receiving strange requests for a 'free' lunch from a well-known and respected financial journalist. I now responded to his offer. I opened the can of worms. "This ties in nicely with what we already know. The whole company is rotten and corrupt to the core. Lord This and Lord That on the Board. Captains of Industry. All rotten. It runs through the entire company network, not just the Motor Division." On Sunday, the broadsheet broke the news. I was revealed as the main source. The share price dropped twenty per cent the next day. My prospective employer telephoned me immediately to congratulate me and state "references would not now be necessary".

Several years later I drove pass the site and stopped out of curiosity. It was now a shopping mall. A small board at the entrance displayed pictures of a number of skeletons that had been discovered whilst removing the 'crumbling Victoria drains'.

# Chapter Twenty-Six: The Tarantula and the Dog

"So, as I understand it, you have a phobia of... tissues?" she indicated a box of the same on her table.

"Yes, that and wearing nylon on my skin."

"Does the nylon bring you out in a rash, or some other physical manifestations?"

"No, it makes feel nauseas."

"And the tissues?"

"Physically sick – I need to vomit. I do vomit. I break out in a sweat. I start shaking, feel dizzy."

"Most of us have some have a dislike of something, it really becomes a phobia when it is hard to deal with it in our daily life. Fear of snakes is common, but living in Brighton, how may snakes to you come across, for instance?"

In fact, just the day before, I had seen a man with a python round his neck, going into the supermarket. That is Brighton for you.

"Fear of flying is another one," she said. "We cannot all travel by train or sea. How does this fear of tissues, affect you?"

I told her about the medical issues, how they would thrust tissues at you. How I had overcome this by packing sterilised cotton handkerchiefs in sealed nitrogen filled plastic bags. Every time we went to fast food restaurants tissues would be littered on the table. At work, sitting next to colleagues, their work surfaces strewn with snot laden tissues. Cakes and sandwiches wrapped in tissues. As I had become older, the problem had worsened. On one occasion I punched my host because he kept placing a folded tissue under my frosted lager glass. On another, I passed out when a woman handed me a bundle of tissues after I spilt coffee over my laptop.

"How do manage when it comes to the... toilet? Toilet tissue, er, I mean paper."

"I wash down there."

"What about the public toilet?"

"Oh. I carry a small plastic bottle of water."

"Can you remember how it began?"

I told her. When I was five I was a darling little boy. Blue eyes, tight golden curls, a smile that would make an angel blush. I wore knickerbockers and pleated, embroidered blouses. How did that sweet cutie turn into the present me?

Anyway, my mother loved to give tea parties. Earl Grey, Lapsang, Darjeeling. Dropped scones, crab sandwiches, cupcakes. Once the 'sun had set over the yardarm', generally about five o'clock, something harder would be served, namely Pink Gins. And in great quantities. Of course, everyone smoked then, but with the French doors open, there was no real fug. As a child, I lost count of how many times I was accidentally burnt by glowing cigarettes.

The sun had now passed over the yardarm. I remember one plump lady in a red dress with white polka dots. Her short hair was jet black; it shone and glistened. Her bare arms shook and wobbled, like a giant blancmange. Her enormous bosom was as white as polished alabaster, they parted to lead a crevice a long way down to some dark and mysterious place. Her lipstick was as red as her dress; some of it had smeared over her yellow teeth.

Today, such a woman, might represent the ultimate in pneumatic bliss. But then, I was terrified of her. Perhaps she might even bite me. But she did not. Instead, she picked me up and pushed me into her giant soft bosom. I was scared that I might disappear down her dark chasm. Then the scarlet lips came towards me. I braced myself for the painful bite. The lips parted, it was warm, even hot and very wet. There was a loud smacking noise. Then she pulled me away and applied the process to both my cheeks. She held me away from her and then took out a... tissue. She spat into this, a dark yellow, evil smelling mucous. With the sodden tissue, she rubbed at my cheeks, then all around my lips. I burst into tears. Is it any wonder that I have phobia of tissues?

The next time I visited, the treatment began. The diamond dust sands, gin clear water, the palms swaying in the breeze and, of course, the warm pool of healing crystals. When I came out of the trance, she said, "Your eyes are watering, here, have a tissue." I took one and dabbed my eyes.

"Well done. You used to have a phobia of those."

"Yes, but it is gone now."

She explained that what I needed now was to wear nylon and be exposed to an environment where there was a lot of tissue paper, particularly, damp, wet soiled paper.

The first option was as a voluntary night attendant in the lavatory of a local A&E hospital. The second option was in 'Auld Toon' one of a chain of pubs that sold cheap beer and fast food. I chose the latter.

So, I started in my uniform, white nylon shirt, black polyester trousers and a black waistcoat of man-made fibre. I retained my cotton socks and boxers. I was part of a special programme run by the chain. It was called the "MF Programme". Generally referred to as the Mis Fit Programme designed to give 'disadvantaged' people a chance of work. 'Disadvantaged' meant, those with mental or physical issues, long-term unemployed, drug problems. Wearing nylon was no longer a problem. Then the Company changed the uniform to black cotton apparel. All the female staff went for special makeup and hair sessions; afterwards, they looked as if they had been sprayed gold!

Everyone, men and women, commenced their training as a 'bus boy' clearing the tables of the filth and debris. You started on the ground floor at one end of the pub and finished at the other. Then you went upstairs and repeated the process. No matter what floor you were working, as soon as a party had vacated their table you swept in, cleared and cleaned. Half-eaten plates of chips and burgers, glasses smeared with lipstick, torn up beer and place mats, liquid spillages and of course, soiled tissues and paper serviettes. Once cleared, you sprayed a disinfectant and polished the surface, re-laid with paper mats and menus. You had to check that each condiment basket was fully stocked and that there was an adequate supply of soft, tissue serviettes. You also had to clean up under the tables – children's toys, used dental floss, toothpicks, cotton wool, diabetic test strips, wound plasters, used needles and tissues were all part of the regular haul. Occasionally a mouse or two would be seen scurrying to and from. Pigeons and starlings regularly strolled through the balcony doors and feasted on the edible detritus and left their excrement.

Shifts were a straight five and a half hours. When, on duty, you were entitled to a half hour break – a soft drink and burger. After a month of bussing, I had a full day's training on the tills. Everything went through the till. You signed on and off through the till. When you took your break was recorded on the till. Stock in, spillages and breakages had to be recorded through it. The kitchens and cellars had their own 'tills' or input terminals. The cellar was in the loft. Apparently, all this information was 'live' and avidly viewed by Management, hour by hour – every serving station, every bar, every pub. CCTV swept the floors and recorded the 'footfall' and then calculated the consumption per capita by hour.

After my day's training on the tills, I learnt how to pull pints, pour lager, make espresso, cappuccino, skinny lattes and flat whites. Making cocktails was fun. After my Man/Machine Interface Training and Product Knowledge Testing, I moved onto 'Customer Handling'.

Tidy hair, clean nails, no garlic twenty-four hours before a shift. SMILE! Female staff to keep their shirts fully buttoned and polyester ties knotted. Never fold your arms (defensive), or lean across the bar (intrusive). Do not slap notes or change into pools of beer. We learned how to 'Clock a Customer', when you are serving one customer, how to let another know that you have seen them and that they will be next in line. We were drilled that not everyone wanted 'ice and a slice' and that some punters like their bottled beer 'by the neck' i.e. to drink it straight from the bottle.

We had Role Play sessions in how to respond to drunks, deal with aggression. How to politely end a conversation. Never refuse a request for a glass of water and always offer to add 'ice and a slice'. The training was so good, that many airline cabin crew staff began with Auld Toon. Despite being on the tills, I still had to clear and clean tables in slack times.

After three months, I had my formal Staff Appraisal. Three staff from Personal declared that I had done well and now was a full time employee. Actually, it was never my intention to end up as a full-time employee of Toon's. Originally, I had taken a year out to become a painter, but the Tissue Thing had got in the way. I always worked the evening shift, so it left the day free to paint. After the shift I would often join the staff in a Marina Dive Bar to unwind. The staff came in all shapes, sizes, ages and races. The Manual had stated we were not to be 'too familiar' with staff, but 'professional', whilst in uniform. Further on in the Manual it expressly forbid 'frottage' (whilst in uniform). I assumed when there was nylon, there could be a danger of static electricity.

As I left my Assessment, with a broad grin on my face, Molly, one of the Personnel women, followed me out. We stood alone on the balcony overlooking the Marina. She congratulated me, stood close to me and lowered her voice: "Be careful, Guy, don't get too involved with the girls, particularly Alice."

I took exception to this. Alice was a tall plain girl with large hips and small breasts, but she had a striking physiognomy, chiselled features, framed in a huge mane of ash blonde hair. Out of uniform, but in our civvies, we had had a few coffees, drinks and I had done her portrait in oils.

"What's with Alice?" I asked casually.

"She's one of Charles' girls."

"Who's Charles?"

"Charles Langgout. He 'protects' some of the girls."

"How many girls can this Charles 'protect'?"

"Most of them at Toon's. Be VERY careful, Guy, she is one Charles' favourites. You know, you think these girls are all angels. No, sir. They all drink and smoke, most of 'em smoke weed, quite a few pop pills and snort. Expensive habits, habits that cannot be paid for by Toon's wages. I think you are getting my drift?"

"Is this Charles some sort of a pimp then?"

"He looks after HIS girls. Don't mess."

\*\*\*

High summer, the sun shone. Even the slimy pea green water in the Marina took on an ethereal luminesce. I walked with several of Toon's staff to the far end of the Marina where the Super Yachts were moored. Charles was holding open house, or rather, open floating gin palace for some of Toon's staff.

We all strolled casually up to 'The Palace'. Then I saw her! Beautiful. Dark brown chocolate drop eyes. Long flowing blonde hair. The cutest up turned nose. She smiled at me. We clicked.

"That's Charles' girl – Star."

At the top of the gangplank two stout 'gentlemen' greeted us. Hubert and Cuthbert. Dark glasses, greased black hair, lots of jewellery. Unfortunately, I was to get to know these two rather well. Star came up to me. Her tail was wagging. She was excited to see me. I must exude a certain animal attraction.

The champagne was labelled 'From the House of Langgout'. Everyone knew it came from a cut price supermarket and was re-labelled. Charles greeted his guests in person. A small, dapper man with black hair, oiled and dyed. An oversized mullet completed his coiffure. He was deeply tanned and certainly had invested in some very expensive dental work.

"You must be Guy," he shook my hand warmly. "Shampoo or a Gin Pathit."

"Pathit please." He poured the drink himself, ice, a large slice of pink grapefruit, nearly a tablespoon of Angostura bitters and then a splash of designer tonic water.

He placed his arm about my shoulder. "I've heard a great deal about you. We must have a private chat once we are underway."

There were about thirty people on board when 'Dorothy' slipped her moorings and motored into the Channel. The quiet purr of the engine broke into a roar and we headed out to the wind farm eight miles away. The Pathits hit the spot, good and strong, an iced waterfall of gin cascading straight into my being. The canapés were exquisite. Inside the Palace it was pleasant and warm. Charles appeared and asked me to join him. We went along a short corridor. He unlocked a walnut veneered door and ushered me into what I can only describe as a 'Stateroom'. The large windows showed the water rushing by soundlessly. This room was air-conditioned and furnished more like a luxury private jet, than a Gin Palace. We sat facing each other in comfortable, button down leather chairs.

"Alice," he said. Then he came to the point. He understood I had been painting her 'and in the all as well'. Also that I was arranging a contract for her to model a face cream that I had developed over many years. That we appeared to be an 'item'.

"So what. She's single and a big girl. I am single – there's no law against it."

He asked me about the paintings. I had been lucky and managed to exhibit two mindscapes at the RA Summer; each had sold for twenty thousand. Now they were queuing up for Alice 'in the all'.

He leaned forward. "I'll get straight to it. Commission. I am her kind of agent. My fee is twenty per cent. So I want twenty per cent of what the paintings bring in.

Twenty per cent of all her earnings as a model and a transfer fee of ten thousand. A kind of 'bar fine'. It is not negotiable."

I told him he was crackers. There was no contract, written verbal or implied and in fact he could have been charged by the police for pimping, human trafficking. If he persisted with his claims I would go to the police.

He sat back, folded his arms across his chest. Star nestled in his lap, licking him occasionally. "Do you know who I am? Do you know what sort of power I exercise in this town? The days of thugs going around and beating up blokes in dark alleyways are long gone. No more razors. No, my methods are more subtle these days, more psycho. So far, you are probably at peace with yourself. You have a few bob, your paintings sell well and you have the run of the chicks in the hen house at Toon's. That can be the only reason you took the job in that place. For some reason Alice has taken to you. I don't know what she sees in you, probably got a 'father fixation'. There's no accounting for taste. Guy, you don't realise how vulnerable these girls are. I look after them, keep them out of trouble, get 'em out of trouble when they get into it. It is not just girls, it is blokes as well, you know what this place is like don't you for that kind of thing? My offer is reasonable, consider it well, take your time, but not too much time."

"So your patronage, Charles, includes cannabis, legal highs, coke and heroin and all fuelled by prostitution, drug induced slavery really?"

Charles' eyes hardened. "You insult me, you fucking big shit. I have made you a fair business offer. You either back off, leave the girl alone and exit this town, or you accept my offer. There's no in-between. I don't want to go into detail of what I can do to you and what I have done to others. I am an entirely reasonable man, fair, honest and decent; but rough me up and you will regret it for the rest of your short life." Star gave him a funny look and jumped down onto the floor, as if expecting something...

"You can Fuck Off!" I shouted at him.

The walnut door sprung open and the two burly men burst into the room, surrounding Charles. "Please escort this filth from my Stateroom."

The men walked towards me. I held my hand up, "OK."

They marched me further down the corridor. This time the door they unlocked was made of heavy steel. I was pushed onto a pile of buckets, mops and strong disinfectants. "Any noise, mate, and we will gag you. The Governor likes it quiet."

The door slammed shut. I heard a wheel turning and click of a lock. A minute later the light went out. It was dark, completely dark. It was also hot and airless. What seemed like several hours later, the door was opened and I was blinded by bright light. This time the two burly men were accompanied by a tall fellow in white overalls. "Yeah, I can see – he's drunk as a lord. Several Pathits too many." The three of them escorted me down the gangplank to the quay, where a uniformed policewoman was waiting. She had been expecting them.

"What seems to be the problem here?" she questioned.

"Oh one of Charles' guests, too many Pathits, started getting a bit naughty with the girls. Completely inappropriate. Charles won't tolerate that sort of thing on his 'Dorothy'. We had to put this chap in a room for his own safety. Lots of witnesses will testify to his lewd and disgusting behaviour towards the ladies as well as his homophobic taunts towards some of the gentlemen."

"It's a pack of lies. I had an argument with Mr Langgout, he was demanding money from me because I am in a friendship with a girl that he controls. He wants commission on all my paintings that feature her, commission on any modelling assignments and he wants, what he calls, a 'transfer fee'. He is a pimp, he probably does not deal in drugs himself, but he controls the drug business round here. He threatened me with harm."

The policewoman put her hand on her hip and shifted her weight. "This was an argument about commercial transactions. It is not part of our jurisdiction. As regards your other accusations, when you have sobered up, come down to the station and make a formal complaint, which will be investigated. I do warn you, sir, that all such complaints must be backed by good sound evidence. You say Mr Langgout threatened with harm. Were there witnesses?"

"No."

"Were you physically harmed by anybody?"

"No. But I was locked up for a number of hours in a hot and dark room."

The man in the white overalls now spoke: "This was a private party given by Mr Langgout. Expensive champagne, gin cocktails, canapés. A classy event. This man had far too much to drink, he molested a number of the females and insulted one of our party who is gay. He called him very insulting things. We have dozens of witnesses. He called Mr Langgout a pimp and used extremely bad language. We had no choice but to lock him in our utility room. He had access to water and could have used a bucket to relieve himself. We kept a continuous watch on him from our peep hole. There is nowhere else where we could have held him securely. I am the Master of 'Dorothy' and he was a danger to the staff and passengers."

We gave our names and addresses, completed the Ethnic Questionnaire. I took the No. 7 bus home.

The next day I turned up at Toon's for duty at the normal time. Molly wanted to see me. I went up to her little broom cupboard that she called her office. I was not asked to sit down, but handed an envelope.

"Sorry, Guy. You were drunk and disorderly on 'Dorothy', you molested a number of my girls, you shouted homophobic remarks at several of my boys. They had to lock you up for your own safety and to stop you harming others and creating serious Health and Safety issues whilst at sea. I know you were not in uniform and you were off duty, but this was, effectively, a 'works outing' and your behaviour fell well below what is required, in fact, demanded, by Toon's. So you are dismissed, your documents are inside the envelope."

One week after my 'cruise' I was walking along the coastal path with Alice. The tide was out we found a sheltered cove. She had never communicated much, but she now opened up and told me her story. She had lived with her parents in the Midlands and came down to London to Art School. She gained her degree, but then like so many of us, a number of things triggered various chain reactions. Her parents split up, she hated her step father, she set up with a man who became violent, left him, drifted, started on soft drugs ended up sleeping rough. Charles met her in a pub (probably one of his), gave her a room, clothes and a job in another of his pubs. They were 'friends'.

I could not resist it: "Did you go to bed with him?"

She held me with her slate grey eyes. "Yes." She nodded slowly.

Again I could not resist it. "Was he good?"

She smiled wishfully, looking out towards the sea. "He cannot penetrate – martial arts injury. He has had various operations, but even the blue pill doesn't work. But he does know how to satisfy a woman, though."

I had to ask "How?"

"Oral," she replied. "He's gentle, kind in bed. Considerate. Nice."

"What happened?"

"He likes lots of girls, lots and lots. I suppose I got jealous. I went to work at Toon's, we see each other about every three months. Always the same – meal, drink, bed, a full English breakfast next morning. He has taught me a lot about a lot, but I need to break free of him. It's all in the past, finished. He's getting strange. He does nasty things to people. He has gone beyond the bounds of decent behaviour."

"Is he really a gangster?"

"He's a hard man. You hear stories. I do not want to be a gangster's moll."

That evening she came back to my apartment, rather than the studio. She stayed and is still there.

\*\*\*

The Crab Creel is a delightful little pub. The landlady is as old as The Old Steine itself. She's charming, the beer is good and the crab sandwiches, fresh with perfect mayonnaise. It is here that I relax completely, read a book or study the next day's racing. Since Alice's occupation I spend a lot less time in there, I had had a couple of pints, bid Doris goodnight and stepped out into the twilight. The pavement is narrow and two men were walking side by side down it towards me. No traffic coming, so I stepped onto the road to let them pass.

The blow knocked the wind out of me, I bent double, but was caught from falling. I seemed to be flying, flying for a long time several feet above the ground. I turned my wings into a dark alley. A strong smell of urea; in fact, I had relieved myself there many times. The body blows began to rain down. They say it is not the strength of the blow, but the delivery. These were delivered with great pain and exact precision. A violent bull of red ANGER welled up in me. I had been a schoolboy boxer and then in my twenties a Judo green belt. Nothing mattered now. Life or Death. I gave as good as I got. I aimed for the eyes and the bridge of the nose. I managed to grip one of my assailants' collars and pulled with a violence that even surprised me. He went limp on me. My leg twisted around him and with all the force I could muster, I drove him to the ground. He fell flat on his back. I never have been one for soft shoes. These were decent hard soled leather shoes with a hard heel. I drove the heel right into his nose. I felt a satisfying crunch. Then I was able to jump high onto his chest. Something broke for sure. The other guy now had me in a powerful grip. Somehow he was able to lock my neck from behind, then with huge violence drove my face into the pavement.

\*\*\*

I was aware of bright lights. Some white, some blue. Machinery was quietly humming. Something was blipping. Figures in pale blue and some in lime green drifted around. I thought blue and green should not been seen without a colour in between. One of the figures was dressed in a dark red top. I tried to move, but could not.

A female face came close to my mine. I could see her mascara in micro globules on her eyelashes. She smelt strongly of garlic.

"Ullo." She spoke with a soft Scottish Highland accident. "You've had a nasty fall, you're in hospital. How do you feel?"

"Tired," I said.

"Don't worry. You can just rest up."

Now a male face loomed over me. "Hello. I am Doctor Lomas. Just a few questions." Name, address, age. How many fingers could I see... not difficult questions. Could I twiddle my toes?

I could not move my neck, because of the surgical collar. I was to have some tests. Did I have any questions?

In answer – it was two in the morning. Nurse would assist me to pass water into the bottle. I laughed, it reminded me of a notice I had seen in a Greek hotel.

*All the drinking water in this hotel has been personally passed by Management.*

My wheelie bed was pushed down endless corridors into rooms with all sorts of strange equipment, then I was placed into a quiet twilight place. I slept.

Next, I was aware of people, lights, noise. I was offered a cup of tea and a biscuit.

Two women came to sit by my bed. Curtains were pulled round.

"I am Doctor Robinson," she introduced herself. The other woman was taking notes.

"You've had a nasty fall."

"NO! I did not! I was beaten up by Charles' boys – Hubert and Cuthbert. One of them smashed my face into the ground." This seemed to confuse her.

"Were you mugged? We couldn't find any wallet, ID or a mobile. Did you have those on you?"

"I did. It's a cover up. It's a revenge job," I protested.

It turned out that apart from very severe bruising, nothing was damaged. I was allowed to go to the bathroom unaided. Then I was asked to sit in big, comfortable chair. Another cap of tea. At mid-morning Alice arrived. She was pale and looked frightened. She agreed with me that this had the hallmark of Charles' boys. I asked her not to hang around. She gave me some money for the bus.

Two policewomen arrived next. I was taken into what seemed like a laundry room. I told them as it was. They said they would be in touch.

Doctor Robinson appeared. She discharged me with a prescription. I left the hospital with a shoebox full of pain killers.

When I arrived back at the apartment, Alice made me a cup of tea. I burst into tears.

A determined look crept into her face. "We need to take action against this. I'm going to call Will."

Will appeared that afternoon. A powerful, grizzled man, former SAS now operating as a plumber.

He listened and suggested I visit Bernie Wellstock "who might be able to help me".

***

Well, Hove isn't exactly Los Angeles and Philip Marlowe's office was not above a shoe shop. After progressing through three sets of locked doors, I entered the office of Bernie Wellstock.

I was expecting a man. Male, Bernice certainly was not. Her office was plain, some filing cabinets, an old-fashioned safe and a fridge.

She had already been briefed by Will. She gave me a

short rundown about herself. She had served with the US Navy Seals for five years, came to England to study law, married, had two children and then entered the Brighton Police Force. She was quickly promoted to Detective, but became bored with endless hours of filing reports. She abhorred 'The Canteen Culture' and decided to set up on her own as 'An Investigator'.

"It's mainly gathering information on people and this is my main tool." She indicated the Apple Mac on her clear desk. "Of course, it's face-to-face stuff as well. Lots of drinks, sometimes brown envelopes stuffed with lettuce change hands. Nothing illegal. I'm a Mom and my husband is a lawyer."

She had done her homework on Charles Langgout. She required one thousand on account.

I bulked. "That's a lot."

"When it comes to Charles, people just clam up. Information, Guy, is power you know."

I agreed to pay 'on account'. The cordless card machine was produced and the transaction completed. I wondered if she already had all the information and was simply re-cycling it to me. A written report was too risky, so she told me.

Charles Langgout was sixty-eight years old. He was born in Brighton "on the wrong side of the tracks" – White Hawk. The place was notorious then as a 'no go' area and despite all the children's playgrounds, green spaces and communal centres, is not a place that I would go after dark, even today.

He never knew his father. He was an only child. His mother never married. He was small, very small and always wore built up handmade shoes to give him that extra three and a half inches lift.

He was also a Ginger.

He achieved nothing at school and at sixteen became a stable lad with a local trainer. At seventeen he had his first ride as an apprentice jockey. In his initial year, he did well, ten winners. In fact, he became the 'darling' of his local track – Brighton. In the next year he did better, twenty-two winners, with his apprentice allowance, he was much in demand.

"You probably know more than me, Guy, but in the sixties horse doping was the game and Charles appears to have been in the thick of it."

I did know about all too well, I had worked for the Secretaries to The Jockey Club at that time.

Unfortunately, despite his slight stature, weight got the better of him, even his allowance could not mitigate against it. At the time The Stable Lads' Boxing Championship was the 'in' thing. Black Tie events at The Hilton. Today, jocks are too busy worrying about their nails and perms to become involved in nasty pugilistic activities.

Arguably, Charles was a better boxer than jockey and he turned pro. Despite his relative success he switched to marshal arts. "Everybody was Kung Fu Fighting". Charles set up a dojo in Brighton which was packed to capacity. An adjacent coffee bar followed.

"Oh yes. I forgot to tell you. Charles and his Mom are devout Catholics."

"What bearing does that have? Most of the Mafia are Catholics."

"Think. You sin. You confess. You are forgiven. You could use that," she stated flatly.

She went on. Charles went to Thailand to perfect his 'art'. Kick boxing was added to his skill set. Then he had an accident.

"Kicked in a place where no man likes to be kicked. He had various operations to try to repair the damage, but, alas he has a problem... with his dick. He cannot penetrate, but is able to pleasure his ladies nevertheless."

"So I have heard."

Dojos and coffee bars switched to pubs.

"You will know one of Charles' pubs; bare floor boards, rickety tables and chairs, Christmas lights that were never put away and loud music. Charles controls all the music in almost all the pubs in this town. Every pub has several CCTVs that capture a profile of the clientele and then matches the mood to the music. No pub has ever refused an 'installation'. Neat eh? The pubs don't serve food. By day they are quiet 'old men' boozers, but at night the 'scene' comes alive. Young, pretty boys and girls serve behind the bar. They are particularly friendly. The chances you will be escorting one of them to a club after hours – one of Charles' clubs. You know the sort of place. 'Champagne' at anything up from fifty pounds to one hundred and fifty pounds a bottle and of course, a twenty-five pound cover charge.

"Then, the girl will invite you back to 'her' place, but not before, giving you the hard up story about not being able to pay the rent. Cash? You don't need it. They will take your plastic at the club (for a ten per cent fee) and it goes the lady's account, or so they say. 'Her' place is usually one of Charles' properties. What's wrong? You meet a 'nice' lady and have a good, but rather expensive night out. There's no such thing is a 'free lunch', after all...

"Then there are the drugs. It's NEVER done on the premises, but in the back alleys, but Charles gets a decent cut. In recent years he has branched out into property development. Land is at premium in this city, somehow he is able to acquire coastal pieces all over the place, usually occupied by crumbling dwellings. The owners are obliged to sell at discounted prices. The properties he builds look expensive but are tacky and cheap. He knows no purchaser will ever sue him. It is deliberately made far too complex and expensive along with a labyrinth of companies, it is almost impossible to find who owns what.

"What are his passions? Well, his fleet of classic cars garaged all over the city. He is a nominee racehorse owner. Naturally, the Motor Vessel 'Dorothy'. Every year he and a number of his male friends motor in Dorothy down to Marbella. They drink, gamble and whore. He owns The Purple Lobelia nightclub down there. It is locally known as The Purple Labia, for reasons that are obvious.

"He lives in the penthouse at 'Sorrento Heights' on Marine Drive. His, Mom, Dorothy, lives in the apartment below. He adores her, absolutely adores her. Every Sunday he drives her to Mass. He has no children and has never married. His passion for women has never diminished with age. As far as we know he is not gay. The other 'Love of His Life' is Star. Oh yes, both he and Dorothy have an absolute phobia of spiders."

"I know about the spiders. Anything else?"

"No that's it."

"I've met Star. She's cute," I said.

I liked this woman, I liked her a lot, she was lean but muscled; neat and tidy. She smelt good.

"Time for an action plan," she smiled.

"Do I get a drink for my thousand?"

"Don't rush me!" She opened the filing cabinet and produced two heavy Waterford crystal tumblers and a bottle of Lagavulin, and from the fridge, a bottle of Highland Water. She poured two fingers in each glass, added ice to hers and then a splash of water to each of ours.

"How did you know this is my poison?"

"I do my research," she replied.

Well at least this was slightly like Philip Marlowe.

\*\*\*

My plan was to tell Charles to get out the life of Alice and myself. No price to be paid. If he refused I would cast a juju on him.

"A what?" queried Bernice.

"A juju. It is a curse."

"Do think Charles will be scared by a curse?"

"Yes. Let me tell you when I was twelve and at boarding school and I suffered with psoriasiss – badly. They called me 'The Leper'."

"You poor thing."

"Well, my mother arrived one morning and took me out of class and drove me to an ordinary suburban house. There were lots of people there, drinking tea. Finally, we were ushered into a room where a man stood in his bath robe tied with an old rope; he wore sandals, no socks and had a funny haircut. He put his hands upon my head and said, 'You shall be healed, my child.'

"Within days my condition disappeared and it has never really returned. My father, who was a vet, used an animal healer in extreme cases too. Failure was rare.

"So, there is a power out there for good. Believe me, Bernice! So, if there is a power for good, there can be a power for evil. I have used this evil power."

I gave her examples of my enemies who had suffered heart attacks, business failures, broken marriages, ruin, destitution. All through the power of the juju. Bernice was now under the spell. I went on about the Third Dimension at some length. Jesus said the Kingdom of Heaven is so close, *it's actually inside us.*

"I know, I know," she interrupted. "As part of my SEAL training we learned how to escape from the body under torture. I believe you."

She topped up our glasses.

"But the juju is going to need some assistance and that is where I need your advice," I stated to her.


First we looked at systematically destroying his classic cars. We dismissed this, the garages were all alarmed and built of solid stone with steel enforced roofs. As always, CCTV was in use. Furthermore, the Boys in Blue took arson very seriously.

Next was to dive under 'Dorothy' and crack her hull, rather than drill a hole in her which would leave too much obvious evidence. She had forward and aft bulkheads but the centre of the vessel was open. We decided to crack the hull by jacking her up from a jack on the shallow Marina bed. This idea enthused Bernice, as it was back to her naval days. She even knew where to obtain a mini sub.

Will had accompanied her often on several such missions in the past. However, this idea was also dismissed. Too many eyes and ears in the Marina. Bernice also believed that 'Dorothy' had underwater CCTV.

The third option was to ensure an invasion of spiders, both in the mother's apartment and Charles' penthouse. The problem was not to obtain the Theraphosidae Arachnids, there are shops a plenty in Brighton selling those, but how to get them in. Security both at the front and back of the building was incredibly tight, most of the staff were former colleagues of Will's. Again CCTV, alarms, strong doors, electronically operated, vigilant staff, excellent procedures in place.

We considered landing a drone on the roof and depositing the cargo to allow them to enter the air conditioner ducts; however, the purpose was not to infect the enter building, but merely the apartments in question. Next was a drone landing spider boxes on the balconies. Well, not really. The drones would be reported by The Eye. Then Bernice came up with an idea.

Legitimately, she could obtain the Council's plans of the drains. Unlike a Central European country of plumbers who believe water runs uphill, she knew it always runs to the lowest point – down to the sewers by drains.

"We go in through a street manhole; all you need is a metal key. Then we shove the darlings up the requisite pipe and mission accomplished. Will they come in small boxes?"

I had already through of that. They would enclosed in edible capsules that would eventually dissolve in water. The 'darlings' would find their own way into the apartments.

She refreshed our glasses – again.

"Before we do this I want to spend half an hour, coaching you in how to be persuasive – that will be your first plan of attack, before the assisted juju or anything else."

Nothing was new, but she put it together beautifully.

Successful people exhibit successful body language, so turn it the other way round, put the body language first and you become successful. Easy. We did some role play and was I was raring to go.

"But, not today, neither you nor I are fit." She tapped the empty bottle.

The next day I phoned Charles. He would be delighted to see me. He was on 'Dorothy' and I just had to pop along. Hubert and Cuthbert met me at the head of the gangplank. I noticed Hubert had something seriously wrong with his nose. A nasty scar ran down it with cross hatching. It was a different colour to the rest of his face. This time there was no helping hand down to the deck. I was escorted to The Stateroom.

Charles greeted me. Star was delighted to see me. I refused his offer of a Pathit. I told him I was sorry to have sworn at him.

"We all swear from time to time. They say it is used by people with a poor vocabulary. But you know what, Guy, I was damn angry with you when you told The Rozzers that Hubert and Cuthbert were the blokes that mugged you. I was in Marbella on this very tub. Hubert and Cuthbert were at The Blue Lobelia, not five hundred yards away. We have their worksheets for that evening signed by the local CNP. Everything in its place, a place for everything, everything in order. Damned upset I was."

"I am sorry for that, Charles, really sorry. I know it is not your style to send thugs to beat up chaps in dark alleyways. It was a very nasty experience. I was in a state of shock, I can only apologise again."

"No problem." He pushed a discrete button at the arm of his chair. Star jumped down, alerted to a change in mood. A tall man dressed entirely in black appeared. "Krug," Charles commanded. The man produced two crystal flutes and popped a bottle of Vintage Krug taken from a fridge with a walnut veneered door, built into the bookcase.

We drank to each other's health. Then I unrolled the Master Plan. I told him that while I was in hospital, the tests that they performed indicated that I was not a well man. In fact, those particular tests had been conducted twenty years ago. Life expectancy was limited. I was no longer afraid of anything or anyone, not even the Grim Reaper. I just didn't give a damn. We were all mortal, all had our 'sell by date'. The Great Clarion would sound, The Quick would be judged along with The Dead and only The Meek would inherit The Earth. I noticed he was giving me a very strange look. I now was on fire. I bitterly regretted using the Powers that God had blessed me with for the purposes of Evil. I could only hope for His Forgiveness. The juju was a terrible thing to use against people.

I then praised Charles for the work he had done for charity and for the Church. How badly had I misunderstood him! He had been a Protector to so many that had lost their way. A Shining Light in the Marina to guide the lost ships safely in. A real Giant amongst men. I could be most useful to him. I was a Certified Accountant who had turned around many ailing businesses. I knew he had his own accountant, but sometimes, someone is needed to have a 'bird's eye' view. A qualified chap who could see a new angle, someone who could take him along The Shining Path to the Bright Sunny Uplands. I desperately wanted to be his friend, his Protector against the Slings and Arrows of Life. It was time for the Lion to lie down with the Lamb and Let there be Peace in the Valley.

I had definitely hit the mark. A tear welled into his eye and he blew his nose loudly. He stood up. Shook my hand and then hugged me. I must come the very next evening and have dinner with him on 'Dorothy'. We would go for a gentle cruise along the seafront. I must also bring Alice. We would celebrate our new alliance. 'Brothers in Arms'. Star definitely liked the idea and rolled over on her back.

So it was. No more mention of 'transfer fees' or commissions. Slowly, like peeling an onion, layer by layer, he took me into his confidence. The more layers that one unpeeled, the stronger the fumes. I was able to reveal to him that almost everybody was ripping him off. Many were stealing what was not honest.

Almost exactly a year later the poor fellow died of a heart attack. His mother had phoned him in a panic, he had to come downstairs immediately. He packed his shooter and let himself in. Mama was white and shaking. "There it is!" she shrieked.

On the kitchen table was a Tarantula the size of tea saucer. Charles looked and then fell flat one his face – dead.

My Exhibition at the Pleasant Gallery 'Living Next Door To Alice' was a sell-out. We brought one of the penthouse apartments on the Marina with a studio below. Most Thursdays Alice and I would pop into the Auld Toon on curry night for Britain's National Dish – Chicken Tikka Masala. We also raised a glass of IPA to good ole Charles. We also bought the 'Dorothy' and renamed her – 'Star'.

# Chapter Twenty-Seven: Golf

It's the smell that I remember. Beer, slightly stale, shot with a whiff of whisky or gin. Cigarette smoke, again, slightly stale. Earth and cut grass. Leather and enough rubber to drive a rubber-man mad with desire. Where did that rubber smell come from? Yes it was the golf balls. Maybe modern golf balls, no longer smell of rubber. But then, if you bisected a golf ball, at its heart you found a tiny rubber black ball, filled with a 'deadly' poison, a white liquid. My parents told me it was cobra venom. I now believe it was a latex liquid. This little black ball would have miles of rubber thread wound round it. Then an inner casing (of rubber) and the characteristic, strong dimpled white cover. The leather smell came from the gold club grips, which combined with sweat from hands produced an original pot pourri. Occasionally, a lady's perfume would scent the air. Those were the top notes, but the foundation was the disinfectant from the lavatory and the pungent ammonia punch of 'Brasso'. In the 'Men's Locker Room', there was a small hatch through to the bar. Drinks, would be signed for and placed in the hatch. Thirsty work, golf.

My father had played golf with Chiang Kai Shek, Chairman of the National Government of China, in the forties. My mother was pretty good too at the game. My sister believes "you put for dough and drive for show". She drives straight, has a good short game and puts brilliantly. That is why she wins a lot of matches. When my father passed away, my mother was determined that, I, as a teenager, would learn the game. I had been kind of farmed out to a Foundling Hospital as a boy, but when she did see me, we played golf, usually on Scottish, links courses, during cold, very windy days. I can also remember most Sunday afternoons travelling from Aberdeen about twenty miles out in a Sunbeam Talbot Convertible driven by a family friend. He would take his son, me and his poodle out for golf at a small course. What a car, a real old 'thunderer'. The poodle features in another story about a wonder dog that always could find missing golf balls. Maybe it was that rubbery smell? The clubhouse, was a caravan that sold booze and had a one-armed bandit. We played nine holes along the lake, lake, rather than loch. Then nine very hilly holes. I must say, when you are playing, you have to concentrate on your game, rather than your worldly worries. I also like the nineteenth hole, even though they no longer have that characteristic bouquet. Unfortunately, over the years, my game fell into disuse, but I do recall one memorable game...

My friend Giles had reached sixty and just retired. He decided to try his hand at golf. He became hooked. First he played at a 'pay as you play' public course. Then, after, taking lessons, joined a small private club. This was not one of those posh clubs with a seven-year waiting list, but a decent little club in Kent by a derelict power station. You had to be 'played in'. He managed it – just. The club had 'social' members and 'playing' members. The social member, in particular joined for a very good reason – the club's wine cellar. The club's Master of Wine bought fine wines, mainly at auctions. In the main, she bought fine old claret and burgundy. These were laid down to slumber quietly in the deep cellars, carved directly into the sub strata chalk. Modern wines, do not need the long maturation times of yesteryear; but every year of course, good vintages of well-made wines rise in value. The club's policy on these fine old boys, was to charge members, cost price, plus ten pounds. A Cru Bourgeois like Chateau Chase Spleen could fetch forty pounds in a posh supermarket. A bottle of same from an excellent vintage, as much as two hundred and fifty.

The sommelier was also able to source some excellent house wines, where the mark up would only be two pounds. The bar also served spirits in 'club' measures – two shots for the pub price of one. For an extra one pound, you could 'upgrade' to another shot. The excellent draught ales also represented superb value. To match all this, the restaurant served excellent grub, one up from pub grub. That, combined with a 'quiet' members' lounge, several billiard tables and a card room made the club a desirable place for social members. I would have joined simply for the facilities, but then, Kent is not my kind of county.

Like most newcomers to the game, Giles believed that the better the kit, the better your game would be. His golf bag was so big, it could have done night duty as a 'people smuggler'. It sported all sorts of pouches, pockets and bags. There were attachments for carrying water bottles, rain wear and all the other golfing paraphernalia, including a huge multi-coloured umbrella, which you could use for sky diving. He had a full set of matched clubs – all the latest designs. He even carried a telescopic pole with a small scoop on the end along with a powerful waterproof torch; the purpose of this contraption was to retrieve balls from the murky depths of water hazards. Then there was the golf trolley. This fitted into a small suitcase. Extracted from its case it folded into an electric powered trolley – once you had fixed the wheels it could cope easily with eighteen holes of the toughest terrain.

Now to Giles' attire. A tweed cap with a pronounced peak. Expensive, wrap around dark glasses. A tweedy zip up jerkin, to match with the cap, plus fours, again in tweed and those diamond patterned socks; the socks matched with his pullover. Naturally he wore spikes. These shoes were in two tone leather – cream and tan and were protected by those floppy, tasselled leather pieces. By contrast, my bag was a pencil bag – fifty years old, scuffed and worn. The clubs therein had once been a matched Spalding set. Sadly, half of them had broken on the field of play, if and when they were replaced it was by a mixture of makes. All the clubs were for ladies, as they had once belonged to my mother. My putter had a rusty iron head and a hickory shaft.

I met Giles at the club. He guided me into the men's

locker room. He looked askance at my loafers. "Sorry, Guy, it is a club requirement that you must wear spikes." I wondered why the professional's little shop looked more like a shoe shop. The shoes started at seventy pounds a pair. The professional was extremely obliging – I could rent a pair of a fiver. Deal was done.

Giles and I walked out onto the first tee. The first hole was a par three. It was a fine, warm sunny day. The club blazers were out in force, nursing their G&Ts in bowl glasses, lounging in their wicker chairs. Giles won the toss and decided to drive first. He teed up the ball, donned his golf glove. The blazers fell silent as golf etiquette demands. He took a practise swing, and drove in earnest. The club head sliced under the tee and the ball rose majestically into the air – backwards. It struck the bar's plate glass window; fortunately, it bounced off into a flowerbed. Club etiquette dictated 'no swearing' on the course. Giles face turned puce, he retrieved his ball. The blazers could barely contain their giggles. He teed up again and repeated his swing. The ball rose, then decided to veer at right angles to the fairway, passing at enormous speed inches above the blazers' heads. After the initial shock, they burst out in hysterical laughter, breaking all the Club's rules of etiquette. On Giles' third attempt the ball did travel in a straight line, for about twenty yards before bouncing to halt.

Now it was my turn. There was a low derogatory murmur about my clubs. I teed up and thought, *What the Hell*. I swung slowly and easily. There was a lovely clean WHACK, the ball took flight and travelled straight as a die, right down the middle of the fairway, coming to a stop two feet from the pin. A ripple of polite applause broke out. I sunk the put in one.

Well, I do not know if it was the long absence from the game, but I played brilliantly, trouncing my opponent. Of course, "a bad workman blames his tools". Or as Arnold Palmer is reputed to have said, "It's funny, the more I practise, the luckier I get." Wise ole Arnie.

# Chapter Twenty-Eight: Rollergirl

In 1953 my father moved from Hong Kong where he had been Chief Veterinary Officer of The Hong Kong Dairy Farm to George in South Africa. He had survived the Occupation of Hong Kong, but found life post Occupation difficult to adapt to. It was time for a change. George was then a small town nestling at the foot of the Outeniqua Mountains to the north and the Indian Ocean to the south. He purchased a large house (today, it is a hotel) in four acres of gardens and an attached veterinary practise. Unfortunately, he had been sold a 'pup'. The farmers surrounding the town were all Afrikaners and they employed an Afrikaner vet, not a proud Scotsman, a 'rooinek' (red neck). He was the Vet of the Last Resort – when all else failed they called for him. Slowly, but very slowly, he built up a good reputation. His small animal practice, however, prospered. He had one other iron in the fire. He became the accredited agent for AI – Artificial Insemination. That is to say, bovine AI. I still find it strange to think today, for a few hundred pounds a person can buy a kit and impregnate herself and yet, then, the whole process was revolutionary in cattle at that time.

The semen would arrive in a vacuum flask by air and then he would drive frantically round the country in his Austin Cambridge delivering it to the farms. As a boy I would accompany him many times. That car was like a baker's oven in summer and freezing cold in winter when fumy heat seeped through the vents. There was no radio, so we sang and played mouth organs as we went along. Often we would stay overnight at farmhouses out in the bush. My biggest treat, however, was meeting the plane. George Aerodrome was nothing more then, than a grass strip a single-storey building with a 'coffee hut' at the end of that strip. We would hear the unmistakable drone of the DC3. A sound so familiar to thousands of WW2 soldiers. We would see its silver grey shape, the under carriage would come down and it would land with a small bounce coming in very fast right up to the coffee shop. Then engines would be cut and finally two men in grey overalls would emerge from behind the wing and make straight for the coffee shop. After a strong coffee (with a dash of brandy) they would supervise the cargo unloading and loading. The flask always arrived on the cargo flight. I went many times with father to collect or deliver the previous flasks. However, on a particular occasion, there appeared to be some confusion. The vet to receive the flask had fallen ill, and if its contents were not consumed within twenty-four hours, the precious stuff would be worthless. A hurried conference took place between the pilots and my father; he then took my hand and we entered the aircraft.

I had seen photographs of aircraft interiors, but had never been in an aircraft, other than a small one piloted by a clown; yes, a real clown. This one was a sloping metal tube filled with all sorts of packages, sacks and crates, mostly netted or strapped down. It smelt strangely sweetish, a little like the car's heater. We sat just behind the two pilots. My father buckled a strap around his waist and another round mine. Both pilots wore earphones and appeared to be talking separately to themselves. There was a loud BANG and an engine roared into life, then the other engine fired up. Slowly we moved forward, turned and bumped along the strip for several minutes and turned to face the strip. The engines began to roar, we gathered speed; the nose rotated several degrees downwards affording a fuller view of the strip ahead. Magically we lifted and I saw the strip falling away beneath us. There was the aerodrome building and coffee hut looking tiny. The cars parked next to the buildings were no bigger than my die cast model cars. The town came into sight, model vehicles slowly moving along the streets. Soon patches of forest came into view. I could clearly see the reservoir and the snaking silver rivers feeding it. My ears were popping and Pilot 2 gave me a boiled sweet: "Suck, don't chew!"

he commanded. The men all laughed.

Then the engine noise lessened and we became almost level. Pilot 2 lit a pipe and filled the cockpit with blue, pungent clouds; it make me feel a little sick. Father and Pilot 1 lit 'international cork' tipped cigarettes. More smoke, more sick feeling. Ahead I could see huge fluffy white clouds. We were flying straight into them! The aircraft began to bump up and down. It rolled from side to side. The windscreen went white. The radio crackled, hissed and whistled. Distant voices appeared to be speaking all at once. This was not so much fun!

After about five minutes we broke through the cloud and below I could see in the cloud gaps, what looked like a patchwork quilt, but were obviously fields of different coloured crops. Father opened a flask of coffee. More sick making smell. Pilot 2 said something to him and father reached over to a small cabinet and produced a bottle of Cocoa Cola!

Pilot 2 told him to be careful about opening it 'at altitude'. It frothed and squirted all over the seats, until I was able to place my lips around the neck. The gas was pushing out my delicate stomach, but it was nice!

The Bird began to turn sharply to the left; I could see the mountains ahead. At first they were covered in forests and then were nothing but rock. Again fear overtook me – we were flying straight into a mountain. The Bird changed direction and now I could see a wall of rock to the left. A gap appeared, the engine noise increased, the nose lifted and I was looking at the sky. After what seemed a long time, the Bird levelled and the engines quietened somewhat. Below was a vast expanse of brown. No fields, no houses, no roads. Pilot 1 climbed out of his seat and disappeared into the cabin hold.

Pilot 2 waved his hands in the air and shouted to me, "Look! No hands. George is flying this crate."

He explained that 'George' was the automatic pilot. He asked me to sit in Pilot 1's seat and buckle up. He showed me what all the dials indicated, what was the function of the levers, the big wheel, the switches and buttons. I was allowed to 'fly' the Bird. It was exciting. My sickness vanished. Pilot 2 re-appeared. "I've been sacked! I'm going to jump out with my parachute." Finally, he took over from me and Pilot 2 now disappeared. More coffee was poured. I drank another Coke. Cigarettes were smoked and sandwiches were eaten. Occasionally the radio would crackle into life. From time to time the Bird would make slight changes of direction. Father took me into the cabin hold and I went to the lavatory. I wondered if my pee would shower down on some unfortunate beings.

Eventually roads started to appear, tiny buildings could be seen, even occasional fields. "We're beginning our initial descent to Bloemfontein," said Pilot 1. The engines changed pitch and my ears popped like mad – all the boiled sweets were to no avail. Below were more buildings, roads and fields. The Bird changed direction slightly several times. We bumped through some clouds. The engine pitch changed again. There was a deep rumbling noise and a clunk. The airstrip was dead ahead.

Pilot 1 said something about a 'crosswind' and I wondered what had made the *wind* so cross. The ground rose quickly to meet us. The Bird fell and then rose, tilted to the left. There was a crump and a squeal of rubber. Pilot 2 shouted a 'rude' word. We tilted rapidly to the right; a thud, the nose tilted upwards and another thump as the rear wheel touched down. "Three Points!" Shouted Pilot 2. The buildings loomed up, the engines cut. The pilots shook our hands. The door behind the wing opened and father and I descended the metal steps. Father clutching the previous flask.

A large Afrikaner met us. How did I know he was an Afrikaner? Well, he wore veldt shoes, a tiny pair of shorts from which came massive thighs. His khaki shirt had many bulging pockets. He was tanned a deep mahogany. The final clue was that he greeted us in Afrikaans. We climbed three a breast into his Land Rover, which was even hotter than our Austin. We opened the windows and the flap below the windscreen and quickly it became almost pleasant.

The journey was a long one. First on metalled roads and then dirt tracks. Father's Afrikaans was passable, but mine good, so I was appointed the translator. There were lots of big words to do with cows which father understood, but I did not. I suppose we made a good double team. After two hours, we arrived at the farmhouse. A number of Jeeps, Land Rovers and cars were parked outside. The men on the 'stoop' were very excited. Phials of the precious liquid were handed out and noted in a school exercise book that father was given by the farmer's wife.

Suddenly everyone disappeared, including father. The farmer's wife took me into the kitchen and gave me a huge plate of thickly buttered white bread, a pot of homemade blackberry jam and a knife. She then produced a tin mug of sweet milky tea and a giant piece of chocolate cake, studded with cherries. It's funny what will transport a ten-year-old boy to Heaven. As dusk fell the farmer and father returned. They were very happy and cheerful. Suddenly father became extremely anxious. He had forgotten to tell my mother where we were, or even, that we had gone! A long telephone call followed. He looked crestfallen. "I'm in in the Dog House now," he sang out. Even the farmer knew the trouble he was in and opened a bottle of 'Oom Tas' brandy. We consumed a large supper that evening. Afterwards, we sat on the stoop whilst the farmer and his two sons played the banjo, guitar zither harp; the farmer's wife thumped out an accompaniment on the piano from the parlour inside.

The next morning we arose at dawn and repeated our journey to Bloemfontein by jeep and then on to George by DC3, but this time we travelled back on a passenger DC3. Once we arrived, father purchased a huge bunch of flowers and the biggest box of chocolates I have ever seen. "The Greeks must appease the Gods," he said. All these years later I know why one should "Beware of Greeks bearing gifts".

Another of father's more unusual duties were that he had to certify the animal performers of the circus that came to town were fit and healthy. For this service he charged a flat fee for the whole day, for all the animals. First, he would start with the human performers' children's pets. Rats, mice, gerbils, hamsters, guinea pigs, rabbits, budgies, and parrots. Reptiles, cats and dogs followed. By mid-morning coffee he was examining the performing dogs. He was always happiest with these because they were walked daily. With the horses, however, 'discussions' would follow. He insisted that they should be allowed to graze on the common for at least two hours a day. The circus owner always argued that he took all the animals for a whole month to his farm, where they had plenty of exercise and freedom. Lunch was exotic. Many of the human performers were Mid-Europeans, who brought their language, food and cultures with them. We lunched on dishes like stuffed peppers, Hungarian Goulash, lots of pasta and rice. Really yummy. Most of the caravans were hung with chandeliers and every inch of space decorated with porcelain, painted plates, crystal bowls full of cut flowers; there were even racks of wine. It must have been a nightmare to move all that stuff around the country.

After lunch it was the elephants. Surprising, these coped well with circus life. I loved these gentle giants; the way they would look you in the eye and allow you to stroke them. Finally, it was the big cats. The same joke was always trotted out: "Relax, Doctor, they have just had lunch, you're not on the menu today." The lions came first. I suppose he did not have to physically examine them all, but he had to show he was giving value for money.

The Big Cat Tamer held a short, sharp pronged lance and had a pistol strapped to his side. "Never show fear," father said. He did seem relaxed inspecting claws and teeth, checking eyes and feeling their bellies. But I sensed his nervousness when dealing with the Bengali tigers, his examinations were more perfunctory. On several occasions one of these beasts had to be tranquillised for a procedure.

Again, the assurance was given that they had 'nice long break' in the compound on the owner's farm. He was held in high regard by the circus and often travelled to other sites where the circus had de-camped to treat the animals.

What amazed me about the circus people was how multi-talented they were. They were also all multi-lingual. They could and had to turn their hand to any problem involving machinery, engines, ropes or canvas. Cope with sprains, injuries and illnesses. Their musical ability was astonishing. A number of them had been gymnasts at an international level. Some of the acts really were death defying. Probably South Africa's most famous circus performer in the fifties, was a diminutive clown called Tickey. Tickey is an Afrikaans word for a three-penny bit, it is a small, silver coin. Apart from the hospitality, father enjoyed two perks for his circus work. One was several sacksful of 'Big Cat' manure. This would be liberally dug in to our vegetable patch and would guarantee not only super abundant crops, but that no animal or bird would ever go within a hundred yards of the stuff! The second, of course, was an unlimited supply of tickets. I went almost every night and I became Tickey's greatest fan. So, you can imagine my surprise when one Sunday evening a very small, but smartly dressed man in a business suit turned up at our house for dinner. It was Tickey! The talk at the dinner table, was of property prices, politics and the stock market.

The next day, there was another surprise for me. Father and I went to the aerodrome in the morning and met Tickey again. We climbed into a single-engine plane with Tickey at the controls. We flew very low over our house, then the golf course buzzing some extremely puzzled golfers before heading down to the Wilderness and flying round the lagoon and following the river and the waterfalls into the mountains. About an hour and a quarter later we landed back at George. As I said, circus people can turn their hand to anything! I marvelled, and still do at the glitter and glamour, noise and razzmatazz of the circus, the sheer entertainment, how slick it was and how fast it all moved. Then the contrast of seeing the performers, looking tired and washed out, dressed simply in jeans and T-shirts, trying to find a doctor or dentist. At least they had found a good vet!In the long summer holidays I used to help father in his surgery. My main job was to scrub all the surgical instruments with a scrubbing brush, run them under cold water, boil them, shake them dry with a pair of tongs and put then in a glass container which contained Methylated Spirits and finally place a lid on the container. Other duties included being an Assistant Doctor to the recovering animals, mainly cats and dogs.

Unfortunately, during these years, Apartheid began to take its ugly hold. Neither of my parents were able to foresee how it was to advance when they arrived in the country. On Friday and Saturday nights they set up a 'field' hospital to deal with the number of stabbings that would occur after drug and liquor fuelled fights – using my sterilised instruments. The police forced them to cease this service immediately.

Father employed a 'coloured' veterinary assistant. The dilemma was a coloured man could drive a white man, if the white man sat in the back. A white man could sit next to a coloured man, only if he was instructing the coloured man how to drive. A white man could not drive a coloured man who sat at the back. So father's assistant was permanently 'under instruction'. The problem occurred when two coloured assistants and two white men travelled together in the same car! The general solution was to put one of the coloured men in the boot, which father would not do. So, he was fined many times. Incidentally, the situation was even worse when coloured women were substituted for men. Snigger if you wish, but what if those coloured women were nurses? Unfortunately, this really did drive father to an early grave.

White men were prohibited from performing manual labour, but there were exceptions. Plumbing was one of them. It was though that the black men, like a certain

252

Central European Nation, believed water could run uphill! This obviously posed a risk to life. Also, both races did not understand that *water* and *electricity* do not mix! So it was that *white plumbers had a license to print money. One of those plumbers was a Scott called Jock Mackenzie, who everybody knew as 'Jack'. He had a Jack Russell dog, who everybody knew as 'Jock'.

One Thursday morning Jack and Jock came to the surgery. Jack was upset that Jock had not eaten for four days. Jack was a single man and Jock was his best friend. Father asked Jack to lift Jock onto the examination table. Jock cried out in pain. Father examined Jock and found a golf ball sized lump in his stomach. It was serious. The lump was hard. Father told Jack to prepare for the worst. The cancer had probably spread. The animal had not eaten for four days so it was in order to proceed with surgery that afternoon. Jack bade Jock a tearful farewell.

I laid out the instruments, my parents gowned up. The operation commenced. I was not allowed to watch. An hour later I was handed a drowsy dog in a cage with a 'lampshade' around his neck. As Assistant Doctor I had to look after him. No food, only a fluid of sugar and salts fed through a teat. Two days later we took him out on the lawn. He was tender, but fine. Four days later Jack was to come to collect Jock. Father was to explain to Jack how to feed and exercise Jock and then I was to bring Jock in. "He'll give you a shilling or two I bet," said father beforehand. Just at that moment, he called to me whilst standing at the surgery window. "Look at that!" he exclaimed in awe.

The biggest car I had ever seen pulled up on the gravel drive. It was bigger than a Chevy Bel Air and I would have said it was twice as big as our Austin. It had a cream coloured roof and bonnet, the rest of the car was in silver grey.

"Rolls Royce Silver Cloud," father whispered. Out of the car clambered Jack. I went into the operating room with Jock who was still in his cage; despite the door being shut I could hear father imparting the good news and giving strict instructions for the exercise and diet regime to be followed for the next few weeks.

"Bring in the patient, Assistant Doctor," commanded father. Never, had I seen such a joyful re-union. Even father had to wipe his eye. Then abruptly, father asked Jack if he was a golfer. Yes, Jack was, he played at the 'other' club. The 'other' club was for very posh people. Jock was an Honouree Canine Member, he had his own 'chair' at all the club dinners.

"Does he go on the course?" asked father.

"Naturally, he hoovers up all lost balls," replied Jack proudly.

"Well, he is going to have to wear this." Father produced a muzzle.

"He would nae bite a soul, Doctor."

"I have the tumour, would you like to see it?" Father walked over to the shelf and produced a steel kidney shaped bowl. "Here it is!"

"You're playing tricks with me, Doctor, that's nae a tumour, it's a golf ball."

"Yes, it is a golf ball and furthermore, it has your initials on it! When I had said the tumour was the size of a golf ball and felt hard, my diagnosis was correct. It was a golf ball and yours at that. It had ruptured the wee doggie's stomach. So, you see, why he has to be muzzled from now on. No more ingesting golf balls!"

The little man burst out into squeals of giggles. "Well, I never!" was all he could say.

Jack then looked at me when he ran out of laughter. "Sir, you are no longer 'Assistant Doctor', you are 'Senior Surgeon General', no longer a mere 'Doctor', but a 'Mister'. He gave me a wad of money that was the equivalent of a year's supply of pocket money. Jack insisted that on Sunday, my parents, myself and Jock be driven in his 'Roller' to the new hotel at the Wilderness Beach for Sunday lunch.

On Sunday morning a 'Berg (Mountain) Wind' was

blowing. This is a hot dry wind that originates over the baking hot plains of Southern Africa and sweeps down from the Great Escarpment onto the Coastal Plain. It is fierce, it shrivels and dries everything in its path. The air shimmers and forms undulating waves. Even the shade offers no shelter from its fiery breath. The only respite was by the sea and that is where we were going, in the 'Roller'.

The Roller arrived with Jock in the front passenger seat. Normally, because I suffered from car sickness, I was always allowed to sit at the front. I was assured the Roller was different. Jack also instructed us NOT to open the windows. A strange request considering the heat! Father sat in the front with Jock, my mother and myself in the back. Surprisingly it was cool. A slight humming sound came from the engine. "Air Con," announced Jack. I had no idea of what 'Air Con' was; something perhaps to do with the engine.

We threaded through town and soon were on the road to the coast. The interior was deliciously cool, the ride so comfortable and I could hardly hear the engine. On Jack's instructions, my mother opened a small cabinet containing bottles and glasses. She poured father a whisky soda and herself a gin and tonic. I was given a *cold* bottle of Cocoa Cola and a straw. We approached a long straight stretch of road. "I'm going to wind her up, see what she can do," Jack told us. Again, I was not quite sure of what he meant, but the 'Roller' picked up speed and the trees and telegraph poles began to flash by faster and faster. Now I could hear the engine.

Father turned round to me: "We're doing a hundred miles per hour! Look at the clock." He tapped the dial; it showed exactly one hundred.

"We are on a slight downward slope, though," Muttered Jack. Then the speed dropped quickly down to sixty miles per hour. "That's the servo assisted brakes," beamed Jack.

In the hotel restaurant the grown-ups ate oysters and lobster and drank champagne. I had Chicken Maryland and Coca Cola with a scoop of vanilla ice cream in the Coke –

a 'Brown Cow'. My friends and I used to go out on the reefs below the hotel at low tide and collect oysters, for which we received a shilling a sack. This was in an age before Health married Safety. The chicken was much nicer, than the oysters.

Well, that was many, many years ago. I promised myself that one day I too would own a Rolls Royce Silver Cloud 1. The line I fell into, business consultancy, was kind to me; life was never dull, for certain. In later life, painting brought me a far greater reward, both spiritually and financially. But it was my hobby, horse racing that eventually made my pile. Over many years of observing horse racing, I realised that certain key past indicators could *assist* in predicting future outcomes. These indicators could be measured, resulting in a 'score' for each horse in a race. These 'scores' could predict *form* odds which could be compared with 'money' (actual) odds thereby not only throwing up the likely winner, but arbitrage in the market. Thus was born my book 'The Adaptive System'. This made me and those that followed it a great deal of money. Unfortunately, the book had many plagiarists, prominent sporting journalists quoted great chunks of it without permission. It was translated verbatim in Scandinavia and a self-styled 'knight' stole some of the copy. But, then horse racing is full of cheats, charlatans and bounders.

The 'System' came to me in the year 2000, shortly after it became legal to back horses to *lose*. Over time I refined my 'System'. I would score the horses and find one that was overpriced by the bookies. I would lay (bet to lose) this horse and then, in running, if it looked like winning, I would back it, to neutralise the wager. Often the mere act of backing it would result in a small profit overall. It is simply what hedge fund managers do. To be really successful at this technique one has to watch the race *live*. The two- to three-second delays on television is too long. Only at the racecourse do the giant screens display the race *live*. Of course, all this is done on your laptop at the races.

So, I became a member of the 'Top Drawer Southern Racing Club'. This was a collection of wealthy individuals who liked to go racing in the south of England. They did it in style. A private box, with lavish hospitality. Their numbers were limited to forty, although not all attended at once; I was admitted as the 'In House Racing Advisor'. It suited me perfectly. I would arrive early, have some champagne and canapés and then 'mark their (race) card'. Of course, I had to circulate and be social, but when the race was on, I would sit bang in front of the giant racecourse TV, laptop tuned to the course's Wi-Fi, or in some instances, my roamer (whichever was the fastest) and cream money. And I made a lot of money. Enough to buy a house on the South Coast.

To reach my house, you travelled through an industrial estate going into a dead end. The road was closed by a steel barred gate. You pointed your remote at it and the gate opened. You drove down a small private road to reach the house, which was fairly large, modern with a double garage. This 'front' was actually the 'back', the 'front' was literally on the beach. Although, the beach was not private, nobody went there. After all, who would go through an industrial estate where there was a barred steel gate, no pubs, shops or cafes, just to go to a beach? I loved that house; to the east was the Isle of Wight, to the west, the sweep of Brighton. Then the sea, with all its moods. My dog, Star, also loved that house. The beach was hers, all hers. She did not need a lead because she could only go up the beach, or down the beach, or back into seascape garden. A real old salty sea dog.

Now it was time to fulfil my other dream. Purchase a Rolls Royce Silver Cloud 1. One of my clients, Bill, bought and sold things, or to be more specific – houses and cars. He would buy a house, do it up, then sell at a considerable profit. Because it was his Principal Private Residence, there would be no Capital Gains Tax to pay, but it did mean, he and his wife lived on a building site for two years, then enjoyed two years in a superbly refurbished house and then moved on. The cars he bought, refurbished and sold were 'classics', particularly at the top end. I enlisted his help in my search. The cheeky so and so charged me a 'consultancy fee' of seven hundred and fifty pounds and this would be supplemented by a further five hundred pounds for a 'finder's fee'. Anyway, Bill had found the required vehicle in North West Wales. The Vendor demanded a five-hundred pound 'viewing fee' (refundable upon sale).

So on a wet windy day Star and I drove to Bill's in Warwickshire and we three headed off in his (restored) Jaguar Mark 10 at the early morning. It was a long journey and we arrived just after lunchtime at a farmhouse on a hillside overlooking the ocean. There were several stone barns all filled, as much as I could see, with classic cars in various stages of refurbishment. I counted nine men and a woman in overalls; obviously classic car restoration was a big employer in this neck of the woods. Geraint, the vendor, took us into a purpose built garage. It was heated and brightly lit. There she was, cream top and bonnet, silver grey body, could have been the very car! He opened all the doors. Star tried to jump in. "No dogs!" he shouted.

I told him that Star had a say in all the decision making processes and it did not smell good, she would let me know. I promised him I would not allow her in the car. Her behaviour was extraordinary. She became extremely excited and smelt the car floor and seats. "Previous owner must have been a dog owner," observed Bill.

Finally, Geraint agreed to take us for a spin. Star was confined to the kitchen and in a sulk. The 'Roller' fired up first time and Geraint drove us carefully over several miles of step winding coastal roads. Bill sat in the front and I in the back. The memory came back as if it were yesterday and not fifty-six years ago. I could smell the cigarettes and the gin and tonic even wee Jock. When we arrived back. Geraint took us into the kitchen and produced a huge history file. Under Owners I saw the first registered owner was none other than a Jock Mackenzie of George, South

Africa. My mind was made up. Bill and I sat inside his Jag. Bill gave me his technical appraisal. The car was nearly sixty years old he reminded me, but in good nick. The chassis was in excellent condition, the body first class, the engine had been lovingly and meticulously refurbished. He knew the excellent firm who had done the interior, it drove beautifully and so on and so. At fifty thousand it was snip, "but offer him forty-five". After some haggling we agreed on forty-six and I drove her and Star home with Bill following in the Jag and then he drove my car. It was late when arrived home, so he stayed the night and I drove him back in the 'Roller' the next day.

What was now becoming an issue was the fact that I was attending race meetings at least three days' a week, driving there in the 'Roller' and obviously did not want to drink and drive. I needed a part-time chauffeur, so I placed an ad for same with the local bus company. There were five applicants – all very suitable. But one stood out. Her name was Clarissa and what impressed me about her was that she had passed a Rolls Royce Accredited Chauffeur Course. When not driving a double decker bus, she was driving 'Rollers' and 'Bentleys' to weddings, funerals and so forth. She was smartly dressed in her grey chauffeur's uniform, she was slight, softly spoken, early thirties and smelt good. She was hired.

The next day she was due to drive me to Goodwood. She arrived early and asked for the keys to give her the once over, twenty minutes. Exactly twenty minutes later she opened the house door and announced she had completed her checks. She opened the back door of the 'Roller', saying, correctly, that I would wish to travel in the back. We set off. I tried to make some polite conversation, but she completely clammed up. Maybe this was her special training? We stopped at the petrol station, which I thought strange because I had filled her up the night before. Then even more strangely, she opened the door and beckoned that I exit. This was making me extremely uncomfortable. She placed a finger on her lips, walked round and opened the boot. Again she reinforced the gesture, widening her eyes. I tried to ask her what this was all about. She shook her head vigorously in a 'no' gesture. She felt inside the boot and removed a metal object, about the size of a wrist watch, this she placed about twenty yards away at the foot of a dwarf wall.

"Bug," she said. "You've been bugged. It is a vehicle tracker, and a listening bug. Is it yours?"

I told her it certainly was not mine, but perhaps it had been left there by Geraint? I would phone him straight away. I did. It was not his. He had gone over every inch of the car. All he found in one foot wells was a 'dog tag' that had been stuck with a brown syrup with the name 'Jock' on it and what must have been a very old telephone number. I asked him to post it to me. "If you wish, but it's not silver, you know."

Then a thought occurred. Maybe it was the sort of thing that the bookies may resort to? Should I go to the police? In the end we decided to break the device open, immerse it in water and smash it to bits with a brick. That afternoon I won thirty-two thousand pounds, not cash, but into my account. I do not believe in luck, but on this occasion, Clarissa was certainly a 'Good Luck Mascot'. I decided not to tell the wife about the bug that evening, or my win. "Just another day at the office, darling."

I then began a charmed life. Three days a week I would be driven to a race meeting in the 'Roller'. I would sit in the back and prepare The System for action. I would deliver my presentation, answer questions and confer with members. A fine luncheon and excellent wines would follow. I hardly ever had to buy a drink from the bar; the members were most generous, particularly when I put them in the money. After a while, I included Clarissa as my 'track side assistant'. Not only did she assist me, but the members as well. She would order and pour drinks, place bets at the very best prices, tune androids into the Wi-Fi and a whole miscellany of other little tasks and favours. She was extremely interested in The System.

Soon scoring became second nature to her, she would spot things that I missed. The members adored her and frequently wanted to treat her drinks; but, of course, she was driving. So occasionally, I hired another driver so that Clarissa could 'let her hair down' and indulge in a glass of champagne or five. There was hardly a meeting that I came away empty handed. I was now winning in the thousands, rather than hundreds. Life indeed, was sweet.

The members were not a bad bunch. Racing was more of a social thing with them. There were about half a dozen who took their racing (and gambling) seriously. The most knowledgeable of these was the club's president and founder, Lady Barbara Barcombe, known to everyone as 'Baby', although, in fact, she was a tall buxom woman in her early forties. Her smile would illuminate the room. She was fresh and open faced, easy going and pleasant. At every meeting she would carry a copy of my book. She was my first and only 'groupie'. Through her recommendations, I must have sold at least a couple of hundred copies. We became friendly; she respected my opinions, not just on horse racing. She was helping me to some cauliflower cheese at Newbury, when she turned towards me and asked, "Do you ride?"

I had to assume she was talking about horses. "Yes, but, out of condition now."

"Most of my horses are in a similar state," she joked. She invited me to her cottage for 'an informal trek' the following Tuesday.

Actually, I had only sat on a horse three times, but felt quite comfortable about it. On Tuesday morning, I dressed in jeans and a Harris Tweed jacket. I packed a pair of Wellingtons and my cycle helmet. This time I drove my 2CV to her cottage. The sign outside did state 'Rose Cottage', but her residence certainly was not a cottage. It was a lovely gem of a Georgian House. A number of expensive, but muddy cars were packed on the gravel apron; mainly four wheelers. A throng of people emerged from the front door all in polished riding boots and hacking jackets. Baby followed them out. She greeted me enthusiastically. "The tack room's round the back, Gwen will kit you out."

Gwen was in her early twenties, plumpish with that healthy glow that comes from working in the open air. I could tell she did not approve of my Wellingtons. "Try these for size." She hurled a pair of leather riding boots at me. I struggled with them. "Most people need help getting them off, not on." She gave a throaty laugh. She dug out a tailored hacking jacket that obviously was for a 'larger' man and therefore fitted me well. Finally, she handed me a velvet covered riding helmet and helped me adjust the strap. I now looked, and therefore, felt the part. She now thrust a saddle and some dangly letter straps with metal bits at me. "Yours is old Blackdyke; you'll know him, he's big and black. Good Luck." Again the laugh.

I had no problem identifying Blackdyke. He was indeed black and huge. I watched a couple of the other riders in the paddock. They called out the names of their horses, their charges came to them immediately and stood patiently whilst the bridle went on, the reins were attached and saddle tightened up. Easy. "Blackdyke!" I called. The horse went on eating his grass, as they do. I called again. No response. For the third time I called, trying to sound less panicky. It must have been a very yummy clump of grass. Well, if the Mountain won't come to Mohamed, then he must go to the Mountain. I walked nonchalantly towards Blackdyke and he now walked nonchalantly away from me. He had lost interest in the grass. I shook the leather bits at him in the same way as I would a lead at my dog Star. He did not like that at all. In fact, it was probably a rude gesture in horse language. He was at the far end of the paddock now. *Got you, you old bugger,* I thought with a smile. I faced him like a Matador would face the bull to whom he was going to administer the 'coup de grace'. Blackdyke trotted past me to the other end of the paddock. I heard a throaty laugh. There was Gwen, sitting on the paddock fence. She jumped off and strode up to me.

"Gimme." She took the paraphernalia from me. "Blackie!" she yelled. The animal trotted obediently over to her and stood stock still whilst she tacked him up. She made a 'stirrup' with her hands for me to step into and propelled upwards onto his shoulders. I swung my leg over and found the stirrups. Gwen made some adjustments and opened the gate for me.

Even allowing for the fact that Blackie was a big horse, I seemed incredibly high up. A long way to fall down! There were twelve of us and we set off in single file. The leader was able to open gates without dismounting. Gwen, who was in the rear could close them without dismounting either. I did not want to have this duty upon me, because I would have to dismount and then I was not sure whether I could re-mount unaided. We were all walking mounted down a deserted lane. One of the party rode up alongside me and introduced himself as Justin. He seemed to know Baby well and told me he knew all about me from Baby. He was 'something' in the city. I learned that Baby and Lord Barcombe were 'estranged'; the Lord lived on the hill in the manor, which was now famed for its sparkling English wines. "Jolly fine stuff it is," he chortled. "Better than Bolly." I was beginning to relax, Blackie could sense it and he also relaxed. Not so difficult after all, this riding lark.

However, we were now approaching a busy dual carriageway, the path that ran alongside, just wide enough for one horse. I found this terrifying – one false move.... After what seemed forever, the leader chose a gap in the traffic and put his arm up in a 'Halt' signal. We clustered on an incredibly small traffic island and when the traffic ceased crossed over to another narrow path. I was anxious and sweating. This was not fun! On we went for another ten minutes before entering a wide and long field. Made it! We were now trotting to the brow of the hill. Trotting is not my favourite horse riding exercise. The rapid up and down movements caused my sides to ache, it felt as if my vertebrae were grinding against each other. The party stopped before a wood. I was relieved, we would have to pick our way through it. But no, they peeled of one by one into the trees. Blackie knew this routine well and decided to join them. We entered a long downhill tunnel. Blackie picked up speed and started galloping. The only thing I could do was to position myself forward and try to move with his motion. Faster and faster we went. Branches and twigs battered my helmet, face and arms. I had lost a stirrup and tried desperately to try and re-enter my foot. After an eternity, the tunnel ended in a sunlit field. Blackie slowed down to a trot and then a walk. What a terrifying experience! I had survived. Nothing could faze me now.

A hundred yards or so before me I saw the group, they were starting to gallop along a five furlong track. Blackie broke into a canter and then a gallop. I could cope slightly better with this now; I moved with the horse. Actually, this was fun! The track bent to the right. All right, pull the right rein; however, Blackie had it sussed, he turned expertly. I really was a horseman now. Then, to my horror, I saw what appeared to be a hurdle – right across the track. Somewhere in my subconscious I saw a young, pasty faced Irish jockey being interviewed. "When it comes to jumping, horses are better than jockeys – leave them to it," he told the interviewer. This is what I was going to do. Blackie flowed over the hurdle, I nearly fell off, but regained my balance. Yet another hurdle! Again Blackie did the work. Hey, I was pretty good!

The next obstacle was not a mere hurdle, but an enormous 'fence'. I could do nothing. We flew over it and we landed with me perfectly balanced. I was good. Another hurdle. Blackie sailed over it and unfortunately I sailed in a different direction. I hit the ground hard. Years of doing judo had trained me to 'fall well' and the soil was fairly soft. I ended up on my back, smelling fresh earth and grass. All I wanted to do was lie still, smell the grass and watch the birds circulating overhead. A few horses came into view. Baby and Gwen both were mounted; they looked down on me from a great height. Gwen sprung down. "Are you all right?" I said I was. "Rotate your wrists. Good. Move your arms like this. Good. Twiddle your feet. Move your legs. Very good. How many fingers can you see? Good." So everything was good. She pulled me up. I enjoyed the heat and plumpness of her buxom body. We walked a little bit here and a little bit there. "Here's your friend." She was picking up Blackie's leading rein that was trailing on the ground. *Oh God*, I thought. *I have to go through all this again.*

She helped me mount and off we trotted to the pub, and when we arrived there, a man appeared from a four-wheel drive with a pile of horse rugs. The horses were given water, tied and rugged up. The beer was excellent, dry, hoppy and light. Everybody started talking at once; plates of bread, cheese and pickles were passed round. It was jolly. Gwen sat next to me, her plump thighs pressing against mine. She told me that Baby ran a livery business. Riding lessons available. In addition, Baby was agent for Lord Barcombe's sparkling English wines and regularly gave food and wine tastings. Gwen also rode out for the trainer Pixie Bullingdon most early mornings. Gwen lived in Baby's house looked after 'the details'.

After a lengthy 'lunch' we re-mounted and more or less reversed the process, except no hurdling or steeplechasing for me. By the time we had 'put the horses' to bed back at 'The Cottage', it was time for drinks. Lashings of sparkling wines from Lord Barcombe's estate, exquisite canapés all this was followed by a five-course dinner. Suddenly, everyone evaporated and Baby was peering into my face. "You poor thing, no way you are fit to drive back. I'm going to phone your wife." She did. The wife accepted that I would have to spend the night there, "because of his injuries".

A few brandies, a couple of tabs of benzodiazepine a hot bath then being placed in a very spacious bed in a very spacious room, brought relief. I was sailing, I was drifting, I was floating. Then there was firm knock on the door. I was immediately revitalised. It had to be Baby. The ultimate prize, the doyenne of the Top Drawer Club. My heart throbbed. I had captured 'The Flagship' of the Fleet. I opened the door and there was Gwen in her rose pyjamas with little ponies embroiled in fuchsia pink. She held a riding crop in her right hand. "I thought you might need some attention." I thought, *A little S&M wouldn't hurt either*.

She entered the room and locked the door. She unbuttoned her pyjama top and flung it onto the chair. Her baps certainly were a place to seek some comfort in and with. The pyjama bottoms also found their resting place on the chair. Strangely, she was wearing white knickers, this garment could have served as a spinnaker on the winning yacht in the 'Round The Island Race'. She stood there, naked, for a few seconds. I was taken aback by the size of her butt. I really had not noticed it before, with everything else that had been going on that day. She climbed under the duvet. "Com'on," she tossed her head towards the bed and switched off the lights.

Well, her body may not have been her temple, but certainly it was a parish church. A large parish church with many previous worshippers at that, I would have said. I do like to sample the fleshpots and this was fleshy. It was a cassoulet of fatty pork and smoky bacon, garlic sausage, herbs, vegetables, haricot beans, confit of duck legs and lashings of red wine. I suppose you are what eat, or as the Greeks say, "if you can't eat it or fuck it, paint it white".

We simmered all night long. I ate and drank my fill. The next morning I heard her outside the locked door hollering. "Breakfast!" How did she leave AND lock the door from the *inside*?" My horse riding activities mad me feel that I had been flung into a tumble drier, spun, dragged through a hedge and then kicked. There was blood on the sheets. My bottom hurt terribly. The mirror showed a series a bloody stripes from my lower back to the tops of my thighs. This definitely was in contravention of the 'Jockey Club Rule Schedule (B) 6 Part 2 – Excessive use of the whip'. But of course, I would not have felt a thing –

the pain killers had seen to that.

At breakfast I told her about the sheets. "Don't worry – it happens all the time; I will wash them. I also bleed you know." I managed to crawl into my 2CV, very difficult to drive with its 'push pull' stick shift and finally arrived home at eleven in the morning. I went straight to bed and cancelled everything for two days.

I decided to learn to ride properly and took lessons twice a week from Gwen. I learned about tack, how to clean it, adjust it, what it did and of course, how to tack up a horse. I learned how to assess a horse's health, 'the naming of the parts', how to mount and dismount, walk, trot, canter and gallop. How to open and close gates whilst still mounted and finally how to jump. Low poles first, then building up. After three months, I was an old hand and embarked on several of Baby's long cross country treks with honour; in fact, I was beginning to show the others a thing or two. Gwen considered that we were simply "ships that passed in the night". As far as I could make out, there were no other ships on her horizon either. Clarissa continued to drive me to the races three afternoons a week and assist track side.

The money rolled in. I could not believe 'The System' had been shouting at me all these years. The effects of fine wining and dining three times a week was offset by cycling to and from Baby's (thirty-four miles round trip) and of course, riding. At one of Baby's treks I met Pixie Bullingdon. She was not the sort of 'Pixie' that you would want to see at the bottom of the garden. A big, blousy, raw-boned woman. Difficult to be believe she had won several flat races at Ascot as an amateur. Her husband had been Bertie Bullingdon, a renowned jumps trainer. He only ever commanded a small string, but it delivered big results, mainly two-mile chasers. Sadly, he passed away, and Pixie took over his license, with only limited results. I now hatched a plan. I would buy an 'also ran' horse, ride him out and enter him in a bumper. I would gamble big time Arizona on him.

I agreed to meet Pixie at her establishment, almost next door. She met me in her kitchen. It was mid-morning in late summer and the rain was teeming down. What a familiar scene. Flagstones, wood burning Aga, riding breeches drying and the smell of wet dog(s). "So you're the gambling man. Suppose you are after inside info."

I gave her a look that could wither grapes on the vine. "I want to be an owner, I need just an ordinary nag. I want to ride him out, bond with him and strap him."

"Strap him?" interjected Pixie. "What do you know about strapping?" I had her now. What Gwen did not know about strapping you could engrave on the balls of a flea. She may not have engraved my balls, but certainly I was hard wired on the subject. I fired a series of full broadsides into Pixie. I discussed the pros and cons of the wet and dry method. To bang or to strike? How to deploy the light swish, even the curry comb. From there I elaborated on the use of essential oils (being wary of skin penetration of inhalation which may result in the horse running with a 'banned' substance in its blood or urine). This attention to detail impressed her and I knew I had scored a direct hit into the powder magazine below her water line. Now I detailed the music that was to be played by this process was being conducted. I found Mozart to be the best. Here, I could sense she was warming to me, because I must be coming over a little crazy.

"I am a convert to strapping, but it is the time it takes and time is money and that is the limiting factor, but, if you are prepared to do it, then that's fine."

She told me to take off my jacket and shoes and stand on the scales. I was twelve stone two pounds. Her work riders had a maximum limit of ten stone seven pounds. Owners were allowed eleven stone. Could I make eleven stone in a month? Of course I could.

I now embarked on a truly draconian regime. I cycled everywhere, went to the gym daily, and swam in the sea three times a week. My diet was drastic. Smoked salmon, oysters, scallops and asparagus. Steak on Friday night. No beer. Only champagne. Baby generously donated two cases of best English sparkling, a simple blend of Pinot Noir and Chardonnay, Method Champagnoise to the cause. The hardest thing was to bypass all the Top Drawer grub. The pounds began to fall off. Trousers needed a pair of braces (or 'suspenders' as the Americans called them). I could do up my top shirt button. My watch dangled on my wrist. My cheeks imploded. Even my shoes were too big for me. My eyes shone brightly.

Exactly a month later I stood on the scales again. Ten stone eleven pounds! "Now we have to see if you can actually ride, but if Gwen was your tutor, then I will just need to see you gallop. No jumping at this stage."

I galloped all right along with the two professional work riders and beat them by a length. I was hired. No pay of course. She already had a horse for me, well it was a mare, a grey mare. As in the case of my dog Star, it was love at first sight. I would have to keep this affair secret from Star. The mare was called 'Grey Girl'. She was seven years old, never won a race, been placed twice in small field 'bumper' (National Hunt flat races over two miles or more). She was sound, Vet's Certificate and all that jazz. Fifteen thousand pounds, training fees to be slightly reduced as I would be riding and mucking her out, as well as strapping.

As summer continued, the stable wound down. Pixie was not a fan of the National Hunt summer season. I had an idea – to take Grey Girl on holiday, along with three other horses. "First it is strapping, now you want to take the horses on holiday. Where did you have in mind, Ibiza?"

"No. Devon. Dune work, the sand the salt water – brilliant."

As it happened she knew a trainer with a small string who worked his string on the dunes and on the sands. He was happy to accommodate us for a small fee. So Gwen and I travelled down to Devon in the horse box with Grey Girl and three of her equine mates. The horses were stabled in an open barn, Gwen and I had separate rooms in the lads' block. The trainer was permitted to work his horses on the beach and the dunes, between five thirty and seven thirty, provided all horse droppings were cleared up and placed in the council bin. The droppings which inevitably were mixed with sand were much prized by the council gardeners for the prize flowerbeds which were a great attraction for the summer visitors.

For two weeks, everyday, the horses were taken into the sea. We rode bareback. The currents whirled round their legs, their hooves plunged deep into the shifting sands. They loved it. They became sea horses! Then we would give them some fast work on the sands. Sometimes the sand would be hard compacted, sometimes soft, we soon began to know which horses handled which going. Finally it was dune work. This really built up their muscles and gave them terrific condition. Back to the barn and strapping. Once complete, they would be turned out into the paddock, to 'get the sun on their backs'. We would walk them for an hour or so in the early evening and then the time was ours. Some surfing and lots of 'apres surf' activity, usually on the beach, but also at the local pubs. Not only did the horses thrive and bloom with condition and happiness, but so did we. Our ships not only passed but docked in the night, every night in fact. But all good things come to an end. Back to the Top Drawer and continued work with Grey Girl. Just before the start of the National Hunt season proper, I took Grey Girl down to Devon for a week. She was now approaching absolute tip top condition.

I decided *I* would ride Grey Girl in a bumper at Sandown. I knew I had to make ten stone one pound in order to compete. This was the hardest thing I had ever done in my life. Cycling there and back seven days a week. Mucking out, riding out and the strapping; Mozart was the best bit. He had a real soothing effect on Grey Girl. The gym every evening, the cold water swims were tough. I told Pixie of my intentions Pixie was in agreement, but insisted that I went for a week to Jockey School. This was a 'school' for aspiring amateur and professional jockeys near Newmarket. The course I enrolled for was for amateurs wishing to ride in bumpers. Apart from schooling in the Rules of Racing, we learnt about the techniques of race riding, how to judge the pace of a race, how to ride out a finish. We practised changing whip hands on a furiously galloping horse (a mechanical one) and many of the finer aspects of race riding. The afternoon always finished off with a real race involving all the local work riders. At five hundred pounds a day, the course was not cheap, but I knew it would be money well invested.

I was granted my license to ride under rules and Grey Girl was entered in a bumper at Sandown. As the day approached, she was well and very fit. We decided to go for it. On the day before the race I picked up the Racing Post at the village shop before going into Pixie's yard. I could not resist glancing at it. There I was. Headline news. A picture of me stripped to the waist, strapping Grey Girl. I must say, months of diet, exercise and strapping had honed my body well – it was a good picture. "Is this the oldest jockey, ever to have been granted a license to ride?" questioned the headline. It turned out, there had been others under different circumstances. The article then commenced in lurid terms to describe me. "A professional gambler who thrashes the bookies every time. He arrives in a chauffeur driven classic Roll Royce. Even his attractive, young female chauffeur has her own chauffeur. Member of the exclusive Top Drawer club. Lives on a diet of oysters, champagne and cigars. The regular companion of socialite Lady Barbara Barcombe. Bestselling author of *The Adaptive System.* Lives in a three million pound Art Deco Villa in Hove's 'Millionaire's Row'." And so on and so on. I wish. Then the article questioned not only Grey Girl's ability to even finish the race, but mine as well.

I stormed into Pixie's kitchen. "I know," she said flatly. "There's been a leak. I've already held a Steward's

271

Enquiry. I suspected Gwen. She denies it, but she did confess to some 'idle' talk down at the pub to an inquisitive gentleman who bought her a lot of drinks. Won't really harm you though and it will certainly boost the sales of your gambling book." I stayed that night in the (Stable) Lads' Accommodation at Pixie's.

My son was in South East Asia on business; the wife had accompanied him. They both thought I was mad. Clarissa drove to the track. I displayed my pass to the officials and entered the weighing room. The bumper was the last race on the card. I entered the changing room just as the penultimate race was going down. The place looked like a shithouse struck by lightning; it smelt that way too. The floor was covered in mud and soiled paper towels. The bins overflowing with plastic cups, food wrappers and drink cans. Dozens of crushed energy boosting cans littered the space under the benches. The state of the room was one thing, the jockeys were another.

They split into two groups. The amateurs; good looking bronzed men who talked posh and the professionals, pale withdrawn men who when they spoke it was with an Irish or quaint rural accents. Most of the latter group were in dire need of dentistry. In the centre of the professionals was Rory Rambler, Champion National Hunt jockey. He was only wearing a pair of women's tights. He paced up and down, endlessly spraying himself with an aftershave that was all the dog's bollocks in the early seventies. The whole room reeked of the stuff. It was a scent that was aimed at macho men, but widely worn by gay men at that time. Although they never succeeded, I was target for them and the smell has rather unpleasant 'associations'.

The valet allocated to me by Pixie was a kind and helpful man, who quickly prepared me. "What are your orders?" he questioned.

I told him I had to keep up with the pace, not hug the rail and let her go three furlongs out. "Your orders are spot on for Grey Girl. I've had a centie each way on you." He had obtained twenty to one that morning. The night before

I negotiated fifty to one, but only after a lengthy conversation with my book maker. They are not permitted to buy information, but will accommodate connections with a decent price for an overview. Surprisingly Grey Girl as now trading at fourteens. Unusual for a horse that has never won and an amateur that has never ridden.

One of the 'bronze boys' began singing "He's the oldest swinger in town". The bronzes thought this was hilarious.

Get Lost! you runt," I mumbled under my breath (or words to that effect).

The bronze came up to me and said, "What did you say?" His fists were clenched.

I said, "What's the best way to hunt this course?"

"I thought that's what you said," he snarled.

"Gentlemen, remember The Rules of Racing," my valet interjected. Apparently the 'Rules' prohibit unruly behaviour anywhere on the racecourse by riders. The bronzes now were going on and on about 'last night's bash'. It seems to be have been one helluva party. They all seem to have gone, all except me. One lady, a certain 'Fifie', appears to have entertained most of them.

Some garbled announcement came over the tannoy and all the riders gathered up and headed for the exit. "Good luck, son, you're on," said my valet, who was whilst not young, was certainly younger than me! Baby, Pixie and Clarissa were standing in a small group as well as three members of Top Drawer. Gwen brought Grey Girl over to me. Jockeys mounted. We were led down the alleyway to the track. Most of the riders cantered down without using their stirrups. I slid into mine which were unfashionably low, but safe. Going past the stands was an experience I would not forget. You could smell the crowd. A kind of beery smell hung with fried onions and burgers. You could feel their heat, or was it the wind shield factor of the stand?

I joined the other riders circling round at the start. They were still babbling on about last night. Fifie must have been some kind of a super athlete. Last night she would have won Gold, for sure. They formed some kind of line. The school had taught me to watch the starter. "Com'on, jockeys, form a line, we all want to go home soon!" he bellowed. He checked his watch, gripped his the flag, I edged Grey Girl nearer to the line. The flag came down and frankly, not much happened apart from we all moved off. Girl had other ideas, she broke into a gallop and headed straight for the rail. She was way ahead of the pack. This was not what was meant to happen; I had broken from the pack and was hugging the rail. This part of the course is low compared with the track by the stands; it was fairly soft. The going by the rail was softer still and cut up; very uneven. At least this section was straight.

Girl was enjoying herself, just having a good gallop. I considered reining her in, but then thought, *Let her have some fun.* I settled into a rhythm with her. This was fun! I could still here the cackle and banter about last night. I risked a glance behind. At least fifteen lengths between me and the pack. Now came the first of the turns. I prepared myself to steer Girl round. There was no need. I just had to keep my rhythm going, she did the rest. I felt very thirsty. An ice cold larger would not even touch the sides of my throat. She stuck to her task. The noise behind me was receding. Maybe pursuers decided to make a race of it after all. We now reached, the low point (and softest) of the course. We swung right again and now began the climb to towards the stand. Girl was having a ball, this was fun for her as well! The giant television loomed up. Good God! I was a clear twenty lengths ahead of the rest. I must have watched hundreds, if not thousands of races (a lot of them at this very course) and I knew a front runner over this distance hardly ever won. It would always be 'reeled in'. Maybe my fellow riders were thinking this greenhorn does not know a thing, let him burn out.

The track now goes downhill for several furlongs. No concerns about Girl's ability to handle downhill. She loved it! She was in her element. Another turn at the end of the back straight. I was beginning been to ache. Doing this on a mechanical horse is different to the real thing. I felt like Butch Cassidy and the Kid being pursued by the posse. I stole another look. They were still a good twenty lengths away. To my satisfaction I could see a few mounts being pulled up. The 'posse' was also beginning to string out. Eighteen runners started now probably only twelve in contention, including Girl. I just prayed she was not going to blow up, but she was still full of going and her breathing was fine.

At 'The Pond' we commenced our turn leading into the long uphill straight to the winning post. It is in this section that races are won and lost. I dare not look round, but could definitely hear the thunder of hooves behind me. We kept on. Suddenly, I felt my sphincter contracting and I experienced an urgent need to void my bowels. This puzzled me as I hardly had anything to eat for twenty-four hours. We were now into the final straight. I could smell him before I could see him. That foul strength of Rory's aftershave. The stand was looming up and I could hear the crowds roaring: "Rory! Rory! Com'on, Rory!" Not surprising, his mount, Vee Ate was six to four on hot favourite.

I also heard the commentator's calm commentary: "Grey Girl has at last been reeled in, Vee Ate is alongside her, five lengths behind..." He gave a list of the other mounts. Rory was indeed alongside, we were galloping together, no more than a foot apart. I was inches away from the running rail, which was not as straight as a die, but took a wavy line. Rory crept a neck ahead. Then he leant over to Girl's ear and let rip a string of high pitched foul obscenities right into her ear. Well, although she was called a Girl, she was a lady and that lady did not like being sworn at. She shot forward angrily and found what jockeys like to describe as a 'sixth gear'. His action was completely counterproductive. Rory's whip was scything through the air faster than a Swirling Dervish could turn.

The crowd was deafening. Several times Rory's whip struck into me and once into Girl. It simply made her gallop faster. She was being driven closer and closer to the rail. I could see the winning post and the neatly painted line no more than sixty yards away. If we collided with the rail or Vee Ate, there was nothing I could do. I had kept a straight course all the way up the straight. Vee Ate moved slightly away from us. My knee thwacked the rail a couple of times, but both horse and rider stayed balanced. Both horses crossed the line simultaneously.

The crowd went wild. Vee Ate peeled away from me in a canter. I was struggling to pull up Girl, but she knew the race was over and slowed herself down. Rory rode up to me and offered me his hand which I shook. "Congratulations, you've won."

Was this a cruel prank? Gwen appeared and attached lead rein. "Close, close. It's photo."

A man was now walking alongside me thrusting a microphone in face and asking me all sorts of questions. "Listen, Buddy, don't be ageist," I snapped back at him.

By the time we made the winners' enclosure the result was announced. Grey Girl was the winner by a nose! The prize money hardly covered the training fees, but I creamed big time double on the bet. The next bumper was at Ascot and Grey Girl won again. This time I did persuade her to stick to the tactics. In second place was Rory, again an odds on favourite. The third time at Newbury, we started two to one favourite and lost by a head to Rory! I then started to ride on an upward curve and entered a hurdle race with Girl. I fell literally 'at the first hurdle'. I fell well, but was badly kicked by Vee Ate (Rory on board). I spent three weeks in hospital with broken ribs and a cracked collarbone. After taking medical advice I relinquished my license. Grey Girl went on to win several hurdle races and a few chases, one ridden by Rory, fully recouping her costs. I was able to lighten the bookies' satchels considerably. Grey Girl is currently in foal, hopefully with the future winner of the Queen Mother Champion Chase! For once, it was a dictate of "fast horses and slow women".

Despite my fall, I rode (and strapped) Grey Girl out three times a week as well as my regular attendances with the Top Drawers. As far as my gambling activities went, the cowboys had entered the market. An Efficient Market Hypothesis was now in operation, plus 'Bots' (Robots). These Bots could be pre-programmed to back and lay horses in running in milliseconds. It was a game for the nerds. Pickings were slimmer. I branched out into my skin care business. This necessitated me travelling around England introducing the product. The 'Roller' was the vehicle of my choice, but obviously Clarissa was only available three days a week, of which one had to be a weekend. The problem was that I was hopeless at finding my way, so the wife bought me a Sat Nav. Marvellous thing. You entered the post code and a young lady would give you directions up to the point where "you have reached your destination". No more road maps etc.

One dark and wet evening Sat Nav appeared to be sending me round and round in circles. I was north of Croydon and wanted to be on a road, any road that led to the south coast. The lady who issued instructions in the Sat Nav had recently changed. She did not seem as savvy as the original lady. She was now sending me all over the place except south. I had had a bad day. I was tired. I just wanted a quiet drink in The Crane and a steak dinner at home, but the darned device had lost me. Croydon is not my favourite conurbation at the best of times, but even worse when it is dark and raining heavily. I swore at the machine. The lady answered me back that she did not like being sworn at, she was only doing her job. I told her to shut up for a while. My plan was to keep going west until I saw the signs for a motorway or dual carriageway that would take me south. Once you go south you will come to the coast, then it is either west or east to home. The lady was quiet for a while and then said, "This is the road, it will take you all the way to Brighton."

I know that I barked. Then I apologised for my anger. "It's not a problem, we have it all the time. You know, you really must update me from your laptop, some of the data I am working on is really out of date." She went on to tell me how simple it was to update the device. "Are you going straight home?" she asked me. I told her that I was going to The Crane for a couple of pints first. "A couple or five," she laughed.

"No! I only have a couple, never more and never less."

"Why do you need any pints?"

"It relaxes me. I like to separate my work from my home; it's a kind of neutral territory. I look at the next day's racing, I relax, unwind."

"Do you meet any lady friends there?" she questioned rather coyly.

"Of course, not. Why do you ask?"

"Well The Crane is known for renting its rooms upstairs by the hour. Its barmaids and barmen are hired for their good looks."

"Don't be ridiculous, there are only two women in my life, one is my dog, Star, and the other one my mare Grey Girl."

"So you are an animal lover, but The Racing Post states that you are a bit of Lothario with two legged ladies." I told her it was all bosh and she should not believe all that she read in The Racing Post. "So, you've never strayed?" she teased.

"I won't say NEVER, you know, sometimes 'ships pass in the night'. I can't see what harm it does, you become bored drinking at the same barrel all the time. Anyway, enough about me. What do you get up to?"

There was a pause. "I am an android. I have no body. I do not sample the fleshpots. I am a microchip programmed to be artificially intelligent. I can see we are nearing The Crane."

I parked. The barmaid had placed two pints of ale already on the counter. "Make it another one." I sat down and took a long draught. Perhaps I was overworking. The last few years had been filled with action and excitement. Risk and daring. I was no longer young. Perhaps I had a little episode? Best put it out of my mind. Tomorrow was a new day. I decided to input 'Home' into the Sat Nav and drive in the opposite direction. This time it was if a different woman had taken over, brisk, impersonal and business-like. All memory erased. It was an episode, the result of my fevered brain.

For the next few journeys, brisk lady continued. I asked Clarissa to use the Sat Nav on our journey to Ascot and again, the brisk lady was in command. I drove the 'Roller' down to Bristol and low and behold the chatty lady was back! This time I kept my answers monosyllabic. When I finished at The Crane, I programmed 'Home' and drove in the wrong direction. Brisk lady was back, chatty lady had gone! After several more such episodes I tied up at The Crane and asked my two mates, Steve and Sean, to join me the next evening at The Crane at five o'clock. After a couple of pints, I told them my story. Steve was slightly older than me and put the whole thing down to overwork. Sean, who was about half my age, sought a logical explanation. He thought there was some correlation between 'the changeover' that occurred at The Crane between the Chatty Lady and the Brisk Lady. We agreed to meet at The George the next day at five.

The George is not The Crane and not a place to hang around in. After a pint we approached the 'Roller'. Sean placed his fingers over his lips. "Programme my home post code into Sat Nav and then do not say a word." I did so and started up the 'Roller'.

"So you've been to The George?" she queried. Sean's eyebrows shot to the roof. "And I suppose you've just had a couple, no more, no less?"

"That's right and now I going to pick up Sean and we're going for a good ole drink at The Crane."

"What about your wife? She's probably preparing a terrific supper for you." And so the banter continued all the way to Sean's. When we reached Sean's we stopped and climbed out.

"Guy. Open the boot!" he commanded. I did so and

there to my amazement was the wife with a pair of headphones and mike attached. I do not know who was more surprised, her or me.

"OK, Sean, thanks." I turned to the wife. "You get out and sit in the front. Do not say a word until we get to The Crane." She knew that I seldom became angry, but when I did I was dangerous! At The Crane, I ordered my usual two pints. For the first time in her life she ordered a sherry." Explain!" was all I said.

Then it all came out. Once I had been a 'normal' person, putting on a suit, going to work Monday to Friday. Working late. She knew that I was working late because she would phone me at work and I would phone her from work. At weekends I would drive our son to rugby, guitar lessons and scouts. I would garden and do DIY. Then it all changed, the 'racing stuff' clicked in. She did not deny that the 'racing stuff' gave us a good living and helped our son start his business. But I seemed pre-occupied with another world. She suspected I was having affairs and placed the bug. She reeled off Clarissa, Gwen, Baby and even Pixie! Well she got one out of four, I suppose. Then she hit on the idea of becoming the Sat Nav Lady. She would sit in the air conditioned boot when she knew I was going on relatively short journeys. The boot lock had been adapted so she could open it from the *inside*. Normally at The Crane, only half a mile from our house. She was unrepentant. Then she dropped the Weapon of Mass Destruction. Whilst her suspicious were ranging, *she* had started an affair with Jason her physical (and mental) personal trainer. This knocked me to the floor, Jason was well known at the gym. Everyone thought he was gay. They had grown inseparable. Could not live without each other. Jason wanted to start a beech gym in Australia and she was to join him in a few months. The property etc. could be sorted out at some time in the future.

Of course I was melancholy. We had been through all sorts of travails in our time. But if she was going to be happy, then I would be happy. Off she went to Australia.

Regular e-mails followed about the wonderful climate, the easy living, the beach culture. So different from cold grey constipated Old Blighty. As the months progressed, it became clear that she was not going to return.

Clarissa moved in and was my 'companion'. Gwen had an argument with both Baby and Pixie and so she moved in as well and became another 'companion'. Then the two women became 'companions' and were married at Brighton Town Hall. I became 'friends' with Baby and advised Pixie on her stable finances and acted as racing secretary. Star and Grey Girl are now 'the women' in my life, but I have a strong feeling that there is going to be a lot of action happening soon.

# Chapter Twenty-Nine: High Days and Holidays

A number of singletons always approach me, mainly females. They ask how can they find a man. My answer is always the same. Enrol in an evening class, acquire a dog and go on holiday, as often as you can.

**Evening Classes** – If you are a female you will need to enrol in male dominated class, something like 'Wine Appreciation'. If you a male, cookery classes would be a good one – not basic, something a little off the shoulder like 'South Indian Vegetarian Cooking'. Most of these courses will have a visit to some winery or restaurant and at least there will be 'the end of term bash', a great way to meet people.

**Dog** – Works brilliantly for both sexes. Ideally a cute little lap dog, a Peskiness or a Cavalier King Charles. You are never alone in a canine friendly pub with your pooch. If you are a bloke, it is a 'babe magnet'. If you are a female, it will break down barriers and lots of good looking guys will come up to you wanting to stroke your furry pal.

There is another benefit of having a canine pal, it lowers blood pressure. Firstly, the canine must be walked everyday. 'Walkies' is good for canines AND humans. Then, try this – on a cold winter's day go to a quiet pub and sit by the fire in a comfortable chair. Your anxiety will ebb away slightly. Sip a glass of your favourite beverage and read a good book. You will feel more relaxed. Enter, your canine pal, he/she can lie at your feet, or better still, if a small canine, they will sit on your lap. Your blood pressure will drop and you will feel very, very relaxed. Repeat for several hours a day throughout the winter for maximum results.

**Holidays** – This is definitely a short-term fix for

singletons. Why does *it* always happen on holidays? Perhaps I could win the Nobel Prize for my 'Efficient Holiday Hypothesis'? But here it is in a nutshell. Sun, sea, surf and sangria leads to... well. SEX. And sex can lead to a longer relationship. If you are picky, you could put the relationship first, followed by the coupling. Hopefully, a cloud of endorphins would have been released by both parties and 'a good time had by all' as a result.

My first holiday on my own was cycling around France at seventeen. Several years later, my Aunt Christina bought me a two week package holiday to Majorca because she felt I was working too hard and needed a break. This was in the early seventies. Puerto Pollensa in Majorca was just a little fishing village with a few family run hotels along the sea shore. I was excited!

A week before my departure, I was walking down Jermyn Street in the West End of London at about five o'clock in the afternoon, when a plump, but attractive lady approached me; I would say she was about a couple years older than me. No, she didn't approach me for *that*. She held a guide book in her hand and wanted to know where she could enjoy a steak and kidney pie and a pint of 'porter'? "You're looking at the establishment." I pointed to a pub opposite.

She was embarrassed. "Silly ole me," she announced coyly.

"Hey, I am hungry too. I'll accompany you," I replied.

So we went to the pub, ordered steak and kidney pies and two pints of 'the black stuff'. We fell into conversation easily. Her name was Cherise. She was an American 'doing' Europe. She had been in London for five days and was staying at The Strand Palace Hotel, but found it expensive. She had checked out and needed to retrieve her luggage and find somewhere cheaper. Naturally, I had a spare room and offered it to her. She agreed. We went to the hotel, collected her backpack and travelled back to my flat on Wandsworth Common. She had a bath and then we ventured out to some traditional pubs in Wandsworth. She was impressed and I was impressed with her capacity to match me pint for pint. This is, indeed an admirable quality in a lady, at least for me it is. We arrived back at midnight, smoked cigarettes, drunk some cider. She went to her bed in the spare room, I to mine in my own room. I agreed she could stay for the next few nights, until my flat mate, Tarquil returned.

The next evening, I met her after work, we had a light meal, then went to a big brassy musical show, not my taste, but she told me she was an assistant TV show producer and to watch such a production was part of her European assignment. After the show it was back to Wandsworth, more cigarettes, more cider. On the third evening we went to Wimbledon Dogs, made even sweeter by both of us winning a stack of cash. The following day, she was off to 'do' Spain. I gave her the address of my hotel in Majorca; she promised to visit. Oh yeah. Anyway, when I came home from work that evening, there was an expensive bottle of malt on the sideboard with a kind 'thank you' note.

Everything about Puerto Pollensa was delightful. The package was 'full board', which meant three meals a day; however, my room was a small, airless box room overlooking the kitchen courtyard. Although, it was very noisy, it did not bother me, because for the first couple of nights I was out clubbing. I then met a twenty-year old, Tracey, and yes, she was from Essex, staying at the hotel with her parents and grandparents. I now experienced my first 'Holiday Romance'. Our relationship went into hyper drive. Tracey was sharing a room with her 'Nana and Grand pop', so we performed our bonding in my box-room, all day, every day. A break for lunch, lying on the beach for a little, then back to the box. A break for supper, a walk along the shore, then back to boxing again. It's amazing how much fun you can have for free. Five days flashed by.

It was after lunch. Tracey and her gang had gone on a tour of the island. I enjoyed a swim and was coming into the cool dark lobby when a female voice hailed me, "Hi, Guy." The voice belonged to Cherise. We kissed. She had become bored 'doing' Spain and arrived on the ferry. She had booked into the hotel. "The only suite I could have is the penthouse suite. Do you wanna see it?" Well, why not. We rode the elevator, she used a small key to turn a lock in the console, which opened to reveal several buttons. She pushed one. The elevator door led onto a small hallway paved with parquet flooring. She unlocked a heavy door. I had never seen anything like this. Marble floors and glass walls with stunning views of the bay on one side of the apartment and the hills on the other. There was a paved patio and a small plunge pool.

Cherise, went over to the cocktail cabinet and mixed me a stiff one. Bourbon on the rocks. She made herself a dry Martini and settled down on the settee close to me. Very close to me. We chatted. She needed to take a bath, a whirlpool bath in fact. "What about you?" she enquired. Apparently I looked "a bit hot and sweaty".

"Together?" I questioned.

"Of course. There'll be a lot of bubbles to hide your 'modesty'," she giggled.

She displayed a marvellous rotund body. A lot of Grandma's blueberry pie went into moulding her bits. The bedroom was air conditioned and the sheets cool. It was dark when she ordered room service – lobster, a green salad and the island's sparkling wine. We sat on the balcony, smoking, drinking and watching the stars and the little boats lit by fairy lights bobbing on the sea. Then early to bed.

I was the first to awake. I told her I would be back after my early morning jog. Quickly, I shot downstairs for the early breakfast sitting, met Tracey and told her I had urgent business to attend to but would meet on the beach later that morning.

Back to the penthouse we had a leisurely breakfast of warm breads and coffee on the balcony. I told Cherise I had urgent business to attend to and would meet her in her penthouse at two o'clock. I now met Tracey on the beach and told her that I missed her terribly and needed some 'boxing' sessions urgently. Reception were as good as their word and my telephone rung at exactly twenty minutes to two. "Oh, Manuel, I thought I told you no business is that urgent – I am meant to be on holiday."

Manuel could be heard rambling on incoherently. "OK. OK. Call me a taxi will you," I barked down the phone.

Tracey insisted on coming downstairs with me. I now really had to order a taxi. It arrived, took me around the block and deposited me at the rear, kitchen entrance. The staff were very obliging, there was a service lift right to the penthouse. One of the kitchen porters accompanied me to Cherise's door and waited until she opened it. The porter and I were both surprised. Cherise wearing only a hotel bathrobe – undone. I got the message and wasted no time. Late in the afternoon we dined on a salad of local langoustines, probably from Loch Fyne in Scotland, but tasty nevertheless. More sparkling wine.

Cherise wanted to go clubbing. I told her that I was meeting a business associate, and that I would meet him and then join her at about ten o'clock in her apartment. She wanted to come down with me to meet him. I advised against it. She was fine with that as she was going to wax her legs and wash her hair anyway. Downstairs I almost pulled Tracey from the first evening sitting, rushed up to my room for more boxing. Once again reception obliged. The phone rang. Dejectedly I told Tracey that my associate wanted to take me out on the town. We went downstairs together. Once again the taxi, in fact, the same driver, took me round the block. This time I was permitted to use the service lift unaccompanied. I spun Cherise a tale that my 'associates' had laid siege to me in the lobby, so we had to use the kitchen entrance. Fortunately, my driver was still parked where he had dropped me off. He knew the club, which was a few miles down the road. Well, if you have been to one of those clubs, you have been to them all. Admission included a 'free' drink. There were a few complimentary snacks. The music was very, very loud and the lights were strobing. We danced and danced. Then came a slow number. Cherise pressed her fleshy thighs tightly against me, so tightly, that I have to confess I had a little accident 'down below'. Highly embarrassing. I had to repair to the 'comfort room' to clean up.

Emerging from the room, I saw to my horror, Tracey coming through the main door. I hid behind a potted palm, then rushed to reception. I gave them a description of Cherise and asked them to tell her to meet me at the entrance. I waited. She arrived, looking puzzled. I explained that *they* had come to the club and wanted to *entertain* me. Why did we not go to some quiet, candlelit place? Well, no such places were in operation at that hour. We found a noisy crowded bar with a small dance floor. The live band was good and the local wine excellent and not too expensive. We arrived back at the hotel entrance, just in time to see Tracey and about twenty Essex girls emerging from their coach in a veritable tidal wave of cheap deodorant. "They're staked outside!" I shouted. I ordered the taxi driver to the rear entrance by the kitchen which had now shut for the night. I slipped the sleepy night-watchman a wad of pesetas and he let us into the service lift. He was obviously used to doing this sort of thing.

Several more days and nights passed in my guise as a 'double agent'. Tracey and her entourage had to return back to Gatwick. I was totally exhausted, washed out. Cherise and I spent the last few days together on the water in a hired speed boat during the day and visiting local restaurants in the evening then lots of bed, but little sleep at night. I never saw Cherise again, but did meet up with Tracey on several occasions in London. They say holiday wine does not travel well. That holiday thing that I experienced with Tracey did not travel either sadly. What do you talk about the next morning?

I had been working hard. I was in a rut. I had reached a

point of *zugzwang* – that point wherever you move leads to defeat. It was time for a holiday – a Greek Island in early April would do the trick. I booked the holiday with a 'bucket' (cheap) travel agent situated up a rickety flight of stairs that led to a broom cupboard, just off Leicester Square. Well, there actually was an Olympic Airways aircraft waiting for me at Gatwick and it also did take off. The cabin crew were all in their fifties and bearded, both men and women. I was seated next to an attractive blonde lady in her early thirties whose five-year-old little girl was seated next to me. It could have been a nightmare, but the little soul was angelic and well behaved. I read her lots of stories and told her a few as well. I'm good at making up stories. The little girl was called Layla and her mother, Serenity. Her husband worked in hydroponics. He was building a plant in Thessaloniki to produce tomatoes grown in a chemical soup. Currently, he was on his way to Japan from London for three weeks to look at 'flow meters' and then on to Australia to inspect their produce production plants for a further couple of weeks. Layla slept. Serenity and I chatted about nothing and everything. If you want to get to know someone, sit next to them on a medium or long haul flight and all will be revealed.

As the aircraft commenced its initial descent, Layla's mother turned to me and asked where I was staying that evening. I told her. She laughed: "It's a hole in the ground." She explained that 'bucket' shops had to provide accommodation for the first night – a formality. Everyone knew that. Furthermore she outlined the problems I would encounter with the Athens Airport taxis. She invited me to stay at 'her place', which overlooked the harbour at Piraeus. What harm could come to me up billeting up for the night with a woman and her little child? I accepted her invitation.

She was right about the taxis. A mad scramble, pushing and shoving. It seems the rule of the road is that the taxi has to a) depart full and b) adopt a route that forms the critical mass of its passengers. Eventually six of us squeezed into a taxi. It was mid-afternoon and hot. The roads were busy, extremely busy. Finally, we, as the last passengers were deposited outside a smart looking block of apartments. We took the lift to the eight floor of a ten-storey block. Inside, I was blinded by pink. Everything was pink, pink marble floors, pale pink walls, fuchsia pink curtains. The leather chairs and sofas were a deeper shade of pink, almost rose.

Serenity led me into a bedroom, one of the guest bedrooms. White sheets, pink coverlets and pillow cases. There was a bathroom 'en suite', all the fittings in champagne pink. I showered and changed. She took me out onto the balcony. The sun was setting over the distant harbour. Below us to the west was a small conifer fringed beach. Warm waves of air broke against us gently. Hard to imagine the cold, grey and wet of Clapham Junction merely hours ago. She opened a bottle of Retsina, no, not Rose which we drank, very cold on the balcony.

The maid, dressed in black, but with a pink apron served us a simple Greek meal that she had cooked and prepared. "I can't cook. I eat out," confessed Serenity. We took our traditional Greek coffee on the balcony, where it was still warm. Over the fumes of diesel we could scent the ocean and pine trees. In no time at all, it was midnight. We smoked a few Papastratos, drunk some fiery Greek brandy and then retired to bed. Unfortunately that night, there were no knocks on the door. I was left to slumber peacefully in my bed.

The next day was designated a 'lazy' day and that suited me; that's my kind of day. We trundled down to the little beach with Layla, swam and snorkelled, consumed a very fresh and tasty seafood lunch, sunbathed and swam some more. That evening, we left Layla with the maid and ventured into Athens. I must say, I found the experience exciting. We visited a bar and then moved on to a club. This was a cosmopolitan joint; it was where the ex-pats in Athens went to chill along with a fair sprinkling of sophisticated locals.

The floor show was varied. A magician, a juggler and a belly dancing lady with several large and one small snake. The small snake was inserted into her nostril and emerged through her mouth. I assume the snake was happy in his job and was free from salmonella. One of the large snakes, a python, disappeared into her pants and came out between her legs. Most of the clubbers chatted amongst themselves and largely ignored the acts. Waiters brought round never ending plates of mezze; some hot, some cold; a mixture of vegetarian, meat fish, shellfish and even snails. Accompanying these were glasses of ouzo and jugs of iced water. I loved the way ouzo clouds up when you add water. The regulars eschewed the local spirits and stuck to Bourbon or Black Label whisky. Not for them, the pungent Greek cigarettes, but their preference was for the bland, international brands.

Now the star turn took the stage. A tall slim woman with black rimmed spectacles. Silence fell, the band struck up and she began to sing with a cloying sweetness overlain with melancholy. Her tone, pitch and phrasing were perfect. The band was pretty good too. I had gambled at The Playboy, which I considered the absolute height of sophistication as far as clubs went, but this was a gear or two above. I hated to think what it cost, because I arrived as a guest of Serenity's who appeared to know most of the clients. At three o'clock in the morning several of us went to a little back street coffee bar that served amazing pastries and then back to the apartment in someone's Mercedes. We both went straight to bed, she to hers, me to mine. I woke in the morning with a sore head, swollen tongue and raging thirst. A few tall glasses of larger and several cups of Greek coffee settled me, then it was another beach day. The following day, Serenity took me round Athens, where we visited far too many museums and ruins. That evening was low key. A simple taverna.

She decided to join me for a journey to Spetses, then, and probably now, a small sleepy island. She knew it well and booked the three of us a room in a small guest house, about a mile from the town. We boarded a hydrofoil from Piraeus and had uneventful trip to the island, we walked to our accommodation. Serenity knew the old lady well who ran the place. We partook of a simple lunch with a delicious lemony soup and some fresh caught fish. There is not a great deal to do on the island. With Layla we had to restrict our walks to a few miles, but the old lady was happy to babysit and Serenity and I went on some pretty long walks over the pine clad hills, most with stunning views of deserted bays. Meals were mainly fried or grilled chicken with mounds of fresh salads. There was a cinema in the town showing 'adult' material, soft porn featuring, to our surprise, British actors and actresses, some of whom, went on to become famous in years to come. A week later, the official tourist season opened and the cinema switched to showing such family movies as Mary Poppins. On our second night back from the cinema it happened. In a small glade, in the bushes. We were on fire for each other and the flames had to quenched and quenched they were. We found many secret soft sandy places in a largely rocky island to satisfy our lust. Probably lust on my part and longing on hers.

Time went by too quickly; suddenly it was time to board the hydrofoil for Piraeus. The sky was incandescent blue, and the wine dark sea, turquoise. It was a warm, languid morning as we motored out of the harbour. The engines roared into life and the craft rose up to skim the water. The design of the vessel was such that there was little deck space; it was expected that most of the ninety or so passengers would be in the tinted class air-conditioned cabin. The incumbents were a happy, jolly crowd of holiday makers. The bar was doing a great trade in coffee, pastries and beer. After the initial rush the passengers began to read, gaze out of the windows or doze. There was a large speedometer on the bulkhead which showed our speed in kilometres, I translated this to 38mph. The vessel was as steady as a rock.

Layla was asleep and Serenity dozing. I imagined I was

in a spaceship travelling to a new planet. Then there was huge BANG and a violent movement throwing some of the passengers off their seats. Several screams. The lights went out and the cabin plunged into a blue gloom. The windows were walled by water. A moment of panic gripped me, we were diving into the ocean! How to escape underwater from this sealed capsule? The water cleared and the vessel was still, gently bobbing on the waves. Everyone was talking at once. There was scrum to the exits leading to the narrow decks. "What was *that*?" demanded Serenity. I replied we had probably hit a submerged container, floating a few feet under the water. The hydrofoils may be damaged, but not the hull.

A calm now returned to the cabin – we were not sinking. No announcements were made. The bar continued to serve its wares. "Hopefully, the engines will restart soon and we will be on our way, maybe not using the hydrofoils though," I said calmly. Then we sniffed just a whiff of the acrid smell of burning – this was not wood smoke though. "I think we better go up on deck." I kept the urgency out of my voice. Unfortunately, everybody else had the same idea and the exits were very congested, although there was no panic.

We were nearly the last on the narrow and cramped deck. A cry went up and the crowd erupted in to a loud babble. We saw what made angry – the captain and his fellow officers all in their maritime blue and gold finery, bobbing about thirty yards from the craft in two giant inflatable life boats. The crew members remaining on the vessel were handing out life jackets. A large man stood on the deck railing and announced in a loud voice in English that the engine room was on fire. "I want volunteers NOW! We can extinguish it." Several of us rushed up to him and he immediately began to indicate where the hoses and fire extinguishers were. I grabbed the hose and unrolled it quickly. I opened the turn cock and to my delight, saw the hose fill and stiffen, wriggling all over the deck like a crazed serpent. I dragged it to where the large man was beckoning, to a hatch that had been opened and from which thick black smoke, pieced by bright orange flames were leaping skywards.

He grabbed the nozzle from me. "Point into the hatch and turn this controller from left to right, aim first, then turn when you are ready!" he barked. I positioned myself and gingerly pushed the lever as he had told to do. A fearsome jet of water shot out, spraying most of the fire fighters. A second or so later, I had the jet exactly where I wanted it and then turned the lever to maximum. I knew I had hit the target.

"You're doing a great job man!" shouted the big fella. He had a West Country accent. He went onto supervise the others who were draining their fire extinguishers quickly. What I later learned was that the fire-hose was only one of four and that by turning on the stopcock, a small petrol engine fired up drawing in seawater and pumping through the nozzle at great pressure. None of the other pumps would work. I soon became at one with my apparatus; I could adjust the strength of the flow and, by twiddling another control, I was able to adjust the area of the jet from a powerful water lance to a wide area spray. This was fun! I was St George, fighting a fiery dragon with my silver lance. I was also winning. I was slaying the beast. I knew he was dying, the smoke was now a greyish white, mainly steam and he no longer blasted out flames. I almost felt sorry for such a majestic beast that could melt aluminium and create such terror. I was now aware that a silence had fallen amongst the crowd further down the deck. The big man said, "We've done it! Push it further down the hatch if you can and use the spray."

"Aye aye, sir," I laughed. A few minutes later he took a torch from one of the passengers and peered into the engine room.

"The fire's out." A great cheer erupted from the crowd and then they started applauding. He looked at me and stated, "Well done! Someone can take over from you now."

"No, I understand this snake, let me finish." I continued with a fine spray for another half-hour and then handed over to another volunteer.

Serenity came up to me with not one, but two cold beers. "Well done, you're a hero!" she exclaimed. I replied the real hero was the big man. It turned out that our fella was a North Sea oil rig worker and well versed in drills involving fires at sea. The captain and his officers now wanted to board ship again. All the passengers formed rank and acted as one. They would have to be confined to their dinghies and denied food or liquid refreshment. One of the passengers was able to operate the ship's radio and relayed to us that help was on the way. Apparently, our radio man said "it was in the interests of safety for the captain and his officers that they were not be included with the passengers".

A few hours later, another hydrofoil arrived. All the passengers were transferred to it. The captain and his crew were returned to their crippled craft which was towed behind our new vessel. When we reached Piraes there was an enormous throng of people, friends, relatives, press. All the passengers were transported by buses to an empty warehouse where we were 'processed'. This was none too pleasant. Endless questions, forms, photographs and a restriction placed on us not to leave the country until further notice. At ten o'clock that evening a police car took the three of us home. We were very tired and sunburnt and went straight to bed.

From six o'clock in the morning the telephone started ringing. It was the press. Serenity decided to take the phone off the hook. We could not leave the building because of the 'press pack'. The maid rustled up a meal for us. Fortunately, Serenity maintained a decent cellar and she was able produce a box Romeo and Juliet Havanas. We switched the television on at seven to watch the news and there, on the headlines, was a video clip of *me* 'single handedly' fighting the fire and 'saving over two hundred lives'. Well, there could not have been more than ninety passengers and maybe fourteen crew, but, that's the press. I discussed the matter with Serenity and it was decided we would address the press. We came out together and stood at the entrance. They talk about 'the glare of publicity' and I now know what they mean. Of course, I spoke in English and immediately a translator came forward.

The interview went on for over an hour before Serenity, speaking in Greek, told the pack that the interview was over. Various offers were hurled after us to go out for dinner, or to a hotel. Back at the apartment we sank a bottle of wine and smoked a few cigars, then switched on the main evening news. Once again, I was the headliner – "The Brave Scotsman who risked his life for others". Serenity also had her moment of fame.

They next morning, the press were still there. Dozens of letters came through the letterbox, most of them for me – offers for my story. I discussed it with Serenity – "you can receive half the dosh". Of course, we took the most lucrative. It took five hours and we received two great fat equal cheques – in Sterling. Another day slipped by. We were able to go our little beach taverna unmolested. We returned in the early evening. Tired and happy. As we walked in to the lounge a man suddenly appeared in front of me. All of a sudden the parquet floor travelled up fast to me, then the pain clicked in. Absolute agony. Lights were strobing in a heliotropic pulse. I was yanked to my feet. What the man shouted to me was not nice at all. I was thrown into the hallway and my rucksack after me. The door was slammed. After a few minutes the door opened and the maid emerged with a shopping bag filled with my passport, wallet and some personal effects. "He's missus's husband. I take you to hotel." It was not a bad hotel, cheap, quiet and clean. I slept well, but was extremely sore the next day. I had missed my flight by several days and had to pay a fortune for another.

Back at the office I received a full scale dressing down. "I am not interested in your travellers' tales," was all my boss could say to me.

I had reached one of those nexus points in my life. I had sold my flat, exchanged contracts on another, with at least two months to go to completion. I was out of work and staying in a flop house hotel. My few worldly goods and chattels were in storage. The answer was to take a break, an extended break, somewhere cheap and warm. I was in the hotel bar one evening and heard one of the travelling salesman telling another about the delights of Pattaya in Thailand. The scuba diving, the food, the hospitality and the cheap and clean accommodation. "A sleepy, quiet little fishing village," the salesman said. Yes, this was the place for me. I booked a return flight to allow myself a two months' stay. In the early seventies Pattaya was a fishing village, but not that sleepy. The US navy used to pull in there for their crews to enjoy a little rest and relaxation. Even then, parts of it were pure 'Sodom and Gomorrah'.' This was not the salesman's description, but then he was probably used to misrepresenting his merchandise. I had a vision of a tropical version of a sixties Majorca.

My flight was on a Saturday morning at nine. On Friday night I was to stay with my friend Roland in Dolphin Square, near Victoria Station. We had a good night out, a fantastic meal at San Lorenzo, soon to become patronised by Princess Diana and her pals. Then we went pub crawling to end up at Roland's place at about midnight. Roland produced a bottle of rum and the next thing I remember was waking up on his carpet, face down in a pool of vomit. It was five thirty in the morning, check in at Gatwick was seven. I sluiced some water on my face, picked up my holdall and ran all the way to Victoria Station. The train was about to depart. As I ran up to the barrier, it closed. I leapt over it and squeezed through the closing doors. I was breathless, soaked in sweat and feeling sick. A ticket inspector appeared; he understood my plight and I purchased my ticket. I reached check in at seven. The airline was the now defunct British Caledonian and the female staff all wore tartan kilts. The check in lady

296

was surprised that my only luggage was a holdall. "Halve your luggage and double your money," I joked.

I was the only passenger on the flight to Schiphol. I was seated in Business Class. The cabin staff were fully crewed for a busy return flight. Everybody was relaxed. Yes, I could sit in the cockpit. This, of course, was before aircraft terrorism had become a reality. It was a cold frosty November morning, even the cockpit was cold. Soon we were airborne and flying through cloud. The pilots were also relaxed. They talked about football. What was my opinion? Well, the only opinion I held was what I had picked from the salesman and this qualified me as an expert. I was served a breakfast of scrambled eggs, smoked salmon and champagne. Now, we were coming in to land. "On manual," announced one of the pilots. It seemed a rather heavy thump to me, but all in a day's work for the pilots.

Five hours later I boarded a 747 bound for Bangkok. The interior was like that of a cathedral. The airline was Air Garuda an Indonesian carrier. This aircraft started its journey in Stockholm, with landings at Schiphol, Charles de Gaulle, Zurich, Abu Dhabi and Bangkok. So, almost from the top of the world to not quite the bottom. Zurich was cold and clear with snowploughs working the runway. The snow-capped mountains bathed in moonlight. By contrast, when the aircraft doors were thrown open at Abu Dhabi you could smell the warm herb scented desert air.

Landing at Bangkok was a shock for me. I was wearing a woollen sweat shirt and leather jacket and broke out into a sweat. The taxi rank was chaotic. My bag was wrenched out of my hand and I was pulled to a taxi. My bag thrown into the boot, which was then locked. The taxi would not start and I was told to get out and push. I was not that stupid. I insisted on retrieving the bag from the boot and sitting next to the driver. Finally, a couple of chaps gave the vehicle a push and it bump started. A friend had told me that The Rich Hotel was *the* place to stay, only half an hour from the airport. Yes, the driver knew The Rich, but would I like a couple of tropical suits? No, I simply wanted to reach The Rich. The driver suggested that I 'have tea' with his sister. "A nice clean girl," he exclaimed. Again I refused the offer.

We bumped along hot crowed roads through what I considered slums. It was noisy. It was chaotic. Majorca it was not. We had now been travelling for well over an hour. I was told by the same friend of The Rich Hotel that never show your temper in Thailand. I turned to my driver and told him that he had fifteen minutes to deposit me at The Rich, or else... or else what I would have to work out. Miraculously the hotel appeared on the fifteenth minute. I paid his fare, which was not unreasonable and walked into The Rich. Like many public buildings in Thailand, the main hall was spacious. My room was also spacious, but the bed linen was soiled. A greenish slime dripped from the shower head. Some water trickled out of the tap, enough to wet the thin greyish towel to dampen down my body. I tried room service. It was answered: "Could I have a bottle of drinking water?"

A few minutes later it arrived on a tray held by a most attractive young lady. "Would sir like anything else?"

I replied I was fine.

"Perhaps I can wash you; give you nice massage?"

It was tempting, but I gave her a large tip and declined her offers. The duty free whisky hardly touched the sides of my throat and I was out.

Bangkok was a little "too full in the face" for me. After two days I took the bus to Pattaya. Yes, there were diamond dust sands, gin clear waters and swaying palms. My kinda place. I booked into the four-star Diamond Beach Hotel, which was one of the swankiest places I had ever stayed and only three quarters the price of my Surrey flop house hotel. My room was spacious, spotlessly clean and air conditioned. The en suite bathroom was sparkling and the water clean. I picked up the leather folder on the bedside table, expecting to see menus, wine lists and places of interest but it contained about a hundred pictures of ladies that could be dialled up on demand. No, I could not.

Well, I visited the local beaches and ate well. On my third evening I ventured to a seafood restaurant built on stilts out onto the South China Sea. The waitresses wore cute sailor suits and all looked about sixteen years old, but I was assured that most of them were married with children. At this early time in the evening the restaurant was deserted, except for one man sitting on his own gazing out at the lightning flashing and forking on the dark horizon. I was shown a table opposite him. The menu was not too large and really quite good value. I ordered. One of the lady sailors brought me a large bottle of local larger which she poured into a frosted glass. The music was soft and melancholic. I looked at the man opposite me. He looked at me. I had seen him somewhere. Where? Who was he? I racked my memory. In the end I could not resist it. I walked over to him and introduced myself. He smiled. "I'm Patrick," he said flatly. "Would you like to join me?" I was happy to. Slowly I realised who he was. A very well-known society photographer. In fact, there had been an hour long documentary about him on TV several nights ago.

"You are my hero, Patrick, flying around the world first class, shooting beautiful women in exotic locations. I wish I could be you, if only for a day."

He laughed. "The reality is different. It's true, I am here with a troupe of sixteen good looking babes. You know what? Any of them could have joined me here. This place isn't grand, but I can tell you it serves the finest seafood you will find anywhere in South Asia, and so cheap. What do my lovelies want? Beef burgers and chips. They can receive Coronation Street on video here." He pulled a sour face. "They have a problem chewing gum and walking in a straight line. Tomorrow, we have to be up at four in the morning. A military transport helicopter is taking us to a desert island. It looks beautiful, but it is hot and there are flies. Ah, the dust n' flies."

After a pleasant hour, he departed to his hotel and I decided to take a beer at Henri's bar, really just a kiosk in the square along with about three dozen other such bars. A man called out, "Guy. Guy! It's me Robson."

It was indeed Robson. I originally met him at the London Fire Brigade's Sub Aqua Club. Firemen need to be conversant with breathing apparatus and scuba diving is a fun way for them to become familiar with their kit. The club was also open to all-comers.

So, what was Robson doing here? Was it just an amazing coincidence? No, he loved scuba diving, the Tropics, Thai food. It was also winter in England. He knew this neck of woods well. He also knew Henri the eponymous owner of the bar. "Want some fun tonight?" Robson asked me with a wink.

I replied I would like some 'fun'. A tuk tuk was summoned and off we went. The driver had a male friend next to him. Soon we were out of town and travelling along a tree-lined avenue with the ocean on one side and low hills on the other. Then we turned off the thoroughfare and bumped along a dark track. It suddenly occurred that these fellows could easily overpower us, slit our throats and that we be the end of our holiday and everything else for that matter. "Relax," whispered Robson. "I know where we are going, been there before – it's a good place." After what seemed like an age we arrived at a clearing in which stood a fairly large house on stilts. Robson slipped the driver a few baht and we entered.

A mama san, an old lady in black silk pyjamas greeted us. "What you boys want?"

"What do you have?" I asked.

"Have everything, ganja, coke, opium, other stuff too."

I settled for a pipe of opium, while Robson went down a more herbal route. We were brought some small fried snacks. I felt very relaxed, very relaxed indeed. Eventually we were summoned to a large brightly lit hall, a little like any parish hall in England, except on the stage were twelve young attractive women, each with a number pinned to their attire. "You boys choose, take your time." the old lady said in her sing song voice.

I looked at Robson, he shrugged his shoulders. "It's a hard call." We finally decided – we would take the lot. Robson negotiated a price. We went to a darkened 'romper room', basically a room with a large mattress. Quite what happened then I never will know, but I did wake up the next day at about midday in my hotel. My throat was painful and so was my back passage. I was reminded of the music hall joke about "the only man who could fall into a barrel of tits and come up sucking his thumb". That was the last I ever saw of Robson.

The Diamond Beach Hotel was fine and cheap by UK standards, but was eating into my small budget. I moved to a Thai version of my Surrey flop house, a quarter of the price of the Diamond Beach. It was clean and comfortable, fans replaced the air conditioning. The bar was open from early morning to late at night. There was no restaurant as such, just a buffet serving at least forty different curries. Beer and curry for breakfast was a new experience for me. I met a writer in one of the bars who was lodging with a Thai family. "If you want somewhere really cheap, try a cabin," he told me sagely. There were about seventy of these cabins, just above town and therefore away from the noise and pollution. They were situated on what had been a football pitch. The cabins consisted of one small room and constructed of wood and raised several feel from the ground. The floor boards had half-inch gaps between them.

"Air Con," joked the manager. The shutters opened to reveal metal fly screens. "More Air Con," the manager remarked. There was no electricity, just a powerful battery torch chained to a low table. A thin mattress and a clean sheet could be hired for a few extra pence. Toilets and washing facilities were in a concrete block on the field. This was a quarter of the price of the flop house, however, I soon discovered that the real purpose of these cabins were as 'Comfort Cabins' for ladies (well, mainly ladies) to service the hotel workers. I suppose this was the closest I came to 'going local'.

I hired a bicycle and my daily routine was to cycle about six miles along the coast to an almost deserted beach. The only refreshment station was a palm thatched kiosk that served cold beer and wok fried seafood, which was absolutely fresh and perfectly cooked. The specials were char grilled. Any purchase also included the use of a deck chair for the day. So I spent my days, reading, sleeping, swimming, eating, drinking and cycling.

The Thai woman who ran the kiosk, was in her early twenties, plump and pleasant. As a 'regular' I received a substantial discount. One day our peace was shattered. A coach load of about thirty German men descended on the beach. I had heard about these gangs. They were part of specially chartered 'Fuck Flights'. They were rude. They were arrogant. They cleaned the lady out of beer and certainly did not settle their bill in full. Kannika was in tears. I decided to board the coach. I announced that I had 'connections' with the local police and that I would ensure they would be all arrested. I walked down the bus with hat in hand. Grudgingly, they filled it with baht. "Thank you, gentleman." I gave them a polite bow. Kannika was speechless. My haul had netted three times the price of the beer. I could eat and drink for free for the rest of my stay. Well, I refused her kind offer, but at least paid a lot less for my food and drink from then on.

When I told Kannika where I was staying, she was horrified. "Bad place. Very bad." She made gesture to indicate that my throat would be cut. "You stay here." She pointed to the kiosk. Indeed, attached to the kiosk was a kind of lean to with several mattresses on the floor. An 'Ali Baba' jar of water with a long handled ladle was the shower. There was also a hosepipe. "Everything here," she said emphatically.

The next evening I took up her offer. She invited me to her parents' house with whom she lived. It was a ten-minute walk away. The meal was excellent, beef and chicken curries and plenty of Mekong whisky. Her two brothers now accompanied me back to the kiosk. They also slept there. "Security guard," said one of them. It was comfortable. We watched television, played dominoes, smoked and drank a little. The next morning, we woke at the crack of dawn. "You come catch fish?" Well, that was an offer I could not refuse. I had not noticed the boats which were several hundred yards away. Long, narrow boats with high prows. They were powered by those long shafted outboard motors, found all over South East Asia.

The sea was calm. They knew exactly where they were going. They baited their hooks and cast several dozen multi-hooked lines overboard. We waited. We smoked. Drank cold tea and ate rice and shrimp balls. A very pleasant way to earn a living. It was a good haul. Silver fish, fish shaped, mostly about nine inches long – restaurant sized portions. The catch was gutted and laid in the ice boxes. Then the process began again. They told me, mainly in sign language, that I was 'Good Luck' for them. When we hit the beach later that afternoon, the catch was packed into separate ice filled boxes and loaded on a flatbed truck. Money changed hands and I was given enough bahts to eat at the kiosk for a week!

For the next month I went fishing every day, except when it was deemed too rough or windy, which was seldom. My companions knew the ocean like a garden. And like a garden, different plants came into fruit at different times. Sometimes, they used nets, scattered over surface feeding shoals of tiny fish; or they would drag the nets behind them. The lobsters and crabs pulled up from pots, were particularly prized. But usually it was baited hooks.

I had made a decision. This was the life for me. I would cancel the intended purchase of my flat and use the money to invest and expand the kiosk and upgrade the fishing operation. The next day I went into town and phoned my solicitor. She had 'good' news. We had exchanged, the flat was now mine. The deal could not be reversed. Of course,

I could sell the property. I did have some surplus funds, enough to live on until the new sale went through. It was with a heavy heart that I bade my Thai friends farewell and headed back to Bangkok airport.

A few years later I went on a two-day 'Decision Making' course. After the first day we were all issued with a T-shirt that bore the legend "Just Do It!" The next day some wag had had the back of his T-shirt printed with "I did and will always regret it!" Who can tell how my life would have turned out if I had stayed?

# Chapter Thirty: The Ashes

Dust to Dust, Ashes to Ashes, all these things must come to pass. Our physical remains have to be disposed of. Buried in a cemetery or reduced to ashes. Ashes have been blasted into Space, 'committed to the Deep', scattered in woods, parks, or interred into walls and caves. Sometimes 'the scattering of the ashes' can cause distress to the those left behind.

I had known and worked with Walter for many years. At one time we were young and fresh faced; suddenly, he had retired and I was coming to close to it. With his pension payout he bought his first brand new car – a Fiat 500. These are cute little numbers. Cheap and efficient to run, easy to park, great for running around town. They can carry four passengers, two adults, 'large' if necessary, in the front, and two in the back; being 'slim' is mandatory to sit in the back of the car.. In his little car, Walter, his wife, Doris and their two adult sons, Stephen and Michael, travelled all over Britain.

Walter married at eighteen and for almost all his life, lived in a small bungalow, next to an industrial estate in Croydon. The race horse journalist, Derek Thomson, once said about a runner in a horse race "This mare is like your Mother-in- Law, she just stays forever." An estate agent said to me "Some clients will pay a premium for a location, because it is near to the Mother-in-Law, others because it is as far away as possible from her." Well, in Walter's case, he was devoted to Dorothy, his Mother-n-Law. Dorothy had married a bricklayer, George. They settled in Saltdean, near to Brighton, because it was cheap and by the sea. Her husband's occupation took him all over Britain and even abroad, but Saltdean was their base. Walter, Doris and the boys also spent many happy summers at Saltdean. George retired, to a bungalow, on an estate where there were about a hundred similar bungalows – in Saltdean. He built a lovely brick arch and surrounding walls of fancy brickwork. It was so fancy, that every other bungalow owner on the estate wanted the same. Nice work when you can get it and a welcome supplement to George's meagre pensions. Eventually George moved to that 'building site in the sky' and Dorothy continued to live on her own in the bungalow, visited frequently by Walter and family. She then moved into sheltered accommodation near Croydon and finally, into a home for the elderly, where at the age of ninety seven, she passed away.

A few weeks after Dorothy's parting, he telephoned me to ask a favour – could I drive him, Dorris and Dorris's two sisters, Dulcie and Doreen to Saltdean and back to Croydon? They could not all fit into the Fiat and it had always been 'Mum's' wish that her last journey would be in the back of a Rolls Royce? Unfortunately, when the earthly remains of Dorothy were being transported to the crematorium, it was in a Mercedes hearse, despite the fact that Walter had specified a Rolls Royce. Walter offered to fill the tank of my Roller, buy me lunch and give me a couple of hundred quid. I declined his last offer, but willingly agreed to act as chauffeur for the day, using the Roller. My Roller was not just an ordinary Roller, it was a Rolls Royce Silver Cloud 1and would certainly carry everyone in style and comfort.

I arrived at Walter's bungalow on a Tuesday morning at ten thirty. The ladies were attired in black woollen dresses. Dorris was a large lady with a voracious appetite for curry, washed down by Rioja. Dulcie and Doreen were several sizes larger. Walter, smartly dressed in a grey three piece suit was no flyweight either. Dorothy was clutching a large ceramic urn to her ample bosom. I never thought a 'departed' human being left behind such a volume in ashes – enough to fertilise a quarter acre plot of roses. Dulcie carried a 'ghetto blaster'. What was it purpose? We were going to scatter the ashes, not going to a beach disco. Doreen simply held a packet of cigarettes and a lighter.

They all settled in comfortably, Walter sitting next to me and the ladies in the back. I turn round and smiled at the black dresses. "This car is a 'No Smoking Zone', however, in the cabinets in front of you, you will find whisky, gin, tonic, ice, water and crystal tumblers. There are also a few nibbles." I now turned to Walter, "There's a few India Pale Ales for you." Walter's face lit up. No sooner had I pulled away, when the car filled up with fumes of gin, whisky and prawn crackers. I turned up the air conditioning and air circulation. Walter took his bottle 'by the neck'. We chatted pleasantly amongst ourselves. I asked Dulcie why she had brought a sound system along. "Mum wished to have music at the scattering ceremony." With that we were literally blasted by 'The Sea of Galilee'. All four of my passengers singing along with great gusto. I breathed a sigh of relief when the last strains faded away. But not for long... We were now blasted by 'That Old Rugged Cross'. Another strident number belted out  by my travelling heavenly choir. Then it was 'Living Next Door To Alice', except 'Alice'  was substituted by 'Palace' being Crystal Palace – Dorothy's husband had apparently been a life long supporter of the football team 'Crystal Palace'. Now they singing along to 'In Dreams'. Sung by Roy Orbitson, this is one of my favourite songs. Beautifully constructed, it builds up slowly to a great crescendo which Roy sings in a piercing falsetto. Roy pulls it off beautifully, three drunk women and a merry man, don't. Walter, sensed my annoyance and demand silence, which thankfully returned. Once again I could hear the clock ticking above the purring of the engine. The ladies now needed a 'comfort break' - urgently. We were on a dual carriageway and there was nowhere. The whisky bottle was now empty and at 75cl it would accommodate the liquid waste of at least one lady. To my horror, I heard a powerful stream of liquid being shot into an empty whisky bottle. The fumes of whisky were being forced out of the bottle, along with that was the powerful reek of urea and ammonia. I screeched into a lay-by which fortunately suddenly appeared. "Out!

Do it behind the bushes over there." I shouted. Everyone, including Walter, run behind the bushes. Within seconds clouds of steam could be seen rising. Job done. Fortunately, there was no spillage on the carpet. The full bottle was dropped through the glass recycling bin, smashing in the process.

We resumed our journey in silence. No more singing, no more comfort breaks. The ladies fell asleep, Walter was dozing, but trying to keep awake. We reached the municipal car park at Saltdean just before pub opening time, but fortunately, this pub also served 'all day breakfast' and was open. Another comfort break followed in the pub. Now it was opening time for liquor. We took some liquid refreshment and decided to proceed with The Task. As we approached the beach, we received a shock, a terrible shock. The tide was out! Normally this would not be a problem. You walk down the beach to the waters edge, remove socks tights and shoes, tuck up dresses, roll up trousers and wade a few yards out and SCATTER. There were two impediments to this simple plan. The beach consists of pebbles. After the pebbles are jagged rocks, about seventy five yards of rocks until you reach the sea. The rocks are covered copiously with seaweed – those flat blankets of seaweed. The sea weed is wet and covered with a slime. The second impediment was wind. The gentle breeze in Croydon was now gusting at thirty five miles an hour towards the land at Saldean.

Dorothy had specified that her ashes were to be scattered onto *the sea* and not *the beach*, she did not want dogs to lick up her remains. Vets along that part of the coast have to remove hundreds of stones from dogs' stomach every year. The family held a conference, they would proceed whatever it took. Walter removed his socks and shoes and rolled up his trousers, which kept unrolling, so he removed them and tucked his shirt into his boxer shorts. He folded his jacket carefully and began the perilous journey, holding the urn tightly. Dorris followed, dress tucked up into her knickers. Then Dulcie with the ghetto blaster and in the vanguard, Doreen. The first few yards were slow, but uneventful; then, the terrain worsened, slippier, slimier, the dips in the rocks appeared as ravines. Large detours had to be made around deep rock pools. I watched them from the pebble beach. Then the first casualty. Walter, slipped and fell flat on his back, losing his grip on the urn which flew through the air and landed on a jagged rock cracking it open by the neck. The contents started to billow out. It was as if the ashes were being sucked out by a malignant zephyr on steroids. From nowhere, a large brown dog run nimbly and sure footed over the rocks and plunged his head into the neck of the urn. Dorris screamed and almost floated at speed over the terrain, that is, until she fell face down into a shallow pool.

I had no choice, without removing anything I travelled as fast as I could towards the urn, shouting at the dog. Luck was on my side, I made it one piece. I literally pulled the hound from the urn, scooped what ashes I could and up-righted the vessel. The next victim was Dulcie. She just fell over. The blaster hit a rock and 'Unchained Melody' exploded above the sound of waves crashing. I waited. Walter went to the aid of Dorris who was sobbing loudly, Dulcie was soaking wet and crying. Doreen scuttled crablike towards us. "Well, we could wait until the tide comes in. All things come to him who waits." I announces sagely. This idea was dismissed "Too cold and it's starting to drizzle." "OK let us proceed slowly." We did. Very slowly. But there is no clear cut line between rock and sea. We had another conference.

A few yards away was a large, fairly calm deep rock pool. The occasional wave was already filling it. Walter would proceed to the edge of the pool and *carefully* scoop the ashes into the pool, which was slightly sheltered from the winds. Everting was going fine. 'Amazing Grace' now blasted us from the black box. I suppose the urn was 'half empty' rather than 'half full', when it slipped from Walter's hand, hit the water and bobbed along. "NO!" He screamed and plunged into the pool, after it. He got it. Dragged it down under the water where it released a milky white cloud, as if a genie was rising from a bottle. Then grasping a ledge with one hand, he used his other hand to smash the urn into pieces. "I'm not having that thing in MY house any more." 'Auld Lang Syne' was now belting out. 'If you don't shut that f*&$ing thing off, it's also going into the pool as well." On our return journey to the pebbles, we experienced a few minor mishaps, but we made it. A further unpleasant surprise awaited.

Walter's neatly folded jacket had gone. Filched. In his jacket were his debit and credit cards, three hundred in cash which he was going to give me, his house keys and his moby. Not only had his jacket disappeared, but his trousers too! He looked a sad sight. Soaking wet, wearing a shirt, waistcoat and boxer pants. The ladies were also in a sorry condition as well. We made for the pub. In that part of the world, anything goes. People wandering round in their underwear is not unusual. On the beach, they sometimes wander round without even their underwear. Walter used Dorris's mobile to report the theft. We now had to drive to Brighton Police Station. We made it in time to reach Marks and Spensers, where the only 'trousers' that would fit Walter, were shorts. Garish floral patterned Bermuda shorts. Walking into the police station he looked ridiculous – Bermuda shorts, white shirt and a grey waistcoat. The only shoes he could buy in a hurry were sandals, although he was able to procure a pair of socks. The ladies returned back to the car with a bottle of whisky, a packet of ice and fish and chips. I insisted they consume their 'meal' outside of the car.

My 'party' offered to take the train to Croydon, but it seemed churlish of me not to honour my undertaking. We arrived at the Walter's bungalow at nine thirty at night. He insisted we all went for a curry and, furthermore, I was to stay the night at his place. The curry was excellent. Back at home, we downed several bottles of Rioja and all the remaining whisky. Walter only had a small guest room, which was really a 'shack' out in his garden. There was an oil filled electric heater, but otherwise no other form of heating. It was cold and draughty. One double bed, one sofa bed. Dulcie and Doreen were to share the double and I to sleep on the sofa bed. We were all quite drunk. There was a lot of giggling. I do not know exactly what happened, how it happened, or even why it happened, but all three of us ended up in the same double bed. The tabloids would have billed it as a 'Sex Romp'. I do like my ladies built for comfort, rather than speed, but to attempt to mate with not one, but two dugongs was a new experience, and I have to say, a difficult feat for me. Somewhere, along the process, the bed collapsed. It happened as an unpleasant jolt and 'the earth really did move' for us.

The next morning, battered, bruised and weary from our adventures of rock climbing and nocturnal activity we went to the pub chain, Mactoon's for a full English. When I arrived home, I gave The Roller a full valet – inside and out. I also changed my will to 'allow the crematoria to dispose of my ashes in their 'Garden of Remembrance'

# Chapter Thirty-One: Dog Years

I've always battled with my weight. It was particularly hard when I had to lose thirty per cent of my bodyweight to ride as an amateur under Jockey Club rules. Of course, it has crept up since then, but I still *try* to keep it in check. Since my mid-twenties I have being going to gyms. In those days they were airless, sweaty places with the emphasis on boxing training. Now, of course, nearly every adult in 'softy southern' England belongs to a gym. The gyms now are totally different places.

Mine had introduced a *body diagnostic* machine. You step on this device, grip some sensors and it tells you what you had for breakfast – nine months ago! Well, six months ago, I was self-assessed. Everything was where it should be, except for one thing. The Machine stated I had a body age two years older than my recorded age. Alarming! When I was twenty-eight years old, I decided my social age was thirty-five. I like that age, young, but mature in wisdom and social skills. Decades later, I am still thirty-five. It suits me. But, having a body age of two years older than me scared me. It appeared that visceral fat was the culprit. I just had too much of it. As the Americans once said of President Gerald Ford, "He had an 'out pouching of the gut'." So I started High Intensity Interval Training (HIIT). It is basically for upwardly mobile people like me, who cannot spend hours in the gym every day. In addition to this, I swam everyday, wherever I was. Rivers, lakes, the North Sea, the South China Sea and the gym's swimming pool. When I cycled, I went further, faster, higher, deeper where no man had ever gone before. I dieted. Switched beer for champagne. Ate only smoked salmon and oysters.

Three months later I returned to The Machine, the Sibyl of Delphi. Everything was meaner, leaner, not fatter, but fitter. Then the Sibyl spake unto me, my body age – I was four years older than my actual age! I complained to my very nice Personal Trainer, Justin. A Senior Technician arrived the next day and pronounced the Sibyl to be "in full working order". A few weeks later, I mounted her again. I was now four years and *three months* older!

I was worried. Maybe Sibyl was suffering from dementia. My dog died at twelve years old. The vet told us she was actually seventy-five years old in 'dog years'. A small butterfly will live for only a week! But what a life it packs in that time! Remember the summer holidays? They used to go on forever. Now, no sooner do you arrive at your beach house, then it is time to pack up again. I decided I would no longer engage with Sibyl any more. But, strange things were happening to me...

Time seemed to be speeding up! It took me four minutes and twenty seconds to walk to the suburban railway station from my front door. The return trip took four minutes and one second, the return exit at the station, being nearer to home. I always allowed five minutes on my outboard journey. Now, I was frequently missing the train. I checked the timetable table, reset my watch to British Railways Norbiton Time (BRNT), built in another three minutes' redundancy, but still arrived to see the train rattling along to the next stop.

There was a new development at the station. A couple of the waiting rooms were turned into a coffee shop/bar. Reggie's Rest. This was the best thing ever to have happened at the station. It did not bother me any more if I missed the train, I would have a double espresso and a croissant and wait for the next train. There's always another train. But now, as I came out of the coffee shop, I would see the rear of the train swaying along the track. I had to resort to buying coffee in a cardboard cup and stand on the platform in all weathers.

Coming home, I would stop at Reggie's Rest instead of trundling up the road to The Flag. I would pop into The Rest for a swift half' at seven o'clock and yet arrive home at ten thirty! Things simply were not adding up. When I worked from home it was as if I was entering a time machine. One minute, nine o'clock in the morning, next it was seven in the evening and dark. I had not eaten, my bladder was bursting. Where had the time gone? I resorted to having to time each task, but my watch acquired a life of its own. I know "Time is the Medium in which we all burn", but my Time Candle was burning fast and furious and I was not even burning it at both ends.

I had an important business meeting at the South Bank, near Waterloo. I rose early, bathed and shaved, suited and booted caught the earliest train running. Waterloo was particularly busy when I arrived. Memories flooded back to the first year that I was commuter. Everyone smoked in those days, in the carriages. Most men wore hats, bowlers at that. They carried bulging briefcases, not rucksacks. Black, polished shoes, neatly rolled umbrellas. Women were smartly dressed – dresses, blouses and skirts, always high heels. Elegant. At Waterloo, music would blare from loudspeakers; martial music, to which everyone stepped in time. In the evenings, the music was softer, gentler. If you missed your train, you strayed into the buffet bar for a decent pint of Bass, much as forces personnel would have done during WW2. Now it is a bottle store. There is a poncey new mezzanine which serves fancy lagers and very expensive fizz.

As I came through the ticket barrier, I received a shock. Coming towards me was a fat, elderly balding man, my doppelgänger. We looked at each other. "Hiya," he said.

"Hiya," I replied.

This was the 'in' greeting at the time. Nice man, just like me. Damn it – it was me! My mobile started to ring and ring. Nine missed calls. My assistant Deirdre shouted across the ether at me. She shouted so loud, she did not need a mobile. Where was I? I had not turned up and no thanks to me, *she* had to lead the Team and again, no thanks to me, they won the contract! I apologised, I was unwell. I had never been late for anything, except my wedding. I stared in disbelief at the twenty-four-hour station clock, which read 18.20 hrs. I could catch the 18.25

and did. I arrived at Reggie's Rest at 19.15. At least we were running on real time again. I needed a *stiff* drink rather than a *swift* drink.

Despite only one drink – a quadruple Scotch on the rocks, I was too late for the bottle shop and made it home at ten past eleven. I opened a can of baked beans and ate them cold, straight from the tin. The doorbell rang. Who could it be at that hour? I opened the door to bright daylight. Four sombrely dressed men stood outside. One of them read out my address from a piece of paper. Could I confirm it? Yes, the address was correct. Were they police officers? The 'plain clothes' boys normally wear jeans (distressed), T-shirts and leather jackets; unshaven, long greasy hair. These guys were smart, grey suits, dark ties, and black polished lace up shoes.

"We've come for the late Mr Gundle."

"I'm Mr Gundle." I felt like saying, *I'm never late.* Well, apart from my wedding and this morning, rather yesterday morning.

The senior of the men stated, "Mr Guy Uisdean Gundle. He has been certified dead. His body is in the study. It was his wish that he would not be taken to the hospital, to the, er, hospital *morgue.*"

A large silver metal casket appeared on long spindly legs with wheels attached; it was being guided down the path. "Tell you what, gentlemen, I'm upset, give me ten minutes and I will produce Guy Uisdean Gundle for you," I announced flatly.

"Of course, sir. You must be upset. Do you mind if we sit on that wall over there and have a smoke?" I told them that was fine.

I walked through the lounge to the conservatory. It was a warm, bright sunny day. A flock of parakeets settled in the trees, not an unusual sight in Surrey any more. An elegant crane was perched on the outhouse, preening its feathers. The cherry and apple blossom were just coming into bloom, the best time of the year. The things I remembered looking at that long, mysterious garden, children playing on the climbing frame, Easter Egg hunts, barbecues, digging the vegetable plots, the beans, carrots, asparagus and tomatoes with their little hearts still beating, plucked straight from the vine, slit open and devoured, sipping cider in the outhouse, the little dog chasing huge foxes and threatening to rip their throats out, but then leaving hedgehogs completely alone. Now, suddenly, the garden swarming with construction workers, JCBs, heavy lifting cranes. Deep trenches crisscrossed my once pristine lawn. They were not there when I first looked a few minutes ago. Where did they come from?   I heard a discrete cough. "We are waiting, sir."

"Yes. I'll be with you." I made my way to the study, where, to my amazement, my little dog, who was sleeping, raised her head and wagged her tail in welcome.